AFTERSHOCK

AFTER

A NOVEL BY
CHUCK SCARBOROUGH

CROWN PUBLISHERS, INC.   NEW YORK

SHOCK

Published by Crown Publishers, Inc., 201 East 50th Street, New York, New York 10022. Member of the Crown Publishing Group.

CROWN is a trademark of Crown Publishers, Inc.

Book design by June Marie Bennett

Manufactured in the United States of America

Library of Congress Cataloging-in-Publication Data

Scarborough, Chuck.
Aftershock / by Chuck Scarborough.—1st ed.
p. cm.
I. Title.
PS3569.C32E24 1991
813'.54—dc20   90-48763
                                                      CIP
ISBN 0-517-58014-4

10 9 8 7 6 5 4 3 2 1

First Edition

*To Elizabeth,
Chad, Allegra,
Al, and Anne*

ACKNOWLEDGMENTS

O f the many people who earned my gratitude during the writing of this book, I must first thank Dr. Robert Ketter, Professor of Seismology at the State University of New York in Buffalo. His warnings, still unheeded, inspired my series of special reports for television, which in turn inspired this novel. I am deeply saddened that he did not live to see the publication of this work.

Laurie McCall's skills as a television news field producer were invaluable during my initial reporting of New York's vulnerability to seismic disaster. Dr. Charles Merguerian, Professor of Structural Geology at Hofstra University, drew a chilling road map of the area's faultlines and helped me understand the peculiar behavior of what we think of as solid ground during an earthquake's shock. Captain Eugene Guerin of the New York City Police Department was an invaluable source, as were officials from the New York City Bureau of Water Supply, the New York City Transit Authority, The Port Authority of New York and New Jersey, New York Telephone, Consolidated Edison and Brooklyn Union Gas Company who explained the maze of conduits beneath our feet through which the life blood of a metropolis flows. WNBC crime reporter John Miller shared his unique knowledge of the other underworld with me. As you'll soon see, for the mob, for anyone with criminal inclinations from Wall Street to Harlem, a major earthquake is an astonishing bonanza. An urban earthquake in the lethal magnitudes releases enormous pent-up energy, both seismic and human, unleashing greed, lust, passion, vengeance, terror, and heroics in equal portions.

I would also like to thank members of the Department of Neurology at New York Hospital; Andrea M. Smith of New York Blood Center; Alex von Bidder and the staff of The Four Seasons; Missy Wood of the Norwich and Norfolk Terrier club; Peter E. Engel of J. P. Morgan; the staff of the New York Racing Association at Belmont Park; Stuart Dodge, mountaineer and a former member of the United States Army's 10th Mountain Division; Bruce T. Kennedy, former member of the NYPD; officers of the NYFD's Ladder 13/Engine 22, the NYPD's Central Park Precinct and the United States Army's 82nd Airborne Division; and staff members at the Schomburg Center for Research in Black Culture, the Central Park Zoo, and New York Yacht Club.

Finally, I must thank my literary agent, Helen Brann, and her associate, Rob Fitz. Without their efforts and constant encouragement this book would not have been possible.

PROLOGUE

obert Ketter, director of the National Center for Earthquake Engineering Research, told a Senate panel today that a major, destructive earthquake—a threat popularly associated with California—is almost certain to strike somewhere in the eastern United States before the year 2010.

The quake hazard east of the Rockies is compounded by the fact that seismic tremors in the East generally cause wider damage than in the West, Mr. Ketter said.

Ketter's testimony went on to underline that earthquakes are a national concern.

Places considered potential sites for major seismic disruptions in the future are the New Madrid–Memphis area, the St. Lawrence River *area, the New York–Boston corridor, and parts of South Carolina, Virginia, and Utah, Ketter said.*

The probability of such a quake striking the East before the year 2010 is nearly 100 percent, he said.

—Associated Press

THE DAY BEFORE

ix miles below the floor of the earth, in a lovely mountain glade thirty miles southwest of Albany, New York, the deformation of a seismic fault that snakes its way down the belly of the state is reaching a critical level. The stress that has been building up over eons this day is becoming uncontainable. Soon the rock masses on either side of the fault, in response to the stress, will slap against each other, grinding along for two dozen feet. Within twenty-four hours, as the pressure builds up, the energy accumulated in the rock will be released, the friction finally unable to contain it. Then the weakest point will give way and the earth will move. Tremendously, violently along an entire 125-mile length that will carry the movement out under the Atlantic Ocean.

The seismologist, Dr. Zimmer, was over two thousand miles away from the cold, dark, deep ocean trench off the eastern coastline. High in the Rocky Mountain range, he studied this trench from his post in the War Room at the National Earthquake Information Center at Golden, Colorado. One of the walls of the room was taken up with a bank of recording drums, each one turning continuously, night and day, displaying readings from twelve key seismograph installations across the continental United States. Those readings he studied this brilliant, sunlit October morning were going into the center's computers to be digested, stored, made instantly available to scientists around the world who were studying earthquakes. Seismic waves from a major earthquake anywhere in the world triggered the alarm in the War Room.

Zimmer was particularly interested in the activity in the ocean trench in the east. He was trained to be calm and unemotional, to study only the data. He was a true scientist, he told himself, as he paced up and down in front of the rotating drums; he did not act on impulse or hunches or fear. He had been up all night for two nights, watching, studying, his pulse quickened, waiting for that hellish siren to go off. He had caught a cold, his head ached, and he longed to go home, have a stiff whiskey, and go to bed. For the past two days he had been in constant touch with his colleague, Dr. Conrad, a professor of structural geology at the Lamont-Doherty Seismological Station at Blue Mountain Lake, New York.

Conrad was as disturbed by the unusual activity in the ocean trench as was Zimmer. The damnable thing about earthquakes, Zimmer and he knew, was that they were unpredictable, the warning signs mainly invisible to all but scientists. Until they happened, scientists could only warn, and those warnings were going unheeded. Conrad had even contacted the executive officer of the Office of Emergency Management in Manhattan yesterday to tell him of the unusual activity off the coast and to try to get him to at least put Manhattan on Phase I—described as a "state of awareness in which an emergency or potential emergency is identified."

Conrad reported to Zimmer that the new police commissioner,

John Maloney, refused to take it up with the mayor on the basis that such a move would trigger widespread panic in the City and its environs, and, to quote Maloney precisely, Conrad had told Zimmer in his German accent, "What have you damn scientists got, anyway, divining rods? I can't set this city on its goddamn ear because you people see fish swimming the wrong way, for Christ's sake!"

Conrad had repeated this to Zimmer and then added, "My German Shepherd, Bavaria, has been acting strange. She has not slept for two days. Off her food. And sits at my knee, looking up at me, whimpering. Remember the St. Bernards who gave an hour's warning when Mount St. Helens blew? I was told that they started to yelp. In Switzerland it means an avalanche is rumbling too far away for humans to hear. I don't know, Zimmer, but we've been having these minor tremors for five months. Sure, no one can feel them, but they show up on our graphs. I've been checking my portable seismographs upstate, driving two hundred miles a day for the last week, and I've found signs of reduced P-wave velocity. Then yesterday was normal. I mean, it's classic, isn't it?"

Zimmer had called his old friend and fellow scientist, Sam Thorne, out at UCLA, where he thought he was giving some lectures. A best-selling writer and highly visible, maybe Sam Thorne could rattle some people in Washington or New York to wake them up. He found that Thorne had left for his mother's home in Colorado Springs, and Zimmer called there and left a message that it was "urgent" for Thorne to call him.

Under the azure Colorado sky, two mountain climbers made their way down the face of Long's Peak. The October noonday sun was hot. They had shed sweaters, which were now tied around their waists over the thick rope that connected them.

A solitary eagle wheeled overhead in a wide circle, and the air was still except for the tapping sound of the hammer they used to place the pitons in the rock crevices, securing the rope in the tradition of climbers for centuries. There was a strong sense of communication between the two climbers though they had not spoken a word for over an hour. The man was lower down the descent than the woman and he paused to adjust the rope that bound them together. If one fell, the rope would hold. It was clear they had often climbed together. The rhythm of their lean bodies was clean-cut and complementary. The man put his dark glasses up on his head and wiped the sweat off his brow with the sleeve of his shirt. Sam Thorne looked up, saw that the woman had moved down to the last piton, and he began to look for the next place to find safe footing, glancing at his watch.

"Sam."

"Yes, Kate," he answered, and found a ledge which would hold the two of them. They were only minutes from the base of the mountain now. For Katherine Thorne and her son, Sam, this climb was just a warmup. She had climbed Everest and had tried K-2 without success. She was one of the world's leading mountain climbers, male or female.

"Are you going to see your friend in Golden on the way to New York?"

"Yes." He looked up and saw her graceful sixty-one-year-old body, foot and hand finding the safe holds and rock to lower itself, until she stood on the ledge beside him. She looked up at him with her clear, bright blue eyes. She was very handsome, with short, curly gray hair, deeply tanned skin, her expression both humorous and intelligent.

"I'll be ready to leave before you are . . . by two thirty at the latest." She smiled at him. "I pack faster than you or your father ever did." She was as strong inside as out, Sam thought. She had no mothering instinct and had raised her children with fond teasing objectivity, saving her passion for the philosopher and poet she had married, and who had died of Alzheimer's a year ago.

On impulse, knowing that it would embarrass her, he leaned down and kissed her cheek. She disregarded his gesture.

"Look down there!" There was outrage in her low voice. "How the hell can they put one of their goddamn condominiums right there at the foot of the mountain. It's sacrilege."

He nodded his head in agreement. He had inherited her love of the outdoors, of the natural world, her talent for mountain climbing, and the dark blue eyes that his wife called "aviator's eyes." Sam Thorne was forty-one, and he and his mother looked very much alike, though his hair was black, flecked with gray. He was tall and thin and sun-tanned and looked as though he belonged here on this mountain.

Sam had grown up hearing Kate inveigh against all who came to ruin her unspoiled mountain range and plains. Her family and his father's family had made millions from silver mining at Cripple Creek over a hundred years earlier. Their marriage in the early fifties had been the social event of the decade in Colorado Springs. The Thorne family had produced miners and rogues and gamblers and bankers and lawyers, but only one philosopher-cum-poet, his late father, Daniel. It was fortunate that there was more money in the combined families than they or anyone else needed, since Daniel Thorne's pursuits had not made enough to pay the gardener, as Sam's maternal grandmother had been fond of saying.

Sam looked at his watch again. "We should be on the plane by three."

"Let me go first," Katherine said. "I'm still better at this than you are."

He tapped the piton in securely, and she started down the rock face. They made the rest of the descent in record time and soon, with Katherine at the wheel of her ancient Jaguar, they were at the door of the Thorne family home, in Broadmoor, where Sam had grown up. It was a large, rambling Victorian house with several acres of well-tended lawns and an excellent view of both snow-capped Pikes Peak and the plains where they could see the Sangre de Cristo range rise purple in the far distance.

"Do you ever get picked up by the police?" Sam asked. He got out of his mother's car. "You were doing ninety and then some." He grinned at her.

"Never. They wouldn't dare. I've known the whole police force all my life. Can you imagine them arresting Kate Thorne!" She slammed the car door and ran up the steps with the arrogance of the rich and well born. Not unattractive coming from her, he thought. She was such a daredevil and always had been. People made allowances for her.

Kate's bedroom was large and high ceilinged, with French doors opening onto a balcony that overlooked the mountain range, Cheyenne Mountain near and already snowcapped above the timber line and in the distance to the northeast, Pikes Peak, majestic against the blue October sky, like a crown jewel in its superiority over the surrounding mountains.

There was an upstairs sitting room off the bedroom, with several overstuffed armchairs, a long, dark red leather sofa, and bookcases filled with volumes that described Daniel's and her tastes in literature. Many paperback editions of poetry from Italy and France, in dilapidated condition, nonfiction books of biography and science and philosophy side by side with mystery novels by Pym and Chandler, first editions of Hogarth Press volumes, picked up in Charing Cross Road years earlier, all of Proust's *Remembrance of Things Past* in French. Flaubert; Conrad; Hemingway (inscribed to her), with copies of her own books on mountain-climbing adventures and her son Sam's first best-seller of two years ago, *The Scorpion Sequence*. It had been his opening salvo in an attempt to arouse the consciousness of the country about the inherent dangers of natural disasters and, in particular, earthquakes.

A large circular table in the middle of the room held family photographs. Most were in polished silver frames of varying shapes and sizes. There she was with Daniel in 1952 on their wedding day, dancing at the reception at the country club, he just back from Korea still in his Air Force captain's uniform, handsome and smiling, and she slender and with shoulder-length hair, looking up at him as he twirled her around to the first waltz. There were pictures of the boys growing up, Sam on skis, Chris holding up the first trout of the spring season, Tom on horseback at their ranch, since sold, in the southwestern corner of Colorado. They could have been three young cowboys in their faded jeans and white shirts with sleeves rolled up. There she was with the Sherpa guides climbing the ascent of Mt. Everest grinning for the camera, with what she recognized was her show-off look. There was the photograph of FDR signed to her father, and one of the Thorne mines at Cripple Creek without which there would have been none of the advantages she knew they were fortunate to have.

A lifetime had been lived in these rooms, she thought, as she undressed with the economy of movement she displayed in all things, getting ready for the shower and dressing for the trip to

New York. A bloody lifetime, and now it had all fallen apart with Daniel's death. She did not allow herself to dwell on the past or Daniel these days, but something about Sam, the promise still inherent in his young life, drew her toward the old photographs and books and gave her a pang of acute pain.

And what a lifetime it had been, she mused, picking up the picture of a group of them at the ranch that summer long ago. The sun had faded the old photograph and at first she couldn't pick out and identify the familiar faces. My God, she thought, a wonderful life at that. Daniel, my precious friend, and the boys, all of them good, decent fellows, talented and bright, the friends all over the world, the position and money so that they knew anyone anywhere they wanted to know, the mountains, her passion, the strength and ability to climb where no woman had ever gone, the recognition of Daniel's work and her talent. Oh yes, that woman in the photo was Edith Jones, one of the summer Texans who came up to escape the heat. A silly woman she was, who drank too much bourbon every night and slept with Joe, the foreman, and there was Dick O'Connor, Daniel's Harvard classmate, standing behind Edith, all of them in riding clothes holding glasses, and there was . . . Gordon Keith. She held the frame in her hand, looking at the faded photograph of the tall man with a serious expression on his face, that lean tanned face, that she remembered laughing, not serious, and then very serious, leaning toward her, whispering to her on that long ago summer night.

She put the picture down and went into the bathroom for her shower.

Sam was packing in his room when the maid came in to ask him to sign a copy of his book, *The World That Was*, for her. She handed him a note with a message from Abe Zimmer at Golden asking him to call. It was "urgent." Sam autographed the book and asked, "When did this call come in, Josie?" He was irritated that she hadn't told him sooner, but he managed to hide it.

"About an hour ago," Josie said. She was pleased to have a signed copy of handsome Sam's book, though she knew she would never read the book, which was about prehistoric times.

"Thank you sir, will you and Mrs. Thorne be wanting lunch before you go?"

He was punching in Zimmer's number. "No, thanks. No time."

After Sam had listened to Zimmer's news, he called Conrad. Then he called the governor's office in Albany, New York, to be told that Governor Fleming was on a business trip in Europe. He did not know the new black mayor of New York City, Bruce Lincoln, but he did know the president, and he punched the number of the White House. The Thorne family had worked for the election of this president and he was greeted warmly by the president's secretary, but told that the president was going to be unavailable until late afternoon. Sam gave her his New York number and decided to try him again from their plane en route. The chances of getting any action taken in Manhattan on the basis of two top scientists' data was slim, but he had to try.

He called Zimmer back and told him what he had done.

Zimmer laughed. "I guess I called the right person. The president? Now I call that action."

"He'll think I'm having a case of my usual earthquake jitters. But why not? We should have them, especially if we live in New York City in a house built before steel beams came in."

"Jesus, Sam, I know you feel that way. Everyone knows you feel that way, from Johnny Carson to the president. The trouble is, old pal, I *know* too much. So does Conrad. So do you. We've warned and warned and what good does it do? Except for the West Coast, the rest of the country is asleep."

"Go home, Abe. You sound terrible. Get some rest. I'll keep in touch with Conrad, and when I know something, I'll call you."

"Okay, Sam. I think I will. I'm bushed. Talk to you later. You got my home number? Good." Zimmer put down the phone and went over to the revolving drums and studied them one more time. He blew his nose and gave a dry cough. His eyes stung. He drew a cigarette from his pocket, lighted it, and yelled for some black coffee. He could no more leave his post now than abandon a life raft in the middle of a hurricane.

Thousands of feet below the surface of the Atlantic, off Montauk at the tip of Long Island, the crevasse that ran up the center of the Mid-Atlantic Range was, as it had been for eons, in constant, tortured flux. Shocks radiated outward as the Ridge, cut by fracture zones, strained against itself. One large shock struck westward, toward the eastern seaboard of the United States, but the shock was unfelt, seen only on scientific devices as just another in an endless series of seismic events. Hot lava from the center of the earth welled up, chilling quickly and hardening to create another escarpment on the face of the Ridge. Then the tremor subsided for a short time, only to begin once again, reaching out with its immutable tentacles. It was like a sick heart, scarred by attacks, still beating, beating, sending blood, like waves, through the threatened body.

Sam thought about his conversations with Zimmer and Conrad as he packed. He sympathized with the seismologists. To know what they knew and not to be able to do anything was like sitting on top of an atom bomb, knowing it was about to go off and not being able to get anyone to stop it. Sam had been writing and making speeches for years about the threat of a major earthquake on the eastern seaboard. Even his fellow scientists thought he was overdoing it, exaggerating the danger. He thought about the recent catastrophe in Brooklyn when an exploding gas main shook the Park Slope section. Brooklyn Union officials did not know what caused the blast, but it brought down several of the older, historic buildings in the area and killed twelve people in addition to causing extensive damage in the neighborhood in general. The president of Brooklyn Union flatly denied reports that its natural gas system was being improperly maintained, saying the company was making every effort to determine the origin of the explosion and to see that such an event did not recur. What was known was that something had failed, people had been killed, water and electricity to the area had been cut off for days, firemen had been injured in the flames while trying to rescue area residents.

As soon as they got on the family Lear jet Sam tried to reach the White House again and was told that the president was unavailable, had gone to an official dinner of some sort, and would try to return his call in the morning. He returned to his seat and sat down next to his mother.

"Why does she want to divorce you?" Kate asked, sipping her vodka on the rocks. "Or you her? Which is it? Is there someone else?"

Kate had on her navy-blue Chanel suit, custom made in Paris by the designer herself in 1959, and she looked ready for Manhattan. She was going with Sam because it was time to do fall shopping—all women from Colorado Springs who had money did their serious shopping in New York—and she had to address a meeting of the Sierra Club on Wednesday night.

"We haven't talked about getting a divorce," Sam replied, careful about telling Kate too much. He was not at all sure she liked Diane, his actress wife, and he did not want to give her ammunition. Things were too delicate at the moment to have a ferocious mother lion come to the aid of her endangered cub, if that is how Kate saw him.

"We are thinking about it, I suppose, simply because we don't seem to be very close anymore. There's no one else." He didn't add, not for me, anyway. He was fairly certain Diane was having an affair.

"And what about young Dan?"

"He doesn't know anything yet, and until we are sure we won't tell him."

Kate took a long swallow. She looked at her son quizzically. "You'll pardon me if I say I do not understand."

Sam sighed. "Look, I just think that after ten years when we spend so much time apart, things happen. She's been in the TV series, I've been teaching in New York, and you know my work takes me all over the world. Somewhere along the line we stopped knowing one another. Or sharing. Except for Danny."

"Do you love her?"

He reflected for a moment. "I remember loving her a great deal.

I've been crazy about Diane for so long. Yes, I love her. I like her, too. But we both are ambitious. And . . . well, we're not doing anything right away anyway." He furrowed his brow.

"You look like your father. Which is to say, handsome and confused. How does Diane feel? I ask these questions," Kate looked at him over the rim of her glass, "because I think divorce is a terrible mistake unless it is absolutely necessary. Our families don't go in for divorce, easy as it is in these days. Of course, there is our money. Is Diane after a hefty settlement?"

"Kate! For Christ's sake, no!" He pushed the button by his arm. A steward appeared. "Joe, get me a Jack Daniel's on the rocks, please." He turned to glare at his mother. "She makes a small fortune with her series, her commercials, and now the play. She is not after our sacred dough. And I think she feels about me the way I do about her. I just don't know why we should stay married if we never see one another and when we do we aren't very close anymore."

"Your son. Tradition. Old age."

Sam laughed. "You sound a hundred and ten. You could be Grandmother Thorne."

Kate glared back at him. "I do, do I? Listen to me, Sam Thorne. You young people make me sick. Heedless, feckless, silly people, squandering life as though it went on forever. Well, it doesn't! My most brilliant child, you are, the handsomest and the best, and you end up sounding sappy."

He grinned at her, loving her anger. "Hey, wait a minute—"

"*You* wait a minute. What about a child being split up emotionally between two parents? What about the vows you took? What about a lonely old age? If one of you beat the other or took dope that would be one thing, but you seem content to drift into divorce as though it were some inevitable outcome of marriage in the first place. Dear God!" She took a moment to take a swallow of her drink.

He waited, knowing she had to finish, knowing that she was hurting terribly because of losing her husband—his father—and facing her old age alone. Of course, she would have family. But it wasn't the same, and Sam knew it.

"I don't understand why you don't apply the same guts and spirit and brains to your marriage that you apply to your work. You are an outstanding scientist and writer. You play the meanest game of tennis of any of my children. You can attack a mountain almost the way I did at your age. You never give up on anything that I know of, and then you talk about your ten-year marriage as though you were some effete milksop."

Sam began to laugh.

"See! You're not serious. You're not a serious person. Oh, well. I always worried about an actress, and not a very talented one at that."

"Oh, come on, Kate. You've gone too far. We're almost in. Fasten your seat belt. We'll get home in time to see Danny before his bedtime."

She leaned back in her seat and closed her eyes. She did not like the landing part of airplane travel. After a moment she said, eyes shut, "I'm sure Diane won't be home yet."

Sam smiled. He knew Kate's digs were good-natured, and that she secretly admired his beautiful, successful wife. But as he sat waiting for the plane to make its descent into Kennedy, he felt a lingering sadness. He knew that, indeed, Diane would not be home when he got there.

━━━━

Seven miles below the surface of New York City, the fault that underlay 125th Street had reached the limit of tolerance of the stress it was under. The deformation along the edges had become profound, and friction would soon fail to be a containment factor. It was as if a rubber band were slowly but surely being stretched to its breaking point. In several hours that breaking point would be reached, and all the energy that had accumulated over thousands of years would be released in the form of great seismic waves that would roll outward.

The fault slipped—minutely, almost imperceptibly, as it had done innumerable times before—and for a few minutes stress was partially relieved. Then it began to build once more.

━━━━

On the ride in from Kennedy to Sam's brownstone house on East 63rd Street, Kate was silent. He thought about Diane. They had met when he was on the West Coast teaching a course in geophysics at UCLA. She was an established actress, divorced, in her early thirties. They were introduced at a Beverly Hills party given by an old MIT roommate of Sam's who had left the world of science to become a movie producer. When he saw her he thought she was the most beautiful woman he had ever seen, a cross between Elizabeth Taylor and Joan Collins with a little Jacqueline Bisset thrown in (a British accent having been fostered during her one year studying at RADA). He had known and had affairs with many women, but Diane Taylor was a knockout, and he remembered how he had maneuvered an introduction to her.

She had just been in a hit movie, and all the hangers-on, agents, directors, and producers were circling her at the party as though she were a hunk of rare meat and they a pack of sharks. She had turned away from a short fat man, given Sam a straightforward look with her large dark hazel eyes and smiled at him with her full, sensual mouth, and he had asked her to leave the party right then to have dinner with him. Within ten minutes they were in a restaurant and within two hours they were in her bed.

They stayed in bed for two days with occasional pauses in the proceedings for a bottle of champagne or a swim. She canceled every appointment; he called in sick to the university. The phone rang and rang, and some faraway maid took messages. They laughed a lot, told each other everything about themselves—how she had been a Hollywood brat who went to Hollywood High and segued into the business without a stop along the way; how he had grown up with two imposing parents who expected him to be great at something and how many times he had doubted that he would be able to fulfill their ambitions for him; about all their loves before that night, and how inconsequential they now seemed.

The limousine stopped. Sam sat still in the darkness of the backseat for a moment. He was not sure what to expect; his homecoming left a sharp feeling in his gut. He pulled himself up and helped Kate out of the car and into his home.

Danny's Norwich terrier, Copper, hurled himself at Sam and demanded to be given a grand hello. The lights in the kitchen were on and a note in their housekeeper's handwriting on the table was propped up against a bottle of Perrier. *Danny and I are at the movies. We'll be back by ten. Welcome home. Mary.*

Sam scratched Copper's belly and checked his watch. He saw that it was almost time for their return.

"I find flying to New York very tiring," Kate said, kicking her shoes off and starting up the stairs with them in one hand and her suitcase in the other.

"Come on, let me take that." Sam grabbed the bag out of her resisting hand—she hated to be helped—and put it in the first-floor bedroom.

"Will you give Danny a hug for me and tell him to come in and see me first thing tomorrow morning before he goes off to school? I've got to go to bed right this minute. Say hello to Diane when she gets home from the theater, will you? Good night, love."

"Good night, Kate. I'll take you to lunch tomorrow at The Four Seasons if you'd like. My interview is over by twelve thirty."

"How grand! I'll see you there at one."

He leaned down and kissed her. Then he went downstairs and looked at the stack of mail on the kitchen table, deciding it would wait until tomorrow. He poured himself a beer.

Several minutes later, as Sam was reading the morning's *New York Times*, the phone rang. It was his agent, Carlton Ames.

"How was your trip?"

"Okay. I've gotten very tired of hearing my own voice saying the same things about the book. Amazing."

"I talked with Michael yesterday. They're doing another printing of fifteen thousand copies. My hunch is that you'll hit number one by two weeks from now. Not bad. Now let's see if your publisher can keep you up there. You're set for the show tomorrow morning? The car is picking you up at ten thirty. The City is madness. The traffic is shit. You'll need the full hour to be sure you get to NBC on time."

"Next time, Carlton, can we get them to do a satellite tour? I'm getting too old to spend nights in hotel rooms eating cold cheeseburgers."

"Oh, come on, kid. You go first class all the way. Can't you find some cute bimbo to have fun with on the West Coast? From what I hear, or I should say read in Liz's column, Diane is getting around. Why shouldn't you?"

Sam felt his irritation level rise. Carlton was a damn good literary agent, one of the best, hardworking and honest. But he was a bitchy gossip, too. "You believe what you read, huh," he said, giving a lame imitation of disinterest. "Just what did you read?"

There was a slight pause. "I'm sure it's garbage. Pay no attention. One of her blind items. You know, about Diane and her leading man. Pure nonsense."

"Hey, I hear my son outside the door, I'll talk to you after the show."

"Do me a favor, Sam. Don't talk about earthquakes on the air. It's a real downer. Doesn't sell your book. Bye."

Danny ran in ahead of the housekeeper, Mary, and flung himself into Sam's arms. With all of his six-year-old strength he hugged his father.

Sam held him aloft, with the big upward swing that he knew Danny loved. He looked up into the boy's laughing, delighted face, a replica of Diane's with its raven shock of hair, hazel eyes fringed with dark lashes, and slightly crooked mouth. He brought him safely down and rumpled his hair.

"You look great, Danny. What movie did you see?"

He looked over his son's head at round, ample-breasted Mary, their life saver, who traveled from coast to coast without complaint as Diane worked one place or the other and Sam arrived from wherever he had been. They said to each other at least once a month, "Without Mary, where would we be? Thank God for Mary!"

She held out her hand. "Hi, Mr. Thorne. We saw the latest Eddie Murphy. I hated it, he loved it. What else is new. Want some fresh coffee?" She poured milk into a glass and handed it to Danny with a cookie.

"There were lots of funny cops and lots of animals from the zoo. There was a big gorilla that was running around." Danny's eyes were wide with excitement, more at seeing his father than the movie. He stuffed part of the cookie into his mouth. "It was awesome."

"Before I forget, your grandmother is here and wants you to wake her tomorrow before you take off for school."

"Will she walk me and Copper to school? I hate that old bus."

On fine days Mary, Copper, and Danny often walked uptown the twenty blocks to Grove, the private school he attended.

"We'll see." Sam looked down at the Norwich, who looked up at him. The dog had been bought from a breeder near Philadelphia after the breeder had put Diane and Sam through the Spanish Inquisition. You might think we were adopting a baby, Diane had complained. But it had been worth it. Copper was beloved. He was small, ten pounds, with a hard, wiry red coat, bright and keen dark oval eyes. True to the American Kennel Club's official description of the breed, he sported sensitive prick ears and displayed a gay and fearless disposition. The Thorne family, Danny in particular, was enamored of him. "Cops, would you like to take Danny to school tomorrow?" His short tail wagged furiously.

"Listen, it's past your bedtime. Why don't you go upstairs and I'll come up in five minutes to check you out?"

"Okay," Danny agreed and swallowed the milk in one gulp. He bounded up the stairs and as an afterthought called down, "Night, Mare." They could hear his delighted giggles at himself and his joke.

"You're wonderful for him, Mary. He seems to be in grand shape."

"He's a good boy, Mr. Thorne. I've been with some families when the children were a mess, but Danny's got sense and he's easy to care for. You and Mrs. Thorne must be doing something right. Even if you are away so much." She couldn't resist a reproving word.

"I know. I intend to spend more time with him from now on. When does Mrs. Thorne get home from the theater?"

"She said to tell you she's going to Orso's for a bite after the show and she should be back by midnight."

"Good. Thanks for everything. See you tomorrow morning. Do you see Danny off to school?"

"The school van comes by the door. And they bring him back around three in the afternoon. Good to have you home, and goodnight. Breakfast from eight on."

Sam entered his son's room. Danny sat on the edge of his bed in his fire-engine-red pajamas. All around was the mixture of toys and adult technology that boys of six treasured: a computer, a television, baseball mitt and bat, stacks of video games, and blown-up photographs on the walls of elephants and lions that Sam had sent him from a trip to Kenya the year before. Sam sat down beside him. "It's late, so we'd better skip reading time."

"Tomorrow night, then?" Danny loved having his father read to him from one of the books that lined the shelf by his bed. Kipling stories, Oz, tales of far-off lands and adventures. He wanted to be like his father, an explorer of some kind.

"Into bed with you." Sam pulled back the covers.

"Will you be here when I get back from school?"

"Sure. Let's you and I go to your mother's play tomorrow night and we can all have dinner afterward." He pulled the blanket up and tucked it around Danny's shoulders.

"Great!" He flashed his grin up at Sam. "How long are you going to be here? Can you come to the baseball game this weekend?"

"I think so, son. We'll work it out tomorrow. You go to sleep now." He kissed Danny's forehead and turned out the bedside light. "Sweet dreams, old buddy."

The satellite had been orbiting the earth for just over seven years, monitoring surface and subsurface temperatures for a group of scientists at fourteen universities around the globe. Since March it had been acting erratically, the signals it beamed home varying in intensity and thus in accuracy, sometimes disappearing for several days at a stretch only to come to life again unexpectedly. Now it had been out since the thirtieth of September and no one was bothering to monitor it any longer; the scientists had agreed that its useful days were over and it had been calculated that the satellite would plunge back into the earth's atmosphere early in the fall of 1997.

On the night of October 4, 1994, in a darkened room in one of the laboratories at Cambridge University, a screen that had been dead for nearly a week but that had never been turned off suddenly flickered to life. Had anyone who understood the signals it was receiving been there to see it, he or she would have raised an alarm, for the screen indicated a major increase of subsurface heat in North America, in a line extending from the U.S.–Canadian border southeast toward Long Island and well out into the Atlantic.

The intensity of the buildup would have shocked those scientists who had seen the satellite report similar events, for it was occurring in an area of the world where it was least expected. But no one was there to observe it, to lock the satellite onto its target, to send out a warning.

The satellite looked away. The screen faded.

From Sam's den he heard the front door open and Diane's footsteps on the stair. She appeared in his doorway, dark hair tousled by the autumn wind, her cheeks pink with the early cold outside, her eyes sparkling. He felt the same intake of breath he always felt the first moment he saw her beautiful face.

"Hi, darling." She came in and he stood to put his arms around her in greeting. Their lips brushed and they both stood back.

"How are you?" Sam asked.

"Glad to see you."

They stood looking at each other for a long moment.

"Want a nightcap?" He turned toward the bar.

"Yes, please. Whiskey, neat." She threw her mink coat on a chair and sat down on the sofa that she had had Mario Buatta cover in English cottage chintz. She tucked her feet under her and took the glass Sam proffered.

"Congratulations again on the show," he said, lifting his glass to her. "I'm sorry I couldn't be here for the first night. We would have your opening and my book tour in the same month." He sat opposite her. He had sent her two dozen Sonia roses, her favorite flower, and a fax to the theater, but still felt remiss.

"I'm sorry too, love, but it couldn't be helped. We're doing great business, I'm happy to report, and my reviews were to-die wonderful. Especially Frank Rich. What did he say . . . 'Diane Taylor, sensual and witty, particularly refreshing when one realizes she is an actress straight out of a TV sitcom . . . she illuminates the stage with her considerable talent . . .' Oh, it was delicious."

"No more than you deserve." Sam pushed the ice around his

glass with his forefinger. "Hey, Danny seems great! I saw him just after Kate and I arrived. I'll bring him to the show tomorrow night and then we can go out for dinner."

A frown flickered across Diane's brow. It was gone in an instant. "What fun! I'll take us somewhere, well, I suppose Orso's. It's the best for dinner after the show, and Danny loves their pizza."

"He's been there?"

"Oh, just once one night when Mary had the night off. During rehearsals. Some of the cast and I and Danny and some other kids, children of . . ." She paused, realizing she was overexplaining. Whatever else was wrong between Sam and her, it was not their ability to pick up on one another's clues.

"How is Kate?" Diane asked.

"Loaded for bear." They both laughed. "She was at the top of Long's Peak this morning, and bawling me out on the plane this afternoon." He glanced out the doorway as though expecting her to materialize. "She is outraged at the idea we might call it a day."

Diane fought the urge to take a cigarette from the drawer in Sam's desk where she had locked them a month ago to keep them away from her. She knew she was right to have been nervous about this homecoming. They had not parted on a happy note over a month ago, and nothing had been resolved in the few phone calls in between.

"And are we . . . I mean, are we going to? Call it a day, as you so quaintly put our ten-year marriage."

She smiled her very sweetest smile across at him, the one she had faith in because she had practiced it for so many hours in front of the mirror years ago for an ingenue role. It was meant to convey her innate sweetness combined with a strong bitchy streak. She knew Sam was not fond of this approach.

"You know we have to talk," he murmured.

"What? I didn't catch what you said."

"Talk." He raised his voice a notch and looked directly at her. "You and I have to decide something, anything. Relationships don't stand still. They either go forward or backward."

"Or die because of benign neglect."

They gazed at one another, at an impasse, neither wanting to take the conversation one more step.

Diane drained her drink and unfolded her long legs. "I'm

exhausted. Come on upstairs and let's talk while I take a bath."

He nodded and followed her up to their top-floor bedroom, actually two rooms joined by an oversize bathroom, his room serving as a second bedroom for times when one of them had a cold or, more recently, when Sam had come into town very late at night or early in the morning and did not want to disturb Diane. This night he sat on the king-size bed in her bedroom while she ran her tub and got undressed. Suddenly he realized that he did not want to talk while she was naked in her tub in front of him. It gave her far too great an advantage.

"I'm going to shower and get ready for bed. I'll see you in ten minutes." He went over and kissed her neck as she dropped her bra on the floor along with the pile of clothes that Mary would pick up tomorrow.

Minutes later she was brushing her hair in front of her large dressing-table mirror and Sam came back in his pale blue pajamas with the navy-blue piping.

"You look adorable," she drawled as he stood behind her. "So clean I could eat off you."

"What an admirable idea."

The scent of her Floris bath soap filled the room. She was wearing a satin nightgown cut so low that her breasts were entirely visible. Sam began to think that conversation was going to be a ridiculous waste of time. But in the way that they always seemed to be slightly out of sync these days, Diane turned serious just as he wanted to forget what he had started downstairs.

"Darling," she began. "You know that game we played when we first met, Tell the Truth and to Hell with the Consequences? Remember?"

He crossed the room and got into bed. "Of course."

She gave her hair another couple of swings of the brush and turned out the dressing-table light. "I'd like to give it a try tonight." She joined him on the other side of the bed and sat propped up by several pillows. "Remember the rules? No matter what is asked we have to tell the truth."

"Don't you think it's a little late to start tonight?" He held his watch in front of her nose. "It's after midnight and I have to get up early for an interview. I'd also like to see Danny off on the school bus."

She smiled her sweet pussycat smile at him. "Let's limit it, then, to five questions each. With a half-hour cutoff."

He sighed audibly.

"Darling, you *loved* the game the last time we played it."

"I was younger then."

"I'll start, shall I?" She leaned back and closed her eyes. After a long moment, "Who do you love more, the Goddess Science or me? Or to put it another way, do you love your work more than you love your wife?" Her eyes opened wide and she shifted her position to face him squarely.

"What an original question!" He grinned at her.

"I am serious and I want a serious answer."

"Do I get to ask the same question at the same time?"

"Absolutely not!"

He thought for a moment. "We both love our work. It's a dumb question."

"I don't believe the rules of the game say anything about our editing one another's questions. Proceed, please."

"No, I do not love my work more than I love you or Danny."

"Then how come . . ."

He interrupted her. "The rules do not allow for follow-up discussion. Simple questions, simple answers. It's my turn. Are you having an affair with the guy who's in the play with you?"

"Nonsense. Where did you hear that?" Diane gave him her most sincere expression.

"Is that your answer? I'd like a yes or no please. And remember, we have to tell the truth. Otherwise there is no trust."

"Okay. Yes, I am."

Sam got out of bed and walked toward the door.

"Hey, wait a minute. You asked. You had to ask."

He turned around and came back. "My agent told me. It's been in Liz Smith's column. Everyone in New York knows, why not me?"

"I get the next question. Did you or did you not sleep with Grace while you were on the West Coast? My old friend and your old roommate's ex-wife, Grace?"

Sam's face was grim. "No."

"No?" She was trapped. "No. Then that means I am the first-class slut, right? And you are Mr. Perfect as usual. Of course,

I see you once every two months if I'm lucky, while you follow your glaciers, vanishing species of all kinds, and earthquakes around the world. Damn! I could have sworn I would get you with the Grace question. She's wanted you to jump on her bones for years."

In spite of himself, Sam smiled. This woman had a way of making him want to laugh at the very moment she was breaking his heart. It was strange. And true.

"My question. Are you in love with your leading man?"

"No. Of course not. It's just one of those theater things. I mean, one always ends up sleeping with one's leading whatever, doesn't one? It is tradition. And sex. I mean, Sam, I do miss you. And I love sex. You did too, once."

"You just broke the no-follow-up-discussion rule. I don't want to talk about your affairs or hear about it again. Okay?" He got back into their bed. "It's your turn."

"Do you want a divorce?" Her voice was low, and her eyes serious.

He reached out and took her in his arms and held her. "No. Do you?"

"No."

"But there are a lot of things wrong."

"Yes." She put her hand down on his leg and ran it slowly upward.

"And we have to try to figure out how to fix them."

"Yes, darling." Her voice was muffled against his chest. Somehow the thought of her with another man simultaneously pained and aroused him. He slipped his hand inside her satin gown and began teasing the erect nipple of one breast.

"I think we have had our five questions." He leaned his head down to kiss her other breast.

"Who's counting?"

She slept on her side, first in his arms, later turned away from him. Sam lay awake in the deep darkness of the bedroom, the heavy curtains pulled against any possible intrusion of light. The day swirled through his mind. Too many places, too many people, too many mixed emotions to allow sleep to arrive. He looked at Diane, her naked back and shoulder and tangled dark hair, one arm flung over her head as though to ward off a blow, her even breathing so calm after the remembered passion of her breath, her sounds in response to him inside her, of only an hour ago. There was some sense of power in being able to arouse passion, some finite sense of control over another being, gone in a flash, gone to make humble the man who dared to feel it. Sam had never felt things so out of control as he lay there trying to go to sleep. He had the strange sensation of everyone and everything swimming away from him, just beyond his reach, so close and then just out of his grasp—his father; his son growing up without him there; his marriage; his wife beside him, fused to him for minutes of shared joy in perfect tune, and now turned away, perhaps lost to him; the phone call from Golden and the sound of Zimmer's agitated voice. He pushed the thoughts away, using the mental discipline taught him years ago by mountaineers. The ability to rid the mind of any destructive element was part of the ability to climb mountains. Kate had taught him early a kind of meditative technique, and he used it now, and eventually sleep came.

THE FIRST DAY

THE FIRST DAY

October 5, 1994
5 A.M.

olcanic activity had been minimal in the Adirondack Mountains for centuries. The mountains were a safe refuge for wildlife, protected in recent years from hunters.

This morning as the sun's rays began to streak the eastern sky with a delicate pink over the mountaintops, deep beneath the meadow that lay between two small hills, named Foxwatch by the locals, the molten core that extended down toward the center of the earth bubbled and boiled. A tremor that had started out in the middle of the Atlantic Ocean reached it, a tremor strong enough to create a crack in the solid granite that underlay Foxwatch meadow. Quickly, eagerly, the magma thrust itself into the crack, widening it as it rose upward toward the surface. Within a few seconds inertia set in and the magma subsided, having penetrated to within several hundred feet of the surface of the meadow. The crack had been formed. With another, more powerful shock, the magma would rise again.

Feeding time at the Bronx Zoo was nearly over, or at least for the majority of the animals; some were fed at different times of the day according to their own biological needs; others fed slowly all day long. But by nearly six o'clock, food had been laid out for most of the four-thousand-plus inhabitants of this big park in the heart of the populous Fordham section of the Bronx.

The food was left untouched. Keepers, veterinarians, and zoo officials alike were mystified by the lack of appetite being shown by virtually all their charges. And the attitudes of the animals were disturbing: The great cats, normally alert and pacing their cages at this hour of the morning, were strangely subdued; the fallow deer stood frozen at attention in tightly packed clusters in their open enclosure; the polar bears took to their caves, unwilling to venture out even for the hunks of meat and fish left them; at the elephant house, a closely watched pregnancy had ended abruptly in a miscarriage; and the entire ape house was bedlam, with the occupants of the cages hurling themselves madly about and screaming shrill cries of alarm.

The senior staff members made a tour of the zoo to ascertain that the phenomenon was general. None of the animals appeared to be sick, yet all were obviously apprehensive. The zoo's director looked around him; nothing could possibly be wrong on this beautiful fall day.

The animals knew better.

At 5:40 A.M. that October morning the shedrows at Belmont's training track were coming alive, the grooms carrying fresh water to the stalls, the exercise riders drinking coffee and looking over the horses they would soon be mounting. Large pots of abundant scarlet geraniums and white petunias decorated the area and the Rizzo colors, red and white bands, adorned the blankets neatly folded over the dutch doors. Early morning fog misted the track, the dawn light turning it into a sultry curtain about to be pierced by the first horse out to circle at a gentle gallop, hoofs thudding into the perfect raked surface, under the scrutiny of the trainer standing railside, stopwatch in pocket, binoculars raised.

Domenico Rizzo with his wife, Rosemarie, drove into his parking space in his black Jaguar that had a pencil thin red-and-white line painted along the side of its shiny door. Behind him another car, a nondescript Chevrolet, drew up and the four men inside it did not come out. They were bodyguards.

Domenico was short, just over five-foot-seven, but he carried himself like a tall man. He was dressed in faded blue jeans, cowboy boots, an immaculate white shirt, and an old World War II Air Corps leather jacket. He waved at the men in the car and gave them his famous smile. At fifty-three he had the unlined face of a choirboy. His cheeks dimpled, and under his bright hard black eyes, his small short nose, his mouth was full and wide, his teeth perfect. His black wavy hair was cut long, full in the back, and he ran his hand over it now, as he opened the car door for his wife.

Rosemarie got out and dropped her binoculars on the ground. He picked them up and handed them to her. She was a pretty woman, twenty pounds overweight, wearing heavy eye makeup, whose expensive Ungaro pants suit seemed out of place. She took Rizzo's arm too tightly as they walked toward the shedrow.

"Good morning, Dom," their trainer, Joe Factor, greeted them. "Good morning, ma'am." Factor had been a jockey, and he barely reached Rizzo's shoulder. "She's looking good."

He walked them over to the stall of Rizzo's latest potential star, a two-year-old filly, Capri, from Lady's Secret by Mr. Prospector. She had broken her maiden and won her first race that summer at Saratoga by five lengths. Today she was entered in the first race at Belmont, an allowance race, which went off at 1 P.M.

They peered into the stall. Capri was lying down, sound asleep.

"I'll be damned," Rizzo said.

"Is she all right?" Rosemarie asked, her eyes full of anxiety.

"The sign of a very good racehorse, like any terrific athlete,"

Factor told them. "She's relaxed. And she knows she's racing today because we changed her feeding schedule."

The dark bay filly lifted her head and gazed at them. She put her fragile-looking front legs out and raised herself up and walked over to them. Rizzo unlatched the dutch door and went into the stall. The filly nuzzled him. He had a way with his horses, and like everything he did he had studied assiduously about thoroughbreds before he bought his first one several years before. His late father, the head of the Barbetta family, the Godfather, had taught him this rule: "Never trust anyone. Not your wife, your best friend, your brother. Trust only yourself. And learn about every endeavor. If you know more than anyone else, you can't be cheated or betrayed as easily." Rizzo could remember as a ten-year-old boy listening to his father's advice. And it was good advice. Rizzo patted the filly's glistening neck and stooped to run his hands down her legs, taking care to feel if there was any heat in her tendons.

"She is so beautiful," Rosemarie said. Capri looked at her with her huge dark brown eyes, tranquil and intelligent and spirited. She had a white diamond in the middle of her forehead under the coarse black forelock. Her head was exquisite. One could never mistake Capri for a colt. She was every inch a filly.

Satisfied, Rizzo left the stall. "We got any other horses out on the training track today?"

"Sure, Dom. Two. The Seattle Slew colt and the four-year-old New York bred by Talc. Let's go take a look."

Factor walked them out toward the track. Rosemarie walked behind the men. She was worried about Capri no matter what Domenico and Factor said. If she had her way, all the horses would be at their horse farm beyond Oyster Bay, Long Island, where she could treat them like pets.

She adored all animals, but none more than horses. Her father, once the best friend and underboss to Domenico's father, had given her a pony when she was twelve. She remembered him still, and as she walked behind her husband and the trainer a picture came into her mind of a day long ago when Alfredo Rizzo had brought his young son on a visit to her father.

She remembered Domenico that day, shy, silent, so handsome he was almost pretty, and how they had played together in the barn, brushing her pony and taking turns riding him and how just before he left, in the hay loft of the barn, Domenico had kissed her on the mouth, the first boy to have ever done so, and put his hand inside her blouse. She remembered his fingers on her breast, and his knee between her legs. She pushed him away, giggling, and he chased her around the loft until she stumbled and fell. "You're a scaredy cat," he said, and threw himself down beside her. "Scaredy cat, scaredy cat."

"I am *not!*" She was in fact slightly frightened by this determined boy whose smiling face came very near her own. He pushed her down and kissed her again, this time putting his tongue in her mouth and his hand between her legs. She struggled but he was on top of her and he was not rough, just insistent. She felt dizzy and hot and the sensation he was causing between her legs was new and exciting. He forced his hand inside her panties. "This is a game I play," he panted in her ear and took her hand and placed it on something hard and stiff. "You do to me what I am doing to you, okay?" Just then, her father's voice rang out from below. "Children? Come down now. Domenico, your father is leaving. Pronto."

The boy withdrew his hand and abruptly got up without a word. He started for the ladder and then, as an afterthought, looked back to where Rosemarie still lay. "Someday we'll play again." He smiled at her.

She remembered that moment as though it had happened yesterday and not nearly forty years before. That was where and when Domenico's power over her began. Ten years later they had had an arranged marriage. She had given him a daughter, Angelica, not a son, and then could have no more children. She knew Domenico would have left her if it had not been for the Church and the family's tradition. At first they had been passionate lovers, but he had not touched her in bed for years.

She knew about his mistress. She knew everything. Too much. Her knowledge about the mob frightened her. Everything frightened her these days about Domenico, particularly the thought that he might put her back in the hospital, where she had spent several months after her last miscarriage. A very fancy place up in the Berkshires for crazy people. She had hated it there.

She leaned against the rail of the track fence watching, thinking. The men were oblivious of her. Horses with their riders trotted by, or walked, and on the inside of the track some went as fast as they could go. She watched them, the beautiful fragile animals, and felt sorry for them. They were trapped too, by their blood and fate, to be raced with no more choice in the matter than Rosemarie had had over her own life.

Domenico had told her this morning that he was going on a two-week business trip. She knew better. Of course, he was going on a vacation with her—the girlfriend. The nightclub singer. The one who had married into the family, married Domenico's cousin, Stefano, and, not Catholic, not Italian, no part of their lives, she had destroyed poor Stefano and divorced him and now was in bed with Domenico. Rosemarie's knuckles whitened as she clutched the railing.

Suddenly, near her, a horse reared and threw its rider. The horse bolted. The rider stood up, a young girl, and brushed herself off as they all looked up the track to where an outrider managed to capture the loose horse.

Factor frowned. "I don't know what's with this morning. We've had more action than we do when there's a big wind storm and all the horses get wired."

Domenico stared through his binoculars. "That's a nice colt, Joe, the one you bought for me at Keeneland. The Slew two-year-old. How do you think he's doing?"

"He's fast. I think we can see a race for him when we go down to Florida. February, March." Factor would not let Rizzo rush him.

"Not until then? You baby these horses. They were bred to run, not sit in stalls and eat."

Factor glared at Rizzo. "I'm the boss here, Dom."

Rizzo was about to get tough with his trainer, then changed his mind. "Sure. You're the only guy in the world who bosses Domenico Rizzo around." He gave Joe his widest smile. "All I do is write the checks. No questions asked. You're the big capo here, Joe."

"Jesus!" Factor yelled. The Slew colt had jumped the infield fence. Joe ducked under the railing and ran across the track along with other grooms and trainers while Rizzo and Rosemarie watched.

By now the sun was up. The horse had shied at a shadow and jumped over the inner railing, leaving its rider in the dirt. He streaked counterclockwise around the track, his neck lathered with sweat. Usually these mornings were quiet. This morning was haywire. Down the track, once again, the errant horse was captured and walked slowly toward the shedrow.

Rizzo turned his attention to his wife and noticed her scowl. He did not want trouble with her. He put his arm around her shoulders. "Come on, I got our Wednesday meeting at the Club in town. Let's go home. You coming back for Capri's race?"

Rosemarie loved the touch of his arm. She brightened. "Yes, if I get through at the hairdresser, I'll come watch her for you."

"Good." He gave her a hug and dropped his arm. "Put a thousand on the nose for me. The odds ought to be okay. She's only won one race and she's got some seasoned competition."

"You'll have to give me the money."

He frowned at her as they got into the car. "You out of dough this month already?" He put twenty thousand into her housekeeping expenses account every month. "For Christ's sake, what do you spend it on? As though I didn't know. Redecorating the house for the fourth time in four years, clothes up the kazoo, Jesus, Rose, my mother never did this to my father."

"Your mother . . ." Rosemarie stopped. She started again. "Times have changed."

Domenico pushed the car up to seventy-five mph on the Northern State Parkway and in his rearview mirror he saw the car with the bodyguards caught off-balance, trying to catch up. He loved losing them. One of the few things he disliked about running the Barbetta family was the need for constant protection. The rest he enjoyed. He was not the new breed who went to college and business school and resented the mob, though he had gone to Columbia and gotten his MBA. From the time he could remember being a little boy at his father's side in the big Cadillac limousine going to church he loved everything about his father's position in the world, the power he had to dispense favors and take them away, to give orders.

In spite of Rosemarie's extravagance, Rizzo felt good this morning. He had two weeks ahead with Nancy. The tickets for the Concorde were on his dresser top. She wanted to go to Paris and he had never been there, so that's where they were going. It would be the first time he had taken two weeks off in his life. Things were quiet right now, the latest indictment for ordering the murder of a union boss had been warded off by his lawyers, and he would turn over the day-to-day business to his underboss, Frankie Scarpino, a Queens loanshark and bookmaker originally from Jersey City. He and his bodyguard, a Romanian, Tom Rufala, were going to be there today at Rizzo's Manhattan headquarters, the Da Vinci Social Club. Rufala was a drug dealer. Together Scarpino and Rufala ran another social club uptown in the 80s, where they had a gambling casino. Highrollers from Westchester came to play poker, blackjack, and craps behind two steel doors to protect them from the police and robbers alike. Rizzo felt that they would take care of things just fine while he was away. And with the network, now international, of spies and operators, no big decision would be made without contacting Rizzo no matter where he was in the world.

In the 1990s most of America's traditional Mafia families were fading out of existence due to aggressive investigators and incompetent leadership. From Philadelphia to Salt Lake City, Mafia leaders had been deposed and their hierarchies dismantled. The exception was the New York City area. Domenico Rizzo was a brilliant businessman who still had the muscle to run his family with its nearly five hundred members with much the same kind of skill and daring and ruthlessness his father had shown.

Rizzo and Rosemarie wheeled into their long driveway lined with birch and maple trees leading to a large whitewashed brick mock-colonial house. It gave Rizzo a laugh every time he saw the house to think what the prior owner, a rich Protestant banker, would think of Domenico Rizzo, the boss of the Barbetta family, living there. On either side of the pathway to the baronial door,

Rizzo had put metal jockeys sporting his colors, red and white, and two Irish wolfhounds bounded out to greet him and Rosemarie. Anything those fucking snobs from Oyster Bay can do, he thought, I can do better—including horses, dogs, and women. Wait until one of my horses beats old Ogden Phipps in the Kentucky Derby.

The door was opened by the maid, and without waiting for Rosemarie, who was petting the dogs without caring that they were putting their muddy paws all over her suit, Domenico Rizzo entered his house and went upstairs to change for his meeting at the Da Vinci Club in Little Italy at noon.

5:48 A.M.

"That was Ed Ingles with sports, now let's have a report on traffic and the weather. First, up to Chopper 88 and Tom Kaminski."

"Thanks, Jim. Traffic is backed up on the approaches to both the Lincoln and Holland tunnels for forty-five minutes and one lane of the Lincoln has been closed due to repair work under way. Your best approach to the city from Jersey would be the lower deck of the George Washington. Avoid the upper deck; a fender-bender involving three or possibly four cars is being sorted out by the police now, and traffic on that deck is being funneled down to one lane. In Brooklyn there is a twenty-five-minute delay on the Gowanus and traffic is slow going past the Elmhurst tanks in Queens. On the East Side, traffic on the Drive is crawling from the Forty-ninth Street exit south to Fourteenth Street, so avoid that stretch if you can. The Queens Midtown Tunnel is backed up twenty minutes. I'll have more for you in ten minutes on our next report. Down to you, Mr. Allen."

"Thanks, Tom. Sounds like a pretty normal day in the life of a commuter. At least the weather will be good, and mild for October. We are having the best Indian Summer since October 1990. The high today is expected to be around seventy-five degrees with a low tonight of fifty-five. Humidity will be a comfortable forty-five percent, and breezes will be out of the northwest at five to seven miles per hour. A cool front will be moving in tomorrow morning, and we can expect a continuation of this beautiful weather through the weekend. I'm Craig Allen, and I'll have more weather for you in ten minutes."

"Thanks, Craig. I'm Jim Donnelly."

"And I'm Bridget Quinn. It's five fifty A.M. and time for a break. Then we'll be back with a story of a lady and her dogs followed by all the financial news, including the latest on the upcoming takeover of Allied Signal by Grumman."

Battalion Chief Brendan Ahearn rolled over and pushed the button on his alarm clock. It was 6 A.M. He lay back for a minute, waiting for the darkest moment of his day to pass. It was still there every day, the sick pit-of-the-stomach realization that he was alone in his bed, that JeanAnne was gone forever. Even after a year, he awakened expecting to see her beside him. Dead, he forced his mind to say, she is dead. Believe it, buddy. You've got to get it through your thick Irish head. He pitched his forty-year-old body up and out of bed and into the bathroom. This was his day shift with the Fire Department. Wednesday, October 5. Firemen worked two shifts, from 9 A.M. to 6 P.M., and the night from 6 P.M. to 9 A.M., and the shifts rotated. Two days on the morning shift, then off duty for forty-eight hours, and back for two days on the night shift.

Toothbrush in hand, he yelled out the bathroom door. "Time to get up, you guys. On the double!" When he heard sounds of response from his two sons, Nicky, eight, and Willy, six, he went back in to shave. He looked in the medicine cabinet mirror. His forty-first birthday was next month. A one-day stubble darkened his strong chin and ran right up to his graying sideburns. He had a mustache, neat and black with tiny handlebars, that the guys at the Third Division Station House—the 13 Truck, 22 Engine on 85th Street between Third and Lexington—teased him about. His dad had been a fireman for forty years, moved up the ranks to borough commander of Queens, and had sported the lushest set of handlebars in the department. Brendan trimmed his mustache. His dark brown eyes with their dark circles stared back at him, at the look he now recognized as sadness so foreign to Brendan Ahearn before JeanAnne had been killed in a car accident. Brendan loved to laugh, and they had both laughed a lot. She was a bright spirit, and nothing the kids did ever got her down. She got angry with them, but her sense of humor came back right away. She had a way with them . . . and with him. Straightforward and funny.

He would never forget when her brother, his best friend in the Fire Department, Joe Gdowski, rang the doorbell of their semi-attached house in Port Washington on one of Brendan's days off. When Brendan opened the door, he knew. Joe was crying, his eyes all red and puffy. He threw his arms around Brendan and held him, sobbing. "Some bastard kid didn't stop at a light. JeanAnne. She's at the hospital . . . she's hurt real bad."

They had driven to the hospital and when they got there a solemn-looking doctor in operating green came down the hall and told them she had died on the operating table.

"Can we go sailing this weekend, Pop?" Nicky asked, spooning cereal into his mouth. Brendan kept a thirty-eight-foot Hinckley docked at the marina. "Yeah, Dad, can we?" echoed Willy.

Brendan downed his second cup of coffee. "Sure. Don't see why not. Sunday. I'm working night shift Friday, Saturday. Did you feed Timmy?" The yellow Labrador retriever sat at Nicky's elbow begging.

Nicky made a face. His brown hair was cut across his forehead and he looked like his mother. "Of course I did."

"Good. I'm going out to run and by the time I get back I want you two ready for school. Okay?" He ran his hand over Willy's blond head. Willy took after him. Short, square, strongly built, a good tackle. Nicky looked like a baseball player, a pitcher, long and lean. "Come on, Timmy. You come with me."

After his morning jog, Brendan Ahearn packed the boys off to Holy Name and drove toward Manhattan thinking about the day ahead. The tour of the day began with roll call, and he'd be there after parking his car in a lot at 86th and Second Avenue just in time. Today, after the ever-necessary cleaning and maintenance of the equipment, the fire rigs, engines, and trucks, their own lifesaving gear, the breathing apparatus worn by every fire fighter, they had to conduct a special inspection of a new office building on Third Avenue. Brendan, as the battalion chief, was in command of three lieutenants and twenty-five firefighters. He worried about each and every one of them. To do their job, it took more than strength, more than courage. You had to love danger. You had to like looking down from great heights with smoke billowing all around you. You had to like the other men—and now a few women—on the force, and the life. Brendan believed you had to be born with it in your blood, the way he had. Most of the guys on his tour had a father or son or uncle in the Fire Department. It was like the Police Department, only more dangerous. A car swerved from the right lane in front of him. "You asshole," Brendan yelled through his closed window. Nothing was more dangerous than the Northern State Parkway.

Domenico finished dressing in his dark blue silk Brioni suit, picked up the tickets for the Concorde and put them in his inside jacket pocket. He went down to his den and unlocked the safe. Inside were stacks of bills. He took a thousand dollars and put it in an envelope on his desk for Rosemarie to take to the track to bet on Capri. Then he went downstairs, in a hurry, two at a time, and got into the back of his chauffeur-driven black Mercedes limousine. He rested his head on the back of the seat. Two bodyguards knew enough to be silent, one sitting in front with the driver, and one in back with him. He patted his jacket. Tomorrow night at this time he and Nancy would be in the Hotel Ritz in Paris opening a bottle of champagne. He could not wait to get away with her, away from all the demands of his work, the never-ending crisis that was his job. He allowed his mind to drift, as the car sped toward Manhattan. He thought about Nancy Thayer.

Almost two years before, on a rainy night in September, Domenico Rizzo had taken Frankie Scarpino, Tom Rufala, and a couple of his bodyguards to the Gray Cat Club to hear Nancy Thayer sing. She was the ex-wife of Domenico's cousin, Stefano, and the purpose of this visit to the cabaret was not to listen to some dumb broad warble, but to teach her a lesson she wouldn't forget. Stefano, since the divorce, always a weakling in Rizzo's opinion, had sunk lower than ever. He was a drunk, probably on drugs, and a disgrace to the family. Before Nancy Thayer, Stefano had been a useful "soldier," good-looking and smart, able to "pass" in social circles most of them couldn't get into, which, Domenico mused as he twirled a straw in his scotch highball, is how Stefano got mixed up with this society singer in the first place.

Frankie yawned audibly. "When does the canary sing? I'm beat."

Rizzo checked his Cartier tank wristwatch. "Any minute now. Have another drink, and shut up."

The piano player appeared and sat down, and the lights dimmed.

"See," Rizzo bragged. "All I have to do is ask. . . ."

From somewhere, he didn't see where, a woman in a simple black evening gown stepped into the pin light. She wore a single strand of pearls. She was tall, slender, and her auburn hair fell straight to her shoulders. She had no discernible makeup on, and her pale skin and almond-shaped green eyes fringed with black lashes gave her the look of some exotic jungle animal. The room fell silent. She turned her back on them and leaned down to whisper something to the pianist. Her black gown was cut very low in back, and the white skin showed her backbone running down to the curve of her buttocks under the shiny black form-hugging material. She turned around and faced the tables of attentive listeners. In a low, husky voice she said, "Good evening. Thanks for coming. I'm going to sing some Gershwin, some Rodgers and Hart, some Kern, and some Porter. So sit back and enjoy yourselves."

Was it his imagination, or was she looking right at him? She had a low-down, impudent look no matter how classy she was supposed to be. Rizzo stared back at her, as she began with "It Never Entered My Mind." Her voice was sure, strong, and melodic. He tried to think who she reminded him of, and the name Anita O'Day crossed his mind, but Nancy Thayer was more fragile, the voice in a higher range, something ladylike that maybe she had tried to get rid of, but he saw she couldn't, anymore than he could shed his background. She went on singing, and every once in a while her green eyes would find him and he felt a singular sensation. Women had always been there for him ever since he could remember. He had been seduced at ten by the eighteen-year-old girl his father had brought over from Italy to take care of him and his brothers and sisters. From then on his prowess with women was something he took for granted. And he was bored with his conquests as soon as he had gone to bed with them. His world was a man's world, filled with male pursuits. Women were to satisfy an itch, a momentary desire. His wife and daughter he would protect to the death. But Rosemarie had become a big liability, unstable and extravagant, and he had long since left her bed. This woman stirred some feeling close to anger in Rizzo, an uneasiness, something over which he had no control.

She finished her set and disappeared into the darkness. When the lights came up, Rizzo said to his companions, "Okay. Now I've seen what Stefano was married to. You can all go home. I'll take care of family business. You hang around, Joey," he indicated one of his bodyguards. "Just follow me at a distance. I don't want her to see you, *capisce?*"

He went to the captain and asked how to get to Nancy Thayer's dressing room. When he found it, he knocked on the door.

"Who is it?"

"Domenico Rizzo."

She opened the door, and he walked into a small room with a dressing table and chair and a chaise longue, on which was scattered sheet music. "How do you do, Mr. Rizzo," she said with a faint smile. She ducked her head as she spoke. He noticed that she was taller than he. "Come in, want a drink?" She held one in her hand.

"Sure. Scotch."

She waved him toward the bottle, glasses, and ice bucket. "Help yourself." She watched him as he poured some scotch into a glass neat.

Domenico raised his glass. "You have a terrific voice."

"Thanks." Nancy Thayer sat down at her dressing table. "Aren't you Stefano's cousin?"

Rizzo took off his camel hair polo coat and draped it over the back of the chair. "Yeah. He sends his regards."

She laughed, a short mirthless sound. "I doubt it."

"Oh, yeah. He did. And, well, I was in the neighborhood, so I thought I'd check out your act. He's always telling us how great you are." He gave her one of his famous smiles, open, cherubic, sexy. He ran his hand over his black hair. "Too bad you guys didn't make it."

"Yes. Too bad." She looked at him without any expression, her green eyes unblinking.

"It's only after midnight. Do you do another show, or would you like to go hear some jazz with me? I know a great place."

She sipped her vodka. "I'm finished here for the night." Everything she did seemed deliberate, not spontaneous. She took another sip. "Sure, why not. I'll be ready in a moment. Wait outside, please."

He took his coat, drained his drink, and went to the hallway. In moments she was there, wearing an old man's tan raincoat over her black evening dress. "Do I need my umbrella?"

"I have a car. Come on." He took her arm and held it close to his chest. "Let's go."

The driver pulled up the black Mercedes limousine, and they got in back. Rizzo poured her another vodka, and himself a weak scotch. She was quiet as the car sped through the rain-soaked streets to the Village. "Where did you meet Stefano?" Rizzo asked.

She cupped her glass and stared out the window. "At a party my brother gave for me when I came back from Europe. I'd been over there trying to paint. When I found out I wasn't an artist, I came back. My brother's into all kinds of crazy schemes. I guess that is how he knew Stefano."

She turned and gazed at Rizzo. "I know what you think. You think that I was a spoiled rich girl who was slumming and I married your cousin for kicks."

Rizzo smiled at her and said nothing.

She put her glass down, empty, in the circular container built into the bar, and looked him squarely in the eye. Her lower lip was fuller than the top one and gave her that look of impudence, of daring him to make a move. "You're dead right," she said in an even voice. "I'd never been with a Mafia guy before. My family went crazy when I told them I was going to marry Stefano. A Catholic and a member of the mob." She smiled at Rizzo. "My parents went into orbit."

That was precisely what he had intended to accuse her of, marrying poor Stefano for kicks. And, of course, he also planned to let her know how damaging it might be to her health if she ever opened her mouth about anything Stefano might have told her about business. Christ knew what that lovesick weakling might have bragged about to try to impress this fancy WASP broad. But at the moment Rizzo was feeling more than a little disarmed.

"Where do you live?" Rizzo asked.

She gazed at him for a moment without answering. Then she leaned forward and said to the driver, "Take us to Forty-one Greenwich Avenue, please."

Domenico Rizzo followed Nancy Thayer up the two flights of stairs to her apartment. He was amazed that she lived in such a crummy place. Where was the money? He had thought she was rich. The parents must have cut off her supply when she married Stefano.

She unlocked the door and stepped inside the dark apartment. He followed her and closed the door. She walked across the shabby living room and turned on lights, until she reached the kitchen, where she pulled out an ice tray. He took off his coat and threw it on a chair, glancing at his reflection in a wall mirror. He ran his hand over his hair and straightened his tie.

She came back to him and handed him scotch, then sipped on her vodka.

"You drink too much," he said.

"So what else is new. You must have known that from Stefano."

It was very late now. Rizzo should have been tired. Something about this beautiful, strange woman made him feel wide awake, though, and he had difficulty reminding himself why he was there.

"So you married my little cousin Stefano for kicks? He was a good little boy until he met you." Rizzo sat down next to her on the sofa. She had drawn her legs up under herself and was curled up against one end of the sofa. She reminded him of a cat, a surly, sassy, unpredictable cat.

"Sure, he was just fine," she said. "A killer, but just fine."

"What did he tell you?" Rizzo leaned forward. "Some tall stories, I guess. You think we all go around killing people? You've been seeing *Godfather* reruns too much. Those days are over."

Rizzo smiled, sipped his drink, then added, "But a little loose talk can bring back the good old days." The smile remained frozen on his face.

"I introduced Stefano to some of the finer things in life, that's all," Nancy said with a shrug. She uncurled her long body and got up to put a tape in the tape deck. Billie Holiday's voice tuned low sang some song he knew but couldn't place. She came back to the sofa and sat closer to him. She put a hand casually on his thigh and leaned toward him, her face no more than a foot from him.

"You trying to scare me, Rizzo?"

He could feel the heat of her hand on his thigh. He smelled her perfume and the faint hint of vodka on her breath.

"Didn't I just explain to you that I married Stefano for kicks?" Her voice was just a throaty whisper now. She moved even closer to him, her lips almost touching his, her hand sliding slowly up his thigh. "Danger, Rizzo," she breathed, "danger turns me on."

Whatever remained of Domenico Rizzo's original game plan for the evening evaporated at that instant. The hell with Stefano and his problems, he told himself. His irresistible desire for this sensual, fearless, intoxicating, green-eyed beauty was all that mattered at the moment. Rizzo put one arm around her and pressed her to him, trying as discreetly as possible with the other hand to reach into the watch pocket of his trousers to extract the condom he usually carried. Just in case the fancy bitch has something, no sense giving Stefano the last laugh.

A week later, Domenico Rizzo had made a decision. He had tried for two days to stay away from Nancy Thayer but couldn't get her out of his mind. His thoughts kept drifting back to their night together, to the sight and feel and smell of her. For Rizzo, women were recreation and for a man of his position there was plenty of recreation available. But this woman had stimulated him so completely, he was becoming obsessed with her. The third night he went back to the Gray Cat Club and sat there with his heart pounding like a schoolboy's as she fixed her green eyes on him and sang. He had been with her every night since. Now, as he lay in her bed with his arm around her sleeping form, his decision was clear.

Nancy stirred. "What time is it?" she asked.

"Eight."

Her head was in the crook of his arm, her face against his chest. He lay there in the semidark, the morning light from the window just enough so that he could see the room. His body felt languid. He was pleased with himself. My God, at fifty-one to be able to make love all night was pretty damn good. And what a woman. He knew this was crazy. Every instinct he had told him that she was trouble, but he wanted more of her. He knew that, too. He wanted to possess her.

"I got to get you out of this dump," he said. "I'm going to find a beautiful apartment for you uptown."

"I love this dump. I've lived here for a long time, since Stefano and I got divorced. Three years at least. I can't afford better. Even if I could, I like the Village and it suits me."

"What happened? Your family threw you out?"

She ran her finger up and down his arm, which was muscular and covered with black hair. "Old WASP money thins, and my trust fund ran out years ago. And I think at forty I shouldn't take money from my parents. They've barely got enough to keep up appearances. I earn enough singing to pay the rent. It's all I need."

Rizzo thought this over, then said, "Families are there to help, no matter what age you are." She puzzled him. And something else had been bothering him. "When you told me to wait outside your dressing-room that first night," he asked, "did you take a hit? Is that what you were up to?"

"Sure," she replied without hesitating. "Why not? I've been on coke since the year of the flood. You guys provide it for me and make a buck, so what's your gripe?"

"Us guys?" Rizzo sounded stunned. "You mean you think I deal in coke? No way."

"Not since the Jamaican Posse up in Harlem cornered the cocaine market a while back, right? But up till then the mob was my supplier. And all the rest of us." She got up, put on a blue silk robe, and sat on the bed beside him. "Don't kid me, Rizzo."

"You're one smart woman, right? Know all the answers. Stefano must have blabbed his little heart out to you. What else you know about?" He drew her down to lie beside him and with genuine concern in his voice said, "Hey kid, you got to stop with the drugs if we're going to be together." He kissed her gently. "I got a place already picked out for you. Trump Tower. You'll love it. I'll buy you a duplex as big as Donald's . . ."

"No, Rizzo," she interrupted. "No vulgar Trump Tower."

Rizzo ignored the rejection. He got up and went into the bathroom. She heard the shower running for several minutes. He came back with a towel wrapped around his waist and got back into bed.

"You've got a dynamite body, Rizzo, for an old man."

"The same to you, sister." They smiled at each other.

"Vulgar?" he continued. "A million-dollar co-op is vulgar?"

"Yes, sweetie. You can't boss me around the way you do your gang or your wife or Stefano."

"Why'd you dump Stefano?"

"I got rid of him because it occurred to me shortly after we got married that I was more of a man than he was. Smarter, braver, more loyal. It doesn't matter. The point is that Stefano is a gutless shit. He's my mistake. I couldn't bear him after the first month."

"You're right." Rizzo took her chin in his hand and kissed her gently. "Now listen. I got to get you out of here. I can't have my girl living in a dump like this. It's not good for my reputation."

She burst out laughing. "You're serious!" She looked at his unamused face. "My God, you *are* serious. What I don't understand about the mob. Listen, Rizzo, is it true you had Big Paul Castellano gunned down outside Sparks Steakhouse? Is that how you became such a powerful Mafia boss?"

Rizzo got up and started to get dressed. He ignored her questions until he had his pants on. Then he sat down beside her. He put one hand on top of her head and patted it as though she were a pet dog. In as sinister a tone as he could muster, he said, "Listen, girl, don't say things like that to me."

Her green eyes were as cold as the sea in December. "I say

anything I want to anybody," she shot back. "I don't move to the Trump Tower like some cheap tart you want to dress up in those awful overpriced clothes you are so proud of. I don't stop drinking and taking an occasional hit of coke. And I most certainly don't censor my questions or my language for you or anyone else."

He removed his hand and sat quietly on the side of the bed for a long moment.

"Are you trying to decide whether to hit me?" she taunted, "or just how to regain your wop dignity?"

He stood up. He went over to the mirror and tied his tie. He picked up her comb and ran it carefully through his hair. Then he put on his navy-blue silk Brioni jacket and brushed off the shoulders, tweaking the kerchief in the pocket into proper points. It matched his paisley tie. She watched his every move like a cat watching a bird.

When he was ready, he picked up his coat from the living-room chair and came back into the bedroom. He stood at the foot of the bed and said, "Everyone knows about Rizzo's temper. I held it down for you. For your sake. You want to see me again, you got to have some respect for me."

"I don't know you well enough to know if I respect you. You can't force people to respect you." She got up and ran her fingers through her straight auburn hair. "My God, I feel as though I met a Mack truck last night." She walked over to him and put her arms around his waist and leaned up against him. "What did you do to me, Rizzo?" She ducked her head for a moment, then looked up at his angry black eyes. She put her arms around his neck and pulled his head down to her so she could kiss him. He tried to resist, but could not.

Almost two years ago, Rizzo mused, as he remembered those fabulous nights he and Nancy had spent together in her apartment, then how he had gotten her to begin meeting him at the Plaza, where he had a room overlooking Central Park. Sometimes their trysts began with lunch. They'd order up room service after Rizzo phoned home and told lies to Rosemarie. They'd make love. Rizzo would conduct some business on his portable cellular telephone, an ideal instrument for his line of work since it used random frequencies, making conversations impossible to intercept. They'd make love again and hold each other and talk, then phone room service again for dinner. He'd get her to the Gray Cat Club just in time for her first set of songs and he'd sit at his usual table listening to her as though he'd never heard such a wonderful voice or seen such a beautiful woman before. She'd sing every torch song right to him. God, how he remembered those early days.

In the end, he had won the Trump Tower debate. She lived now in a sumptuous apartment. He had even set up an office in one of the many rooms, complete with fax machines, computers, and other paraphernalia. Rizzo spent as much time with Nancy Thayer as he could, and even now after almost two years, he couldn't say he understood her. Or that she respected him. He remembered her words. Maybe she did. Maybe she didn't. All he cared about was holding her and being with her and taking care of her. He had come to realize that she needed taking care of, and that for all her bravado, she was in need of his love and protection. He was sure she had given up cocaine and, most of the time, booze. She had made some records for CBS and had an offer to sing at the Algonquin. He had been good for her, and that pleased him.

9:00 A.M.

Howard Tate's limousine drew into the circular drive of New York Hospital. The driver jumped out and went to open the passenger door.

"Thanks, Jim. I'll be about half an hour."

Tate walked through the revolving door and down the marble corridor toward Dr. Gordon Keith's office. As he walked, he read the gilt-engraved names of the great benefactors of the hospital: Rockefeller, Sloan, Kettering, Vanderbilt, Guggenheim. A tall, thin man of seventy, Tate squared his shoulders under his expertly tailored British suit and tried to put a pleasant expression on his unusually tense face. He had tried to dismiss the odd twitches in his muscles and sudden weakness in his hands and legs, which came and went without reason.

"Good morning," he said to the young nurse behind the desk. "I'm . . ."

"I know." She smiled at him. "Mr. Tate. Dr. Keith is waiting for you. Please follow me."

Gordon Keith, as famous as a neurologist as Tate was as a real-estate entrepreneur, stood up and shook his hand. Keith was in his late fifties, a man with erect bearing, his brown hair receding over a high forehead, his large, heavy-lidded eyes alert and direct. He smiled at Howard. But was the smile reassuring? He had all the tests back now. This was The Talk. Doctors always had to schedule The Talk to tell you the bad news. Maybe it was good news. He couldn't tell a thing from Keith's expression.

"All ready for the big event?" Dr. Keith asked.

"Don't stall, Gordon. The big event can wait." The doctor had referred to the opening ceremony planned for one o'clock that day of Tate Acres, Howard's penultimate plan for New York. "I want to know what's wrong with me." Howard's gray eyes, stern behind rimless glasses, demanded an answer.

In his unthreatening voice, as though talking about any everyday occurrence, the doctor said, "Howard, I've studied all the tests and scans as have several of my colleagues, including Dr. Posner over at Memorial—he is probably the best diagnostician in the country when it comes to neurological problems." He paused and gazed at Tate with a look that said: You all *say* you want the truth, but do you really, Howard Tate?

"Shoot."

"Amyotrophic lateral sclerosis. Lou Gehrig's Disease."

Tate said nothing but looked away.

"Howard, there is a lot we can do now that we couldn't before. I'd say you can expect to lead a full life, have a full lifespan."

Tate smiled without mirth. "You mean at seventy . . ." He let it hang.

"Exactly." Dr. Keith knew that the last thing this complicated and powerful man wanted was for him to be sympathetic at this moment. "Several more years without any severe problems, and who knows after that. New scientific approaches, new medicines are being developed, some of them right here. This is not the death sentence it was in the forties. It's rotten. But you've got some good time."

Tate stood up and held out his hand. "If you don't mind, I'd like to wait until after the ceremony today to hear all the grisly details, what I won't be able to do, what I will be able to do, you know. How about next week?"

"Of course. Make an appointment with Janie as you leave."

"Any chance of you getting over to the ceremony today? I want you to reconsider my offer to head up the neurological staff at the new hospital at Tate Acres. I won't hold today's news against you, I promise." He held out his hand. The Tate charm was universally recognized and it was operating even now.

"I'd love to be there today, but I have to take a rich lady to lunch at The Four Seasons hoping to pry some money out of her for this hospital. You know I can't even think of leaving here right now. But I am honored, you know that too." Dr. Keith shook Tate's hand. "Come to see me next week and we'll work out the details of your medication."

Tate left Keith's office, made his appointment with the nurse, and strode back down the vaulted hall and out into the purest of October days. The air was cool and clean, and everything seemed in harmony. He leaned back in the car and closed his eyes. After a few moments, he pulled himself upright. "Jim, swing by the apartment first. I want to see my wife before we head downtown."

On the way into Manhattan, Rizzo ordered the driver to stop in Roslyn at his daughter's place. "I'll be ten minutes," he said and bounded up the steps to Angelica's big Victorian house, set back off the main highway and surrounded by a twenty-foot-high wooden wall. The driver shrugged. It happened all the time. Domenico Rizzo never missed an opportunity to see his only child.

Rizzo rang the doorbell, tried the door, and went inside, calling out, *"Figlia bella.* You there? Where are you?"

"In here, Papa," Angelica called back from the kitchen. She appeared in the doorway, a short, square young woman, with heavy dark eyebrows and a brilliant smile like her father's. They embraced, and he held her back from him. *"Come' stai, bella?* Okay?"

"Sure, Papa. Come on in. I'm just making some dough to bake your favorite bread. I'll leave it off later today with Mama."

He sat on a stool by the wide countertop and watched Angelica roll out the dough like his grandmother had done many years before when he visited her in Little Italy in an apartment she would not leave no matter how rich the Rizzo family became.

She stopped and went to the stove. "Here's some good coffee, not like that stuff you get at home." She poured some *caffe filtre* into a small cup and handed it to him. "How's Mama?"

"Okay, okay. You know. She's not a happy woman. I do what I can. Money. She buys and buys and shops and shops. Listen, *bambina*, I don't know what to do about her, but maybe going to watch Capri win the first race at Belmont this afternoon will cheer her up."

Angelica was not interested in her father's horses. She frowned. "She told me you were taking a trip?"

"Yeah. Me and some of the boys. We got to go over to Europe. You know, the business is going worldwide these days. I'll only be gone a couple of weeks. You look out for Mama, okay?"

Angelica looked up and gave her father a long, quizzical glance. "I hear things, Papa. Alfredo tells me things."

"How is that son of yours, anyway? What the hell would he hear, he's too busy getting into trouble." Angelica's husband had been killed in a shoot-out with the Biambelli gang five years before. Their son, Alfredo, was fifteen now, and hung around with Rizzo's bodyguards every chance he got.

"Alfredo's not good. I need your help. He tells me you got a girl, Papa. And this time it's serious. How about it, is it?" She had her hands on her ample hips and reminded Rizzo again of his own mother.

Angelica was thirty-three. He had been only eighteen when he married Rosemarie and they had had her, and she, in turn, had married at eighteen and had Alfredo the same year. She was old enough to know what was going on, and besides, Rizzo confided in her as he had only done with one other person in his life, his late mother.

"Yeah. It's true. It's been going on awhile."

"How long?"

"Couple of years. I met her after she divorced your cousin, Stefano." He drank down the bitter coffee.

"So, she's one of us," Angelica's voice was relieved.

Rizzo threw back his head and laughed. "She's about as far from the family as you can get. Old Protestant money. How do you say, WASP? She's like the rebel in her family. The black sheep. She's a nightclub singer. She gave that sap Stefano one hell of a time." He grinned at his daughter.

"And you. What kind of time does she give you?"

"One hell of a time." He laughed again. "I got her to give up the pills and booze, but she's a bad girl." He became serious. "Listen, *carrissima*, I'm crazy about her. She's not like any other woman I've ever known. I . . . she's got her hooks right into me where I live."

Angelica came around the counter and stood near her father. "You be careful, Papa. Not in the family. It's dangerous. And Mama. What about her? Is this woman very young, is that it?"

"No. She's in her forties. She's been around. I can't explain. Look, I'll never leave your mama. You know that. And Nancy understands that I never will leave your mama. She doesn't want to marry me, she doesn't want my money or my power. She's the only woman I've ever been with who only wants me." Rizzo felt that what he said was true, that Nancy wasn't interested in money or power. But he didn't know why.

Angelica kissed his cheek. "Papa, be careful. And I want you to talk with Alfredo. Can you come over some Sunday to see him? He's getting into more trouble all the time. I have a suspicion about drugs. Will you talk with him?"

Rizzo glanced at his watch. "Of course. When I get back from Europe. I got to go now, but I'll see you three Sundays from now after church. I'll talk to Alfredo. Don't you worry. When I'm finished with him he'll be okay. Kids. My God, these days it is terrible. When I was a kid it was different." He kissed her and walked to the door. "Don't worry about me, I'll be okay. You check on Mama when you take over the bread, okay?"

"*Va bene. Ciao*, Papa."

At eleven thirty that morning, Brian Kelly, the founding partner of a small brokerage located in the World Trade Center, had had his regular meeting with his partners, Kline and Farnsworth, to review the business activity that past week. Among the subjects for discussion was their young hotshot broker, Dave Hartnett. Glenn Farnsworth's patrician brow was creased with a deep frown. "I had a very disquieting lunch on Monday at the Union Club with Sam Gaites, you know, Dave's last employer at Morgan," he drawled.

Brian sighed. These WASPS could never spit it right out, they had to chew on it while you waited for the other shoe to drop. "So?"

"Well, you know we've been discussing making Dave a partner. After all, how old is he, thirty-two? He's been here three years and we started him at a salary of one hundred thousand plus commissions, and the last time I checked, which was last week, he was earning over five hundred thousand from commissions alone. In fact," Glenn smiled and lowered his glasses to look at the bored faces of his two dear friends and Columbia University classmates from '78. "In fact, he is doing better for the firm than some of its partners."

"We hired Hartnett because he's the best whiz kid we could afford at the time," Brian reminded him. "I know six firms that would like to hire him away from us."

"Yes," said Aaron Kline. "I can't stand the guy, but he's good, all right."

Glenn gave Kline a victorious look. "Right. Which brings me back to my lunch. And to my second look at Hartnett's résumé. We may have been a bit hasty. Gaites tells me that Hartnett is a compulsive gambler."

"Oh, yeah. And Kline's an alcoholic," Brian said, giving Kline a fond look. When Brian and Farnsworth were savoring their end-of-the-day martinis, Kline had a Diet Coke.

"Everyone knows, like my grandmother said, there are no Jewish alcoholics or homosexuals," Kline replied with a straight face.

"I am serious, gentlemen." Farnsworth persisted. "We know that the vice which is most dangerous for us is not wine or women. Gambling can wreak havoc with a financial firm, especially one as small as ours, with no ability to withstand either a hint of scandal or a major financial indiscretion." Farnsworth rested his case and gave the other two a somber stare.

Brian made doodles on the pad in front of him. Kline was thoughtful.

"Where did Gaites get the information?" Brian asked.

"It seems that Morgan's had hired a young man with the same problem, and, in interrogating him, Hartnett's name came up. Of course," Farnsworth added, "Morgan's had no recourse but to ask for their young man's resignation."

Brian was irritated. He did not need this problem. The firm did not need it. And if Glenn was right, he hated to address the possible irregularities that Hartnett may have caused in the conducting of business that could have gone unnoticed. "Okay. I am going to have a chat with Dave and clear this up. Let's get on with the rest of the list you have there, Glenn, and I'll speak to Dave before the day is over."

Dave Hartnett gazed out his office window overlooking Battery Park City as he talked to Domenico Rizzo on the phone. He had never spoken to Rizzo before and he was worried. His contact was much lower down than the mob leader, Rizzo, and he did not like it that Tommy "The Mouth" Sereno had been superseded. Hartnett had his feet up on his desk, and his baby-face, pale blue eyes topped with a crop of curly, sand-colored hair, was pink with nerves.

Domenico Rizzo had started the conversation, calling from his cellular car phone, by saying in his mellifluous deep voice, "I hope you are going to catch the first race at Belmont today. I got a horse running. Capri. She's a beauty. Two-year-old filly, broke her maiden at Saratoga and won an allowance race last month. Her dam's by Secretariat. You know what a great broodmare sire he was. Going out? I can give you a lift with one of my boys."

"I'm afraid I can't get away, Mr. Rizzo, but I'll take a raincheck."

"Call me Dom. I'll call you Dave. Now, Dave, we got a problem. I dislike talking about it over the phone. Tommy should have brought it to my attention before this."

There was an ominous pause. Hartnett could see the white lights on his phone blinking while his secretary put his other calls on hold. He glanced at his watch: twelve seventeen.

"You got a line of credit with us. Tommy tells me you bet anything that moves, right? Boxing, football, baseball, basketball, Atlantic City, the horses, the works, right?"

"From time to time." Hartnett gazed helplessly out his window at the Cesar Pelli four-tower World Financial Headquarters and the Wintergarden, with its towering glass pavilion and its 120-foot vaulted roof gleaming in the October sun.

Rizzo's voice sank to a low whisper. "From time to time? That's good. That's real good. You yuppies are real good." His voice came back into Hartnett's ear full volume. "You owe over eight hundred thousand bucks on a credit line of one million. You haven't made a payment to reduce the debt in four months. Yesterday your betting receipts for the past week brought your overage to eight hundred ninety thousand. We need to talk, Hartnett. We are patient, but we need more than interest payments. We'd like to close the account now, all simple and direct. You pay up, and we shut up."

Hartnett could feel his heart thumping in his chest the way it did after a four-mile run. His mouth was dry. "But Tommy said—"

"Tommy says nothing. I say. And I say we are closing your account. See, Dave, we need clients who keep their credit line under control. We're like the bank. Now I'll give you a week to pay up. That's fair. Domenico Rizzo is fair. This time next week I'd like a certified check in the full amount plus interest. I'll call you at this number and we can discuss where to meet." The phone clicked.

Hartnett sat motionless, ignoring his buzzing telephone. He watched people crossing the pedestrian bridge connecting it from Battery Park City to the World Trade Center, tiny specks behind the windows enclosing them. People were specks in Hartnett's feverish mind, to be manipulated as he manipulated the market. He tried to think. Almost two million dollars in a week. And he had about fifteen thousand in the bank and a one-bedroom condo on the Upper East Side. Gambling losses had been the worst he had ever experienced these past seven months. No matter what system he used no bet had paid off big, and in his league of gambling either you won big or you were in deep trouble. There was a knock on his door. "Come in."

The senior partner and founder of the firm, Brian Kelly, entered his office and said, without smiling, "Dave, we've got to talk."

Rosemarie lay in her unmade bed upstairs in the house, hearing the slam of the Mercedes' bulletproof limousine door. Dom would be sitting in the backseat with two bodyguards, one in front, one in the back with him. The car was equipped with two cellular phones, a fax machine, television, and bar. She envisioned Dom, who would be wearing one of his Brioni silk suits, the material stretched across his heavy, muscled thighs.

Rosemarie had undressed when they got back and taken a shower. Instead of putting on a dress to go to the hairdresser, she had gotten back into bed naked. She had called to cancel her appointment and then used the intercom to tell the maid to wake her at eleven thirty, in time to dress and get back to the track for the race; until then she was to be undisturbed.

She had weighed herself after the shower and saw that she had gained another five pounds. Her breasts felt heavy. She lay in bed and closed her eyes, thinking about Dom. She had been excited and now, thinking about him in the car and his hard, muscled body, flat stomach, narrow hips and thick, sensual thighs, she was aroused. She imagined for a moment Dom's touching her, starting to make love to her. Then the tears came, tears streaming down her face, the eye makeup running in black tracks down her cheeks.

After a few minutes, Rosemarie got up and went to the small refrigerator that had been put in her dressing room and took out of it a large chocolate bar, which she took with her to her bed. She sat naked, cross-legged, and slowly ate the delicious candy. The sun shone in the windows of her bedroom. Her mind was blank. After she finished the candy, she lay back against the pillows and went to sleep.

Sam Thorne answered the phone. He was ready to be picked up for his television interview.

"Sam, it's Abe Zimmer. Any luck with the president? Or anyone else for that matter?"

"Sorry. I haven't been able to reach him. If only we had more real data I could do something here with the mayor and the Emergency Management people. Anything new from your end?"

"My friend Conrad has been feeding seismological data from off the coast of Long Island into our computers and it's a muddle. We've got seismic waves of every kind, size, and velocity out there. We've got rebounding waves going on top of the original ones and it looks like it's earthquake time, but we are not able to sort it out. I don't like the look of it. But if you asked me pointblank should we order New York City evacuated, I'd say don't blow the whistle yet. Let's see what today brings, Sam. I'll call you this afternoon around three your time, okay?"

Along the coastline off Fire Island the shifting ocean rocks encountered the continent and the steel spring was tightened and twisted. Immense forces had been imperceptibly but implacably driving the ocean bed underneath the land mass a few inches a year for centuries. The agonized rock deep beneath the surface was nearing its breaking point. Above, the early morning fishermen were trolling for bluefish and beginning to return home to their docks to unload their catch. This morning they lingered since their quotas had not been met. The fish were not biting. They swam in agitated circles, round and round, darting out and then back, then round and round some more in a crazy watery dance.

Ingrid Tate sat in the stark waiting room of her psychoanalyst. The ashtray by her side already had two crimson-tipped butts in it. Ingrid was pencil thin, blond, fiftyish, what one gossip columnist had called a "beautiful rumpless woman of mysterious origin."

Ingrid tapped her Charles Jourdan shoe impatiently. The doctor always kept her waiting. Once Ingrid was used to waiting. She had been in the chorus line of American musicals in her native Germany and she waited then—waited for men, waited for auditions, sometimes taking money for her favors simply because she was hungry. She did not think of herself as a whore ever; it was an acceptable way of augmenting the skimpy salary she received for dancing and singing rather badly in A Little Night Music and other shows.

Howard Tate had met her after she got to New York via a boyfriend who paid her way over. She was waiting on tables at a

Greenwich Village bistro that he frequented after off-Broadway theatergoing. The first time he had seen the plump blonde in the mini-skirt, he had asked her to have dinner with him the following night. Six months later she had lost fifty pounds and married one of the richest men in America.

The door opened and the doctor motioned her inside his office.

She sat down opposite him, lighted a cigarette, and said disdainfully, "Well, the old bastard's dying."

———

Kate was reading *The New York Times* at the kitchen table when Diane came down from her bedroom carrying her teacup, which Mary had brought her at eleven.

"Darling," Diane exclaimed, and Kate looked up, accepting Diane's European kiss on either cheek. "How are you?"

"Just fine. And you? You look wonderful as always."

"God, without makeup. That *is* good to hear." She went to the refrigerator and took out a banana and milk. "Where's Mary?"

Kate peered at her daughter-in-law over her reading glasses. This young woman was to her like a creature from another world and though she did not necessarily approve of her she was fascinated by her. "Doing the laundry." She sipped her coffee. "I saw Danny off to school with Mary and Copper. He is a terrific little boy. So intelligent."

Diane sat down at the table and peeled the banana. "Can't have too much potassium. He is great, isn't he? Are you coming to my show tonight with Sam and Danny?"

"Alas, no. Tonight is my speech at the Sierra Club."

"Right. Of course. But you are coming to see the show? You must. How about tomorrow?"

"I'd love it," Kate lied. She had seen Diane on her television series and had not thought she was a very good actress.

"Good. I'll set aside a house seat at the box office in your name. Or do you want to bring a friend?"

"No, I think not. On such short notice, all my old pals will have plans. I'll look forward to it on my own."

There was a brief silence. Kate returned to the *Times*. Diane finished her banana and drank her milk, giving her handsome, youthful mother-in-law a quick glance. She admired her but thought her cold as ice.

Kate, without looking up from the page, asked, "How are you and Sam getting along?"

Diane had forgotten how direct Kate was. She got up and took her plate and glass to the dishwasher. "What has he told you?"

"Not much." Kate gave her a piercing look. "That you're thinking of getting a divorce."

Diane felt pinned. She decided to try to deal with Kate rather than escape, though she had to get ready to leave for the theater soon. She sat down again and looked directly into those clear crystal-blue eyes. "We've discussed it. Frankly, I don't know what I think at the moment." She was remembering last night. Sam was a very good lover.

"Is there another man?"

None of your business, Diane thought. "Of course not, Kate. And I don't think Sam is involved with anyone. But for the past few years we've seen each other very seldom, and when we have, it hasn't been the same. Our careers seem to come first, it's that simple. And neither of us is willing to give up any part of our work. You of all people should understand."

Kate smiled at the younger woman. "Daniel always came before my work, if you call mountain climbing 'work.' And my children did too. But, to be fair, my career as a climber could be planned around them."

Diane smiled back at Kate. "Always? Wasn't there ever a time when you went off to Mount Everest or wherever when Daniel and the boys wanted you at home with them? I've seen your clippings, remember? You were famous."

Kate thought a moment. "I suppose you have a point. But Daniel was always home. His work as a poet and his other writing was done in his study in Colorado Springs. Or we traveled together, and sometimes took the boys if they weren't in school. Sam's work does require a great deal of travel. It's a problem," she conceded.

"Look, Kate, I don't want a divorce. But I need a man in my life. And what about Danny? He needs both of us. He adores Sam."

Kate nodded. She went back to the *Times*. "All I can tell you, Diane, is that it can be a lonely old age."

"You? Old? Never. I know how you miss Daniel. But looking ahead is no reason for Sam and me to stay together. I need him now."

Kate murmured, "But if you weren't tied to acting you could travel with him."

Diane had had enough. She stood up, her husky deep voice at its most emphatic. "Look, Kate, don't try to make me feel guilty, okay? It won't work. Sam knew I was an actress when he married me. He knew how hard I'd worked to achieve whatever success I've had. I'm not from money, the way you and he are. I'm a California girl whose parents were low on the totem pole in the movie studio's hierarchy and not well paid. What I do for a living keeps me independent, so I can tell any man to take a walk when and if I want to, and I want to keep it that way. I'm never going to let any man support me. So, if there's going to be any changing done, it is going to have to be done by Sam, not me."

She made her exit, as Kate stared after her in amazement. Then, in spite of herself, she chuckled. Her appreciation of Diane Taylor had grown in the last few minutes. She must talk with Sam again at lunch today. My God, she thought, I am becoming an interfering mother, and I had better watch it. On the other hand . . .

———————

Dr. Patricia Kelly was late for an appointment with the police commissioner. Three months ago she had been appointed head of the Emergency Medical Services by the new mayor, Bruce Lincoln. Even though she knew she deserved the job, she also knew she had gotten it because of a political favor, and this knowledge gnawed at Pat Kelly's proud second-generation—on both sides—Irish soul. Her father and John Maloney, the commissioner, were best friends from boyhood days in Queens. A car from the commissioner's office had come to pick her up at her office in Maspeth.

They were on the East River Drive. The driver cursed the traffic, which was inching along because of some construction around 30th Street. One Police Plaza was near the southern end of the island of Manhattan. Pat Kelly looked at her watch. She was going to be twenty minutes late to her first meeting, professionally, with Maloney, but that was the story of her life. She had known him all her thirty-six years, and had always called him Uncle John. Today she would try to be more formal.

Pat Kelly was used to doing things for herself. She pushed the car forward mentally, argued the decisions the driver was making about lanes, and grew more irritated as the minutes ticked by. From the day she beat her older brother in a race from their house to the corner candy store, Pat Kelly had known that no man would dominate her, and her independent spirit was well known among her colleagues. She had graduated from New York–Cornell at the top of her class and done her internship and residency at New York Hospital. Dr. Gordon Keith picked her to be his second in command in the Department of Neurology when she was twenty-eight. She was small boned, five-foot-four, with cornflower blue eyes and a cap of jet-black hair that she wore short and straight so that she could wash it in the shower each morning, run a comb through it, and be ready for the day. Feisty and smart, Pat Kelly had no time for frills. "Does this car phone work?"

"Sure, go ahead."

She punched in her husband Brian's number at his Wall Street office.

"Kelly, Farnsworth and Kline," the receptionist answered.

"Hi, Shirley. Let me speak to Brian."

"Hi, Pat. Sure. How're the girls? He's on the other line."

"They're fine. Tracy wants to be a commodities trader when she grows up and Abigail wants to be a cowboy. All she can talk about is horses. When I was a kid we were so poor all I wanted was a catcher's mitt signed by a Yankee player, *any* Yankee player. These kids are spoiled, but what can you do?"

"Wait a minute, he's off now." Shirley put her through to Brian Kelly.

"Hi. Where are you?"

"I'm stuck in traffic on my way to see Uncle John. Want to have a quick lunch late?"

"I'd love to but I have that British guy for lunch. You know, the one that thinks he wants to buy us."

"Jesus Mary and all the saints! You aren't going to sell to the enemy are you? All the Kellys in Mayo will rise from their graves."

"We could go live in London. The girls could go to one of those fancy British schools."

"You're a sellout, you are. You've forgotten Easter Sunday if you ever did know what it was. Don't you think we're getting to be too upwardly mobile for two tough kids from Queens?"

"You know it will never happen. Have fun with Maloney. He's a real hard-ass, a stickler for going by the book, all the stuff you love."

"I'll be home late tonight. Don't wait on me, okay?"

They hung up and she tried to stop pushing the car. The water of the East River glistened in the bright October midday sun. Pat thought about Brian. She had worried for years about the possibility of neglecting him and the girls. She had given up any social life and maintained old friendships by phone, hoping the people in her life, mainly the Fitzgeralds, her family, and the Kellys would forgive her for not going to birthday parties or first communions and know that she had made a decision early to devote every moment of free time she had to her daughters and Brian. That way she did not feel too guilty about her fierce pursuit of her medical career and now this new job. It helped that Brian, whom she had known since she pushed a piece of ice cream cake in his face at the age of three at a cousin's party, was a financial wizard. He came from the same lace-curtain Irish background as she did, and when he graduated from Columbia he put together his own money management firm with two classmates, Kline and Farnsworth. Brian, she mused, was about twelve years old emotionally, for all his brains. She loved him because he needed her and was funny and smart—not, God knows, because he was there for her when she needed him.

"Can't we get any nearer than this?" she asked the driver, who had pulled up at the street corner in back of One Police Plaza. He shook his head. She jumped out of the car and crossed the street. Workmen were doing something to the outside of the large dark brick building that had sort of a purple hue. The cops who worked there derisively called it "the purple palace." There were plastic yellow warning ribbons stretched across part of the plaza, sawhorses scattered around aimlessly, and scaffolding up one side of the many-sided headquarters. She ignored the yellow ribbons, walked through the plaza and past a long line of mostly black or Hispanic young men waiting to be processed for possible recruitment to the police force.

She went to the desk, gave her name, and showed the woman her official I.D., but still had to go through the metal detector equipment, and that was another line. She was not known for her patience. She tried not to bite one of her nails, a habit she had never quite outgrown. While she waited she glanced at the ugly mosaic on one wall of the lobby and the lists engraved in bronze of policemen's names, men killed over the years in the line of duty. So many names were Irish. She felt the sudden pride she always felt about being Irish, on both sides at that, that sudden sense of identity she had gotten as a little girl looking at the big photograph of John F. Kennedy her pa put in their living room in Queens as though he were part of their family.

Finally she got off the elevator onto the eighth floor and followed the sign to the commissioner's office. The halls were painted institutional green and the atmosphere was that of a down-at-heels endeavor. She recognized a lack of money to run things everywhere she looked.

Commissioner Maloney got to his feet when Dr. Kelly entered his small square office. He held out his hand in greeting, "How are you, Pat. Sorry to bring you all the way down here, but I have a meeting first thing this afternoon. How's your dad? Haven't seen him in far too long."

"He's in good form, thanks, Uncle John."

He puffed on an unlighted pipe and shuffled through some papers. "What I wanted to go over with you today is the new Emergency Management Plan. You've got it?"

"Yes. It was faxed to my office yesterday. And yesterday we had another hazardous-waste-material incident out on the Long Island Expressway. We wouldn't have been involved, but several people were badly injured when a tractor trailer overturned and spilled some sort of acid all over the highway. There was a three-car pileup. I have to tell you, John, I did not like the way the systems worked on our end, so I'm very glad to have this meeting."

She knew he wouldn't have heard about the incident. There were at least two hazardous-waste incidents a day, and they usually did not involve her EMS and certainly not the police commissioner, who was the director of Emergency Management and only became the temporary head of not only the police but all other government agency personnel—the Fire Department, Red Cross, Sanitation, and other departments—when there was a Phase II crisis in Manhattan. Phase I was a state of awareness in which an emergency or potential emergency is identified. Phase II activated the Command Center, which was down the hall from the commissioner's office, but no broad policy decisions were made and the emergency was treated as an isolated local event. Only Phase III brought the mayor, the police commissioner, and all the available agency heads together at the Command Center—a large room with a dais where four red phones were located along with about ten regular phones. A huge map of Manhattan hung behind the dais and several flags from various police battalions hung from high on the wall, below which many desks and computer terminals were arranged.

Pat knew that only the blackouts and Hurricane Gloria had triggered Phase III alerts for the past fifteen or twenty years. What she had learned when she accepted this government job of heading the EMS was that her predecessor, not a doctor but a civil-service type, had let the Service fall apart. It was this challenge that had enticed her into accepting the job, for which Maloney had recommended her, from Mayor Bruce Lincoln. She was flattered, too, since no woman had ever been asked to run the Service and she knew that as a doctor she could do more than had been done in the past. Her colleague and then-boss Gordon Keith had been horrified. "Politics, Pat, you'll hate it. And your work is here. I need you. Don't take the job. It leads nowhere except to frustration and fury at the bureaucratic mentality. Look how upset we get at the hospital bureaucracy. Ye gods, don't jump from one frying pan to another." She had said she'd think it over, but she already knew it was a job she couldn't turn down.

"Let me ask you some questions, John, if I may?"

"Sure, fire away. Want some coffee?" A square, stocky man, with a ruddy face and a shock of pure white hair, John Maloney got up and fetched a mug for himself as he acknowledged the shake of her head. The boredom he felt about this aspect of his job was assuaged by being able to look at Fitzgerald's girl, who had grown into such a pretty young woman. What a tomboy she had been! They had despaired of getting Patty Fitzgerald into a dress.

"I'm going to go through this list in my head as though I hadn't studied any of the material in my files or talked with any of my team. I need to hear what you say, John, and then I'll understand better how you and the mayor feel about the Emergency Services of the city and the EMS in particular."

He swirled the powdered milk around his coffee mug.

"Go ahead."

"Okay. We have a major disaster. Let's say Hurricane Gloria hadn't swerved out over Long Island but had hit the City full force, or that some Third World nut hits us with a nuclear device. Let's say the Command Center here is rendered unoperational for days. On a regular weekday there are approximately twelve million people in the city—five million commuters and visitors and about seven million residents. What happens?" She leaned forward slightly in her chair.

Maloney looked up at the ceiling for a moment, sucking on the pipe. He lowered his head and gave her a look, part belligerence and part Irish charm, which she found reminiscent of her pa when she had asked him something he did not have a ready answer for and knew he should have had.

"First of all, the Command Center might survive. This building is made of steel and concrete and unless the hit were direct it would survive. The mayor and I would be in charge. We have a video room at Command Center. Cameras are placed at strategic sites throughout the city, including, I might add, my office and Mayor Lincoln's, so that we could monitor the situation. We have backup emergency generators for our communications systems. Why, Pat, we have twenty-seven thousand police in this city, plus four thousand transit police, and seven thousand civilian employees and over ten thousand fire fighters. We are the best equipped city in the world to deal with a major disaster." He paused. When she did not speak, he went on.

"As the man in command, I would do many things as quickly as possible. I'd use our Emergency Coordinating Section with its Command Vehicle, which can move around the city and to which officials from all the agencies can go to coordinate rescue and relief efforts. That would include yours, Pat. We have a Public Inquiry Unit manning dozens of phones to answer calls from citizens. We have an evacuation plan, which . . ."

She interrupted. "How many people can it move out of the city or to another part of the city?"

"Over a day or two, approximately one hundred thousand. And we have a Voluntary Egress Plan for people to evacuate the City drawn up at the direction of the Federal Emergency Management people in Washington. As you know, they fund most of our disaster costs."

"That's the bad news." She smiled at him.

"Not enough you mean? True, but . . ."

"Not enough and bungled when it counts."

Annoyed, he decided to barge ahead. "I would get in touch with all the senior police officials who are automatically in charge of any particular disaster site. Even if it's a fire, our police officer is in charge of more senior fire officials present at the site. I'd get in touch with all these guys and coordinate through them the Red Cross . . ."

Pat said, "I'm sorry to interrupt you, John, but one of the major problems would be our blood supply. You may not know it but we have about a four-day supply for normal emergencies, which would be used up in about six hours."

Maloney held up one hand to stop her. "I know, I know." He shook his head. "I'm a regular blood donor. I wish more people were. Now then, we'd use the schools as emergency shelters—they are all supplied with blankets and cots—and I'd order the use of our 'victim locators,' which sense heat through piles of rubble in order to find people trapped by collapsed buildings. We have a Press Information Unit here at One Police Plaza used to release information to the news media for public awareness. And a dedicated radio channel for communication with your rescue teams, base stations, and portable units. The mayor, under Article 2B of the State Executive Law, can declare a state of emergency, and he would request assistance from the governor, who could in turn send in the National Guard if needed and possibly request assistance from the president."

He paused, pleased with this recitation, which to his ears sounded damn impressive. And reassuring.

"Have you any questions, Patty?" he asked, using the diminutive that she hated and knew was his way of patronizing her.

"Lots, John. Mainly to do with my Services function, but one big question. What happens if this building is destroyed, if One Police Plaza is no more?" She used her lightest, most reassuring voice, the voice she tried to use with very sick patients, but she could see that Commissioner John Maloney was not fooled.

"Christ, Pat. How do I know!" He got to his feet. "Go down the hall and talk to Captain Driscoll. He knows more than I do. It's been a pleasure, and give my best to your dad. I have to run. Sorry. I'll have my secretary call Driscoll and say you're on your way. He's executive officer of our Emergency Control Board. He knows where all the bodies are buried." With a cheerful wave of his hand she was dismissed.

———————

Evie Lincoln, the daughter of Bruce Lincoln, New York's second black mayor, strode up and down her small office. At twenty-eight, she was one of the ranking assistant district attorneys in the Manhattan D.A.'s office, and the only black. She looked at her watch. It was almost noon and she had a dental appointment uptown at two o'clock. There was never time enough to get the pile of homework done that sat on her desk. This morning she was agitated. A case she was on was defying her, eluding her usually quick and highly intelligent grasp.

She was model-pretty, with high cheekbones and a slim, excellent figure. She wore a dark gray Calvin Klein suit with a white silk blouse, and small gold earrings, the only jewelry she had on. Evie Lincoln, she knew, was the very picture of success. But last night had upset her. More than her mother, with whom she quarreled about almost everything, more even than her brilliant father, she adored and revered her paternal grandmother, Mattie Lincoln. Last night she felt she had let her grandmother down, and as she paced and, finally, sat down at her desk thumbing through a brief she did not pretend to be reading, she remembered the scene at Gracie Mansion where, the night before, the Lincoln family had celebrated Mattie Lincoln's eighty-fifth birthday.

On the way to Gracie Mansion, Evie had thought about her father. Bruce Lincoln had held the office of mayor for less than a year, the second African-American to do so. At sixty-one he was in robust good health. Square-jawed and handsome, not given to showing emotion on his face, he was a reassuring and comforting figure to his family as well as his constituents. A graduate of Harvard University, Bruce Lincoln had worked his way up the City's political ladder, but he had not been taken seriously as a mayoral candidate until his predecessor unexpectedly announced that he would serve only one term. Then Bruce Lincoln went into action.

In a matter of six weeks in the early summer of 1993, in a campaign in which Evie and her brother Charlie had worked, Lincoln had managed to win the support of a broad spectrum of Democratic leaders, Irish, Jewish, Italian, and Spanish as well as his own power base among the blacks, through a combination of cajolery, promises (which he intended to keep), and mild threats typical of the political life of the City. With the endorsement of the incumbent mayor and Governor George Fleming in Albany— Fleming and Lincoln had disliked each other for years, but the governor had had little choice other than to get on the bandwagon—Bruce Lincoln had easily defeated his Republican opponent and, in January of 1994, been installed as the 107th mayor of New York.

Evie was ushered into the big living room at Gracie Mansion, where there was a fire in the grate, her mother and Charlie deep in conversation by it. Her father was in the library with her grandmother.

Evie interrupted her mother, who was just telling Charlie about the long waiting list at the daycare center she ran, and how, because the welfare rolls of the Department of Social Services had climbed through the eighties and into the nineties, neither the public nor private sector could keep up.

She leaned down and kissed her mother's cheek. Then she gave Charlie a hug.

"Hey, big older sister, how're you doing? Slaying dragons as usual down at the D.A.'s office?" Charlie got up to greet her. At twenty-seven, he was in his second year of residency at New York Hospital.

They were so close in age that they might as well have been twins. Charlie had a rebellious streak, too, and it had been hard for him growing up in their father's compelling presence. Growing up in the seventies and eighties, Evie and Charlie had both had a difficult time with their peers and their parents, a tug-of-war on both sides either to stray, to run with the wild gang of kids who drugged and fell into crime, or stay on the straight and narrow. They had both chosen the latter way, but it had not been easy.

"How's my favorite sawbones?" She grinned up at her handsome brother. "Liking being a doctor any better than the last time we met?"

He laughed. "It's the hours I love. You know they keep talking about shortening the 'on call' hours, but we're all still up sixteen hours or twenty, so it's the patients you should be asking about, not me. We're all staggering around like zombies."

"It's good for you," Evie said, going over to her father for a hug, and finally to her grandmother, around whom she put her arms and held her tight. "How's my favorite person in the whole world?"

Mattie Lincoln had hugged Evie and then pulled away and held Evie out, looking her over as she had done ever since this beautiful, willful child had been old enough to walk. "My, we are looking fine," Mattie had approved.

"Come on, let's go in to dinner," Bruce Lincoln said. "The chef will quit if we're late."

The dining room in the private quarters of the residence of Gracie Mansion was ablaze with candles. They lighted the two-hundred-year-old handblocked wallpaper illuminating the scenes of Paris painted on it. The table, which could, and often did, seat twelve, was set at one end for five, crystal and sterling glittering on a softly patterned Irish linen cloth. This night, the mayor did not sit at the head of the table as was his usual custom. That place was occupied by his mother.

Evie's father sat to the right of his beloved mother, Martha—or Miss Mattie, as she was known to one and all at her church, the Abyssinian Baptist on 138th Street—as she finished saying grace over the meal they were about to begin. Evie watched her grandmother carefully as Mattie intoned the words of the grace Evie had listened to ever since she had been big enough to come to the dining table at the apartment on that same street in Harlem where her father had been raised. Evie looked for signs of age, of weariness, but at eighty-five, Mattie Lincoln's face, lined and creased though it was, showed only the same combination of vitality and serenity that had marked it for as long as Evie could remember.

"And for those who are absent or departed, Lord, we ask Thy special blessing."

The waiter poured red wine into the Waterford crystal goblets. Mattie had ended her grace as she always did, and Evie knew who her grandmother had in her heart as she said those words—her uncle and aunt and their families who were absent, living in far-flung corners of the world, the former a career diplomat, the latter married to an Army lieutenant general. And the one who was departed, Mattie's firstborn, a rising young star of the City's police force when he had been senselessly cut down in a gun battle with a doped-up hippie nearly thirty years before.

Her grandfather would not be included in that group for whom her grandmother prayed. Alcoholic, unable to hold a job for more than a few days at a time, he had deserted his family when her father, the second child, was only six, leaving Mattie Lincoln to bring up her three boys and a girl by herself.

Evie doubted that her grandmother was capable of hatred. She had simply shut her heart to the father of her children. When her grandfather's body had been discovered in an alleyway off 125th Street, it had all been resolved for Mattie Lincoln, and though she had later had several suitors and had received proposals of marriage from them, she preferred to make her way alone.

That Mattie Lincoln had raised her children successfully had never been in doubt, and was proven once more by the fact that they were sitting here in Gracie Mansion. The three boys had all gone on scholarship to colleges, Bruce to Harvard, their sister to Wellesley. Though they had followed different paths, all had in some way gone into public life, and their mother's pride in them knew no bounds.

"Well, Mother," said the mayor. "Let's hope that this is only the first of many birthdays for you that we'll celebrate here."

"If the Lord is willing, Bruce."

"I'm sure he will be, Mother," said Evie's mother, Paula Lincoln.

Evie studied her mother as the others talked. She took a sip of the red wine. She marveled at the faith that predominated the lives of her grandmother and mother. She had tried since childhood and with little success to achieve the faith that seemed to come so naturally to these older women.

Her mother had been married to her father for over thirty years and in those three decades had always kept herself in the background of his life, raising Evie and her brother Charlie, and keeping their home a safe refuge for her father to come home to after a day of political struggle and strife. In her teens and early twenties, Evie resented her mother's self-effacement. It drove her wild to see how her mother always without question put her father first. Everything in her rebelled against what she considered to be her mother's abdication of her own pride and self-determination. In the ten years or so since she and Charlie had been considered old enough not to need their mother's constant attention, the focus of her mother's life had at least allowed her to have one other outlet than her father—daycare for working mothers. Her mother had gone back to school and finished a master's in social work. Then, with funding from both public and private sources, she had opened a daycare center in a building on 127th Street that had been renovated by Jimmy Carter's Habitat for Humanity group. Evie had found new respect for her mother because of this new passionate interest in something outside her father's every need.

The conversation was lively around the table, as in this family it had always been, but this night Evie felt removed from the rest of them. They were all talking at once about the visit of Father Diaz to the United Nations to speak the next day. He was the controversial Gandhi-like figure who had risen from nowhere in Peru to become the great hope for bringing Central and South America together and ridding them of the powerful drug cartel.

Mattie Lincoln was saying, "He is the greatest world figure since our blessed Martin Luther King."

Charlie broke in, "I'm not sure I trust him, Grandma. I mean, what do we really know about him?"

Bruce Lincoln added, "We'll find out more tomorrow when he speaks. Unfortunately, I have to be at the opening ceremony for Tate Acres or I'd be at the U.N. to hear him."

"I wish I could go," Paula said. "I've got a big day at the center tomorrow."

Evie listened and her mind went back to religion and the question of faith. Where had she lost it? Or had she ever really had it? In the intellectual games that Paula and Bruce Lincoln insisted their children—only eleven months apart—play when they were growing up, games designed to hone their young minds at every level, Evie had excelled in those that required the skills of rhetoric, Charlie in those that demanded scientific analysis. Maybe it was way back then that her mind started to reject the kind of blind faith, for this was how she saw it, of her mother and grandmother. It made her feel isolated from the core of her family, and particularly from her beloved Mattie.

The rest of the evening passed with much laughter and conversation, and as they sat over coffee and cookies baked especially for Mattie Lincoln by the chef who knew she loved brownies, Bruce Lincoln asked, "Do you want me to order up one of the cars to drive you home, Mother? We can't have the mayor's ancient mother dragging her old bones onto a bus at this hour, though I'm sure you'd prefer it."

"Ancient old bones, indeed," Mattie replied. "And won't you get in trouble with some Republican," she pronounced the word with distaste, "for letting your ancient, old-boned mother use an official car? That's the way it usually starts, isn't it? Abuse of privilege, or some such?"

The mayor chuckled. "Of course, you're right, Mother. It would probably be safer for me if you walked."

"It wouldn't be the first time, Mr. Mayor."

"Come on, you two, stop wrangling," said Charlie. "Give me a kiss, Nana. I have to be back at the hospital by midnight. I'm off on Saturday. May I take you to lunch?"

"Noon sharp, and don't be late," his grandmother replied.

"I can take you home," Evie offered. "Call me, Charlie, when you get off duty."

"You sure it's no trouble, sweetheart," Mattie asked her granddaughter.

"No, Nana, really. I had the car service coming anyway."

"Well, it's nice to be alone with you even if it's only a few minutes."

"Yes, Nana. Nice for me, too." Evie steeled herself for what she knew was coming. Her grandmother was the one person in her life with whom all her rhetorical skills went out the window.

"I won't probe, sweetheart. And I won't ask you to make any commitment you don't want to. I just want you to know that all of us—everyone at church who knows you, and that's just about everybody—misses having you there, not least Pastor Stevenson." With patience born of age—once Mattie had been impetuosity itself—Mattie waited for her granddaughter to reply.

"He's a good man, Nana, and a kind one." She felt the old woman's body lean into hers as the car turned a corner. "It's just that when I hear him preaching about loving your neighbor and being kind to your fellow man on Sunday, it seems kind of empty the next day when I have to deal with thieves and murderers, pimps and prostitutes and child molesters and people so depraved that I wouldn't want you to know they exist. I miss church, Nana. I really do. It's not so much a loss of faith as it is a crisis of conscience. I've just got to work it out, try to find some balance so that I can continue to believe in the essential goodness of man even though most of the men—and women—I have to deal with don't have an essential let alone a goodness." Evie stopped speaking and laughed softly. "Boy, can I get carried away with myself. But do you understand, Nana, at least a little bit about what I'm saying?"

"I do, sweetheart. Maybe even a little more than a little bit."

"And . . . ?" Evie asked, an unfamiliar uncertainty in her voice, as the car pulled up in front of the beautiful old brownstone on 138th Street where her grandmother had lived for half a century and more.

" 'And?' Evie? There is no 'and.' " The driver opened the door, reached in a hand to assist the old woman. "There's only the Lord, sweetheart, who is watching over the lives of all of us."

Evie's secretary barged into her office and interrupted her reverie. "Miss Lincoln, that man from the Lower Court has been waiting for fifteen minutes. Will you see him now? And don't forget your dental appointment."

At the base of a six-story tenement building on the Lower East Side between Spring and Prince streets, a very important meeting was held every Wednesday. The building was a wood structure but the façade was made of red brick. Two high, blacked-out windows flanked the single door. An air conditioner that had seen better days jutted out above it. The meeting place for New York's most powerful organized crime family was called the Da Vinci Club. There Domenico Rizzo and his capos met at noon, and the business at hand usually kept them there until midafternoon.

The black Mercedes limousine rolled to a stop and two burly, dark-suited young men jumped out, one from each rear door. Following them was the short, dapper figure of Domenico Rizzo. He stepped briskly across the sidewalk, glancing up and down the street and running his fingers through his hair as he entered the building. He was over an hour late.

Inside, the long table in the back room was lined with men, drinking coffee and chatting, waiting for Rizzo. The furnishings consisted of several deep leather chairs drawn up around an unused fireplace, a bar the length of one wall, the conference table, and some card tables off to one side. Though the sun was high in the October sky, the room was dark and all the lights were turned on.

After the usual greetings, the meeting got down to business. There were reports on the drug trade, now cocaine since the Chinese mob had taken over the heroin trade. Then there were the numbers games. The mob had up to fifty thousand runners all over the city taking care of over two hundred fifty thousand customers. Another ongoing business was property, the restaurants, the nightclubs, and many other real-estate enterprises that the mob, now in 1994 numbering over five hundred members, controlled. Rizzo's particular passion was gun-running, and each Wednesday he gave a report on new shipments coming into Kennedy Airport. He wanted today to tell them about the new Beretta 9mm coming in from Brazil and the Taurus Berettas coming from Europe. Since each mob member had at least two guns in his possession, both long guns and handguns, this subject was of great interest to them all.

These mob leaders were a mixed brew, with some of the old men from another era still in command of various enterprises, wearing ill-fitting suits, playing pinochle and smoking cigarillos; the balance of the men might have sprung from the graduating class of the Harvard Business School, and, in fact, several of them had gone to Ivy League colleges and on to various graduate schools.

At fifty-three Domenico Rizzo, whose late father had been the leader of the Barbetta family in league with John Gotti's Gambino family, had risen through the ranks and when Max "The Ox" Cinetti was gunned down nearly a decade earlier, Rizzo took over, his place earned by his courage, cunning, and personal charisma. He dominated by his very presence. Today his long, jet-black hair was carefully styled to brush the top of the collar of his white poplin shirt and black jacket. As he talked to the men assembled there, his deep voice carried conviction and strength. They watched him. His skin was creamy, without blemish, and except for a slight puffiness under his eyes, his choirboy face with its full lips and suggestion of dimples, gave him a deceptively young and innocent air. His chin was strong and his black eyes were restless. They watched his every move, these men, looking for signs of weakness or betrayal or favoritism, joined in a fraternity of criminal activity as strong as Yale's Skull and Bones, and as secret. They knew about his mistress, the singer Nancy Thayer. They knew Rosemarie Rizzo had had nervous breakdowns. These were weak links in Rizzo's strong chain. Also, that he hadn't had a son. On the other hand, among his strong links were his inherited brains from his great father, a man of principle and dignity. And Rizzo's single-minded devotion to the family's aims. There wasn't a CEO in the country more dedicated to his business than Domenico Rizzo, and these men knew it.

An ancient waiter had brought them a lunch of fresh trout and salad and a good white wine. Rizzo glanced at his watch. It was one fifteen. The first race was finished and Capri must have won it. He ordered someone to call the result line. He decided to put off the discussion of the new guns until after lunch.

———————

At eleven thirty the maid knocked on her door. Rosemarie Rizzo arose and took another shower, put fresh makeup on, and dressed for the track in a Calvin Klein tweed suit, feeling the skirt too tight across her buttocks. Fortunately the jacket was full and covered her hips. She went downstairs and into Domenico's study, where he had left an envelope with ten hundred-dollar bills in it for her to bet on Capri. Then she took her binoculars and the *Racing Form*, which was delivered each morning, and got into the Jaguar. Thirty minutes later she was at the Clubhouse entrance to Belmont, and the parking attendant opened the door of the car. "Good morning, Mrs. Rizzo," he said, handing her a ticket for the car. "I'll put it right over there in your parking space." He pointed to a row of expensive cars parked near the entryway.

"Thanks, Jimmy." She gave him five dollars, and after she placed Dom's bet she went to the paddock. It was twelve forty-five and the horses were being led by their grooms to the row of open stalls. The huge old maples were yellow and red and scarlet in the high October sun that glinted off the golden statue of Secretariat in the center of the paddock. She saw Joe Factor and went over to the number-three stall where Capri was being saddled.

Factor was busy and did not look at her. Rosemarie watched the men working at getting Capri ready. The black beauty, Rosemarie thought. The horse was excited now, nostrils flaring, eyes flicking looks at the other horses and all the activity in the paddock.

Rosemarie wanted to pat her and whisper words of encouragement, but she did not dare invade the male world that surrounded the filly.

"Jockey's up!" rang out the cry, and a boy who looked about twelve but must have been twenty, climbed up onto Capri's back. Rosemarie looked at her program. Jose Cielo. An apprentice. Why would Factor allow an apprentice to ride Capri? She supposed it was all right, but still. The horses seemed unusually nervous today, many of them breaking out in sweat though the day was cool. Something in the air this morning. She felt their nerves. Factor and she walked through the Clubhouse to the Rizzo box on the second floor.

———

Backstage at the Music Box Theater, Diane Taylor was applying her makeup, getting ready for the matinee. As she studied her face in the mirror, she noticed new lines that she hadn't seen before and made a mental note to go to her collagen lady next week. As she put a delicate amount of purple eyeliner above her green eyes she was thinking about Sam and last night. Divorce? When he was still such a good lay? She smiled at her reflection. Fiddle dee dee. She'd think about it tomorrow at Tara!

The Rockettes at Radio City Music Hall were kickstepping to end an early show, in red, white, and blue costumes.

Schoolchildren all over the city were playing outside on this glorious day.

At the Metropolitan Opera at Lincoln Center, there was a full-dress rehearsal under way of Giuseppe Verdi's *Nabucco*.

The mayor's wife, Paula Lincoln, was playing with a one-year-old Hispanic baby who had not stopped crying since her mother dropped her off at her daycare center. Paula was trying everything she could think of, but nothing made the baby any happier.

The third game of the World Series was under way at Yankee Stadium—finally, a "Subway Series" between the Yankees and

Mets. Dwight Gooden was at bat with two outs and Ron Darling, pitching now for the Yankees and eager for revenge, had his mind on making this a shutout day. George Steinbrenner, though still an exile from the game, was in his box, having chosen to be here rather than at his friend Howard Tate's celebration. The stands were filled to capacity and it was perfect baseball weather.

High up on the thirtieth floor of the Trump Tower the bodyguard outside Rizzo's duplex apartment searched a well-dressed man who carried a brown paper bag and an attaché case.

"I'm Nancy Thayer's brother, for God's sake. And I don't carry a gun."

"Sorry. Orders." The burly bodyguard apologized, and finished patting the expensive navy-blue suit. "You can go in now."

Nancy had been buzzed by the doorman from downstairs, and stood in the doorway. It was almost noon, she had just gotten up. She was wearing jeans and one of Rizzo's Armani sweaters and was barefoot. "Hi, Timmy," she gave her brother a grin. "Come on in. How are you? What's in the bag?"

"Jesus!" He closed the front door behind him. "That goon really thought I was carrying a gun, for Christ's sake." He grinned back and handed her the paper bag. "Edna Valley. Your favorite Chardonnay. Two bottles and it's cold. So this is where you live these days. I don't believe this . . ." He spread his arms out and surveyed the large living room overlooking Fifth Avenue. "Some difference from your pad in the Village. Have our parents been invited up?"

Nancy led him out to the kitchen and opened the wine. "Thanks. Here," she handed him a glass and took one for herself, held onto the bottle, and led him back to the long sofa near the grand piano. "How are you, baby brother? No, I haven't asked them; our parents I mean. Somehow it just didn't occur to me." She lifted her glass to him.

Timothy Thayer was thirty-seven, a partner in a real-estate firm in Greenwich, married, with two teenage children. He had inherited his father's looks, tall, thin, and square of jaw, and his posture gave away the years spent at a second-class military school in an attempt to pound some discipline into his soul. "No, I don't suppose they'd approve of all this . . ." He waved his arm to encompass his surroundings. He took a long swallow of wine and gave Nancy another big smile.

"It's good to see you, Nan. Do I get to meet the hood, or the gangland figure, or whatever you call him, that makes all this possible?"

Nancy did not smile back. She studied her younger brother with her green eyes narrowing slightly, as though looking at him to find out something. "I'm sure anything you and Joan hear in suburbia is colorful."

"Very." Timothy surveyed the trim nails on one of his hands. "Domenico Rizzo. Wasn't he indicted recently for some crime or other? No wonder those goons sit outside the door. I mean, Nan, from Stefano to his boss? What would the girls at Ethel Walker say? What would *anybody* say?" He arched his eyebrows and did a perfect imitation of their mother.

Nancy burst out laughing. "Oh, God, Tim, who the hell knows and who the hell cares?"

Timothy nodded in agreement. He poured them another glass of wine and went to the piano. "Sing me something, sis." He sat down and began to play "Bewitched, Bothered and Bewildered."

She went over and leaned on the piano. "You could have done something with your music, Timmy."

"Thayers don't go to Juilliard. Thayers go to Harvard. Then," he started to play Cole Porter, "they Marry Money, since the family fortunes have dwindled to tiny trusts in which the principal must never be touched, and live happily ever after." He stopped to take a drink. "To us, Nan."

Nancy listened to him play for a minute. She had not seen her only sibling for months. Once he had called her old apartment and left a message on the answering tape—she had kept the pad in the Village as an escape hatch if she ever needed it—and the message was slurred as though he had been drunk. "I need you, Nan. Call me back at the office tomorrow. I need to see you." She had called him but when she reached him, he made light of it.

Once she and Tim had been very close. A million years ago, she thought, listening to him play. He had become such a straight arrow. Still there were moments when he was still the impish, irreverent boy whom she had protected and adored as they grew up in that cold household peopled by disapproving Thayers.

He stood up and they went and sat on the sofa again. "How come you're not out in Greenwich selling another five-million-dollar estate on such a beautiful day?"

He shrugged his well-tailored shoulders. "Hard to come by these days. The recession. You know how it is. I took the day off." He leaned toward her, his old playful expression lighting his pale eyes. "Let me buy you the most expensive drinkiest lunch in town. You name it. I take."

She thought of her afternoon appointments. The hairdresser. The practice session with the new accompanist. The hell with them. "I'd love it, Timmy. But where, darling?" She rearranged her face and did *her* imitation of her mother. "Now that the Colony and Pavillon are gone, what's left?"

"Oh, God," he laughed. "Ain't it the truth."

"What about Aurora? It's so pretty. And expensive enough for your mood."

Tim looked at Nancy intently, the smile turning serious. "You know, babe, you look more beautiful than ever. Rizzo must be good for you."

"Thanks." She returned his gaze. "You didn't come to spend your day off with old sis for no reason. What's going on? Trouble with Joanie. That would please me a lot." Nancy could not stand her sister-in-law.

"No. She's okay. I've been toeing the line since she found out about my girl. Or I should say the wife of one of my partners. No, it's not the home front. It's money." His expression was bleak. And something more, she thought. He was scared.

"What about money?"

"Things have been rough the past two years. Nothing has worked out." He got up and paced. "All my best deals have fallen through. The kids' schools. God forbid they darken the door of a public school, or wear anything that doesn't have a fancy label. And then there is the Round Hill Club. And Joan's entertaining. And the high interest rates." He paused and stood before her. "You name it. And it's gone wrong for me. I'm broke and what's more I borrowed a little money from the firm and the senior partner has caught on, or is about to, and . . ."

Nancy looked up at him. "What you mean is you've put the Thayer hand right in the cookie jar?"

He sighed. "Yes."

"How much? And how much do you need to get you out from under for enough time?"

He looked immensely relieved. "I should have known you wouldn't give me the lecture treatment. I've always been able to count on you, Nan. Well, frankly, I need two hundred thousand."

Nancy smiled. "You knew enough not to go to any of the respectable members of the family. Okay. *I'll* do a little borrowing, and explain it later. Wait a minute." She went to Rizzo's office, opened his safe, took out several packets of bills, and returned to her brother. "Here."

"No questions?" His lower lip trembled.

"No, Tim. I already know all the answers. But this is the last time. I won't be able to do this again. And I am doing it now for old times, you and me together against them all, understood?" She reached up and gave his cheek a kiss. "Get yourself out of trouble and stay out, hear?"

"I'll never forget this, I—"

She put her finger on his lips. "No, Timmy, don't. I can't stand hearing any of that."

He put the bills in the attaché case. "My God, Nan." He could not resist saying it. "Rizzo must be some rich guy. You sure landed in a pot of honey. I hope that murdering Mafia chief takes good care of you. He's got the reputation of a vicious criminal, and . . ."

Nancy stepped back. Her eyes grew very cold. "You know, Tim, that's your problem. One minute you're a human being asking for help and the next you turn into a Thayer. Get out of here."

"Hey, I didn't mean . . . I just think you deserve better."

"All you know about Rizzo you read in the papers. He's the first real man I've ever known, and I'd put his code of honor or ethics or whatever you people want to call it up against yours any day." She was angry, angrier than she had allowed herself to become for a long time. "You're happy enough to take his money. Just get out of here, you poor confused son of a bitch."

She opened the front door. "Show Mr. Thayer out, Joey. He's got business to settle and he's late."

The number 3 train crawled into the Chambers Street station where Evie Lincoln waited impatiently for it. She disliked the subway and avoided it whenever she could, but finding a taxi had been impossible and she didn't want to be late for her two o'clock dentist's appointment on West 72nd Street. If the way this subway was creeping along was any indication, she'd barely make it.

She began to tap her foot and glanced at the overhead clock—it was 1:11 P.M.—as the train sat in the station for several seconds before opening its doors. When they finally did open, she was nearly bowled over by an old lady muttering various curses to herself and pulling a shopping cart full of things Evie didn't want to contemplate. Like most New Yorkers, she was used to such rudeness and barely gave it a thought as she entered the first car of the train and sat down.

It wasn't rush hour, and there was plenty of room in the car. She looked around her with the practiced eye of a criminal lawyer, seeing and registering the other occupants of the car. In the corner opposite the motorman's closed door, a young Hispanic couple was engaged in some serious kissing. Evie nearly laughed aloud at the mock horror the girl expressed as she kept her boyfriend's hand from encompassing her breast. No one was in the two-seater opposite them, but at the beginning of the next long bench, a lanky boy in his teens with a tattoo proclaiming "Rick" on one bicep and a heavy-metal haircut lay stretched out, cleaning his nails with a hunting knife.

The chimes rang, the doors closed, and the train lurched forward. A woman at the back of the car who had gotten on just in time stumbled and nearly fell trying to take her seat. The other people at that end of the car pretended not to notice; it was, after all, none of their business if she was going to be foolish enough to have an accident. Evie looked from one to the other. They were all perfectly normal-seeming people, and normal in New York was defined as someone who didn't get involved. Without meaning to, she sighed audibly and was surprised when the black man sitting on the bench across from her smiled sympathetically. She was further surprised to find herself smiling back.

People had always thought Evie Lincoln's smile dazzling and, encouraged, the man got up and then sat down beside her as the train gathered momentum.

"We haven't met, but I believe you're Evie Lincoln from the Manhattan District Attorney's office."

Evie was both startled and relieved. Usually people who recognized her made reference to the fact that she was the mayor's daughter. It was nice to know that someone knew she had a persona of her own.

"Yes, I am." She waited for him to continue.

"I'm Allen Young. I joined the Brooklyn D.A.'s office last August and was in the audience for the seminar you participated in last month on victims' rights."

Evie smiled at him and held out her hand, which he took in a warm, firm grasp.

"I thought you were terrific," he said. "That schnook from the ACLU and his 'balances between the rights of the victims and the rights of criminals' "—here Allen drew himself up in parodic severity—"made me want to punch him, but you took care of him without resorting to violence."

"Thanks. It's just that I didn't want him to be a victim and have to balance his rights against mine."

Allen threw back his head and laughed resoundingly.

The brakes on the train screeched loudly as it slowed down to enter the 14th Street station.

"How far are you riding?" Allen asked.

"Up to Seventy-second Street. I have a dentist's appointment at two," she checked her watch and was reassured that it was only one nineteen, "and couldn't find a cab, so I decided on this." She made a disgusted face.

He smiled again. "I know what you mean. I still haven't gotten used to the subway, and it's been four months that I've been riding it."

"Wait until you've been doing it for twenty-eight years," she replied, as the train ground to a stop and people flowed in and out of the car. "I take it you're from out of town."

"Yes. Tuscaloosa."

"Why did you decide to come here?"

"I've always liked New York. When I was a teenager I used to come up during the summer to visit my aunt. I had cousins about my own age and they used to drag me all over the City. It was really eye-opening for a kid from the sticks. Just playing in front of an open hydrant in Harlem on a hot day in August was a thrill."

"I'll just bet." She thought him very naïve but attractive, and that was rare in her line of work. "But why the D.A.'s office? Why not a private firm?"

"Private practice just didn't hold any appeal. When I finally decided to go to law school, I knew I'd come out and do something in the public sector. I went to Annapolis. Then eight years of the Marines before I resigned my commission. Georgetown Law."

"Why did you resign your commission?"

He paused before replying. "The truth is that there's still a lot of racism in the services. I was a pilot, and it wasn't noticeable when I was in the air—how could it be, I guess—but on the ground it was very evident."

"So you left and went to law school," she said, and thought how typically idealistic. He'd learn after a couple of years in Manhattan. The doors closed and the train stumbled forward again, picking up speed for its run to 34th Street. Then the lights went out and the train began to slow.

"Damn," she muttered, and glanced at her watch again. Under the dim light coming from the emergency system, she could barely make out that it was one twenty-three and a few seconds.

It was quarter to one and Kate Thorne sat at banquette table one in The Four Seasons Grill. The autumnal sun shone through the huge scallops of bronze metal curtain devised by Mies van der Rohe for the three-story-high windows overlooking 52nd Street, and the light from the windows made the rosewood walls of the Grill Room glow. While she waited, Kate thought about her Vassar friend, Phyllis Bronfman, and how her friend had persuaded her father to build not just another office building, but to use Mies and Philip Johnson to build a masterpiece. The bronze and glass tower was magnificent. Then Phyllis had gone on to become an outstanding architect herself. She was the kind of woman Kate admired. She looked around. Every table was filled by now, though Julian

Niccolini had complained when Kate arrived that the celebration across the river at Tate Acres had caused a momentary lull while he and Alex von Bidder decided which of the reservations on the waiting list took precedence—there would always be takers for these tables when the "regulars" were absent.

Some of the latter were here, having opted not to go to the ceremony. After all, this restaurant filled up by twelve thirty and was emptied by two o'clock most weekdays because the elegant men and women who frequented it were, on the whole, serious businesspeople in a hurry to get back to their offices.

Tina Brown from *Vanity Fair* was at the banquette table three down from Kate; Philip Johnson—he must be well over ninety, Kate guessed—was seated at his accustomed circular corner table; and Michael Korda, tow-headed, was at his usual table across the room. He was the famous editor/novelist from Simon and Schuster and he was waiting for his lunch guest, too. Michael had been the editor for her book on her ascent of Mount Everest that had been published twenty years ago. Michael never aged. He looked a perennial thirty-five. He saw her and got up to come give her hand a kiss.

"Kate, you look magnificent. As always. What brings you to New York?"

"I'm having lunch with Sam. Some speaking engagements. Shopping. You know how it is for us folk from the hinterlands of the Southwest, Michael. But, of course, you have your wonderful hideaway in Santa Fe, so I don't need to tell you. We migrate here in the autumn. You look fine yourself. I loved your last novel."

"Let's have a drink while you're here. I'll call you this afternoon. At Sam's?"

She nodded and he departed for his table just as Sam came up the broad staircase to be ushered to the table.

"Hi, Julian," he greeted the young maître d' who had risen from waiter to partner in the outstanding restaurant.

Julian made a mock bow and chastised, "You are late, late, late for your mother!"

Only Julian in all of New York City could get away with his combination of irreverence and playfulness. He was simply the best at his job. Nothing, absolutely nothing, escaped his eyes.

"Hi, m'love." Sam slid in behind the large, heavy, angular table and ordered a Pellegrino from the hovering waiter.

"How did the interview go?" Kate was sipping an Absolut martini straight up with olives.

"Boring. I thought the day wouldn't ever come when I couldn't stand the sound of my own voice, but . . ." He grinned at her. "It has arrived."

"My, my." She studied the menu. "Shall I do the right thing and have the Spa Cuisine? No. I shall have what I want, which is the crab cakes. After this lunch I am going home and having a long lovely nap. Jet lag at my age is awful."

"Did you see Danny this morning?"

"I sure did. We played one round on his TV of some dreadful video game, which, of course, he won. He's a joy, Sam. How you two have produced such a sturdy soul I simply don't understand. Helter, skelter, all over the place, both of you more in love with your careers than anyone or anything else. He is a gem. It must have skipped a generation and he goes back to his grandparents."

"Sure." Sam nibbled the currant roll. "Whatever it is, I'm grateful. I thought I'd surprise him and go over to the school after we leave here and pick him up."

"Good idea." Kate smiled approvingly and hailed the waiter. "Encore," she said and indicated her martini glass. "And you may send Julian to take our order."

A tall, distinguished man stood by their table and looked down at Kate. She looked up at him prepared to be annoyed at the interruption.

"It's Gordon Keith, Kate." He bent down to kiss her cheek. "Hi, Sam. I don't expect you remember me, since you were in college the last time I was a visitor at your house in Broadmoor. How are you, Kate. You look marvelous."

"I'm fine, Gordon. What a surprise. You look well, too."

Sam listened to the two of them exchange more banalities and was amused at his mother. Kate was not often caught off guard. Something had caused the color to rise in her cheeks, and he was fairly certain it was not the vodka. The gentleman was about her age, tall, thin, with a dark Savile Row suit on and an air of seriousness. But his smile was wide and his deep-set dark eyes never left Kate's face as they chatted. "Oh, Sam, you remember Dr. Keith. My old friend."

"Of course I do. You beat me in three straight sets, as I recall. I'd ask you to sit down, but these damn tables are so heavy I can't move."

"No, no. I must join my own table. I'm fund-raising for New York Hospital today, part of my job—though what it has to do with neurology, I don't know. Kate, I heard about Daniel. I'm very sorry."

"Thank you, Gordon. Daniel hadn't been himself for many years."

"Are you going to be here long enough for me to ask you to dinner?"

"I'd love it. Call me at Sam's," and she gave him the phone number. He nodded at Sam and went to his table where a white-haired, heavyset woman sat nursing a white wine.

Sam turned to his mother. "Well?"

"Well, what?" She sipped her fresh martini. "I am famished. Where is Julian?"

"Tell me about you and Dr. Keith."

Kate gave him a blank look. "He is an old family friend of mine and your father."

"I don't remember your talking about him much if at all after that summer he visited us."

"No. I haven't seen him except once on a visit to New York since. That happens to friendships. You drift apart if you live thousands of miles away unless you work at keeping the friendship going."

"And you didn't. Unlike you." Sam studied her expression for a clue. "You're like a barnacle about old friends. Did you have a falling out?"

"Of course not. Why are we going on about Gordon Keith? You are hinting at something and I am not about to discuss it with you."

"Okay. But you admit there is something. I've wondered if in all that long idyllic marriage to Dad you ever, either of you, got interested in someone else." He felt a grim reminder of Diane in his teasing words. "I mean, we kids never sensed anything. And you'd have us believe that in over forty years you never had an unfaithful thought. But you'd be doing me a big favor if you'd tell me the truth." He paused and waited.

Kate signaled Julian again, who nodded vigorously from across the room. She turned her whole body toward Sam on the banquette seat so that she cut off the view and hearing of the next table. "You want to know so that I can help you?" She smiled at her favorite son and gave a shrug. "You know as well as I do it doesn't work that way. My story isn't your story. Much as we love one another, we are isolated completely when it comes to our separate passions. What good will it do you to know that Gordon Keith and I fell in love that summer? As unwanted a love, for me anyway, as any that ever started in a garden after a dance sitting in old rickety lawn chairs watching the others inside in the light dancing a waltz, and then a fox trot, and then another waltz. Watching the couples sway with the music, the strains of Cole Porter and Irving Berlin songs floating out over the dewy grass to our moonstruck ears." Her voice was low and suddenly angry. "Will it help you to know that I gave him up that summer? That from the moment we knew we loved I knew that everything I cared about except him was in the balance and that for a brief moment in time I could have given it all up—Dan, you children, the works—but I didn't, and I sent Gordon away and saw him only once again in all these twenty years."

Sam saw the tears darken her blue eyes. He was amazed at this outburst. But in some strange way not surprised at the revelation.

With superb timing, Julian arrived at their table.

———

Promptly at one o'clock the horses were loaded in the gate and Tom Durkin called out over the loudspeaker system: "They're off!"

Rosemarie held her binoculars to her eyes. It was a six-furlong race. She found Capri, running on the outside, about fifth off the leader. "Come on, girl," she cried out. "Come on Capri."

For such a short race it seemed to be going in slow motion for a few moments until they reached the turn. Then it speeded up and Capri moved up to be second. Factor was beating his program against the metal rail of the box. Rosemarie started to yell. "Capri, Capri, go, girl, go!"

The beautiful dark horse continued to move up on the leader, and on the near turn took over the lead and then, in front of them all, Capri took a bad step. She crashed to the ground, all one thousand pounds of straining flesh, muscle, and heart, head over heels. The jockey flew over her head. The other horses managed to jump over Capri and the jockey and finish the race. Capri lay without moving, as did the jockey. At the edge of the race course a huge white horse ambulance started to make its way slowly toward them, and the smaller human ambulance sped out in front.

The crowd had moaned at first when they saw the tragic sight. Now, though, they were looking at the tote board to see what the results would pay, some tearing up their tickets on Capri in disgust.

Rosemarie stood transfixed. Factor had jumped to his feet and rushed down to the infield moments after the accident and she could see him running toward the horse and jockey along with other track officials, and the ambulances as sure as doom making their terrible journey toward Capri and Jose Cielo.

For the second time that day tears flowed from Rosemarie's eyes. She found she could not move. She wanted to go down and hold Capri in her arms, take the beautiful animal's head and hold it to her breast, tell her she loved her and that the cruel men who had bred her and made her race would pay, but she stood rooted in the same place where moments before she had cried out for Capri to win, to win, to win.

Somehow it was the culmination of all the injustice in life, all the destruction of great beauty, all the cruelty of existence, the sight in front of Rosemarie's eyes. The horse ambulance positioned itself between the track and the grandstand so that the patrons would not have to see them loading the horse into the back of it. The doctor leaned down over the jockey who was alive, and sitting up, and after another minute or two the horse ambulance lumbered away leaving an empty space where Capri had fallen. Rosemarie sobbed as though her heart would break. She rushed from the Clubhouse and found the parking attendant.

"Mrs. Rizzo, I'm sorry. I heard. Is there anything I can do?"

"Give me the car keys," she pleaded. "No, nothing. I want to get out of here. Please."

"Right now," he said and trotted over to the Jaguar. She's in no condition to drive, he thought, but I'm not going to try to stop Rizzo's wife from doing whatever she wants to do. He wondered if she realized the filly would probably be all right. The horse had been stunned for a few minutes and broken her leg, but it would mend and she would make a fine broodmare. The parking attendant knew. He, like most people around the racetrack, knew and loved horses and owned an old claiming horse he kept for a pet.

He watched her hurl herself into the driver's seat and take off. He glanced at his watch. It was 1:16 P.M.

The president was flying in for the dedication ceremony of Tate Acres, a 150-acre development on the Brooklyn side of the East River, centered on the old Brooklyn Navy Yard and including landfill out into the river as the basis of a lovely public park.

The development itself consisted of six thirty-story office buildings located around a central plaza with an attendant shopping mall including a theater, which was to be the home of a new Performing Arts Center and a "quad" movie house with state-of-the-art acoustics and sound insulation. There were thirteen apartment buildings, ranging from fourteen to twenty-eight stories in height— the architect's aim being to create Tate Acres in harmony with the surroundings, not dominant over it—with condominiums for the rich ranging from $750,000 and up and rentals for "middle income" residents as low as $675 a month for a studio. Scattered through this residential complex were daycare centers, restaurants (both fast food and four-star elegant), small pocket petting zoos and aviaries, and several mini-parks for children with slides, swings, sandboxes, and the like.

Most innovative, the architect had designed a low-income housing development on thirty acres of the land containing ten-story buildings that both harmonized with and were as structurally sound as those for wealthier residents. They were grouped around atriums, all of the apartments had terraces and many of those had river views and their attendant breezes, and the atriums and lawns were to be planted with birch and Oriental trees and other exotic flora not normally associated with developments for the economically disadvantaged. These buildings would be occupied by the poor—primarily blacks and Hispanics—and at least one of them was to be given over as a temporary shelter for the homeless.

With its own police precinct, firehouse, and sanitation facility, Tate Acres was a self-contained "mini-city" within the surrounding Borough of Brooklyn.

Among the public buildings, the standout was the Medical Center, a six-story building in the shape of a cross. Built of Vermont granite over steel, it was sleek and spare of design. It was to be used solely for the care and treatment of drug addicts and victims of AIDS, the funding coming from a $350 million trust set up by Howard Tate, the research and treatment facilities staffed by clinicians, scientists, and psychiatrists of world class.

The opening day ceremony was being held in the park, where for one year the landfill had been brought in to fill in some thirty acres between piers jutting out into the East River. The landscaping was perfected so that there were beautiful nature trails, walks lined with geraniums and now yellow and crimson mums, to be replanted with the seasons, magnificent trees brought down from upstate New York and Connecticut, birch and spruce and maple, rhododendrons and lilac and dogwood. There was a wide-open meadow in the middle of the park, ringed by the newly planted trees, reached either by walking from the Performing Arts Center or from a handsome yacht basin where many of the richer apartment owners would keep their pleasure boats. Also located in this area was a large helicopter pad with room for thirty machines since many of the occupants of Tate Acres would want to fly to Wall Street or Midtown or to the airports from this base. If in the mood, they could take their boats to the various landing sites across the East River.

For today, the park groundsmen had been up since dawn, checking the platform where the dignitaries would sit to make sure all was in order. The fifty-man Secret Service detail had set up elaborate screening devices and had been crawling all over the place since early morning. Three hundred spanking-clean white folding chairs had been set up on the grass. The breeze was blowing the American and New York State flags and the flags of many other nations that ringed the plaza leading down to the meadow. Mowing machines and painters were putting finishing touches on the tennis courts and eighteen-hole golf course at one end of the park. The electricians were testing the equipment on the dais. All was in readiness for the ceremony to begin.

One of the first to arrive was Mayor Bruce Lincoln. The most important figures were meeting in the Central Hall of the Performing Arts Center, where Henry Moore and Louise Nevelson sculptures stood and the walls boasted a Picasso and a Monet from Howard Tate's private collection.

Bruce Lincoln's handsome face was square of jaw and impassive, belying the fact that his mind, as always, was on at least a dozen things, but he was looking forward to today. He liked the president, though he wished he could get more money out of him for the City; he thought Cardinal O'Connor a great help to the ills of the City, both practically and spiritually; his wife, Paula, who had chosen not to come today because of her duties at the daycare center in Harlem that she ran, was upset with both men because of their stand on abortion; he respected Howard Tate, even though he considered him a cold son of a bitch. Yes, it was the kind of mixed-up day Bruce Lincoln enjoyed. No politics. Lots of undercurrents.

The cardinal arrived with his entourage. The hall began to fill up rapidly. Soon Howard Tate and his wife, Ingrid, who had come over via the Williamsburg Bridge in their limousine, arrived and started shaking hands with everyone. The governor was traveling in Europe and had sent his regrets. Except for him, all the luminaries of the city and state were now about to take their seats in the park. There was Beverly Sills, ex-mayor Ed Koch, Si Newhouse, Liz Smith, and Donald Trump. Wherever you looked, you could see the rich and the mighty, the talented and the famous. It was one of the 1994 events at which most of the movers and shakers of New York wanted to be. Over there was Tom Brokaw. Dr. Mathilde Krim. Grace Mirabella. By boat, by car, and by helicopter, they had come to pay honor to Howard Tate and his incredible project.

Cardinal O'Connor, Mayor Lincoln, the Tates, the buildings commissioner, and other dignitaries took their seats on the dais. The sun was high in the azure-blue sky. It was almost time for the president to arrive, via helicopter from LaGuardia. The honored guests were being shown to their seats by various uniformed attendants. A Secret Service man approached the mayor from behind with a whispered message. Bruce Lincoln then rose and walked toward the podium microphone.

"Ladies and gentlemen, honored guests, Your Eminence, I have just received word that the president was unavoidably detained in Washington, so our program will not commence for a few minutes. Welcome to you all, and we will begin with Cardinal O'Connor's benediction as soon as the president is here."

1:10 P.M.

"Air Force One is cleared to circle."

"Cleared to circle. Thank you, LaGuardia."

Colonel James Petersen, one of the several pilots who rotated command of Air Force One, turned to the young Navy lieutenant who stood respectfully at attention several feet behind him in the cockpit.

"You may tell the president that we have been cleared to make one or two circles over Manhattan before we go into LaGuardia. The airspace is clear."

In his private cabin aboard Air Force One, the president was fine-tuning the speech he would give later at the dedication ceremony for Tate Acres. Old Howard Tate (old? They were Andover and Yale classmates, both members of Skull and Bones and almost exact contemporaries!) finally had his monument. He was finding it hard, however, to concentrate on what he would say. The speech had to be upbeat, but much of the news he had had for the last few days had begun to get him, one of the most ebullient of presidents, down.

The Chinese situation was the most dangerous it had been since the beginning of his first term, with another change in leadership that was even more conservative than the previous one; after the momentous events of 1989, the countries with newfound freedom, Hungary, Czechoslovakia, Bulgaria, Romania, all were having a terrible time economically and politically; the national debt refused to come down to an acceptable level and he knew that if he could not achieve this goal, that rascal, Governor George Fleming of New York who had become governor in 1991 when Cuomo had stepped aside to run unsuccessfully for the presidency in 1992, would have a real shot at becoming the first Democrat in the White House in sixteen years, a thought the president could not stomach. Fleming was a bad man, he believed. Not because he disagreed with him politically. No, it was something much worse. The values that mattered most to the president—loyalty to family, friends, country—just didn't mean a thing to Fleming. He was a rotten apple. The only bright light on the horizon was the incredible leadership of Father Antonio Diaz, bringing the Central and South American countries together in the war against poverty and drugs. Diaz would fly back to Washington on Air Force One later that day to address a joint session of Congress. He was the new Mahatma Gandhi, a genuine hero.

Thinking about Diaz restored the president's optimism and he was determined to enjoy himself today. Political allies as well as enemies would be there, but it was understood that this was not to be an afternoon for polemics. It was a time for all the powerful and wealthy who would attend the ceremony to show themselves off at their best. His own speech would emphasize all the good things about New York—a city he loved more than perhaps any other in the world.

The president felt the plane begin to descend, then realized that a young Navy lieutenant had entered his private cabin and was standing stiffly by his seat. He smiled vaguely at the man, barely more than a boy, really, and obviously ill at ease. "Yes, lieutenant?"

"Sir. Colonel Petersen has asked me to tell you that we have been cleared to make two circles around Manhattan before we land at LaGuardia. By my reckoning, we should be within sight of the City in ten minutes. Sir," he added, hoping that the president wouldn't think it was just an afterthought.

"Thank you, Lieutenant." When the young officer didn't move, the president smiled again at him and said, "Dismissed." The lieutenant backed up two paces, saluted sharply, and almost marched off. The president had glanced at the lieutenant's hand as he had saluted. A ring-knocker, he thought, using an old Navy term for Annapolis graduates. They're always a little stiff the first few years after they're out of there, the good ones anyway. Takes time, or a war, to loosen them up.

The president glanced once again at his speech, then folded it and laid it on top of his jacket on the chair next to him.

He was going to be late. Couldn't be helped, though, he mused; the prime minister had sounded almost frantic on the phone—probably as much because his power base was eroding day by day—as he told him of his decision to abandon the European Economic Community as "simply not for Britons, although we gave it a jolly decent try." But then he had gone on and on about the mutual dependence of America and Great Britain, which was more nearly an overt pitch for financial help. Well, he'd have to think about that. We couldn't abandon them, of course, but there wasn't a great deal of money to hand them.

He felt the plane begin to descend again, arose, and moved to a window on the port side of his cabin to gaze at the coastline to the west. They were still over ocean—at this low altitude, they would avoid land as much as possible in order not to disturb the residents—but when they began to fly over New York Harbor and move up the Hudson, he would return to his seat on the starboard side to watch Manhattan. They would bank right at the George Washington Bridge, then right again and follow the courses of the Harlem and East rivers down the east side of the city. If he changed seats again, he could get his first glimpse of the newly completed Tate Acres. One more right turn, up the Hudson again, and then Colonel Petersen could take the jet into LaGuardia. The president stared out into the blue, glad that, for a few minutes at least, his world was at peace.

Colonel Petersen turned to Major Davis, something he didn't really have to do since they were both wearing communications headgear. But it never hurt to have eye contact when issuing a command. "Bring her left to three-fifty please, Tony. We'll take her in over the Verrazano Bridge, then cut across the harbor and up the Hudson. No need to terrorize the folks on the ground."

Davis nodded his acknowledgment, then brought the big jet

around to three hundred fifty degrees on the horizontal situation indicator. They were still some thirty miles from the tip of lower Manhattan and about five miles off the New Jersey shore, cruising northward at a comfortable 198 knots.

As the plane passed over the Verrazano, the president moved across the aisle and settled back into his starboard seat. He stared out at the most powerful city in the world, brilliantly sunlit on a crystal fall day, glad to be alive and on his way there.

"Good idea, Tony. Let me just tell them." Colonel Petersen spoke briefly into his microphone. Davis had already begun making the subtle adjustments that would bring the craft around the west side of Liberty Island even before he had air traffic control's permission to do so. Both men knew that it was the president's habit to sit on the starboard side of the plane when it was approaching a landing, and they knew that the boss would appreciate the sight of the lady, even if from the back.

The president, never having lost his pilot's instinct, felt the tiny course correction and knew intuitively what the men in the cockpit were doing. Good lads, he thought. I'll bet on a day like this there's a mob at the statue. It's a heck of a climb to the top, but once you're there it's worth it. The president himself—his wife declining politely—had made the ascent only two years before with several of his grandchildren in tow. As fit as he was, even he was a bit breathless when the bottom step was reached, and one of the Secret Service men looked on the verge of a cardiac arrest. But the kids had loved it, and the president had been glad he'd made the effort.

It was simple. Like the American flag, the Statue of Liberty meant something. Not just something to him, though that was certainly true, but something to everyone, to all Americans. To all the world, in fact.

"Bring it back to three-sixty on the heading, Tony. Very nice flying, I might add."

The big plane shuddered, seemed to be gripped in the talon of some huge beast, and a roaring far in excess of that made by the four engines filled its cabins.

The president sat bolt upright, then in an automatic reflex

reached down to tug the life preserver out from under his seat. Two Secret Service men quickly entered the cabin along with a colonel who had a padlocked briefcase handcuffed to his wrist called "the football," which contained the codes necessary for the president to order a nuclear attack.

The president was staring out the window. "My God! Turn this plane around and head for Washington."

Seconds later, Air Force One rose in a steep climb and banked sharply to the left, taking it over New Jersey. Petersen had taken over the controls from Davis. The president's aide was on the airborne scrambler phone, using a secure satellite communications path and speaking urgently now to the control tower at Andrews Air Force Base, requesting that not only all other traffic between New York and Washington be rerouted but that a pair of fighters be deployed to escort the president's plane back to the capital.

1:21 P.M.

At first, for perhaps ten seconds, the ground rocked gently, a swaying motion, not severe, but back and forth. Then the ground started to surge underfoot in great undulating waves, shock after shock. People sitting in the audience at Tate Acres fell from their chairs onto one another. A roar, inhuman, unfamiliar, terrible, rose. The dais, built only four feet off the ground, crumbled and all upon it were plunged to the uncertain earth.

No one made a sound to begin with. It was only moments later that the screams of fear and pain began. The newly transplanted mature trees at the edge of the meadow crashed down. Flagpoles bent and broke, striking those nearby. A fissure, thirty feet wide, opened at one side of the park, widened, and closed. Another opened at one side of the place where the ceremony had begun and all there fell into it, going down, down, landing at the bottom of a **V** that kept opening. They began to scramble up the sides, trying to get to the top.

Those who could got to their feet. They stared in shock across the East River, as though in slow motion, as though a giant wrecking ball was at work, buildings were coming apart before their eyes, falling outward, collapsing in on themselves. The roar continued, clouds of what looked like smoke rose over the falling buildings, the Empire State swayed but stood, the World Trade Center was firm, the Chrysler Building remained, and much of everything else they could see along the other side of the East River was in an instant flattened. Behind them, the Tate buildings, made of steel and reinforced according to the latest codes, stood. They were three hundred people in some God-given oasis in the middle of monumental, unthinkable catastrophe.

The floor under Kate's feet moved. The swaying motion happened again and Sam grabbed the edge of the table. Julian turned and seemed to be walking uphill at a slant as the shock hit again. And again. All the tableware flew off the tables as though a giant hand had swept across the tabletops. The waiters were tumbling about in crazy motion, some on the floor, others attempting to stay upright by clinging to anything they could reach. Wine coolers hit the occupants of tables. The noise of breaking glass, china, and screams was a roar.

Sam grabbed Kate and pulled her under the table where they crouched as the building swayed . . . and held. He knew immediately from the first motion what was happening, and in his shocked mind came gratitude that they were in a building that was safe and a room that could survive the worst earthquake, but on the heels of that thought was panic—Diane . . . Danny . . . everyone . . . the City.

The nightmare had come true.

When Brian Kelly left his office, Hartnett called his lunch date and canceled. He put his feet back up on his desk and looked out his window. Several minutes later, before his amazed eyes, all of Battery Park City disintegrated in slow motion—as he held on to his desk and then got under it, but not before he had seen great buildings sway in the far distance and then crumble. Hartnett's mind automatically, almost before the shock of the earthquake subsided, knew that there was opportunity here. At first he was not sure what lay ahead, but by the time that day was over and he had settled in to stay the night in his undamaged office, he was certain that the plan that was formulating in his head could work. And if it did, it would free him from Rizzo and Brian Kelly's threats. He would be far beyond their power to harm him.

—————

Copper was sleeping in the sun in the window seat in the living room. He was dreaming of chasing a rodent through the tall grass of a meadow. His tail twitched and his paws made running motions. The field mouse was just out of his reach, but Copper was gaining on him.

Just then a terrible noise woke him up. He jumped off the window seat and ran like lightning down the stairs and into the basement kitchen under the stove. For a long time the noises continued and he cowered. He could see things falling down around him.

After a few minutes it was silent. He saw a small space left and he went down on his belly and squeezed his way out. He found himself outdoors on the sidewalk by his house. He looked around. He knew he was not supposed to be loose outside the house. There was a person staggering out of the house across the way. He ran across the street and greeted her. She ignored him and pushed him away, making terrible noises from her throat. He ran back to his house and saw that it did not exist anymore. A huge pile of rubble. His nose to the ground, sniffing, sniffing, Copper searched everywhere he could climb to find Danny. Or Mary. Or any of his family. Weary after an hour of futile searching, only finding bits of their clothes and other belongings, he found a sunny place in the debris and lay down to sleep. When he awoke to the sounds of people in the street, lots of them, he ran from person to person to see if any of them belonged to him. No one was interested in him. By afternoon, Copper was on his way. He knew the route to the Grove School and he was taking it to find Danny.

—————

Pat Kelly was angered by her interview with John Maloney. She got back into the waiting car and barked at the driver, "Go uptown, Richie. I want to check out the new equipment we got last week at Bellevue."

"In this traffic we could get there by Christmas."

"Just get me there," she ordered, and immediately felt sorry that she was taking out her anger on Richie, a slow-witted young man the department had handed her for a driver. She thought of her late mother's constant comment to her as she grew up: "You have a chip on your shoulder the size of County Cork." Maybe she was right. But damn it, Maloney was a patronizing son of a bitch, and what was worse, he was clearly not going to back the Emergency Services with any organized clout. Probably Gordon Keith was right. She shouldn't have taken this administrative job. Hands-on doctoring was what she was good at, not dealing with red tape and men who thought they could push her around. She stared out the grimy car window at the river. Not for the first time she allowed a thought to cross her mind and then pushed it away fast. Brian. Children. Why had she done it? She should never have gotten married and had kids. Most marriages were traps for the women, and kids were a responsibility that she didn't need or want. She had seen her mother's life go right down the drain.

She pulled a pad out of her bag and wrote: "Make apt. Capt. Driscoll, officer Emergency Management." Richie had turned off the Drive and onto First Avenue. He braked for a light. Suddenly she felt the car move as though it were on a roller-coaster. She grabbed the back of the front seat. Richie had hit his head on the steering wheel. Pat watched the whole avenue in front of her undulate. Their car slammed into another car. Pat was thrown sideways against the door. Then the movement stopped. She picked herself off the floor of the car and moved her arm. It was not broken. A bomb must have hit. She tried to open her door and it was jammed. Richie was coming to, just as she climbed over into the front seat. "What the hell?"

They looked out at the avenue split by a huge open fissure, into which many cars had fallen, and at the tangle of cars that had been tossed about like blowing leaves.

"Come on," Pat said. "Let's get out of here." She opened the front car door.

"Oh, no," Richie sat there. "I'm staying here. It looks safer."

Eleven Wall Street. It was 1:20 P.M. The morning had been a frantic one on the floor of the newly renovated New York Stock Exchange. The afternoon was proving more so. Everywhere the traders looked, at every display screen, on every printout, the prices were down. Genentech, down twenty-one points. IBM down eight. General Motors down a whopping thirty-seven and a half. Panic had begun to spread in the financial community as the volume of sell orders swelled. Investors all over the country had responded to the sudden nervousness, phoning and faxing their brokers to dump one stock or another before the bottom fell out.

The young trader sitting on the recently completed balcony above the floor of the exchange looked at his watch. He was talking almost simultaneously on three phones, had four more calls on hold. Christ, he thought, this can't keep up. Something's got to give.

A rumbling filled the hall, unlike anything that had been heard or felt before. The building began to shake. The cries of the traders on the floor as they sought to deal were nothing compared to the noise that filled the great hall. People began to fall, thrown down by the motion of the building. The largest of the display screens ripped loose from its bolts and plunged down, killing or injuring scores on the floor below.

The young trader watched in horror as an explosion of fire and steam ripped up through the floor from pipes buried in the depths of the building. People—scalded by steam, burned by the flames, cut by flying glass—clawed at each other in an attempt to escape the hell around them. Their screams stabbed through the trader's brain, numbing him. He looked around. Everywhere lights were going off, computer terminals were blank screens, telephones were dead.

Then it was over. But it had just begun.

After Timothy left, Nancy went to the living-room phone and canceled her afternoon appointments. She stood by the ceiling-to-floor window overlooking Fifth Avenue for several minutes, thinking about her brother. Then she went upstairs to shower. Afterward, dressed in a long dressing gown, she went back downstairs and asked one of the bodyguards for a line of coke. She opened the second bottle of wine that Tim had brought and started to drink it after she had used the coke. After another few minutes, she went back up to her bedroom, bottle in hand, and turned on some jazz. She lay in the bed she shared with Rizzo and thought about her baby brother. What a mess he was. But, what the hell, so was she by Thayer standards. Tim depressed her and he brought back the past. All the good times he and she had shared as children and all the bad, too.

She felt very high, and the sadness began to lift. She knew when she told Rizzo about the money he would understand. He was like that about family. Rizzo would understand. He was the first person in her life she could trust and depend on. How strange that this was true. She leaned back against the pillows and dreamed. She was just starting to get good and drunk, singing scat along with a Gene Krupa tape, when the earthquake struck.

The dust had barely begun to settle from the earthquake when the looting began. No part of Manhattan was exempt, from Washington Heights at the north end of the island to the Battery at the south. The targets were large and small—mom-and-pop grocery stores and supermarkets, hole-in-the-wall hardware stores and the city's most elaborate electronics outlets.

The young Chinese man looked around at the destruction on Canal Street. He had been in the street itself, crossing from one side to the other, when the earthquake struck. Paralyzed, he had stood there in the middle of the intersection of Canal and Broadway as traffic ground to a halt around him and glass and concrete from the surrounding buildings rained down.

He had to get to his girlfriend working at Bernstein's on Canal between Baxter and Mulberry.

He waited for the shock to pass, then took stock. He was unhurt except for a cut on his right thigh where a large sliver of glass had torn through his pants leg. The cut was bleeding but not badly, and it didn't hurt more than a bit when he put his weight on it.

He started forward, then was thrown to his knees by an aftershock as it rippled through the city. When he thought the whole thing was over, he rose and looked up Canal toward where it curved to the right to approach the Manhattan Bridge. Canal Street, never easy to negotiate by car, had become one long parking lot. The street itself had been badly torn up by the shocks and drivers had abandoned their cars for what they thought was the greater safety of the street. Now nothing moved forward or backward along the street's entire length.

He covered the three-and-a-half blocks to the jewelry store as quickly as he could. The large plate-glass windows had shattered and much of the jewelry being exhibited behind them had poured onto the sidewalk, the diamonds and other gems winking seductively among the rubble. Already people were beginning to sift through the debris and claim prizes—watches, rings, bracelets, pins—that were quickly secreted away in pockets and purses.

The door to Bernstein's had been wrenched partially open, the frame twisted, and he squeezed himself through and into the store. He heard sounds of a scuffle and tried to see through the dust enveloping the store.

He had been in the back of Bernstein's often enough to know where the door was even in the gloom. He also knew that the safe was there. He moved quickly but was suddenly grabbed from behind by two sets of hands. Then he was propelled through the door to the back room.

He saw her, then saw the slender young Oriental with the black bandanna wrapped around his head pointing a gun at her. The store's owner lay on the floor, blood welling from a wound in his back.

"Now," the bandannaed man said. "I want it open now. Don't tell me you don't know the combination, bitch. Everybody in Chinatown knows how old man Bernstein trusted you. Get it open."

Slowly she turned toward the safe, began to spin the dial to unlock it. Her hands shook and she had to try twice before the correct pins fell into place. Then, soundlessly, the big steel door swung open.

"Start taking things out, put them on the counter. Give me the sack we brought."

"Who would have thought that the day we decided to rob this place we'd get such a lucky break."

"Yeah."

As quickly as they could, the two robbers filled the bag. Finally, they prepared to go.

"What about them? They've seen our faces."

"Leave them. After today, faces aren't going to matter."

Mattie Lincoln's only experience with earthquakes was what she had seen from time to time on the television. Nevertheless, for a woman of eighty-five, when it struck she had the quickness of mind to drop the flowers she was arranging on the altar of the Abyssinian Baptist Church for the midweek service that evening and get under a heavy table that had been left for some temporary purpose a few feet away.

As the church caved in around her, Mattie could hear the screams of the other ladies who were there with her that day. As she began to pray, all the prayers that had comforted her during a lifetime of service in the church comforted her now as she huddled under the table and darkness descended around her.

Rosemarie was on the Northern State Parkway when the earthquake hit. She felt the highway move under the car and instinctively slowed down. Other cars pulled over, but she drove on. Trees had fallen across the road but she avoided them and went forward until she reached her driveway. Sobs had been replaced by a fury that gripped her by the throat. She was consumed with it. Oblivious to the fallen trees, the earth's tremor, the driveway littered with branches and leaves, she braked abruptly and leaped out of the car. She ran to the door and burst through it and started up the stairs, when the maid came after her. "Oh, ma'am, there's been a terrible something going on—the phones are out and the electricity and—"

"Never mind," Rosemarie turned. "Are the dogs all right?"

The maid looked stunned. "I haven't seen them, ma'am. I think we've had a hurricane or something terrible, and—"

"You take care of the house and try to find the dogs. Go out and find the stable boy—he can help you. I have things I must tend to. Go," she ordered the astonished and terrified maid.

Rosemarie went directly to Domenico's study. She went to his desk and took out his favorite gun, the Beretta. He had taught her how to shoot it because he was afraid of intruders breaking into the house and he wanted her to know how to protect herself. She loaded it and put it in her Gucci handbag. Then she sat down and started to think.

The maid and the policeman found her that way an hour later when the policeman came by to check the house for damage to it and its occupants. "We've had a major earthquake, Mrs. Rizzo. We weren't hit too bad, but Manhattan was hit hardest. Where is your husband?"

"In Manhattan for a business meeting." Rosemarie knew Domenico wasn't dead, that no earthquake would kill him. No, he was alive, and earthquake or no earthquake she was going to find him, and kill him and his nightclub singer. Rosemarie smiled up at the cop. "I'm sure Mr. Rizzo is all right. Is there any way to find out?"

Governor George Fleming was in the south of France with a girlfriend for two days between his junket to Italy, Germany, and France with some other governors. They were staying in St. Paul de Vence at La Colombe d'Or, a small gem of a hotel in the walled Roman village overlooking Nice and the Mediterranean. Their suite was down the stone steps carved into the low flower-lined wall along one side of the outdoor dining room. Geraniums in urns, hibiscus, bougainvillaea in profusion. Actually, their suite was a little house, consisting of a large bedroom, huge bathroom, and sitting room. The maid had left a big dark blue vase filled with hothouse daffodils on the table.

Simone and he had spent the afternoon by the swimming pool. An azure oblong with a Calder mobile at one end and a Braque mosaic of a running bird at the top of the ladder to the pool. The sun had baked them, Simone's bikini barely covering her oiled and tanned twenty-six-year-old gorgeous body. Fleming was trying to keep from frying his fifty-nine-year-old skin, white from too many hours in Albany running the affairs of New York State for three years; he was snatching this moment in time before returning to a strenuous campaign for reelection and after that victory, which he did not doubt, starting his serious run for the White House to succeed an incumbent as the first Democrat to win the presidency in sixteen years.

Simone had been introduced to him in Paris, and when he had invited her to join him in the south of France she had been thrilled. She worked as a secretary at the American Embassy and spoke flawless English. Not that they talked a great deal.

At five o'clock they went barefoot in their bathing suits to the bar and got two kir royales and took them down the stairs to their little house. Fleming had her bikini off before she set her drink down on the bedside table.

An hour later he was contemplating how to make this luscious creature come one more time—he loved her squeals in French—before they had to dress for dinner, when the phone rang.

Fleming sat up, naked, in bed, her small warm hand caressing him as he answered. "Yes," he groaned into the phone. "What is it?"

"Who? What? We have a terrible connection." He felt himself growing hard beneath her tender fingers. Not bad for an old man, he thought. "Who? Okay. Put him on. Gus, what are you trying to tell me? Speak up. This frog phone—Jesus!" He jumped up, surprising Simone, his erection bobbing up and down. "New York City? When? How bad is the damage? No, Mayor Lincoln may not take my place with the president until I get back! The National Guard? Not until I get back to assess the situation. Tell Lincoln I'll be back on the first plane I can get. Contact my people in Albany. I want no major decisions taken until I arrive. Hold everything. There's a night plane from Nice. No airports open? Well, they'll divert to Boston or somewhere. I'll get there. I'll call you from the plane. Bye."

He clicked the phone for the girl at the front desk. "This is Governor Fleming. You must have heard the news. I must get back. Get me a car and call my aide in room twelve. Tell him to get us on the first plane leaving Nice. I'll be ready in fifteen minutes."

Simone pouted. He looked at her naked body. He could dress in five minutes. There was just enough time.

In less than six minutes he was in the shower, mission accomplished. He left a thick wad of franc notes for her on the bedside table. "Sweet girl, I have to leave pronto. Here's more than enough to get back to Paris and buy yourself a new car with. Write your address and phone number on this piece of paper. You are too good to lose." He gave her a kiss as she lay under a sheet now, sleepy.

His aide, Bill Harvey, was waiting in the bar, which was full of before-dinner drinkers, most of whom were talking about the catastrophe in New York. "I've paid our bill, George. We have a taxi waiting. The flight is in twenty-five minutes. Madame Roux says we'll just make it."

They had the bulkhead seats in first class and the pilot had instructions to allow the governor access to the long-range communication radios. Bill Harvey looked rattled, which was rare, since he was the most discreet, most poised aide Fleming had ever employed. He knew it made Bill nervous when he had women on these trips, but for God's sake, everyone from Kennedy on and before had had women. It was nothing new.

"Have a drink, Bill. You look shook up."

"Thanks, sir. It's just that I think my wife was in New York City today. She said she might do some shopping and see a show."

Governor Fleming was suitably horrified. He put his big, freckled hand on Bill's arm. "Son, when I get on the horn with the president, if I can get through to him—there's no way to reach the mayor—I'll see what I can find out for you."

Bill's eyes misted over and he took the drink the stewardess offered.

Fleming turned down a drink. He needed all his wits about him. New York City. The campaign. The bid for the White House. There was something here if he could just grasp it. Opportunity. Never during his long climb up the political ladder had George Fleming missed a ripe opportunity. His ambition was so single-minded that instinct guided him toward the opportunities he made where none might have existed. George Fleming was the rising star in the Democratic Party. He was the son of an Irish pol from Newark and had inherited his father's good looks and charm. Where he got his venality no one knew. But then few knew that he had that darker side. George Fleming had a rare ability to make the person he was talking to believe completely for those few minutes that he, George Fleming, was deeply and sincerely interested in whatever the other person was saying. In truth, George Fleming was almost never interested in anyone other than himself.

As the plane flew through the night, Governor Fleming figured out that his opportunity to take advantage of New York in ashes was there for the plucking. His own chances for gaining the nomination two years from now and winning the election could be enormously enhanced. He, George Fleming, would lead the vanguard in the movement to dump New York City, and thereby send a flow of federal money where it would do him most good.

———

Conrad reached Abe Zimmer at his home in Golden. The phone rang ten times before Zimmer picked up.

"Abe, it's Conrad," he said with his distinct German accent.

Zimmer held an amber glass full of whiskey. "Hi. What day is it?" He sneezed and took another Kleenex from the box he carried from one room to the other.

"You know what day it is. Wednesday. How come you aren't at work? Don't they need you?"

"No guilt trips, please. Once the sucker hit New York, there was little I could do that many others there could not do better. My head is not working well. The cold and all. And how are you?"

Conrad was shocked at this show of irresponsibility. He had thought better of Zimmer. He said stiffly, "I am fine and just wanted to know if you were all right. I'll talk to you in a few days. We have our hands full here right now. Good-bye." And he hung up the phone, shaking his head.

"Good-bye," Zimmer mimicked the accent. "Goot-by." He took another swallow and lay down on his bed. He looked at the ceiling. "Nothing I could do." He spoke to himself. "Nothing I could do for any of those poor bastards in New York. They wouldn't listen. No one would listen. And the walls, they came atumbling down." He lay there with his eyes wide open, staring up at the ceiling.

———

Brendan Ahearn had parked his car at a garage on 85th and First. He walked the few crosstown blocks to the station house. A few minutes later as he was calling roll and issuing assignments the strident clang of the alarm ripped through the station house.

The blaze had been extinguished in a very short time. Fortunately it had been confined to a large closet in the elderly woman's apartment and even though she had been overcome by smoke while sitting in her living room, Brendan didn't think she would have any long-term ill effects. Brendan took out his pocket watch. One nineteen. He looked up at the senior lieutenant who was already in the cab of the idling fire truck.

"Get these hoses out of the street and get the street opened to traffic." Then he turned to get into the battalion chief's car.

As he reached for the handle of the car door it moved away from him. What the . . . ? Then, in turn, he moved away from the car, impelled by what seemed to be a giant hand. A roar filled the air and Brendan was thrown to his knees. Something solid slammed into his shoulder and through his own pain he could hear the screams of people around him as they, too, were tossed violently about.

A fissure opened in the street and Brendan began to roll inexorably toward it. He clawed at the paving in a desperate attempt to gain some sort of hold, but nothing was stable enough to support his grip.

A shovel from the fire engine skittered across the pavement and past him, its sharp blade missing his face by inches. A length of hose whipped by and shattered the front windshield of his car. He watched in horror as one of his men, still standing, teetered on the edge of the fissure, then dropped in. Mingled with the other noise, the man's cry stood out sharply.

Brendan was aware that he was bleeding, not badly, but from at least a dozen places in exposed parts of his body where a shower of broken glass had cut him. Thank God he had on his heavy, fire-retardant coveralls. His helmet had been torn from his head and, reflexively, he put his arms up to cover it.

The fissure loomed closer and Brendan wondered if he would follow the doomed fire fighter. His car toppled in and became wedged between the edges of the fissure. Brendan reached out to grasp the front bumper but it remained tantalizingly out of reach. Another large piece of debris struck him in the small of the back and pushed him forward. His fingers touched the edge of the bumper. He gripped it and pulled himself toward the car, praying that it would not fall deeper into the crevasse, but as the shuddering and heaving continued, he felt it sink, heard the scream of metal being tortured as the sides of the fissure squeezed the car's frame, then opened a bit to let it fall further in. Brendan clung to the bumper, knowing that the car's bulk was his best chance at safety.

He went over the edge, dangled from the front of the car by one hand, knew he wouldn't be able to hang on for more than a few seconds.

The car slipped again and the walls of the fissure began to move toward him. The car shook violently as its roof was crushed, and flashes of JeanAnne, Nicky, and Willy raced through his mind. He felt one edge touch his shoulder, knew he mustn't let go of the bumper, prayed to the God he had abandoned when JeanAnne had been killed, prepared to die.

Then, as quickly and without warning as it had begun, everything was still. Brendan could feel his hand slipping, knew he wouldn't be able to hold on much longer. With an effort, he twisted his body so that his back was to the wall of the fissure that had touched his shoulder, then put his feet out and braced them against the opposite wall some four feet away. Now he could let go.

Voices above him, someone peering over the edge of the crack in the street, a length of hose dropped down in front of him. Brendan grasped it. His hands, both of them bloody, slipped along the hose's surface. Gritting his teeth against the pain, he tightened his grip on the hose, then called out, "Ready."

The hose went taut and Brendan felt himself being lifted. He banged against the wall roughly, slipped several inches down the hose, coming precariously near its end. Then his head was over the edge of the crack and he felt hands reaching to take him under the armpits and bring him out of the fissure.

He sat on the crack's edge, feet dangling into it, breathing heavily, aware of how close he had come to death. As he looked into the fissure he saw that at its bottom, some twelve feet below, was a swirl of water, as if a main had ruptured. The water was moving swiftly and Brendan knew that if he had dropped into it he would drown. He began to rise, unsteady on his feet, arms reaching out to support him once again.

The aftershock shook the ground under their feet and Brendan and the men who were supporting him stepped back quickly as the walls of the fissure shut to within three inches of each other. Brendan closed his eyes and swallowed hard, pushing the terrible vision of himself trapped in that vise out of his mind. Then, finally, the earth became calm.

In the Central Park Zoo there was pandemonium. Some of the older structures collapsed or were damaged in such a manner as to release the animals. In the minutes after the first shock, the keepers, a dozen young men and women who saw to the animals' welfare, tried to contain the animals, but could not stop the larger beasts from escaping.

The monkey house was a madhouse of screams and escape. All kinds of exotic primates from gorillas to spider monkeys fled their cages, at first bewildered and frightened themselves, but as the day passed, becoming bolder and hungrier.

An elephant who had given birth two days before would not leave her large enclosure even though the gate had been smashed. She paced up and down with her two-day-old baby crying at her side.

Polar bears, tigers, and lions, set free, began to roam the park.

They had been late to begin with, and this traffic wasn't helping any. Jim Richardson drummed his fingers impatiently on the steering wheel of his 1992 Oldsmobile as they inched along the approach to the Queens/Midtown Tunnel. He looked at the digital clock on the dashboard. Just one o'clock. Damn. Those tickets for the revival of *Annie* hadn't been easy to come by. And Phyllis, his wife, had been really excited when she gave them to him for his birthday.

They had kept the two kids, Kathy and George, out of school on the theory that going to a Broadway matinee was culturally enriching. Besides, the children were only six and eight. How much education would be lost for one day of hooky?

They came up to the toll booths and Jim handed the tollkeeper the six dollars necessary to get into Manhattan. Six dollars. Where would it end? Every time you turned around, something had gone up in price.

In the tunnel now but still creeping at a snail's pace. Maybe it would be better to park the car right outside the tunnel's exit in Manhattan and grab a taxi. Cabbies could always get around the City faster than private drivers. One twenty. About halfway through the tunnel, Jim estimated. They'd just make it.

Directly behind the Richardsons, Joe Mazurski worked the clutch of his sixteen-wheeler carefully, nursing it along. He had started to have problems with it about ten miles back. Nah. That wasn't true. He had known two months ago that his transmission could go at any time, had been putting off getting it repaired because money was so tight, what with Patti just about to have their third child—third in four years. He glanced at the picture of his wife taped to the sun visor. At twenty-four she still looked like the seventeen-year-old he had dated, the twenty-year-old he had had to marry. Had had to, and been glad of it. But she sure did get pregnant easily. It seemed like all they had to do was think about having sex and her rabbit test would be positive.

The transmission groaned as he eased the clutch out, left the toll booth. He should really pull over to the side of the toll plaza, give the traffic a chance to thin out before going through the tunnel. He'd really have a problem if the transmission decided to call it quits once and for all after he'd gotten inside. But he had a schedule to keep. An independent trucker couldn't afford not to make his promised deadlines. Work had fortunately been steady, but that was because he had a reputation for delivering his loads on time. He was due to deliver the full load of electronic equipment from a small manufacturer in Garden City to a wholesaler in Weehawken by four, then deadhead back to his home in Northport for a couple of days off and work around the house before going on a transcon. One twenty. He'd figure out how he wanted to get to Weehawken once he was through the tunnel, had assessed the Manhattan traffic situation.

They'd gotten married on Saturday, but Christine was already coming down with the flu and they had postponed their wedding-night celebration for a few days. Not that it was any big thing. After all, Christine and Toby had been living together for eighteen months. But the parents—both sets—had put the pressure on, kept it on, and now they were Mr. and Mrs. Toby Riley. Christine snuggled against him as she rolled the phrase around in her head. Really, it did sound good. Eighteen months had been long enough for them both to be sure, and now here they were, married and on their way to spend the night at the Waldorf Astoria. They were going to do it up right. Dinner at Lutèce. Dancing at that hot new place, Maybe, down in the Village. A nightcap at their favorite pub on Carmine Street, then back to the Waldorf and the king-size bed in the suite they had booked. Perfect.

Christine looked at the gold Patek-Philippe her parents had given her on her wedding day. One-twenty. The truck they were next to seemed to be having some difficulties. At least Toby was a patient driver. Being stuck in traffic never rattled him the way it did Christine. His arm tightened around her.

Sister Mary Immaculata was driving, as she almost always did. The other nuns could all drive, but Sister Mary was acknowledged by everyone in the convent to be the most skillful behind the wheel. In fact, no one else had ever driven the new Vanagon that had been the gift of a wealthy member of the parish to which their convent was attached.

Once a month, on the first Wednesday, the four nuns traveled into Manhattan to work at the outreach program for teen runaways their order had founded nearly fifty years before. All four had very specific skills that they brought to the children. Mary was a nurse by training, and there were always one or two of the children who required her attention. Bernadette, fluent in five languages, was a reading specialist. Anne had a master's in psychiatric social work. Constance, the youngest of the four, had been on countless Outward Bound expeditions and taught survival skills to these kids who, if they weren't going to go home, needed them to exist in the harsh realities of New York.

They had been listening to the news on CBS and had just gotten the one eighteen traffic report before reception had been lost in the tunnel. The building that housed the outreach program was downtown off Canal Street, but they weren't due until two o'clock. Sister Mary switched to an FM station with classical music and heard the announcer say that it was one twenty and Holst's The Planets would be their next selection.

They were squabbling as usual. Well, not squabbling exactly, but carrying on the low-level dissension that had existed between them for the forty years they had known each other. Not, mind you, that they weren't best friends. It was just that they were diametric opposites and both were strongly opinionated women who each wanted her own way.

As usual, it was over nothing. Where to begin the day's shopping trip that would end with dinner with their husbands. Vivian wanted to start off at a silversmith's in the West Village. Her husband, Derek Gordon, had given her a beautifully worked brooch for her last birthday and she was hoping to find a matching set of earrings. Charlotte Haskins, whose husband, Elliott, routinely forgot her birthday, wanted to make a strike on a boutique in the East Seventies, then go on from there.

The discussion went back and forth. Charlotte knew that Vivian would in the end get her way, if only because they were in Vivian's Mercedes. But it was still worth putting up a bit of a struggle.

They entered the Midtown Tunnel and Charlotte gave an involuntary shudder. She had always hated—feared—tunnels and had tried to talk Vivian into taking the 59th Street Bridge. Vivian, of course, saw that as a ploy on Charlotte's part to be closer to the boutique and flatly refused, pointing out the expressway went directly to the tunnel whereas they would have to get onto 25 to get to the bridge, which would slow them down. Charlotte felt she hadn't put up enough resistance and now here they were, going into the damnable tunnel and probably downtown to the equally damnable silversmith's.

And she wanted lunch and a bloody mary. She looked at her watch. The trip had taken much longer than usual. Twenty past one. Good grief! It would be two thirty before they sat down to eat. Unless she could talk Vivian into eating first, then shopping.

"Vivian, dear," she said. "I think we shouldn't shop on empty stomachs. It's—" she looked again at her watch, "one twenty-one now and . . ."

The Queens/Midtown Tunnel ruptured in three places, all of which were where the tunnel passed through different strata under the riverbed. At the two ends, where the tunnel rose into both Manhattan and Queens, it had been bored through rock. Under the river itself, the construction had gone through silt and sand, then rock, then silt again. The section that the Richardsons and the others were in was the first portion, going from Queens, that went through silt. The violent motion produced by the earthquake caused the wet silt and sand to temporarily liquefy. The section snapped completely from the two adjoining ends that were em-bedded in rock and sank into the liquefied silt some thirty feet below where it had been constructed.

The liquefied silt poured into either end, burying cars and trucks completely as it did so. It had advanced nearly a hundred feet into the tunnel section at each end before the earthquake ceased and the silt returned to its normal density.

The occupants of the cars trapped in this section of tunnel were unaware of the horrifying consequences of the earthquake on vehicles at either end of the tunnel. The lights in the tunnel had gone out abruptly, and several cars had careened into each other, though no one was seriously hurt. As the section began to settle and fill up with silt, people in cars closest to the broken ends sat dumbly while they were buried in the darkness. Few had the wit to put their headlights on during those first few, critical seconds, though all could feel the section sinking and knew that something terrible had happened.

The sinking feeling came to a sudden halt as the silt reverted to its normal state. Jim Richardson flipped on the car's overhead light and looked at Phyllis, then at Kathy and George sitting wide-eyed and silent in the backseat. He could see that Phyllis was trying to control the terror she must be feeling. She had never liked the dark, but had always tried to conceal the fact from the children in order not to pass her own fear on to them.

"Must be some sort of accident," he lied. Whatever it had been, an accident wasn't the answer.

"Put on the headlights," Phyllis replied.

Jim did so and they both gasped at the solid wall of silt directly in front of their car. The Cadillac that had been just ahead of them was gone, buried, Jim assumed, in all that dirt.

"What's happening, Dad?" asked George.

"I don't know, son, but we'll find out soon enough." Jim Richardson, an accountant who was used to thinking logically, opened the door to their car. "Stay here with the kids while I find out what's going on," he said to Phyllis, who nodded without replying.

Other headlights were going on as he got out of the car. The driver of the truck behind him was climbing down from his cab. Two nuns were emerging from the Volkswagen van next to the truck and behind a car containing a terrified-looking young couple. Behind the van, a large Mercedes sat. Jim couldn't see its occupants but the trunk of the car seemed also to be buried in dirt.

Rizzo had just lifted his fork with a delicious morsel of fresh grilled trout on it to his lips when the first shock came. The room seemed to be moving in slow motion. First the old waiter fell to his knees, then the crash of tableware and chairs sliding and the glass bar splintering and on the outside the brick façade disintegrating and tumbling into the narrow street where cars were upended and tossed about like miniature toys. A downed electric line lay sparking within feet of a gas main.

Those who could had gotten under the conference table. One of the older men was having a heart attack, but no one noticed him in the general panic. Rizzo crouched under the table and hung on to one of the table legs, as the shocks came one after the other, and he instinctively found his rosary in his jacket pocket and started to pray.

After less than a minute, the noise subsided and the men began to realize that this old building, or at least the basement floor they were on, was not going to come down on top of them. Above them was another matter. They could not tell what was going on up there. Plaster dust and glass covered the room and the floor.

Rizzo got to his feet and took control. "See if you can help Pauly," he ordered a younger man. "He looks dead to me, but try. A bad heart. Let's clear this room of crap. I don't know what this is, but we got to survive and we will. No bomb this. What the hell—"

"Sir, it must be a quake like they have in California. I was out there once and it felt the same."

"Someone try to open that front door. If you're right, God knows what's out there." Rizzo looked around him. "Anyone badly hurt?"

The fourteen men checked themselves over to make sure and reported no serious injuries. Cuts, bruises, nothing worse. One capo shook his head over Pauly's inert body. "Gone," he announced.

———

Within fifteen minutes of the shock they had cleared most of the debris and after one look out the front door realized that they were safer inside until they knew more than venturing out into a street blocked by cars and fallen debris. Rizzo knew that all of them had families in jeopardy, and he thought of Nancy, his wife, Rosemarie, and his daughter, Angelica. Long Island might be okay. The Trump Tower? Who knew? And Nancy might have been out shopping. He forced his mind back to where it belonged. He was in control of an army, and all his life he had been trained to put the mob first.

"Listen to me." He said it loud. The initial disbelief and stunned reaction were beginning to wear off and he could tell discipline was about to crack. They all had his thoughts about family. "The first thing we got to do is to protect our own. By that I mean our families first, then our interests. We've got to figure out how to do that and fast. The phones are out. We have to get someone to the runners' station and see what we got left. All but Sammy and Joe can leave if you want to try to find your people and protect them. You, Guido, go to the runners' station and round up as many as you can. Get the word out that we need . . ." He paused. What the hell did they need and how was he going to organize when he didn't know what was going on uptown or anywhere else?

Sammy "The Bear" Gennero stood up. "Domenico, we have got to stay here, all of us, until we have time to think things through and find out more. One of us should leave to go out and walk uptown for a few blocks and see what's what. When he comes back, we can make plans."

"Right. Guido, you go on out and get as far as you can until you see what's happened and come back with a report. Listen, we got fifty thousand runners in this city, maybe you'll find one or two." Rizzo smiled without humor. He looked at his watch. "It's almost two o'clock. Be back by three."

Guido came back in two hours. The look on his face told a story Domenico Rizzo had feared. "Boss," he started. He was only twenty-one, Rizzo remembered. Guido—son of the now dead Sonny Compello, one of the best capos Rizzo had ever known— blond and wiry, short and tough, began to weep. He struggled.

Rizzo put an arm around his shoulders. "Tell us, take your time, get him whatever you can find in that bar. Brandy. Wine. Whatever's left, he needs it." He led the young man over to a chair. "Sit down, Guido."

The men gathered around Guido. In the half hour that he had been gone most of the talk had been about families, where they were, what the extent of the earthquake had been, maybe it had only hit lower Manhattan, maybe it was some kind of explosion after all. Maybe the feds were being cute and trying to rid themselves of Rizzo and the leaders of the mob fast.

Guido gulped some brandy. "It's like a war. Like what I've seen in movies. It's all gone." He put his head down on the table and sobbed. Then he pulled himself up and pulled the handkerchief out of his natty jacket pocket. "I walked uptown as far as the Village. I mean, I didn't walk. I climbed over stuff, cars, bricks, pieces of buildings, people, dead, lots of people just laying there or under stuff. You could tell they was dead." He looked up at Rizzo, eyes filled with guilt. "I mean there was nothing I could do. I knew that right away. If I could—but there was people walking around in a daze. Not saying anything. There's hardly a building up and the Village is gone. And when you look uptown it's like an atom bomb hit the city. A few tall buildings standing. And downtown the Trade Center building, a few others. And once in a while one building will be okay like nothing happened. It's weird. And there's fires everywhere. No one doing anything about them. Gas stations on fire. Water coming out of the mains, just shooting up there, no one paying attention. No sign of firemen, no police. Just people wandering around carrying things, the damnedest things, like a book or a doll or a picture. And some of them are digging in the bricks and stuff trying to see if anyone's under there. I . . . I can't. . ." and he struggled to keep from bursting into tears again.

"No police," Rizzo murmured.

"I saw a couple of them. One was trying to get inside his patrol car, which was smashed up pretty good, to use his car phone. It didn't seem to work. Another was trying to use his walkie-talkie and no luck either. But the phones seemed alive, I mean the car phone and the other. Like there was static. I asked them what we were going to do." Guido moved his blond head up and down, "You know how stupid can you be, you know I hate the cops, and how the hell did they know, but it just came out with one of them, the guy trying to get into his car, I said what are we going to do, and he said 'Buddy, how the Christ do I know?' Then he said, 'It hit New York instead of California after all,' and went back to trying to get in touch. Blood was coming from a cut on his head. I started back down here then."

Rizzo took command. He had had time to think. "Sit down wherever you can, all of you, and listen to me. Guido, did you see any of our boys? Any runners?"

"I saw one or two and they're on their way down here. And they said they thought others would think to come here. I mean, where the hell else would they go? They know we meet here every Wednesday."

"Good. Let's hope they got the brains to figure it out. Now. I know all of us are thinking about our wives and children." He paused and looked at all of them. "As soon as we can, when we get the runners here, we are going to send them and their guns to protect our families and other loved ones. That is first priority. Then we got to protect our other interests. There is going to be a lot of looting out there. We got to get men to our restaurants, all our business interests, if we can do it, as soon as possible. Those are the first things. I don't know how we are going to be able to get around the City, but we'll manage. Our runners don't need phones. Their bikes probably won't do them any good. But we don't use communication that can be traced, never have, so I see something in this earthquake. Some things are occurring to me. I see some opportunities." He waited for this to sink in. "Do you follow?"

"No police, Guido says. I mean they are out of commission," said one of the men.

"You got it," Rizzo said. "We got opportunities here. We got the Jamaican Posse, those shitheads who are trying to take over our cocaine business. We got canaries who sing to the police. We don't care about those crazy Colombians and let the Chinks have the heroin. Leave them alone. There's billions of dollars worth of cocaine in the basement at Police Headquarters. How about the U.S. Attorney's office? Those files are full of information about informers we wanted for years. How about the guns coming in to Kennedy? How about the money out at Belmont? We got the manpower and we got an opportunity here." He might have been Churchill for the power he put into this rallying cry. "We can settle some scores, get our cocaine business back, and make a fortune. But we got to do it before the City gets up off the floor. This city is not going to be knocked out by an earthquake. I don't believe it. We got to move fast. Now I want to hear from each one of you about his territory, how many guns you got, how many runners, and any problems you got that we can all help you solve. Let's start with you, Benny."

Guido Compello looked at Rizzo with disbelief. Deference to Rizzo kept him from saying what he was thinking which was, What the fuck are you talking about? You haven't been out there, you fucking idiot. He took another swig from the brandy bottle.

Moishe Dersowitz, now Matt Devon, dress designer, received his mother that morning in the large ward at New York Hospital where he had come to be given the first round of a new drug for AIDS, one which the medical profession hoped would be more effective than AZT.

The resident doctor on call was Charlie Lincoln. He was finishing his examination of Matt Devon's painfully thin but still relatively strong thirty-eight-year-old body when Mrs. Dersowitz arrived. "Hi, Ma," Devon closed his hospital robe as his rotund mother approached his bed. She had her arms full of presents, which she put down in various places. Cartons of food, her chicken soup, her chicken liver, some fruit and candy, and some fresh baked bagels. "You can share with the others," she announced as she put her ample arms around her son. "I brought enough for all."

"Thanks, Ma. That's great. Ma, I'd like you to meet my doctor, Dr. Lincoln."

"Pleased to meet you," she put out her hand, trying to hide her surprise that her son's doctor was black.

"Hi, Mrs. Devon," Charlie replied.

"Not Devon, Dersowitz. Moishe had to change his name. Not me!" She smiled at the young doctor.

He smiled back. "I've got to go. See you later." He had been up all night, then the other resident who was to come on duty that morning had called in sick. That meant another eight hours for Charlie—from 6 A.M. to 2 P.M.—whose first year of residency at New York Hospital had been terrible enough to make him consider giving up the medical profession. For whatever reason, probably, he thought privately, because he was black and visible since he happened to be the son of the mayor, he had been put in charge of the floor that was partially given over to both the ambulatory and bedridden AIDS patients. Whatever movies and books told you about these guys, Charlie had not come across a less appealing group of young men ever. Allowances made for the fact that they were his age and dying, Charlie still could not get past their attitudes. Most of them were black or Hispanic junkies. The white ones were endlessly self-deprecating, ready with a faggot joke every time he stopped to check their charts.

All of them made him nervous and angry, and he had not had the time or the inclination to try to figure out why. The worst of the bunch was Matt Devon. He was the most obnoxious patient Charlie had ever come across. He had had a round of AZT, then a bout of pneumonia, another round of AZT, and was back in the hospital for this new miracle drug. There were three other young men in the room with him this time, all of them white, all of them trying the new drug. Charlie had not known the others before, but Matt Devon he knew. Demanding, arrogant, Matt was a spoiled mama's boy. He never moved a muscle he didn't have to, and he lay on his bed all day reading gossip columns, his Walkman on, unresponsive to Charlie's medical questions, usually not bothering to take the earphones off his head when Charlie came by. When he did, he answered the questions in what Charlie considered a snotty manner.

"Any more swelling of that left knee?"

Matt's lips would curl back in a sneer. "No, doctor, but you can amputate if it comes back." And then, "I need some Kleenex and some ice water. A fellow could die around here from neglect." This was followed by a mirthless smile.

———

Mrs. Dersowitz was watching her son spoon up the chicken soup. She was in her sixties, gray-haired, and very sad. She smiled often in spite of her feelings, and chattered on as Matt spooned the soup.

"Me and the girls went to see the new Sondheim show last week. My, that man can write a good song. You know his father was a dressmaker. Did you know that? He started out in Brooklyn just like us. Did you ever meet him?" Matt shook his head. "No. Well, he has a talented son. And so do I. I saw an ad for some of your designs in *The New York Times* just yesterday. It's a shame Bobby isn't here to share with you." She spoke of Matt's dead lover Bobby, his partner in the design firm until 1991, when he died of AIDS. Mrs. Dersowitz, once Matt had told her that he was gay, had decided to accept Bobby into her family. Not like Matt's father. He had never come to the hospital to see Matt, his only son.

Since Matt's illness he never spoke Matt's name in their home. Of course they had never been close. Matt would never help out in the tailor shop his father owned in Brooklyn, a storefront shop below the apartment where they lived. Matt had gone to Erasmus High, graduating with honors, and then had gone on scholarship to Parsons. His education had made his father both proud and uneasy because none of it brought Matt closer to home and the world of Jewish relatives all of whom lived within minutes of one another in Brooklyn and who celebrated Rosh Hashanah together, observed Yom Kippur, and joined forces to give Seders together. No, Matt had gone away and seemed to look down on his family. The day he told them about Bobby, the man he lived with and his business partner, and what he was dying of, that was the day Matt's father stopped wanting to have anything to do with his son.

"How are you feeling?" She hated to ask but she couldn't stop herself.

Matt put the spoon down. "I feel fine, Ma. Really." She was the only person on this earth he was kind to, cared about, or tried to make the dying process easier on.

"Good, good." She fussed with the sheet. "Don't they ever straighten your bed? You need it made. Get up. I'll have it neat in a minute."

He indulged her and sat on the chair looking out the window at the East River and the Triborough Bridge. The noonday sun was high and the sky clear. He liked watching the boat traffic in the river. A huge tug was laboring against the tide.

He glanced at the other occupants of the room. They were all about his age. One was reading the latest Jackie Collins novel. The other was cutting his toenails. The third was looking at a daytime soap. They all looked fairly healthy to Matt. One day you look great, Bobby had said, weeping into his arms, and the next you're dying. And he had, the next week.

His mother had finished the bed and he got back in it. He felt tired and when she left him he would sleep.

She leaned down and gave him another hug. "I'll be back in a couple of days, Moishe. You be good."

"Sure, Ma. I promise." He gave her a big smile.

He closed his eyes. He had tight curly brown hair. His face in repose was sallow, the mouth slightly turned down, the loneliness and bitterness of the past three years etched in the deep lines by it. His mind would not permit him to sleep as he wished to do, and he played the game that always helped him to sleep. He counted buyers, retail and wholesale, and then he counted up the revenue from his hugely successful business—he had outsold Armani and had almost caught up with Calvin Klein for the past few years. He could feel sleep begin. Then he thought of the new drug they had injected him with that morning. He wondered how sick it would make him. Then the same questions started to plague him as they had done ever since his doctor gave him the verdict a year ago. He was wide awake. When would death come? How would it come? Would he have the strength to kill himself when it got really bad? Was there any hope? Negative. The therapist, whom he loathed but saw anyway, kept telling him to have hope. Bullshit. Matt Devon, Moishe Dersowitz, was going to die and soon, and no one loved Matt except his mother because Matt had only loved Matt. Even Bobby had known that, and they were on the verge of splitting up when Bobby got sick. Now, it was too late to do anything about any of it.

Charlie had stretched out on the cot back of the nurses' station to take a quick nap when the first shock came. He found himself on the floor, the lights out, a tall file cabinet on top of him. He heard terrible sounds of crashing, screaming, and total chaos. He managed to get out from under the cabinet, rubbing his leg where the metal had clipped his shin, and he made his way out into the corridor where people milled about in the semidark, crying, sobbing, yelling for help. Someone found a flashlight. Someone else started down the stairs—they were on the tenth floor—to try to find the engineer or anyone who could pull the switch for the auxiliary generator if it had not been destroyed. Nurses and interns were trying to calm the patients in their bathrobes and hospital gowns who had come out of their rooms in terror. Some nurses were dealing with the respirators. Others coping with the very ill patients who should not have been moved from their beds.

Charlie made his way to the AIDS ward nearest him. He pushed open the door. The bright sunlight from the window shone in on the large room. The four young men in the ward looked all right. Three of them were still in their beds. At the end of the room, Matt Devon stood at the window looking down.

Charlie went over and looked down at the devastation. "My God." He tried to get a hold of his emotions and thoughts. "I have to try to help the other ward. No electricity. And those other guys down the hall . . ." He was referring to the AIDS patients on oxygen and other life-support systems.

Matt Devon bowed from the waist. "Tell me what to do, doctor. I'm all yours."

Charlie glared at Matt. "You stay where you are. You're in no condition to help anyone."

Matt Devon watched the resident doctor go, and then went over to the bed of the young man who had been watching soaps. Just then there was another convulsion, less strong. The water containers, magazines, and Kleenex boxes littered the floor. Matt righted himself and approached the bed.

"What's your name? I'm Matt Devon."

"I've heard of you. I recognized you yesterday when I got here. I'm Elliot." He put out his hand. He was sandy-haired and blue-eyed. "What's going on? Are we being bombed or what?"

The other two young men got up and came over. "I'm Scott," said the tall one with pockmarked cheeks and a short brown pony tail held by a rubber band. "I'm Guy," said the other, who was sturdy with an athletic build. "What's going on down there?"

"This is no Con Ed gas main," said Matt, shaking hands with them. "It looks like an earthquake to me. Take a gander out the window."

They all went and looked out. The East River Drive in front of them had a fissure in it twenty feet wide into which cars had driven, several of them on top of one another, and the ones behind piled up for as far as they could see. People up the line were getting out, bloodied and in shock, wandering about by their smashed cars, some less injured already trying to help. Across the way the huge apartment complex on Roosevelt Island had collapsed in on itself, and the cable across the river had snapped. The overhead tram had fallen into the water and they could see it still bobbing in the river, a few occupants clinging to it, and as they watched, as though in slow motion, it sank and the people disappeared from sight in the fast current.

"Jesus Christ!" Elliot muttered. They were all transfixed. "Look at the bridge!"

The Triborough Bridge glinting in the midday sun still stood, but a section of it—it looked to them as though it was the ramp that fed cars into Manhattan just past the toll gates before the roadway curved sharply down onto the FDR Drive—was twisted in a **V** shape. They could not see what was going on, but the sharp **V** looked vicious, particularly with the knowledge that the traffic on a beautiful Wednesday afternoon in October would be heavy coming into the city.

Matt Devon looked down at the scene below and felt a surge of energy that he had not felt since his last opening in Paris. "I don't know you guys, but I have an idea. See if you agree with me. I'm going out in the hall and take some white coats that the residents and interns use. Then I'm going to take some medical supplies—I know a lot about first aid because I took care of Bobby for the year he was sick. I expect you all know something about first aid, too?" He paused and surveyed his troops.

Elliot, Scott, and Guy were all nodding. "Right on," Scott said. "I think I know where you're going."

"So Charlie Lincoln, the mayor's stuck-up, bigoted son doesn't think we can do anything? We'll show him." Devon warmed to the subject. "We pass ourselves as medical personnel and get down there in the streets and do what we can. Are you with me? It may be dangerous."

Guy looked at Matt. "So? What have we got to lose?"

"My thoughts precisely," Devon said. "I think we should stick together no matter what we find down there. We're a team. Okay?"

The other three nodded in agreement and started getting into their street clothes. Matt, still in his hospital gown, went out into the hall. People with flashlights were running along it and shooing patients back into their rooms. The generator must not be working yet. He thought of the AIDS patients on respirators. Maybe they are better off this way.

He found the doctors' changing room and slipped inside. No one was there. He raided four lockers and rolled up the jackets as though they were a blanket he might be carrying under one arm. He went back out into the swarming hallway and made his way to the nurses' station, where he knew the trays with the various medications would be, and with very little difficulty he took vials of morphine and other medicines, boxes of disposable needles, bandages, and dumped them all in an empty waste paper basket under the desk. Armed with the jackets and medicines, he moved quickly back to the room. No one had paid the slightest attention to him.

The others were dressed. He handed them the white jackets with the blue oval spelling out New York–Cornell Medical Center on the sleeve. Matt changed into his pants and his shirt and sweater and put the medical coat on.

"Listen, which of you has had the most experience?"

Elliot, the soap opera addict, laughed. "What kind are you talking about, Matt. I've had all kinds. Bars. Rough trade. Baths. You name it."

"Medical, medical," Matt put an arm around Elliot's shoulders and gave him a hard hug. "We've all had enough of the other kind, chum."

"Yeah. Or we wouldn't be here," Guy muttered. "I was in charge of the first-aid unit when I played a year of pro football for the Patriots. I know how to tie a bandage."

"Good." Matt turned to Scott. "How about you?"

"I'm a dancer. Chorus not ballet. Don't know a thing about the subject. Sorry. But I'll help out, if you still want me, that is." He looked ready for rejection.

"Of course we want you," Devon said. "So, Elliot, what's your bag?"

"I'm a philosopher king." He grinned.

"Who watches 'Days of Our Lives'?"

"Some of the best minds I know watch 'Jeopardy' and 'Golden Girls.' Why shouldn't I watch my beloved soaps? I have never learned diddly squat about medicine, but I know how to give myself shots so I can do it to others, I suppose." Elliot put on his doctor's coat. "I like this jacket. It gives me a feeling of power."

"Me too," said Scott, flicking his pony tail outside his jacket collar.

Matt finished packing the medical supplies into the large Vuitton shoulder bag he had brought to the hospital. He checked their bedside drawers and tossed into the bag aspirin, poppers, Advil, decongestants of all kinds, and some pills that looked like uppers. "Let's go, gentlemen. If anyone stops us, look stern and medical and as though you sat on the right hand of God . . . just the way Charlie and the rest of these docs manage to look."

Matt Devon led the way out of their sunlit room and into the hallway. He saw a group of doctors gathered around another doctor, who seemed to be giving them all instructions. He motioned for the others to follow him and they joined the group.

"The emergency generators have kicked in, and it is essential that each of you carries out the assignment given to you the last time we had a mock emergency drill. The faster we get this place back to something like normal the better, and the nurses are doing a fine job already calming the patients and taking care of the sickest ones. Our problem is not going to be so much taking care of the people who are already here, as the flood of patients that will start arriving any minute now from the streets," the older doctor said. He went on for a few moments more, as the various doctors went to their posts.

Matt moved nearer him and at the first opportunity asked, "Doctor, the four of us were assigned to try to assist those injured outside the hospital in a radius of ten or so blocks. Is there anything we should know before we go out there?"

The doctor stared at Matt Devon, distracted by the milling people in the hallway. "No, no. Just get on with it. Remember, first aid only, don't medicate anyone. We have to try to bring them in here so that we see what's wrong and monitor them."

Matt nodded and turned on his heel. Elliot, hiding the Vuitton bag, Scott, and Guy followed him down the stairs and out through the great hall onto the circular driveway. Taxis were piled up in a line, one upended on top of the other. People wandered about, and the guardhouse by the entrance had collapsed across the drive blocking it further.

"Where should we go first?" Scott asked.

"How about the Triborough? That looked real bad from the window," Guy suggested.

"Let's go to the nearest place first," Matt said. "Maybe we can't get as far uptown as the bridge."

He waved at the scene in front of them. Thinking a second he said, "Let's try to cut through to the drive without going out to York Avenue. I'll bet that's worse than this. Let's see if we can walk through past Payne Whitney and climb down to the drive."

———

The Grill Room at the Four Seasons remained intact, except for the Richard Lippold brass hanging sculptures in the form of huge tubular chandeliers, one over the bar, the other over the balcony end of the dining room. Both had fallen on the patrons below, and at the height of the lunch hour several people had been badly injured by the heavy tubes of bronze that now lay about the carpeted floor like a child's game of straw sticks.

The heavy, draped metal curtains at the end of the dining room had protected the people at those tables from the implosion of glass shards. As the first shock subsided, the diners and waiters started to get up off the floor and come out from under tables, and the screams of pain and terror became muted almost at once.

Kate and Sam crawled out from under their table and Sam said, "I've got to get out of here and go to Danny. Grove School is not built to withstand this one. I've got to believe that Diane can take care of herself if she's alive. But Danny . . ." He looked down at Kate. Mountain climbing had given him the ability to think fast and clearly in the middle of disaster. And to be cold as ice. She knew he was right. She was the same. When you are on a ledge four feet wide at an elevation of fourteen thousand feet and a sudden blizzard erupts, you don't have time for emotion.

"Of course," she said. "I'm needed here. How bad is this, Sam? Can you tell?"

"Not until I get out of here. My guess is that it's the big one. If it is," he paused, "if it is, we might as well have been hit by a nuclear device. Look, you're all right here. Stay here until I look around outside." He moved quickly through the knots of stunned people and down the stairs.

She looked around the room. Julian was helping an elderly man across to the couches by the staircase, where he sat down. Tom Margittai was trying to use the phone. Dr. Keith was over in the area behind the cracked glass partition by the bar, kneeling down by someone who lay inert. The carpeted floor was littered with plates, food, wine bottles and coolers, broken glasses, and people were milling around in a daze asking one another what had happened, was it a nuclear explosion, what should they do, where should they go—all these beautifully tailored men and women mingling with the green-uniformed waiters and waitresses, some of the richest, most powerful men and women in the City—all brought down to size. Kate made her way to where Dr. Keith was working on the injured, making tourniquets from napkins, already ordering the cadre of eleven waiters, among the smartest, best-trained young waiters in the City, to get him various things he needed. "Tell me what to do," she said.

He looked up. A man was stretched out in front of him, blood pumping from a chest wound. "Take these," he held up a wad of napkins. "Hold them tight in the wound. Press as hard as you can. I'll be back in a second."

Dr. Keith got up and made his way to Tom Margittai, who said, "No phones, no electricity, something's wrong with the emergency generator. I can't reach anyone in the building or outside."

"We have to organize this place as fast as we can," Dr. Keith said. "We need to get all your crew together. If this is as bad as I think it is, we won't have water or electricity for days. God knows what has happened outside. Or above us in the offices. But one thing is certain. For now this place is an oasis. We can turn it into an emergency center for the East Side. I can't do much for the badly injured who are going to die. But I can save a few lives. I need boiling water—what kind of stove have you?—and bandages, and I need to look at the kitchen equipment."

Margittai stood at the entrance to the Grill Room, and just as he was about to call out, his younger Swiss partner, Alex von Bidder, ran down the long hall from the Pool Room, where people had been coming down the hall, past the torn huge Picasso painting, some bleeding, some untouched, gathering at the head of the stairs, unsure whether to stay or try to leave. "Tom," von Bidder gasped, "a mess back there. The glass shattered in on the people. We need ambulances, the phones don't work, I'll go upstairs to our office—"

"Don't bother," Margittai said. "Nothing works. I don't know what this is, but—"

Sam Thorne came up the stairs at that moment, saw Dr. Keith, Margittai, and von Bidder standing together, and approached them. "It is what I thought. A very strong earthquake. It must have its epicenter under Manhattan from what I can see outside. The City is down. Fifty-second Street is filled with rubble from the garage across the street and the smaller buildings toward Lexington Avenue. There's glass all over, people badly cut, dead, and dying. The plaza of this building is filled with people who have already come from wherever they were when it hit. Jesus, feel that!" An aftershock came, and instead of the screams of panic that might have been expected, the people held on to whatever was nearest and waited for it to subside.

"What else could you see?" Margittai asked. Dr. Keith had left Margittai to go back to the bar area as soon as he saw Sam, realizing that Kate's son was better equipped than he to tell everyone what was happening.

"Many of the taller buildings, built of steel beams, are still standing. I managed to get to Park Avenue. Nothing is moving. Buildings all up and down the avenue are collapsed. St. Bart's is completely destroyed. The Pan Am is still there. Cars and taxis tossed every which way. Listen, let me talk to these people. Then we can try to make a plan."

Tom went up the stairs at the far end of the Grill Room to the balcony area. He looked out over his beloved restaurant, at the familiar faces. Most of them had never been in a war or, as he, a Hungarian, had done, fled the Nazis with his parents when he was ten. Most of these people were American born, successful, powerful men and women, of whom he had grown very fond over the years. He checked his watch. It was 1:52 P.M. Usually by then many of the regulars were having coffee, about to hurry back to their publishing houses, their stock brokerages or advertising agencies or wherever, for this was like a select club at lunch for nonfrivolous workers. They turned toward Tom, as he called out,

"Ladies and gentlemen! Please, your attention." The room fell silent.

Sam stepped forward.

"We have had what I believe to be a major earthquake. We don't know anything for certain yet, but I have seen many earthquakes and from what I just saw outside I'd say this is the big East Coast one that was inevitable and for which New York is not prepared." He paused. One dapper man took an unbroken bottle of wine from the floor and found an unbroken glass and drank a full glass down as Sam spoke. "We must find the strength to survive the next days and to help one another. I know we can count on the staff here to give us all as much help as is possible. It is clear that most of us have been very fortunate, and that the damage to this building is relatively minor. There is one doctor here, Dr. Gordon Keith, head of the department of neurology at New York Hospital. He is attending the injured as best as he can. I know that all of you are thinking, as am I, of our loved ones and their fate. I ask all of you to stay here, however, until we can make some coherent plans, both for how to utilize this building best, and in particular the restaurant, and how to deal with what is going on in the rest of the City. I must emphasize that unlike any other kind of natural catastrophe an earthquake, particularly one that strikes an island where over thirteen million people live and work on a weekday, will have rendered Manhattan helpless for the first few hours, perhaps days. There will be no supply of water, and one of the first things we must ask the staff here to do is protect all bottled water, as well as the water from the Pool Room, for future use. There will be no electricity, no phones, in many streets no way for firemen or police to gain entrance."

He looked out at the faces fixed with attention to his words. "I want anyone with any medical experience of any kind, even those among you who left med school after a year, life-guard experience during summers, first-aid courses, anything, to raise your hands." At least a dozen hands were raised. "Good. If you would come over here to the desk, please." Among the people who came forward were Michael Korda, who had taken an extensive first-aid course once; a literary agent, Jonathan Dolger, who had finished two years of medical school; Felix Rohatyn, who had had no medical experience but whose habit of putting himself on the line to help was ingrained; Betty Prashker, a publisher who had had a summer job as a lifeguard after graduating from Vassar and had brushed up on first aid recently; and several other regulars.

"No one can be kept here against his or her will. Those of you who wish to try to leave, please raise your hands." There was a murmur of voices. A blonde woman dressed in a chic herringbone suit raised her hand and asked, "My husband works on Wall Street. Have you any idea of what has happened down there?"

"I'm sorry. None. Except that there are a lot of good strong buildings down there built of steel."

"Those of us who want to leave," a large, heavy young man spoke, "why don't we form groups according to locations where we want to go so we won't be on our own. I am going to try to get to my wife in our brownstone in the East Seventies. I'll take anyone along who's going that way."

Sam held up a hand. "I can't keep you here, but I strongly advise that if you do leave you take this man's advice and stay in groups. There will be looters and lawlessness sooner than you want to imagine. And that leads me to ask, is there anyone here who has any weapons, guns, knives? And any drugs, marijuana, cocaine, pain pills, tranquilizers? If anyone does not want to be identified as having illegal drugs, we ask that you realize that this is an emergency and that any and all drugs can be used to help the injured, both those who are here and those who will find their way here. Tom, can you get one of the waiters to give us a big white tablecloth, and someone volunteer to cut a Red Cross symbol out of anything you can find, or draw on it with red pen, so that we can hang it out on the awning on Fifty-second Street. At least here we have a doctor, a steady roof, space, and some food and water. All of these things are going to be at a premium."

The waiters passed among the men and women with a garbage bag from the kitchen and by the time they had finished, there were three pistols and a small but impressive cache of drugs, mostly tranquilizers and pain medications.

The patrons who had been in the Pool Room for lunch had gathered in the hallway and the stairway to listen. Dr. Keith had already gone down the hall to see what could be done for those cut by the flying glass. Kate had gone into the kitchen and borrowed one of the waiter's extra pair of pants and a shirt. She had grabbed an apron and changed in one corner behind the service bar. The white shirt and green pants fit her and she looked as at home in them as she had in her Chanel suit, which she rolled up and left in the corner. She followed Dr. Keith down the hallway, passing Sam as he continued to answer questions.

"There will be aftershocks, but remember the quake in San Francisco in 1989? The worst is over. So don't panic when you feel the earth move again."

"If we do leave," a publishing executive asked, "what chance do we have of getting anywhere outside? I want to get to my home, I guess we all do, and it's in Greenwich Village. But if I can stay and help here, and if you think I can't make it downtown, then . . ."

Sam knew that both the man who lived in a townhouse in the Seventies and this man who lived in the Village were doomed to find tragedy. Their dwellings, like sixty percent of the buildings in New York City, were built of unreinforced masonry and would have disintegrated in this major earthquake. Sam knew that it was not the quake that killed. The killer was man-made structures.

Right now, Sam was certain, men and women, in firemen's or policemen's uniform or not, were trying to dig the buried victims out from under rubble all over the City. The worst hit, he thought, had to be the East Side, the Village, Harlem, parts of Park Avenue. He abandoned that train of thought. It was too horrible to conjure with. He said, "I suppose by some weird irony of fate I happen to know as much about earthquakes as any scientist in the country. I have no easy answers.

"I would hope that all of you with medical experience would stay at least until we have been able to communicate with someone to get a better grasp on what is going on. I am leaving in a few minutes to go toward my son's school on East Eighty-third Street, and anyone who wants to go my way, come along. I assume that those who can, will go to Central Park, to the churches which are still standing, to any big building still standing. The governor, I remember, is in Europe. The mayor was over at Tate Acres today, but if he can I'm sure he will try to get to One Police Plaza or to

City Hall. The point is, my friends, we are going to have to make our own decisions about what is most important in the next few days."

He went down the wide marble hallway with its now shredded Picasso painting to the Pool Room and found Kate, working side by side with Dr. Keith, bandaging the wounded. The room was empty except for those who couldn't walk, and there were only about a dozen people lying on the floor, their heads on coats brought from the coat room by one of the Pool Room's twelve waiters. At lunchtime there were a total of twenty-three waiters working at The Four Seasons. In this crisis they behaved as though doing their regular jobs, looking for any detail of something helpful to do for anyone, checking and rechecking the injured, running messages back and forth, answering what questions they could from the people who had massed in the hallway by the stairs out to the Seagram Building mezzanine or in the Grill Room. Sam bent down next to Kate. "I'm going now to try to find Danny. I'll try to come back here. Please don't leave this place until I get back no matter how long it takes me. Okay?"

She finished tying a tourniquet around an elderly woman's upper arm. "Now, Dr. Klein, that feel any better?"

The woman smiled up at her. "Not much, but thanks. At least I won't bleed to death."

"You'll be fine. Dr. Keith will give you a tranquilizer in a minute. Too bad you're a psychoanalyst and not a surgeon, Dr. Klein." She gave the woman a gentle pat and got to her feet.

The older woman looked up. "I may come in handier than you think." Kate nodded in agreement.

"Yes, I'll stay here, Sam. I haven't a hell of a lot of choice, have I?"

Sam put his arms around her. She looked like a slender boy in her get-up, vulnerable and young, not a distinguished woman of sixty-one. He hugged her and let her go. "Do you think I'll find him," he heard himself ask her in barely a whisper. "I've got to find him. Alive."

Kate touched Sam's cheek with her hand and said, "Of course, you will, just get going. I'll see you . . ." she paused. "And I love you, Sam."

They stood for an instant staring into one another's eyes, both of them knowing that what lay ahead, whatever it was, their world and the world of all around them would never ever be the same again.

———

At precisely 1:21 P.M., West 45th Street was split down the middle by a giant fissure. On either side of the chasm massive pieces of concrete broken from the façades of buildings cascaded into the street, crushing many of the theatergoers who had been walking along toward one of the nine theaters on 45th Street that were giving matinees that day. A broken main gushed water high in the air. People were trying to scramble up from the soft, dry sand at the bottom of the sharp **V** of the fissure. Buildings were at all angles. Some were erect, untouched it seemed. Others, nothing but heaps of mortar and brick.

The Music Box Theater, halfway down West 45th Street between Broadway and Eighth Avenue, was still standing, though its marquee lay at a crazy angle in the fissure. Diane Taylor's name tilted up at the sky.

The star's dressing room, unusual, for most theaters had their dressing rooms in the basement of the building, was up two flights of stairs. Diane had been seated at her dressing table and her costar, Tony Allister, following what had become a ritual between them, was just coming in the doorway to embrace her before the five-minute warning call came from the stage manager. Diane was still in her dressing gown, waiting until the last minute to slip into her freshly pressed costume.

Diane's first warning was a rumbling that sounded to her like distant thunder. Then she felt, for about ten seconds, the floor under her feet rock gently. Her makeup jars and bottles jiggled on the dressing-table top. The vibrations grew worse, much worse. The entire building began to shake. Instinctively Diane fell down to the floor and crouched under the dressing-table top. She knew what this was. All the years in California. She put her arms over her head. Above her the mirror exploded into shards of glass; chunks of ceiling plaster shook loose and fell. Then the lights went out. She heard Tony scream. Shock after shock slammed into the old theater, and later she remembered thinking, It cannot hold, it cannot hold. There was a roar now, earth breaking and coming apart, glass shattering, timbers giving, snapping, splitting, tearing. It seemed to go on forever.

Incredibly then it was quiet. She stayed in the fetal position for moments, too terrified to move. The only light came from her window, partially shadowed by the fire escape and debris from the building. I'm alive. She began to move her body, first her arms, then legs. Blood was coming from somewhere. She touched her face and realized that her head was cut, but not badly, and she seemed to be all right. She crawled out into the small room where the furniture was upended, glass covering everything. Then she saw him.

Tony was lying in the doorway, pinned under massive-looking pieces of mortar and parts of the roof that had caved in above them. His head was visible, and one arm stretched out. She made her way to him. His handsome face was quiet, the makeup fresh on his eyes and skin, giving him a garishly healthy look. His large gray eyes looked up at her and tears streaked the mascara down his cheeks. "Help me."

"Oh, my God, darling," she started trying to lift the debris off his body. At first she managed to move the top pieces, tearing at the stone, her fingers ripped by the mortar. She moved like a maniac, frantic to save him.

"Oh, babe," he moaned. "It hurts."

She looked over him into the dark hallway by the stairs and saw nothing but heaps of rubble. The whole roof had collapsed onto the top floor. No one could get through to them. Her mind raced. Danny. My son. My little boy. Oh, God. And Sam.

She managed to move all but one heavy beam that lay across Tony's chest and a stone that pinned one leg. She knew she could not move either after trying for minutes without budging them at all. As she moved to lie down beside him he gave a sound of agony unlike any she had ever heard—a low cry, guttural and deep, a primitive sound. Then he was quiet, and she thought for a moment he had died.

She lay down beside him and put her head by his. "Darling, Tony?"

His eyes opened. "It's better now. It's stopped hurting so

much." He gave her his open smile, which had won him so many young women fans across America. "What hit us? A bomb?" He whispered, but her ear was next to his mouth.

She kissed him then, gently, tasting the dry dust from the rubble on his lips. "God, no, an earthquake. I grew up with them. Some were pretty bad, but this is the big one." She thought of Danny. She knew she could do nothing. Was the school safe? Was he safe? And Sam. His warnings. How bored she had been with his sermons on the subject. Where were they? Alive? Dead? Dying, in agony, like this sweet twenty-six-year-old boy? Oh, no. Please . . . no. "Tony, there's got to be someone alive down below us and they'll find us and you'll be fine. I'm going to start yelling for help right now."

"Hope you're right, babe. Don't leave me. Promise you won't leave me."

"Never. I'm right here. Don't be frightened when I yell." She got to her feet and stared out into the gloom. "Help! Help us! Is there anyone down there? Help! One of us is injured. Answer me if you hear me."

For a few seconds, silence. Then a man's voice. "I hear you. We're trying to reach you. Hold on."

"Are you the police?" she yelled.

"No. Tell me who's up there."

"The stars of the fucking show, that's who!" she shouted back. "And Mr. Allister is hurt." She felt tears starting and fought them back. A lot of good it did now to be a star. What a stupid word, anyway. She turned back to Tony and lay down beside him again.

"Hold my hand," he said.

She took it and it was cold. He moaned. She knew he would have screamed if he had had the strength. "Tony, they're coming. Hold on, darling. Listen, I have so many plans for us. We have so many good things ahead. Let's talk about them."

There was a pause. "No, let's talk about . . . about how good it's been. Have I ever told you how crazy about you I am? An older married woman. And me, just a nice American kid from Ohio."

"I'm only ten years older. Perfect ages. I'm crazy about you, too, Tony my darling. You are my wonderful young lover who makes me laugh."

"I wish . . . I wish I'd met you when you weren't married."

There was a gasp of breath and she knew he wasn't able to get enough air. She put her arm under his head to raise it a bit. She could see his face. The pain darkened his eyes. "I'd have married you and wouldn't have let you play around with guys like me."

"I'll bet you would have put me on some ranch with a lot of kids," she answered, looking out over him into the darkness, thinking, I've got to do something, I've got to try. "I'm not leaving you, sweet, but I'm going to get up and try to get some of the crap that's blocking the hall and stairs cleared away so that someone can get here faster. Okay?"

She felt the pressure of his hand in hers, holding on the way she remembered children did: part love, part fear, part a show of strength. Then he released it. "Yeah, try. Anything," he breathed.

Once beyond him, she crawled over some rubble to what once had been the stairwell. She paused and heard the sounds below of something like a hammer or shovel, muffled men's voices. She started attacking the debris around her, using all her strength, panting with the strain of trying to lift unmovable stone. Her back and shoulders ached and her fingers were raw and bloodied from scraping the surface of the unyielding, murderous fallen roof. She kept swearing under her breath, knowing her anger was all that stood between herself and the despair she felt hearing the groans behind her. She had been in a movie once, playing a dying woman, and for some reason the phrase the doctor in the film used came back to her now. "Intractable pain. She's in intractable pain."

She was able to move some of the stones, but there were others she could not make even rock in place, and always behind her, Tony's muffled cries, weaker and weaker. What did they remind her of? Yes, oh God yes, her puppy when she was ten years old that the neighbor poisoned. She remembered the cries and whimpers of terrible agony, how she had screamed at her parents to do something to help, how her father had run for his shotgun and killed the dog in front of her eyes, and how, even at ten, she had been grateful that the suffering animal was out of his pain.

She knew she had done what she could, that it was not enough, and they would have to wait until the men were able to get through to them. She had never seen anyone die. She knew she was helpless to give Tony anything except the knowledge that she cared. As she crawled back to him, she thought, what do I know of real life, what do I know of real life?

"Don't leave me again. It's dark and cold. Promise you'll stay right here."

"I'm right here." She took off her dressing gown and put it over him. She lay down again beside him and placed his hand so that it touched her bare breast. They lay that way for moments that seemed to her like minutes and hours. "Tell me everything, Tony. I want to hear about you when you were growing up. Who was your first girlfriend? Your first lover? Tell. And then I'll tell you everything about me."

"You first," he whispered.

"Me? I was a Hollywood brat. My parents were in the business. Funny we've never told each other about this. Too busy making love, I guess. Anyway, my father was a film editor and my mother was a script girl. I went to Hollywood High and passed photos of R.J. Wagner and Jill St. John and all of them every day when I went to class. It never occurred to me not to be an actress. My first lover? A boy named Clark, after Gable of course. Parents used to do that out there, name their kids after stars. He was terrible, came too fast. I hated it."

"I'll bet," he breathed into her ear. "I'll bet that's the last time you did . . . hated it, I mean."

She kissed his cheek. "You bet. Now you."

"I wanted to be a cowboy. I used to practice lassoing our cocker spaniel. For hours on end. I got a part in the high-school play, and the rest is history. My first girl was fourteen and I was twelve." He stopped, his voice growing weaker, higher. "See, I've always loved older women. She taught me a lot in the backseat of my dad's car. She was great. She . . ." He paused. "She was generous and kind, like you, babe."

"Oh, Tony. I know they're going to get here soon. It's going to be all right. I love you." She took his hand again and sat up, looking down into eyes that stared up at her. "It's going to be all right," she repeated, hating the words. "I love you so much."

There was a long pause with his eyes closed. Then he opened

them again. "What about Sam?" Through the pain and desperation, still so young and jealous.

"He's my best friend, Tony. You know that. But what has that got to do with us, you and me? We have something so special. You're the most handsome, smart, funny, sensitive lover I've ever known, and soon we'll be in that incredibly vulgar king-size bed of yours doing a wonderful variety of things to one another and some new ones I haven't ever tried with anyone."

He closed his eyes, a smile flickering for a moment. Then, weaker still, "You know there's no use. I'm done for. I can feel everything inside me sliding around, coming apart. Shit. Don't go. Hold my hand. My mother died of cancer. I remember her dying. She screamed for days. Don't let it hurt anymore. I . . ." He was taking short, shallow breaths now.

She squeezed his hand and held it hard as it grew colder under her fingers. She yelled again for help, then again and again, and now she began to cry. Even when the voices called back that they were going to get to them soon, she couldn't stop crying.

His breathing stopped, started, paused and started, then stopped. Suddenly blood from his mouth washed over her breast.

"Oh, God," she whispered. "Please don't go this way. Don't give up, my darling boy." But he had, she realized. For a moment she was dizzy with shock, but forced herself to speak. "Oh, Tony, may your everlasting soul rest in peace. I can't think of anything else religious to say, and you should have some words said for you. I can't even think of any Shakespeare for you. What kind of actress am I, anyway?"

She got up off the floor, and yelled. "Mr. Allister is dead. Where the fuck are you people? Too late you are. Too damn late!"

She was shivering, and she took the bloody dressing gown off Tony to put it around her shoulders. She made her way to the window and peered down onto 45th Street, stared at the flames and destruction. "Holy Christ! It's Armageddon."

Father Antonio Diaz had delivered an address to the United Nations on Monday. The speech had been received with enormous enthusiasm by the press and the president and Congress. Not for many years had such a spiritual figure arisen on the world stage. From a village in Peru, the man had risen from obscurity. Until a few years ago he had practiced medicine in the mountain villages, then he had gone into the priesthood. Within a few more years his writings had come to the attention of publishers throughout South and Central America. He'd begun to make speeches, first in small towns and villages, then in cities. His message was both simple and complex. Drugs were destroying their culture and their lives. Civil war and terrorist activity against the United States were destroying their culture and their lives. Only by nonviolent means could the twin problems of civil war and the drug lords be stopped. Only by the countries cooperating with one another with a vision of the future, aided economically by vast amounts of money the U.S. promised if moves were made to stop wars and the drug trade, only then could Central and South America survive and prosper. In return, America would stay out of the region politically.

Father Antonio Diaz was a small, not handsome man. He wore the robes of a country priest. His face was olive complexioned and had the high cheekbones and wide eyes of a Peruvian peasant. Those eyes were luminous, dark, and compelling. When he spoke his voice was deep, a worthy vessel for the passion he felt. No one who met him could deny that this was a spiritual man, and one whose power to move presidents and masses of people was unique to our time.

He was, as well, highly educated and possessed a wily political mind. He traveled a great deal, spoke eight languages fluently, and had a ready, self-deprecating wit. In the past two years he had raised millions of dollars for his cause, money that was kept secure in an American bank until countries started implementing some of the plans set before them to rid themselves of strife and reliance on drug trade.

Father Diaz was attending a private lunch in the suite of the Saudi Arabian Prince Makthoum on the twenty-fifth floor of the Seagram Building. He was to leave that afternoon for a meeting with the president that night in Washington. In fact, he was to join the president and his party that afternoon, after the president attended the function at Tate Acres, and travel on Air Force One back to the capital.

At 1:21 P.M. all that was changed. The sixty-five-year-old priest found himself, along with the Arabs with whom he had just been sharing a nonalcoholic drink before lunch, trapped on the twenty-fifth floor of the Seagram Building.

The large sunny dining room where they sat rocked gently back and forth for what seemed forever. Several men leapt to their feet and were thrown to the floor. Others got under the table. Father Diaz was pulled under the table by someone. Then it was over. But the sound of the tinted glass shattering in the floor-to-ceiling window in the room was deafening, and then it was terrifying to stare a few yards away to the open air twenty-five flights up. Instinctively they all either crawled or walked away from the gaping hole and made their way into the inner sitting room.

After it was determined that no one was seriously injured, they sent a secretary out to check the elevators, other offices on the floor, and the stairs. Of course, they realized, no electricity, no elevators. No phones. No faxes. The secretary returned. The south stairway exit was completely blocked by bricks and mortar that had fallen in on it, and the other stairway exit at the far end of the hallway had been undergoing some kind of repair work and was without railings. Some plywood was thrown across the stairwell. The door on the next landing was not only locked but the brick façade from the walls had crashed down and blocked it too.

There were three banks of elevators in the building that serviced floors two through ten, ten through twenty-five, and twenty-five through thirty-eight. The secretary presumed that the people on the twenty-fourth floor were able to walk down out of the building. She reported back that above that floor they were completely trapped.

Aides began cleaning up the suite of rooms of Prince Makthoum, pulling chairs upright, sweeping up glass from broken picture frames, putting things back on desktops. The Chinese chef was busy heating water with his auxiliary Bunsen burner for tea, once he had swept the debris of broken glasses and china from the floor of the small but fully equipped kitchen.

It was not until an hour had gone by, while the priest was talking quietly and calmly with the prince, that Father Diaz realized he had only enough insulin to last a few hours. No one there knew he was a diabetic. And he had left his extra supply of insulin at the hotel.

—————

The great open plaza of Tate Acres was in a state of chaos. The rich and famous had been tossed to the ground from their white folding chairs when the earthquake struck, and on one side of the park the earth had opened up and a dozen or so guests for the ceremony had found themselves going down a long distance into soft, dry sand at the bottom of a sharp **V** that kept opening more. Trees, stumps, heavy clotted soil like boulders came rolling down on top of them, and they scrambled to stay on top to keep from being buried.

In the mass confusion, after the earthquake's last tremor subsided, Howard Tate, unhurt, saw the mayor get off the floor of the platform and grab the microphone, which fortunately was attached to a battery-powered amplifier.

"This is your mayor, Bruce Lincoln," his deep voice boomed out across the turmoil.

"Keep calm. Do not panic. If we stay calm, we will be all right."

Their faces turned toward him, faces that minutes before had counted on their fame or money or both to lift them above life's more ignominious problems and even tranquilize them against its tragedies. Their faces were ghastly now, with the bare, uncompromising knowledge that nothing had saved them from the ground under their feet giving way or the sight of the skyline of their city crumbling to dust.

"Please stay where you are until we can organize help. All officials please come over here, and any park personnel, please see to the wounded." He put the microphone down.

In spite of his words, many of the people were running, not walking, toward the shore and their helicopters and private boats. Some of them shoved and pushed others in their panic to somehow get away from the disaster. They had no way of grasping its scope.

Howard Tate, a man of great discipline, saw what was going on, grabbed his chauffeur, who was tending Ingrid, and ordered him to run as fast as he could to the helicopter pad and guard a helicopter until Howard could get there. Howard reached into a pocket and before the chauffeur's amazed eyes drew out a small handgun. "Take this, and if anyone tries to take the copter away, tell them it's for the mayor. Got it?"

The chauffeur nodded, grabbed the gun, and ran off.

Ingrid was unconscious. Howard made his way to Bruce Lincoln. "Bruce, I've got a helicopter for you. I can fly it. Let's get going. There's nothing more you can do here, and the City needs you. We'll go to Central Park. At least we can land there, and we don't know about the rest—"

"Right, Howard. I can set up headquarters there and try to assess things."

"Help me with my wife." Cardinal O'Connor appeared, his forehead bloodied by a head wound. "If you've got a ride for me back to my church, I'll take it. I'm needed there."

"Cardinal, you got it." Howard Tate and the mayor lifted Ingrid Tate between them and started off.

When they reached the helicopter pad, the scene was bizarre. Men and women, their fine clothes ripped and muddied, were fighting over the few functional machines. One pleasure boat had sunk a hundred yards offshore because too many people had rushed on board. Other boats were already crossing the East River toward Manhattan. The sun shone down on the rough water, as some sailboats made their way toward the other shore looking like a late-summer regatta.

Howard's chauffeur was brandishing his gun and shouting at the menacing crowd. Howard climbed up into the helicopter and studied the controls as Bruce Lincoln and the cardinal lifted Ingrid into the back of the machine. Despite the disaster of incalculable proportions, Howard could not help feeling a thrill as he sat once again in a cockpit. To be needed, to have a purpose. The verdict from early that morning from Dr. Gordon Keith faded from his mind. He started the turbine engine and listened to it spool up to speed. "This may be a bumpy ride, but we'll get there."

A young couple engaged to be married had been jogging together in Central Park each weekday at their lunch hour. This Wednesday the young woman had provided their picnic. They always picnicked in back of the zoo. They had just settled down on the plaid blanket he had brought to the park, when the earthquake struck. They clung to one another as trees crashed down around them and the earth shook beneath their bodies. Minutes passed while they struggled to regain their wits and decide what to do in the face of such chaos. Suddenly an escaped Kodiak bear, enraged and hungry, smelling their picnic, approached them. Terrified, they stood up, about to flee, but with one swipe of his mammoth paw, the bear killed them both.

───────

When the earthquake hit, the train in which the mayor's daughter, Evie Lincoln, sat talking to Allen Young was caught up in the havoc that was nowhere more devastating than in the subway system. As the earth began to roll, that system, structurally questionable after more than three-quarters of a century of halfhearted repairs, began to come apart. No thought had ever been acted upon that questioned the rock underpinnings of the City; they were deemed to be as solid as anything God ever created. Mayor Bruce Lincoln, ironically as it would turn out, had been a voice in the wilderness in the early days of his administration asking for federal funding to rebuild and repair the bridges and tunnels of Manhattan. Politically this was unpopular. He backed off as other mayors before him had done.

The City was mined, crisscrossed with tunnels that carried not only the subway system but others for the delivery of water, gas, electricity, steam, and sewage. When disaster struck, all these tunnels and systems interacted. When the power went off at 1:21 there were approximately thirty-one thousand people below ground, and the system was plunged into darkness. The heaving of the earth tossed trains around like a Lionel set that had been sabotaged by firecrackers.

In the confines of the tunnel where Evie's train sat, the earthquake's roar was deafening, the shaking of the car the most frightening thing any of them had ever experienced. As the car pitched and rolled, the passengers were tossed about like rag dolls.

The lanky youth—Rick—was launched from his bench and deposited on the bench directly opposite where he had been. His knife fell to the floor but he quickly retrieved it. The necking teenagers were driven apart and the boy's head hit the window behind him with a crack that was audible over the sound of the earthquake. Seeing him slump to the floor, the back of his head welling with blood, his girlfriend began to scream and pray, crossing herself wildly. The passengers at the other end of the car had reacted with equal fear. Most had been thrown from their seats to the floor.

As the first shock from the earthquake hit the subway, Allen Young threw his arms around Evie and took a tight grip on the bench's end railing, thus preventing both of them from being flung to the floor of the car along with the others. In turn, Evie had put her arms around his chest and buried her face in his shoulder.

With a screaming sound of metal being torn apart, the front car in which they were sitting reared up, tearing itself loose from the car immediately behind it. Several of the passengers at the rear end of the car fell forward, and a baby carriage belonging to a woman who had entered at 14th Street struck Evie against one leg. The gash that it made was not deep, but blood began oozing out and down toward her ankle. The carriage itself tipped over and Allen was helpless to prevent the tiny child within it from being thrown violently to the floor. There was a resounding crash as the rear end of the car hit the low tunnel roof. As glass from the car's windows shattered, the rear end began its descent and the car rolled to the right. As the first impact of the earthquake passed, it came to an unsteady rest on the barrier between the express and local tracks.

The silence that replaced the noise from the earthquake was broken by the sobs of the passengers. The young Hispanic woman had stopped screaming over her boyfriend's body and sat numbly, her face buried in her hands, her back to the front door of the car.

Evie raised her head from Allen's shoulder but didn't take her arms from around him, then buried her face again as an aftershock tore through the tunnel. Finally it was over, and it was with an effort that Allen released his viselike grip on the railing. He gently took Evie's waist and held her away from him, looking intently into her face. They stared at each other in shock.

Allen started to speak and found that his voice had deserted him.

"My God, what was that? A bomb?"

Allen shook his head.

"But what, then?"

"I don't know."

Without another word, they both got to their feet and instinctively made their way to the closest of the other passengers. It was a young woman, sobbing softly and cradling in her arms the child who had been thrown from the carriage. Allen touched her and she shrank back from whimpering. Then she looked up, her face contorted with grief.

"My baby, my baby."

She turned her face away from them. It was clear the baby was past help, was probably dead. Evie sat down beside her and put her arm around the mother, who rocked back and forth in anguish.

Allen looked over his shoulder. The passengers in the rear of the train who had not been thrown forward when the car was heaved up were beginning to calm down, beginning to pick themselves up and assess their damage. Evie shook her head and got up to join Allen, whose attention had been diverted by a soft, persistent sound coming from the motorman's booth. As they passed the lanky youth, Rick, still stretched out on the bench, Allen saw the boy's hand reach out to grab Evie's pocketbook.

With a well-placed kick to the boy's arm, Allen stopped the attempted theft, then reached down to grab the youth by the shirtfront. He reacted more swiftly than Allen expected, sitting up and pushing himself out of the awkwardly tilted bench to stand in front of them, knife at the ready. His eyes looked drugged—probably crack.

"Hey, nigger, you want to watch yourself." He shifted the knife from one hand to the other. "Man, the world just ended outside or damn near, an' if I ain't got much time left, I'm gonna take just about anything I want."

"Don't use that word with me. And don't come near the lady—anytime, anyplace, or anywhere."

"Oh, a nigger who can talk like a white man. If I want—"

He got no further. With one massive punch to the gut, Allen doubled him over. The knife dropped to the floor.

"Allen," Evie cried, as the young man named Rick slumped down, unconscious.

"The last thing we need is *him*." Allen rubbed his knuckles.

They each moved up to opposite sides of the front of the car. Evie bent down over the young couple, took the boy's wrist, and felt for a pulse. She put her hand under his chin and his head flopped back horribly, uncontrollably. Instinctively she recoiled from the body, its neck broken, all life gone. She knelt down and put her hands around the girl's elbows, and tried to lift her to a standing position. Surprisingly the girl responded, removing her own hands from her face and allowing Evie to help her up. She looked at the body of her boyfriend.

"He's dead, isn't he?"

Evie nodded.

"I knew. I knew when I heard him hit his head. Like a watermelon dropping off a truck. Same sound." She crossed herself and started to weep.

Allen was attempting to open the door to the motorman's booth. As had become the rule in the crime-infested system, it was locked from the inside. He spoke through the door, in normal tones at first and then louder, telling the motorman to open it. When there was no response, he turned to Evie and the Hispanic girl. "Move away. That lock doesn't look too strong. I'm going to try to kick it in."

With the same effortless movement that he had used on Rick's arm, he kicked once, twice, three times. But the lock, fragile though it appeared, held.

"Okay, mother, let's try something else." He reached up and grabbed hold of the two metal straps opposite the motorman's door, balanced carefully on the edge of the two-person bench, and then leapt, aiming both feet at it. Allen's weight and the force of his spring accomplished what he had not been able to do earlier, and the door crashed inward, its hinges groaning. It moved only a few inches before encountering the motorman on his seat, then stopped abruptly.

Allen let go of the straps and reached around the partially open door to unlock it. He turned the key, then brought his hand out and began to move the door outward. As he did so, he looked in. Involuntarily he gagged, then quickly shut the door. He turned to Evie, who hadn't heard the sound coming from his throat.

"Take her to sit over there." He gestured to the small bench behind the motorman's booth.

Evie looked at him quizzically but said nothing and moved with the girl to the bench.

When he was satisfied that they couldn't see, he turned back to the door. Steeling himself, he opened it again.

Both front and side windows were shattered, the jagged edge of the front one smeared with blood. The motorman sat slumped to the side, his hand still on the train's accelerator, his head gone. The noise that Allen had heard from the booth was coming from the motorman's keys on their chain, still swinging and hitting the column of the booth's seat as the car continued to make small adjustments to its precarious tilt.

Christ, Allen thought. If I look out and see his head, I'll lose it. But even as he thought it, he knew that he wouldn't be able to see anything in the blackness of the tunnel. The emergency light in the booth cast only enough of a glow to see what had happened within it, nothing beyond.

Allen reached out to the corpse and detached the motorman's keychain from his belt loop. Then, looking around, he saw the flashlight that he had hoped would be there. It was partially covered by the motorman's torso, and Allen wondered if he had the nerve to touch the body, move it so he could grasp the flashlight. At the same time, he saw the first-aid kit attached to the wall next to the flashlight. Holding the body away, he took the flashlight out of its bracket and put it tightly between his legs. Then he reached for the first-aid kit.

It was difficult to control the gagging as Allen was forced to work so close to the headless corpse. He could feel heat from the blood that still seeped from the gaping neck, and the smell of it in that confined space was unbearable.

The first-aid kit had probably not been detached from its brackets in years, and was held too firmly in place for Allen to be able to work it loose with one hand. In the smallness of the booth, he knew that there was only one thing he could do. Carefully, gingerly, he brought the dead man's shoulder to rest against his chest, then reached around the headless neck with both arms to grasp the kit. He worked it back and forth in the brackets, gradually loosening it. At the moment it came free, the car settled a few more inches. Allen, unprepared, stumbled backward and sat down heavily on the bench opposite the door, flashlight clattering into the aisle. As he watched in horror, the corpse rolled off its seat and fell to the floor, half in and half out of the booth, the neck pouring blood onto the legs of the Hispanic boy who still lay where he had fallen.

The boy's girlfriend screamed once, a shattering sound that riveted the attention of the other passengers in the car. Then her eyes rolled up in her head and she fainted.

Evie looked, then quickly looked away, directing her gaze at Allen's face.

Allen stood, emptied the pockets of his suit jacket, then took it off and placed it over the motorman's corpse. He said softly to Evie, "If we're lucky, it's dim enough in here that nobody else saw this."

The matter-of-factness of his tone amazed her. "How can you be so, so damn calm?"

"I'm not." He paused and then said, "Look, we're the ones with the least damage, physically anyway. If anybody's going to get us out of this mess, it's going to have to be us."

Evie was beginning to think she had been wrong about this young man. She nodded in agreement. "What's next, then?"

"First of all, let's get this kit open and see if there's anything worthwhile in it. You do that while I see how the other people in the car are. I want to find out who can leave here with us."

He turned away, picked up the flashlight, and moved down the aisle, speaking quietly to people as he did so.

Evie unlatched the top of the first-aid kit and peered inside in the rapidly dimming light from the emergency bulbs. Her eyes found the small vial of ammonium carbonate and she opened it and passed it under the girl's nose. The girl coughed several times, then began to come out of her faint, Evie talking to her soothingly the whole time, telling her to keep her eyes closed.

When the girl was fully awake, Evie said, "Honey, we are in some deep trouble, and you're going to have to get hold of yourself and help both Mr. Young and me. He's trying to find out how the other passengers are, who can get out of here with us and who has to stay here until help comes. So we can't have any more hysterics, no matter how bad you feel. You understand?"

Eyes still tightly closed, the girl nodded.

"What's your name, child?"

"Marisa," the girl whispered. "Marisa Colon."

"Okay, Marisa. Mine's Evie. Now I want you to get up with me and move toward the back of the car. Can you do that?"

"Yes," Marisa replied. "But I want to see Juan one more time, say a prayer for him."

"That's fine, honey. If you want, I'll say a prayer with you."

"Please."

The young woman and the girl stood holding hands. Marisa opened her eyes and looked down. For a brief moment she looked away. Then Evie felt the girl's resolve return as she gazed once more at the broken body of her boyfriend.

Marisa crossed herself and then began a prayer in murmured Spanish. Evie, understanding the intent if not the actual words, prayed silently alongside her, though she did not believe any longer in the religion of her grandmother or this terrified girl. She did not believe in this irrational, cruel God.

Allen returned up the aisle. The flashlight now took the place of the fading emergency lights.

"Two men and a woman are dead. So's the baby. The mother seems to be in total shock. I couldn't get any response out of her. Lots of cuts on the others. One man's pumping blood from a severed artery in his leg. I tied it up with a couple of handkerchiefs. He's not going to be able to move, and two of the others have broken legs and can't come with us, either. Anything in that kit?" he asked, gesturing to where Evie had put it on the bench.

"No, it's outdated. Band-Aids. Nothing we can use."

"Doesn't matter. People can either walk or they can't."

Evie looked at him and made a rapid mental calculation. "Fine," she said. Although her instinct was not to leave any of the living behind, she realized Allen was right. And the last thing they needed right now was to argue among themselves.

"We have to get out of here and up to the surface. Let whoever's in charge up there know that there are hurt people down here."

"What about the people in the other cars?"

Allen deliberated. "I'd like to say let's rescue them, let's bring them along, but I don't think it's practical. For one thing, this car is detached from the rest of the train. Hell, we don't know if maybe all the cars aren't detached from each other. So it's not like we can just go through the train and round up everybody who can walk and lead them out of here. I know that's what you want to do, Evie. It's what I'd want to do if the circumstances were different, but it just won't fly."

Outside, water flooding from broken mains was escaping in subway tunnels and rising in a lethal swell. Natural gas was seeping slowly into the tunnel. One match to light the way to safety could cause a major explosion. Allen did not know what lay outside the car, but he knew it had to be bad. He knew that staying in the car was madness. There were no options. He looked at Evie, her pretty face tearstained, her expression defiant. She was strong, he could count on her. What lay ahead must be better than sitting like trapped mice. Everything in his life—his childhood in Alabama, the naval academy, the Marine Corps— had brought him to this moment of action. You did not sit life out waiting for the white man to boost you up or push you back. It was the same in this situation. You used every ounce of intelligence, courage, and strength to act.

Allen moved to the set of doors behind the motorman's booth. He took the keys he had recovered from the corpse out of his pocket and began sorting through them. "Damn. We're going to be here all day if I have to try each one of these. Why don't you two go and gather up the ones who can make it out with us while I see if I can get one of these to work."

Marisa suddenly stood up.

"I know which key works. My uncle Carlos drove a subway in New York before he moved back to P.R. When we were kids he used to let us ride in the little room with him. Once, when the door wouldn't open, he had to use his key to unlock it. Let me see."

Allen handed her the heavy ring of keys and she began going through them. He played the flashlight on her fingers as they nimbly flipped through the keys.

"This is it, I think. It fits all the doors. It goes down there," Marisa said, pointing to a plate with a keyhole fixed near the base of the subway car's wall.

Allen squatted and inserted the key into the plate for the middle set of doors. It resisted his efforts to turn it. He stood and shrugged his shoulders, then moved on with Marisa following. By the time they reached the rest of the passengers, they could hear Evie speaking softly but urgently to them.

"The reality is, we can't all go. Only the ones who can walk unassisted. As soon as we're outside, we'll get help back to the rest of you."

An elderly Italian gentleman was protesting vigorously. "But we must take my wife. She is too frail to stay here by herself. I insist."

Evie began to respond in a reasonable manner, but the old man was barely listening, his own voice becoming shrill as he continued demanding that his wife be brought with them.

Allen cut through the conversation with a voice that neither Evie nor Marisa had previously heard. "Enough." The old man's demands came to a halt. "I'm sorry sir, but she is right. We can't take anybody with us who can't move on their own. You'll have to decide whether you want to come with us or stay with your wife." With finality he turned away from him and went to the rear set of doors. "Please bring the flashlight," he said to Marisa.

Once more he inserted the key into the baseplate. This time, to his relief, it turned smoothly, though the door remained closed. Either it's the lack of electricity or something happened to the wiring as the car was being tossed about, Allen thought, but it doesn't matter. Now that it's unlocked, I can probably force it open.

He stood up and slipped his fingers between the rubber edges of the doors. As strong as he was—and in as good shape—he was able to crack them only a tiny bit.

He turned to the others, most of whom were sitting and staring blankly ahead. "Come on, people, I need some help. You there," he said and pointed to a middle-aged man who looked less dazed than the others. "Get up and help me."

The man shook his head as if to clear it, then stood up uncertainly. As he moved to join Allen, he stumbled but managed to recover his balance without aid.

"Take hold of that edge. Lot of resistance, so you're going to have to use all your strength. Now pull."

Slowly, exhaustingly, the doors began to inch apart. When the edges were about two feet from each other, Allen signaled that it was enough.

"Everybody should be able to squeeze through this." He turned to Evie. "How many do we have?"

"If the gentleman is coming, nine. If he decides to stay, eight. Counting you, me, and Marisa. So five more." She turned to the old man and gave him a gentle smile. "We can't do more than ask you to make your decision. Will you stay with your wife or join us?"

The old gentleman shook his head sadly. He was holding his wife's two hands in both of his. "I cannot leave. We have been married sixty-three years and we will stay together. Only promise me that you will send help back for her."

"If we can get out, sir, we'll do everything that we can for the rest of you."

"Come closer," he said to her. "My eyes are not so good as they once were and this darkness doesn't help, but are you not Mayor Lincoln's daughter?"

"Yes."

"Then I know you will do everything in your power to get us out of here. Your father is a good man, a fine man. I'm sure his daughter is the same."

Evie leaned forward and kissed the old man on the cheek, then straightened up.

Allen had been peering out into the blackness of the tunnel, shining the flashlight all around but particularly down toward where the train bed would be. For many minutes, through the broken windows and now the partially open door, he had been aware of the sound of water rushing along somewhere. Now he could see where the somewhere was: directly below them.

He felt Evie's presence at his side and slightly behind him. "Look," he said to her, and moved out of the opening so that she could see.

She backed up a pace and turned to him. "How deep do you think it is?"

"I don't know. But of course it doesn't really matter, does it?"

"No, I suppose not. I guess we should just get going."

"Yes," he agreed. "Waiting isn't going to make things better. I can't tell for sure, but I think the level of water is rising. And there's something else—fog . . . no . . . steam—beginning to form. The batteries in this flashlight won't last forever. You know the system better than I do. Where do you think we are?"

"I'm not sure. I was so busy talking with you that I didn't notice how far out of the Fourteenth Street station we had come. I think I saw the station at Eighteenth Street go by, but maybe not."

"I don't see light in any direction. We could be right opposite a station and I wouldn't be able to tell; the flashlight doesn't shine far enough."

"So then, no matter which way we go, we're as much right as wrong."

"Yes, but I'd like to walk against the water's flow. If something's going to come down on me, I don't want to be overtaken from behind."

Evie, still holding the flashlight, had turned to the door opening once again and was looking out. She made a low sound of disgust in her throat.

"What?" Allen asked.

"A rat. Not a small one, either."

"Nothing we can do about it, I'm afraid. If one gets on you, try and knock him off. If you get bitten, get the bite under water as quickly as possible to flush it out. That'll at least help until we can get to a doctor."

Evie gave an involuntary shudder. "Let me get the others."

The passengers who were going—three women and two men besides Evie, Allen, and Marisa—had gathered together, and now Evie brought them over to the door.

Very calmly, very matter-of-factly, Allen said to all of them, "Okay, people, this is how we're going to do this. I'm going down first, then Miss Lincoln—"

"Is she really the mayor's daughter?" one of the women asked.

"Yes, I am," Evie replied. "For whatever good it's going to do us right now."

"Then Miss Lincoln," Allen continued, "will help everybody else down—woman, man, woman, man, woman. Marisa, I'm going to ask you to be the last one. You're young and even if you don't know it, probably stronger than most of these folks. If anyone slips once we start walking, you'll be best able to help. Okay?"

Marisa nodded, mumbled a whispered yes.

"Once we're on the tracks, we go single file holding hands, one arm in front of you, one arm behind. There's water down there. I don't know how much but I'll let you know as soon as I'm in it. Also how fast it's flowing. If any of you think it's too deep or too swift, then stay here. We can't start out being afraid of it; we've got enough other things to worry about. Whatever you do, don't light any matches."

"What about the third rail?" the man who had helped Allen open the door asked. "If the water's deep enough to cover it, we'll get fried."

"I don't think we have to worry about that. It's pitch black out there, there's no electricity at all. And nobody's going to throw the switch to get the power back in here until they know that everybody's accounted for. At least I hope nobody would be that stupid. If no one else has questions, I suggest we get going." He looked from one to the other of them, but they were all mute.

Allen moved to the doorway, turned sideways, and began to squeeze himself through it. The car shifted again and the shoulder that was outside knocked up against the barrier between the tracks. "Hand me the flashlight," he said to Evie.

Once it was in his hand, he shone it ahead. The barrier was in the form of an interconnected series of arches. Allen recalled seeing subway workers standing within these arches as trains passed by. His shoulder was only six or seven inches from one of them.

He wriggled his body free of the car and leaned back against the barrier with his feet on the edge of the doorsill. "Okay," he said to

Evie, now in the doorway. "Take the flashlight again for a moment. I'm going to step down and if I slip I don't want it getting wet."

Evie took the flashlight from him, climbed up on the bench next to the door, and shined the light out the window, careful not to come in contact with the ragged edges of the broken pane.

Allen removed one foot from the doorsill and began inching his back down the barrier. His superb physical condition allowed him a great deal more flexibility than most people but even so, he was not able to slide down far enough for his foot to feel anything underneath except water.

"Shit," he muttered. He looked up at Evie. "I'm going to have to kick off with the other foot and hope I don't break anything when I fall."

Without warning the car shifted again. Startled, Allen uttered a short curse as the foot he had been balancing on slipped off the sill and he fell into the water. He found his footing and balanced on what he thought was the wooden cover for the third rail.

Evie climbed down from the bench and approached the opening.

"Get Marisa to hold the flashlight and I'll help you down," he said as he stood up on the track bed. "Tell the others that the water's only about a foot-and-a-half deep and not running quickly. We're just going to have to take the chance that the train doesn't settle any farther."

He reached out his hand as she came through the opening, her slender body having no trouble fitting through. "Let me lift you down. I'm going to put you inside the arch. I think it's easier if I help everybody."

Evie felt his hands around her waist and put her own on his wrists to steady herself as she was effortlessly lifted down. Her face came to within inches of Allen's and she could feel the warmth of his breath on her cheek as he swung her around and deposited her within the arch.

"God, the water's cold. Where do you think it's coming from?"

He looked at her, wondering how much she realized. He was only beginning himself to understand what might have happened.

"And it's rising, isn't it? I can feel it."

He reached out and touched her face and, instinctively, she leaned forward toward him. The dim light cast from the emergency bulbs within the train played shadows around his eyes and mouth and she felt herself drawn irresistibly toward him.

"Should we start to come out now?"

The moment had passed and Allen turned back to the train and said to Marisa, "Bring them to the door one at a time. I'll help anyone who needs it."

One by one, the other five approached the doorway. Two of the women and both of the men declined more assistance than a helping hand. One of the women, though, said that she had a fear of heights and would have to close her eyes, so Allen lifted her down in the same way he had Evie.

Then it was Marisa's turn. With a final glance at Juan's body she slipped through the opening, handed the flashlight to Allen, who in turn passed it to Evie, and allowed him to lift her down. She thought she heard the old man whisper a blessing as she went through the door, but she couldn't be sure.

Once they had all gone through the arches and were assembled on the roadbed, Allen gave them instructions about how they would proceed. Although he assumed they were all more familiar with the subway than he, he explained to them that they would walk north, against the flow of water, staying on the uptown local tracks for as long as they could until either debris or another train blocked their way. As they moved forward, they would look for emergency exits. When they reached platforms for the line's stations, they would attempt to find their way to the surface through entrances that might not be blocked. They would go in single file holding hands, led by Allen with the flashlight and with Marisa bringing up the rear. Knowing that they would realize it soon if they hadn't already, he did not attempt to minimize the fact or the implication of the rising water, saying that they had to move as quickly—but as safely and accident-free—as possible to find either a ladder to the street or an undamaged station exit in order to make their escape. With nothing further to say, he led them off.

They moved slowly at first, then with increasing confidence as they fell into the rhythm of going from tie to tie. Even at that, however, they were moving at a snail's pace and the water was up to the knees of the shortest of them, Marisa, by the time they had been walking for two or three minutes.

The blast of steam that hit them unexpectedly was both shocking and frightening. Because it had lost most of its heat, however, none of them was hurt. It added, though, to the gloom in the pitch-black tunnel as tentacles of what seemed to be a heavy fog on the darkest of nights reached out to caress their faces.

Allen had been talking quietly to Evie, immediately behind him, while they were walking—nothing of consequence, simply words of reassurance. He could hear several other voices and hoped that the speakers were doing the same. The last thing they needed was for anyone to create a panic. As he walked, he shined the flashlight continuously against the wall of the tunnel, searching for a ladder that would take them to an emergency exit. Finally one appeared through the blackened haze.

In a voice that carried eerily in the confines of the tunnel, he told the other seven to halt but to stay in line and not let go of each other's hands. He shone the light up the ladder but it did not penetrate to the top. He would just have to take a chance that there was a door at its end and that the door would open when he reached it.

He handed the flashlight to Evie and began his ascent. It was not until he reached the sixth rung of the ladder that he realized that the dank odor that he had almost become used to on the floor of the tunnel had been replaced . . . by the smell of natural gas.

From the floor of the front of the subway car where he was now only feigning unconsciousness, Rick watched Marisa pass out between the doors of the train, listened as Allen gave instructions to the group, then heard them begin to move away. Slowly, quietly, unnoticed by the remaining passengers in the almost-faded light from the emergency bulbs, he sat up and looked around. It took him several seconds to locate it, but then he reached out for the hunting knife. He tested its sharpness against a finger, then stood and began to make his way down the car toward the others.

Matt Devon and his team managed to find their way into the drive at the 72nd Street entrance. At the sight of their white jackets, the people standing or sitting by their cars reacted. "Thank God you're here," was the refrain Matt Devon heard most often, as they made their way toward the fissure, stopping by each car to do what they could for the occupants, most of whom were not badly injured. Devon and Elliot formed a twosome, and Guy and Scott another, as they bandaged cuts and reassured everyone that more help was coming soon and that they should try to stay calm. There was no sign of any official person on the scene yet. No police. No emergency medical teams. But how would they get there, Matt wondered? The city was at a standstill. The FDR Drive was impassable. He could see up its length that one of the overpasses was collapsed onto the cars below. "Come on," he beckoned the others. "Elliot, you aren't bad at this," he admired, watching his pupil tie a knot in a bandage on the arm of a young boy who had been cut by the flying glass from the windshield of his parents' car. Elliot finished and stayed squatting down by the little boy. "How do you feel now?"

"Okay, I guess. Thank you, Doctor." The little boy's face was tear-streaked. Elliot gave him a pat on the head. "You'll be all right, sonny boy." He joined Matt. "I can't believe the heady feeling I had. Do you know what I mean?"

Matt smiled. "Isn't it wild? No wonder doctors are so crazy."

As they made their way to the large fissure, they could hear cries coming from the cars that were lodged in the crevasse. The team ran down the highway the last few feet and arrived at the brink of the fissure. Matt Devon took a good look. There were four cars that had been unlucky enough to have been in the wrong spot at the wrong time. All he could see of the bottom two cars were their hoods and one back fender. The two other cars had fallen on top of them. In one of the top ones, a man was wedged behind the steering wheel, his head slumped forward.

A woman passenger had lowered her window and her hair was matted with blood. She called out, "Help. Please don't let me die here."

Matt handed the Vuitton bag to Elliot and lowered himself carefully down the bank of the gaping hole. Then Elliot handed him the bag. "Hang on," he said to the woman.

He looked at the other car that was visible. Its windshield was smashed and the occupants of the front seat did not move, but he saw someone behind the closed windows in the back.

"Guy, Scott, you take that one," he called to them, and Elliot scrambled down to stand beside him, then climbed over the car that rested firmly on top of the buried car to reach Guy and Scott.

Matt tried to open the door of the car. It was jammed. The woman was moaning and Matt put his head in the window and saw that her leg was smashed by the crumpled front of the car. The man beside her looked dead.

She screamed when he touched her. "Help me. It hurts. Oh, God, I'm going to die."

Matt wanted to prepare the syringe and give her a shot of morphine. He remembered what the emergency chief had said: Not to medicate anyone. He inspected her head, gently, to see where the wound was and found a superficial cut that had bled profusely. The leg was a mess, though, and he began to ask her questions. She was overweight and told him she suffered from asthma and heart trouble. He knew just enough to know that if she wasn't freed from the car soon, she would die, too. He glanced over to the other part of the team. They were struggling to open the back door of the car. Elliot, who was very thin, had managed to climb in the window and was giving help to whomever was inside.

Matt pulled at the door of the car and it moved a bit. He reached inside and juggled the handle and pulled again. It opened enough for him to reach inside. He inspected her leg and saw that it was not jammed and could come free. He put his hands under her arms and with all his strength pulled her up and out. "Push, if you can, lady," he groaned and she did push against the dashboard and suddenly they both lay on the ground outside the car. Just then, out of the corner of his eye, he saw two real uniformed EMS men walking up the drive toward them with bags of equipment strapped to their shoulder. He checked the woman, who had passed out, and wrapped a tourniquet around her leg before yelling at the others, "Hey, we've got help on the way. Let's us get out of here."

The other three saw the EMS men approaching and finished with their survivors. They climbed up the bank and joined Matt, who was already heading uptown toward the bridge.

Guy couldn't resist turning around and waving at the EMS men, who did not bother to respond to four white-jacketed doctors who were leaving the scene at a strangely fast pace.

The battalion chief's car was caught in the grip of the fissure as it opened and closed down the length of the street, and 22 Engine was out of commission, having been toppled on its side during the quake. Fires had broken out in at least half of the ruined buildings from gas mains that had ruptured. Within minutes Brendan and his surviving men realized there was no water. Brendan made the first of many painful decisions he would make in the days to come.

"All right, men. Five of you stay here to help rescue any survivors. The rest of us are going back to the station house. Pick up any pieces of equipment you can carry. Let's get going."

One of the men started to say something and Brendan interrupted with, "No questions. Just do it."

When they reached the station house, Brendan found normal communications were out. They were in touch with headquarters in Brooklyn by generator-driven shortwave radio. Brendan took the microphone from the dispatcher.

"Battalion Chief Ahearn here. Who's speaking, please?"

"George Grey." Ahearn recognized the voice of the Chief of Operations. "What's your assessment of the situation in your part of Manhattan?"

"In a word, Chief, terrible. I didn't know anything short of a nuclear explosion could do what this earthquake has done."

"I'm afraid it's like that throughout Manhattan. We were hit in Brooklyn pretty hard, and I understand Queens got about what we did, but everyone I've managed to talk with in Manhattan says the same thing."

"Who's in charge over here, Chief?"

"Rodriguez is dead and LeConte is missing." Chief Grey had named the Manhattan borough chief and his deputy. "I need somebody who can *take* charge, Brendan. That somebody is you."

Ahearn swallowed hard. "Yes, sir. Is the Command Center at One Police Plaza functioning?"

"One Police Plaza fell down, and took most of everyone there with it, including the commissioner. The mayor was at the dedication ceremony at Tate Acres when the quake struck. He's gone to the precinct house in Central Park to set up an emergency command post."

"The Central Park precinct? My God, Chief, that's one of the least prepared houses in the City to act as a command post."

"You know that and I know that, Brendan. Even the mayor knows that. But it's still standing and nothing's fallen on top of it. I want you there within the next half hour, on foot if there's no other way. You're to report to the mayor directly on behalf of the department. I have no word on the police captain in that precinct. For all I know, there isn't one in shape to take over. So get a move on."

Twenty-five minutes later, having successfully negotiated the rubble in the streets, Brendan Ahearn strode through the wooden door of the Central Park Precinct House. What he found there was controlled chaos. The house was one of the smallest in the borough, the structure dating back to the last half of the nineteenth century. It stood on the south side of the 86th Street transverse through the park, more east than west, a low red-brick building of shabby appearance. There was a common parking area in which police cars and those of the Department of Parks, which had a facility to the west of the precinct house, shared. For years the building had been allowed to fall into disrepair, bandages being applied only when absolutely necessary. It was a source of great surprise that the precinct house had survived the earthquake virtually intact, but then everyone who had ever been in an earthquake knew the quixotic nature of this natural phenomenon. Fate, luck, whatever, played a great part in what buildings were spared.

Now, this unprepossessing building, too small to hold any ordinary day's activities, was the center of the largest relief effort ever experienced in the entire country.

Brendan had had to go through an identification and security check before he was allowed to enter the building, and he immediately understood why. If all the people milling about outside had been allowed in unscreened, the tiny lobby with its booking desk and small holding tank would have been overwhelmed. As it was, the twenty or so people in the room made it a tight squeeze.

Ahearn recognized several of the people who had been allowed inside. Ignoring them, he pushed his way through to the desk sergeant, to whom he flashed his I.D.

"Brendan Ahearn, battalion chief, NYFD."

"Upstairs and straight back. The mayor and a few others are in the captain's office. The captain himself is badly wounded. The mayor is expecting you."

The captain's office was the only private one on the second floor, and through the glass of the window, Brendan could see several figures standing around the desk. He entered without knocking. Bruce Lincoln was behind the desk on which a high-powered receiver/transmitter had been set up. He was talking urgently into its built-in microphone. Several other people stood around the desk. Ahearn recognized Howard Tate from numerous photographs.

Ahearn stood silently with the others as Bruce Lincoln spoke. "Fine, so you've been in contact with the governor and he can be back from Europe by tomorrow morning. I can't wait until tomorrow morning. I need some sort of reinforcements for my police force now, by tonight. Otherwise, the looting that's going to go on will make the second blackout look like child's play." He paused, then shook his head. "You mean that you, as lieutenant governor of this state, can't order up the National Guard in the governor's absence?"

The lieutenant governor's voice echoed eerily through the receiver. "That's right, Bruce. I could if we hadn't been able to contact the governor, but when we did, I was given a direct order to take no steps, that he would decide what to do when he gets back. And that's not until tomorrow morning."

"Can I reach him in the air?"

"I doubt it, Bruce. He's trying to get the first flight out of Nice, but we don't even know when that will be. You're just going to have to sit tight until you can talk with him tomorrow."

Bruce Lincoln was not given to profanity, and his "Fuck that," was a shock to both the lieutenant governor and the listeners. "Fuck that," he repeated. "You tell him when he finally gets home that this City doesn't need his help. We've been fine before without the state's aid, and we'll be fine now." Abruptly he broke the connection.

"That was going out on a limb," Howard Tate said. "He's been looking for a way to saw that limb off for some time now."

"I know. But I've got a city to run that's going to be out of control as soon as night falls, which—" he looked at the wall clock, realized it had stopped at one twenty-one, then looked at his watch— "should be in about two hours. My next call is to the president." The mayor turned to a young police lieutenant who stood at attention. "How soon will they be finished setting up the communications facility outside?"

"Within the hour, Mayor. We were able to get equipment hand-carried in from the four precincts on either side of the park, including gasoline-powered generators. Between our supply of fuel and the Parks Department tanks next door, we can run the communications gear full time for at least a week."

"Good. We'll need it." He looked at Ahearn. "You're Fire?"

"Yes sir. I was ordered to report to you. My senior officers, one was killed, the other is missing. My name's Brendan Ahearn."

"Give me your first impressions, Chief."

"Well, sir, there's fire everywhere, as you can tell from the smoke, mostly fueled by ruptured gas mains. And there's no water pressure to fight it. Buildings down, people trapped, no way to move vehicles of any size through the streets."

The mayor's attention was diverted. "He's on," a voice said, and the mayor leaned in toward the transmitter.

"Mr. President, this is Bruce Lincoln. I know you've only just gotten back to the White House and I understand that you saw what happened to New York from the air earlier."

"Yes, Bruce. An unbelievable tragedy. What can I do to help?"

"To try to give you some details, One Police Plaza has been completely destroyed, Mr. President, and with it our police commissioner and our Emergency Command Post. I'm being stonewalled in Albany. Bridges are down, tunnels are out. We're almost completely isolated. The City desperately needs reinforcements for our police—we probably don't have more than a couple thousand cops on the island right now—and George Fleming has instructed his lieutenant governor to do nothing until he arrives back from Europe. That won't be until tomorrow early morning, and I need it before that, or by then at the latest." The mayor knew that the president and the governor were bitter enemies and that the governor was hoping to succeed to the presidency.

"What do you suggest, Bruce?"

"Even if Fleming orders the Guard up the minute he returns, they won't be available for at least twenty-four more hours. I'm receiving reports from all over the City that looting is starting on a massive scale. That has to be stopped, fast. What I'm asking, Mr. President, is that you send me some troops."

The president's response was immediate. "Agreed. I will order men from the Eighty-second Airborne out of Fort Bragg as soon as we finish this conversation. How many do you think you need?"

"Four thousand, sir."

"You'll have them at dawn tomorrow morning."

"Thank you, Mr. President."

"I want you to call me every couple of hours, Bruce. We need to coordinate Washington's efforts, indeed the whole country's efforts, to help you save your great city. I am meeting with the cabinet in emergency session tomorrow morning and need to have the latest update you can give me."

"I will, Mr. President, I will."

The mayor beckoned Brendan Ahearn to stay behind while he sent the others off to do their various appointed assignments. "You know that Police Chief Matara was badly wounded?" The mayor did not wait for Ahearn to respond. "You are the ranking officer here in this precinct. I need you to take over both the police force that is here as well as the fire personnel. For the next few days, you are in charge. You understand?"

Ahearn nodded.

Mayor Lincoln frowned. "I need your help and I know I can count on it."

"Yes, sir."

"Where do you live? Have you had word of your wife and do you—"

"My wife died over a year ago, sir. I have two boys . . . they were at school out on the island."

The mayor nodded and put his hand out to shake the officer's hand. "We are very much in the same boat now."

The mayor gave him various instructions. Brendan was to erect a "tent village" south of the precinct house. Using some forty officers from the precinct who were on duty when the earthquake struck, he ordered them to get emergency floodlights from the Parks Department. Communications equipment had been stripped from vans belonging to several of the precincts surrounding the park, and both gas and diesel generators were being used to power these and the floodlights. He then ordered some of the policemen, as well as citizen volunteers who had come to the precinct house to offer their services, to erect tents that had been requisitioned from the park's zoo. There were thirteen of these and one, when the turret at its peak had been removed, had an open top and was designated as the cooking tent. Most of the other tents would serve as places to sleep for the many hundreds of nearby residents who had survived but were without shelter. The storage space above the precinct garage held fifty cots and blankets, and they supplemented those with more from other precincts. Two tents were set aside for toilet facilities, and portable toilets that belonged to the Parks Department were set up in them.

One of Brendan's men found an EMS van near the entrance to the park. The largest tent, which was not set up with cots and blankets, became the first-aid station.

A truck pulled up to the tents. One of the policemen had found it—Del Vecchio Meat and Produce—stranded on the 86th Street viaduct. They cut the bolt and the open doors revealed a full load of meat and vegetables.

"Good work," Brendan told the cop. "This is going to come in very handy. Now if we only had enough good water. Try to get some new steel garbage cans from the Parks Department. We can cook in them. And I'll try to reconnoiter some water. It may be fizzy, but we aren't at the Ritz, so what the hell, right?"

The cop grinned and loped off to find the equipment.

Brendan Ahearn had been in one of the police vans, utilizing a dedicated frequency to try to call the twenty-one precincts that served Manhattan. Only sixteen had responded. The 25, 26, and 32 precincts in Harlem and the 5 and 7 in lower Manhattan could not be raised on the shortwave frequencies.

With each report, Ahearn's thoughts became bleaker. They were all saying the same things. Streets were blocked. Fires burned out of control. Thousands were trapped in buildings. Looting was rampant already and getting worse as the criminal element, never far from the surface in New York City—or any other city, Brendan thought defensively about the city he loved—were now set free from any restraint.

"How many men do you have left?" He was talking to a police lieutenant in the Sixth Precinct, on West 10th Street. The precinct's captain had been killed by flying glass.

"About forty-six. But most of them are all over the territory. I've only got six with me at the house."

"Are the others out in pairs or singly?"

"Mostly singly. We're a small precinct, but still awful big for thirty or so men to cover, and doubling them up didn't seem like the right thing to do."

"Fine," Ahearn replied. "When are they scheduled to report back?"

"They're not scheduled for any one time. I told them that they were on duty until they were released and I didn't know when that would be. I can get them back if you want."

"No, you've done fine. But now I want you to get word to all of them that the following is a directive from the mayor. Looting must be contained if at all possible. If there is no other way, your officers are authorized by the mayor to use their weapons. We will have help from the Army tomorrow morning. Until then, keep your men in the streets to do whatever they can. But, Lieutenant," Ahearn said, "tell your men also that if a situation is too big for them, they're to back off from it. We're going to need all the officers we can muster, and I don't want anyone to put his life at unnecessary risk. Understand?"

"Yes sir," the lieutenant replied, and Brendan Ahearn ended the conversation. He decided to go check out the medical tent.

Dr. Patricia Kelly had been walking uptown, picking up bits of information from police officers along the way, heading toward the mayor's headquarters in the park. Along the way, she had seen nothing but chaos and terror in the streets. She stopped several times to give aid to fallen pedestrians. She realized quickly that she must coordinate with the man who was running the City to try to pull her Emergency Services crew together, but by the time she had made it to Central Park, she knew that organizing her people would be next to impossible. The streets were blocked with abandoned cars. There was no way to communicate. As she approached the precinct house she recognized an old friend of her brother, Captain Brendan Ahearn, who was coming out of the doorway.

"Brendan," she yelled. "Wait up!"

He saw her and stopped. His face broke out in a wide grin. "Pat Kelly. Well, I'll be damned."

She reached him and they embraced. He held her out from him. Her navy-blue suit was bloodied and her stockings torn. "I hear you're a big cheese these days," he said. His face turned serious. "Mother Mary, we need you, Patsy. We sure do. Let me take you to the mayor." He put a firm hand under her arm.

"I'm okay, Brendan." She pulled away. "Just got shook up when this bugger hit. How're the boys? Oh, geez, I put my big foot in my mouth. How would you know, anymore than I know about Brian and the girls."

"Right." He led the way up the stairs. "No one knows how anyone is, except the ones that they keep bringing in. We've set up one big tent for our medical headquarters. Just finished getting it up a few minutes ago. Here's the mayor."

They waited a minute until the mayor got off the phone and Brendan stepped forward. "Sir, this is Dr. Patricia Kelly, she was just appointed head of—"

Bruce Lincoln smiled and held out his hand to Dr. Kelly.

"No need to introduce us, Chief. I'm the one who appointed this fine young doctor head of Emergency Medical Services. You look as though you could use a cup of coffee, Dr. Kelly. Here, sit down. Are you hurt?"

Pat waved away the chair. "I'm okay. I'll take the coffee, Mayor, and thanks. Who is in charge of the medical tent, sir?"

The mayor looked at his watch. "As of three forty-three, Dr. Patricia Kelly is, okay?"

━━━━

Brendan took her to the medical tent, where two policemen were going over the supplies that the abandoned EMS van had provided. "Christ, Pat," said Brendan. "By morning this is going to be like trying to sweep back the tide." He waved a hand toward a crowd of people standing outside the barricade. They were patient, waiting their turn to have wounds cleaned, stitched, bandaged. While they stood there, policemen carried several badly wounded people through the emergency entrance in the barricade and into the tent.

Pat sized up the scene. It reminded her of old World War II movies, or the hospital scene in *Gone With the Wind*. Too much damage to people and too little medical resources to cope with it. "You say the Eighty-second's bringing in medical supplies and personnel tomorrow morning? We need it now if not sooner."

"I've got some of my men trying to get some supplies from the Red Cross. But I think the park is going to be as much a morgue as a hospital, no matter what we do."

His words enraged her. "What are you talking about? I haven't time for that kind of downer. You keep the supplies coming in, like the mayor said, and we're going to save a lot of lives here." She strode inside the tent, and Brendan shook his head. That's Patsy for you, he thought, just like she was when she was a kid. She should have been a boy.

He left the tent and saw the young police lieutenant coming toward him. They walked together. The smell of soup cooking in big vats over an open fire permeated the October air as they passed the cook tent. They cut through the line of people waiting for food. "Hey, sir. How goes it?"

Brendan shook his head. "Damned lucky that Tavern on the Green had all that bottled water. Warner LeRoy is some kind of gent. He's out there busting his ass helping out. He's set the whole place up as an emergency medical and food facility. Some guy."

They made their way back up the stairs to the mayor. He was conferring with Howard Tate. He looked up.

"Good work." He nodded at them. "I'm going to stay up here because access can be controlled better and I can communicate better from here than down there. I have called a press conference for tomorrow morning, though God knows what "press" will be here. Howard and I have been talking about what I'm going to say. Tell me everything the two of you have learned."

The lieutenant and Ahearn gave their reports and the mayor sat in thought for a long moment before saying anything. "The Eighty-second is scheduled to begin landing at six tomorrow morning. They're using copters rather than parachuting and they'll touch down in the Sheep Meadow and set up headquarters there. Lieutenant, I want you down there to meet them. I want them to understand that they've been brought in to help us, not to be in charge. Agreed?"

"Yes, sir. I'll get the message across."

"Before they start landing, Brendan, I want you to go up in a copter at first light to tour the city, top to bottom, East River to Hudson. Then I want you to come back and tell me whether any or all of it can be saved. That's all, gentlemen."

Brendan left the mayor's office and took a moment to get a cup of coffee from the kitchen tent. He was leg-weary. For a few seconds, as he rested in the October sun before setting out again, the strong impulse to leave and go search for his sons struck him with the force of a physical blow. He was mentally planning how he could reach them, when his years of training and sense of duty brought his thoughts to a halt. His hands sweated with the knowledge of how close he had come to deserting.

———————

Diane had covered Tony's body with her dressing gown, and she shivered even though she had managed to find some clothes in the closet, which was relatively unharmed, and now wore a suit and her fur coat. She knew that below there were men trying to reach her, and their voices were coming nearer. There was no point trying to move any more debris; she had moved what little she could in her attempt to get help for Tony.

She stood looking out the window down onto 45th Street. Her watch said three forty-two. At first she had been so consumed with trying to help Tony that the reality of what had happened did not penetrate. She thought, ruefully, she had always been good at turning away from reality. Now she was beginning to feel and think more clearly, and she put her hands over her eyes and pressed them shut against the garish sunlight outside and the terrible scene below.

Danny. All she could think was that name. Danny. Would Grove School have survived? She knew enough about earthquakes to know that it was improbable. Her little boy was somewhere, alive, dead, in pain, in agony, dying, suffocating? Oh God, she sobbed. No one to hear her sobs, no one to turn to. Sam. He was having lunch with Kate at The Four Seasons. California born, she knew that it was just as likely that the Seagram Building would have stood as it was that Grove School would have crumbled. "Somehow," she whispered to herself, "I have to get out of here and get to Danny." She forced herself to stop crying and calm down. Years of training how to portray emotion, how to discipline herself as an actress came to the fore. I'm alive, I'm not hurt, and I'll find Danny and he will be all right, she told herself. Repeat it, she demanded, and did. And again. Once more. She looked down.

Below there were men and women working at helping the wounded, bringing bodies out of the theater and placing them in neat rows on what was left of the sidewalk; some people had climbed down into the giant fissure that split the street down the middle and were carrying the injured and dead up the banks to try to care for them. The sidewalk on both sides of the street was broken by the huge pieces of masonry that had crashed down from the façades of buildings, killing many, the sight both tragic and bizarre, gargoyles and angels from cornices staring up at Diane from crazy angles, the Music Box marquee tilted up at her from its resting place on the soft underbelly of the fissure. Everyone seemed to be moving in slow motion. There was smoke coming from somewhere down the block and no one seemed to be paying any attention to its cause. No firemen were evident and she could see only two policemen among the people attempting to help. And weirdest of all was the sight across the street of several buildings completely untouched it seemed, though God knows what was going on inside them. There was no point yelling down at anyone, they were in bad enough trouble.

She went to the doorway and climbed over Tony's body and the rubble-blocked hallway. "Hey, down there. How close are you to getting me out?"

A muffled male voice answered. "A couple of hours. Not more. Probably not less."

"Thanks," she called out. And meant it.

As he struggled to bring some order to the chaos around them, Brendan Ahearn realized in the first few hours of the disaster that one of their biggest problems would be drinking water. The bottled water from Tavern on the Green would be exhausted quickly, but they knew that the largest single source of potable water in Manhattan wasn't far away. The Central Park Reservoir. Ahearn had dispatched a police unit to secure it. Three hours later the sergeant in charge of that unit delivered a strange report to the Central Park command post.

"Captain, we got the reservoir secured, okay. But it's weird."

"What's weird?" Ahearn asked.

"The water. It's swirling and bubbling like crazy, sir."

Ahearn took off his hat and scratched his head. "I think I got it," he announced, putting his hat back on. "We got maybe thousands of busted water mains underground out there. I know that because I got no pressure in my hydrants and because it figures after a quake. So the system is hemorrhaging water. The reservoir feeds the system. It's draining fast and being refilled automatically just as fast by the two reservoirs up in the Bronx that feed it. The Hill View and the Jerome. That's gotta be why the water's doing all that churning."

"Where's the water going?" asked the sergeant.

"Like I said, out the ruptured water mains."

"I mean, after that. Where's the water going?"

"Well," replied Ahearn, "into the sewer system, and . . ." Suddenly all the blood drained from Ahearn's face. He swallowed hard and looked into the sergeant's worried eyes. "And into the subway system."

"Dear Christ," the sergeant gasped. "There must be thousands of people trapped down there. Better get the mayor."

After he heard the grim news from Ahearn Mayor Bruce Lincoln fired a series of questions, then made one of his most difficult decisions.

"How high could the water get in the subway system? Could it fill the tunnels?"

"It's almost done that before with just a single water main break," answered Ahearn. "Depends on how fast it's leaking. I'll tell you one thing, Mr. Mayor. Leaks only get worse. Erosion makes the holes bigger."

"You're telling me if we don't do something fast, thousands of people who might be rescued could drown?"

"Yes, sir. And the only thing to do is get someone up to the reservoirs in the Bronx and shut the valves and hope there isn't enough water left in the park here to fill the tunnels."

The mayor pondered a moment, then said, "But to shut those valves in the Bronx shuts off all water to Manhattan, doesn't it?"

"Yes, sir. But there's no pressure in the system anyway. Not much there for people to drink."

"Not much is better than none, though, isn't it, Brendan? For people desperate for water to drink?"

"It's a very tough decision, Your Honor," said Ahearn softly. "But God help those poor souls in the subway if we can't shut the system down."

The mayor looked at Ahearn. There were tears in his eyes. "All right, Brendan. Dispatch a team by helicopter to the Bronx with orders to shut down the water. Good luck."

Allen Young paused only briefly on the sixth rung of the tunnel's emergency exit ladder. The natural-gas smell that he had picked up was only a faint one—disturbing but not alarming, at least not yet. He continued his climb up the remaining rungs until his head touched the escape hatch at the top.

He played his flashlight above him in order to see how the hatch was constructed. Circular, with a wheel attached to the underside that would unlock it, it was of a type that Allen had never had occasion to use but one that should present no difficulties. The wheel itself had a knob attached to it so that, while hanging on to the ladder, he could turn it with one hand. That is, if it would turn.

He balanced the flashlight on a small lip jutting out from the stone face of the tunnel's wall, then thought better of it, switched it off, and forced the butt end into his trouser pocket.

The knob on the wheel was in an awkward position for a right-hander and he first attempted to turn it with his left. When that failed to produce any results, he carefully turned himself around on the ladder so that his back was toward the wall; then he reached up again to grasp the knob with his right hand.

Slowly, excruciatingly, he felt the wheel begin to move, then jam. Preferring not to use up his energy in forcing it, he rotated it back to its original position, then forward again several times, each one making a small advance. He realized that the emergency exit had probably not been used in years, if ever at all for a real emergency, and kept his patience as the process of unfreezing the hatch's mechanism continued its slow pace.

With a sudden give that startled him and caused him to almost lose his balance on the ladder, the wheel moved forward. Steadying his grip on the ladder once again, he rotated the wheel until it had reached what seemed to be its unlocked position.

From the moment he tried to push the hatch upward with his right hand, he knew that if the wheel had become stuck with lack of use and the passage of time, the hatch would be in as bad condition.

He turned around on the ladder again in order to have the best possible grip, then climbed two more rungs until his shoulders and upper back were against the hatch and he was hunched over with his head against the tunnel wall. Then he began to push.

Several inches above Allen, on Seventh Avenue near 20th Street, the hatch against which he was straining lay buried under several hundred tons of rubble. Had the survivors on the surface, who were by then beginning to take stock of the damage that had been wrought, even known that a subway escape hatch was beneath where they wandered dazedly, picking through the debris, they would not have been able to do anything about it.

On the floor of the tunnel, Evie Lincoln and the other six members of the party stood in knee-deep water. She tried to form a mental picture of the two men and three women who were with her and Marisa. If they were dependent on one another for their lives, she should have some idea of who they were. In the pitch dark, she voiced her thoughts.

"Tell me your names and a little about yourselves, and I'll tell you. Then we'll all feel better about this team. My name is Evie Lincoln. I'm a lawyer, twenty-eight years old, and I was born in Harlem and have lived all my life in New York."

A voice, female, said, "My name is Gerta Knessel. I work at Bloomingdale's. I'm not married and I'm not telling you my age." There was laughter.

"My name is Bill Cohen. I'm an accountant, fifty-six, and I have an office on Fifty-seventh and Seventh. I have a wife and three kids and thank God they're in Florida visiting my parents."

"My name is Mary Morrissey. I was on my way to visit my mother in the Bronx. I'm thirty-three and unmarried. I work as a part-time secretary."

"I'm Jake. Divorced. Salesman. Computers. Younger than springtime."

"I'm scared to death. I don't know about you but I am terrified." The woman's voice quivered. "I was in a car crash once, and this is worse. Oh yeah—I'm Peg."

Danny Thorne was lying wide awake during the nap period thinking about going to the theater that night with his dad and then dinner afterward with both his parents. He loved to see his mom act, and he loved even more dinner with the two of them. He was excited about the evening ahead. He looked at his watch that his dad had given him for his fifth birthday last year. It gave the time of day, the date, where the moon was—the time was one nineteen. He got up and walked up to the stairs to the eighth-floor bathroom off the gym and went into a stall to pee.

There was a terrible sound like the strongest clap of thunder he had ever heard and then crashing sounds and screams. Something hit his head and he was knocked unconscious. When he came to, minutes later, he was sprawled in the stall. Above him a beam rested across the steel walls of the stall and the beam held up piles of plaster board, bricks, and chunks of cement. Danny was in a tiny dark cave surrounded by disaster.

The roof of the Grove School had collapsed and fallen in on the eighth floor, which in turn had pancaked down on the seventh floor, the seventh floor onto the sixth, where the pancake effect stopped. Danny was alive only because he had been in the bathroom stall when the roof caved in; miraculously he had been saved by the steel walls and the beam, which kept so much of the roof from falling on him.

Danny sat up and rubbed his head where it had been struck. He was bewildered. He could hear muffled noises coming from somewhere near him. Cries, whimpers. He yelled, "Can you hear me?"

There was silence. Then more whimpers. Someone who sounded a long way off cried out, "Help! Please. Someone help us." Danny yelled again, "Can anyone hear me? It's Danny Thorne. I'm okay. I'm in the bathroom."

Danny kept checking his watch, which was the only light in the space where he was trapped. Fifteen minutes had gone by. He was beginning to realize that no one was hearing him. The black darkness was terrifying. He tried to stand up and hit something above him. Dust, plaster, and stones fell down around him. He lay down again and started to cry. He realized that he had wet his pants.

Danny fell asleep sometime in the middle of the afternoon. He was dreaming. His father and he were in Africa. Huge elephants like the ones in the poster by his bed walked slowly along a path, their wrinkled trunks swaying gently back and forth. Monkeys chattered overhead. Brilliantly colored birds perched on limbs of incredibly tall trees. His father carried him on his shoulders so he could see around him better. The sun was hot on his shoulders and he could feel the strong muscles of his father's neck and shoulders under his legs, a warm secure feeling. The black native men were up ahead of them carrying all kinds of equipment. Tents, food, cameras. Danny was very happy riding up there on his father's shoulders seeing the world from a wonderfully high vantage point.

When he awakened from his dream, Danny lay in the dark sobbing. What was he going to do? How was anyone going to find him? It must have been a bomb that hit the school. The whimpers that he heard stopped. Then started again. He called out, "Hey, can anyone hear me?" There was silence above him and around him and everywhere.

It was over an hour later that Danny heard more whimpers and then a girl's voice. "Help. Help me. I'm hurt."

"Where are you?" Danny called. No answer. He called out again. Silence. Danny decided that he had to try to think about what his father would do if this happened to him. He certainly wouldn't cry. He would try to think of things to do that would help someone find him. And he would try to find whomever was crying out. He stood up and pushed against the stall door. It moved an inch and plaster fell down from the beam above him. He could see light through the crack, sunlight from somewhere. He pushed again and opened a wedge big enough for his foot. "Can you hear me?" he yelled.

"Yes." A moan. Not far away. "I can't move."

"What's your name?"

"Debbie. Debbie Murdoch. What's yours?"

"Danny Thorne. I'm in first grade. Tell me where you are. I'm in the bathroom."

Sobs. Then, "I was playing in the gym. I'm in third grade. I hurt real bad."

Danny pushed harder on the door, and chunks of cement crashed down from above hitting his head, knocking him to the floor. He lay there, dazed. The air was heavy with plaster dust and he coughed. He had to help Debbie Murdoch. That's what his dad would do. But how? Every time he made a move more stuff from above caved in on him. He got to his feet again. This time the stall door was open wider. He could almost squeeze through it. He called out, "Debbie, I'm trying to get out of where I am to help you. Can you hear me now?"

"Yes," her voice was weaker than it had been.

"I'm going to find you, Debbie." He tried to think what his dad would say. "Take it easy. Everything will be all right."

Jim Richardson and Joe Mazurski had assessed the situation in the broken section of the Queens/Midtown tunnel where they were stranded. The silt from the riverbed that had entered the tunnel was as solid as rock and both men knew that even if it hadn't been, there were vehicles immersed in it that would effectively block their ability to tunnel out.

"Tunnel out to what, anyway?" Jim had asked, and Joe had simply shrugged.

"So what are our options?"

"Got me, pal." They had been standing at the front end of the sealed tunnel. "Let's go back to the others. They're going to know the worst soon, anyway. We may as well get it over with."

They made their way back to where the rest of the group waited, next to the nuns' Vanagon. It contained a small refrigerator and bottled-water cooler for long trips in place of the last row of seats. The side door of the van was open and a light from a Coleman lantern illuminated the immediate area.

Jim looked at Phyllis, motioned his wife to take the kids out of earshot. Phyllis complied wordlessly, gathering her two children against her and leading them away. Kathy was crying silently and Jim felt a piece of his heart break.

He looked at the people standing in the glow of the lantern. The nuns were as composed as if on their way to mass. The two elegantly dressed women stood together holding hands. The young married couple was a slight distance away, he sitting on the trunk of their car, she leaning against him between his legs. Not wishing to talk loudly, Jim beckoned them to come to the van.

The nun who had been driving—Sister Mary, Jim thought—said quietly, "I take it both ends are completely blocked?"

Jim looked at Joe Mazurski. "Yes," he replied. "Whatever happened out there, a nuke maybe, broke this section off and it filled up with dirt, probably from the river bottom. I thought I felt a sinking feeling when it happened, so we may be lower than the rest of the tunnel."

"But what does it mean?" Vivian asked. Her voice had trembled slightly. Not like her, Charlotte thought, and gave her friend's hand a squeeze.

"It means we're trapped. Pure and simple."

One of the nuns crossed herself and her lips began to move silently.

"For how long?" Sister Mary asked.

Jim looked straight at her. "For as long as the air holds out, Sister. Or until somebody comes to rescue us. But I wouldn't hold out much hope for that."

Charlotte felt her knees begin to buckle. So her worst fear about tunnels had come true.

"Well," said Sister Mary, all brisk efficiency. "Then we should take stock of what we have and how long we can survive on it." She paused, then turned to Joe. "You must have a radio in your truck."

"Yes, Sister, in the cab."

"How powerful is it?"

Joe shook his head. "It's powerful enough, carries through the air for lots of miles. And I've even used it in tunnels. But I don't know about this. I mean, if we're really blocked in . . ."

Sister Mary, used to dealing with parochial school students, cut him off. "There's only one way to find out."

Sam Thorne left the Seagram Building and made his way up Park Avenue to the Grove School at 83rd Street between Park and Lexington. Once there, he found a scene of horror. Parents who had managed to get to the site were on their hands and knees digging through the brick and mortar, throwing the refuse into the street, some standing in shock, others weeping, some looking up at the caved-in roof, the pancaked eighth, seventh, and sixth floors, and some lucky ones had, Sam was told, arrived to find their children safe and sound, able to get out of the lower floors to the ground floor and out of the building. The basement crafts room was buried. And the sight of the top floors was ghastly.

Sam was all too familiar with the phenomenon. The quixotic nature of earthquakes was everywhere apparent. The lower floors of the school, while badly damaged, had stood the shock, but above some areas of the floors were open to view. Parents below could see desks and gym equipment and crazy angled walls. The whole building looked slanted.

The headmaster was on his knees digging in the rubble. Someone had heard cries coming from the basement area. Sam knelt down by him. "Mr. Thatcher, it's Sam Thorne. Danny's father. He's a first-grader."

The headmaster turned and looked at Sam. His face was grimy, his eyes red with plaster dust or tears or both, "Yes."

"Where would he have been at the time of the shock?"

"The first-graders . . ." he paused and stared at Sam thinking. "The first-graders have lunch at noon and then nap until one thirty. They take their naps on the seventh floor then go up for an hour to play in the eighth-floor gym."

Sam nodded. He wanted to yell, NO!, but he nodded and stood up. "Thank you, Mr. Thatcher. How many children got out?"

"More than half of them. About ninety. About forty are unaccounted for. At least twenty children were in the basement crafts room." The headmaster stood up. "Can you get us help? We need medical and rescue personnel. I've heard that they have detectors that can pick up voices under the rubble."

"I'll do what I can. Has anyone tried to get up there?"

"Yes. It's impossible. And very dangerous. The staircase is blocked, the elevator doesn't work. There is room to slip by the blockage on the staircase but I tried it and got only as far as the fifth floor. I heard cries for help and called out that we would get help for them, but when I tried climbing to the sixth floor the stairs are completely gone. There's the landing but no stairs."

"I'm going to try." Sam ignored the headmaster's attempt to stop him.

Inside the building he saw the stairs covered with bricks and timbers. At the first landing he looked up and saw that the headmaster was accurate. The staircase had disintegrated and half of it hung in midair between floors, swinging slightly. He could see open sky through the walls of the fifth floor. He descended and found the headmaster. "I'll get help. I'll be back. If my wife gets here, Diane Taylor, Mrs. Sam Thorne, please tell her I'll be back as soon as I can."

By four that afternoon, after asking every uniformed person he met where the mayor was, Sam Thorne reached the precinct house. He asked to see the mayor alone.

Mayor Lincoln cleared the room. Sam stood while he talked, pacing up and down. He began stressing various facts.

"We have a twelve-hour 'window' to rescue the victims. After that, people who are marginal to begin with are much less likely to be saved. We found that out in Mexico City and Armenia. Unfortunately," he added, "there is no realistic short-term, twelve-hour response to a major disaster like this one, on anything more than a rudimentary scale."

The mayor listened intently.

Sam stopped pacing and stood in front of what had been the police captain's and now was the mayor's desk. "You have to decide when to put 'triage' into effect. My strong recommendation is that it would be an official order from you today."

Lincoln was silent for a moment. Then he said slowly, "My wife is buried under her day school up in Harlem. I can't give an order like that. Not while there's hope she's alive."

"My six-year-old boy is trapped high up on the floor of his school where the roof caved in. Our personal tragedies . . . well, the City is one big personal tragedy. We have to ask all official personnel and all citizens to concentrate their efforts on those who are above ground and are able to be helped. We have no choice. We'll lose the ones who are alive but seriously hurt if we don't put the policy of 'triage' in place, and you are the one with not only the power but the moral authority to do just that."

The mayor nodded. "You're right. I forgot myself. I am sorry." For the first time that day the mayor gave in to his grief. He put his hands over his eyes. "Oh, God," he said, "we must have the strength to go through this. I must be stronger than I am." He took a deep breath and brought himself under control.

"I know," Sam said, and was quiet.

"I need your expertise, Sam. I need someone to coordinate with Captain Ahearn and the police and fire departments and the EMS in the next few hours. We have four thousand troops being helicoptered into Central Park to help control the criminal element, looting, the like. And we have to figure out how best to deal

186

with the supplies that will begin arriving this afternoon, parachuted into the park. On top of everything else, we have the problem of abandoned cars, thousands of them, left on every side street and main avenue when the earthquake struck and people who were able ditched them. We have set up an emergency medical station at the edge of the park. Then we have the problem of what to do with the dead . . ."

Sam nodded. "Within forty-eight hours we're going to have a problem with disease if we don't cremate the bodies. The heavy-duty equipment to dig mass graves won't be able to get through the streets until too late. We should cremate the bodies after we identify them, or at least take fingerprints."

"Oh, my God."

"It's terrible, I realize. But again, we haven't much choice. The situation is out of control and can only get worse. I saw emergency squads piling bodies north of the precinct as I walked up here from East Eighty-third. There must be hundreds more there by now."

"Yes, I have Captain Ahearn in charge of the personnel doing the identifying."

"Look, I'll do anything I can to help. Can you get your top people in here so I can talk to them?"

In minutes, Brendan Ahearn reported to the mayor's office and was introduced to a civilian of whom he had never heard. At first he was skeptical, but in a few more minutes he was convinced Thorne was all right.

The three of them stood in front of a huge wall map of the City. No one had spoken of the other boroughs, but it was implicit that they would have to fend for themselves as Manhattan struggled for its very life. "One of the first tasks is to alert everyone at the lower end of Manhattan and on the riversides to the tsunamis." Sam glanced at his watch. It was 4:20 P.M. "They are bound to strike the lower end of Manhattan, City Island, and the other shorelines, and soon. We can't do anything except to warn all survivors in those areas to get to high ground and away from the shoreline."

Brendan Ahearn rubbed his neck with his hand. "What the hell are they?"

"They are waves caused by the earthquake and they can be as high as a three-story house. They could crest seventeen feet above the normal water level. They will pick up boats, dock pilings, any small buildings not already knocked down, and wash them blocks into the City. When they suck back out, they'll pull all the debris into the harbor. In the big Alaska earthquake that hit Valdez in 1964 there were at least eight tsunamis after the quake itself."

"How long have we, Sam?" Mayor Lincoln asked.

"No time. We're out of time. If we're lucky, we can somehow warn people before the first one hits, but it may have already rolled in."

"What about helicopters flying low enough so people can hear a battery-operated bullhorn?" Ahearn asked.

"Good. Get it under way," the mayor ordered.

"I can try getting power boats, the ones that still run, to do the same and go up and down the west side of the Hudson, and how about the East River?" Ahearn suggested.

Sam said, "That's a suicide mission if we're too late. A lot of the survivors downtown will be going to the World Trade Center and other big buildings that are still standing. The waves won't knock those buildings down. The same with the survivors on the West Side. The East River is probably too narrow to be a serious problem. Whatever we do, we won't save many lives from these waves, I'm afraid, but at least we can try."

"Okay." Ahearn prepared to leave to get the helicopters and equipment ready.

"You get going, Brendan, and good luck."

"Let's organize the survivors, on a volunteer basis, and start evacuating the wounded over to Tate Acres," Sam said. "That will speed things up until the military gets here tomorrow. That new hospital that Howard Tate is so proud of can be damn useful."

"I've had word that Bellevue and New York Hospital are already sending doctors and nurses over there," the mayor said.

"At some point, I'll go by a friend of mine's apartment, and if he's alive, he can be a big help. He's the ex-commodore of the New York Yacht Club."

The mayor looked sharply at Sam. "How about Harlem? The rescue effort must reach out to Harlem. It is in ruins. I cannot allow either the appearance or the fact of more help going to the rich than the poor in this city."

"Believe me," Sam replied, "boats can dock uptown off Harlem as well as midtown, sir. This earthquake is very democratic."

"Give me your friend's address, Sam, and I'll get one of my men to go on foot to his place and see if he can get started with the private boats."

Sam wrote down the name and address and a brief message: "Dear Preston: Pretend this is Dunkirk. Every person you know who can man a boat should try to pick up the wounded at the East Side hospitals and take them to the dock at Tate Acres. Good luck, old pal. Sam Thorne."

"You sure the tsunamis won't wreck small boats," the mayor asked.

"Look at the map, sir, and see the formation of the East River. Thank God, the waves can't get that far up it. It'll be rough, but that's all."

"Good. What next?"

"Building crematoriums in the park and starting the process as soon as possible."

The two of them were thinking the same thing, and he knew it. Not since the Holocaust. But this was different, and very necessary. They agreed that the Army Engineers should be given the job of building crematoriums the next day, since they could not figure out how to do it without their help. The engineers could start building or mending the bridges which were either destroyed—the 59th Street Bridge—or severely damaged—George Washington and the Triborough. The Brooklyn Bridge and the Williamsburg were down, as was the Whitestone. Throgs Neck was damaged. And on the list went.

"We have to start the civilians who are not hurt getting together in volunteer teams. Every block should be covered by someone. There are thousands of people trapped up in office buildings. Children wandering the streets without knowing where their parents are. By daybreak tomorrow we should have organized these volunteer groups to take charge of their blocks and neighborhoods, to get people down out of the buildings, into church shelters, school shelters, those that are still standing. Those are the places best equipped with cots, blankets, and emergency food supplies to take in the homeless." Sam could not stop his thoughts going back to where Danny was trapped. He forced his mind away from the agonizing questions. "I'll help organize the civilian volunteers if you like, sir."

"I do like, Sam. Thank you. We'll help you as much as we can. Every minute we are hearing from other precincts. The emergency teams are reporting in and so are the other uniformed forces, the firemen and police. But they have their hands full with the wounded and trying to dig out the buried. With the fires most of all. So if you can rally the civilians, and I'll give you as many men as I can to help you, that would be great."

"Okay, I'll do it."

"You'll need a gun. Looters. And worse."

"Hope I can remember how to shoot one of those." Sam grinned. "I missed the wars but we hunted jackrabbits out west when I was a kid."

"Good luck, Sam. And I hope your son is all right."

"Thanks, sir." They shook hands and a young woman entered the room. She did not acknowledge Sam's presence.

She stood before the mayor's desk, legs planted, hands on her hips. Her white coat was smeared with blood. "Mayor, I got to have supplies. We've set up facilities at checkpoints around the park, but this one here is the main one, and I don't have enough morphine, let alone antibiotics. We're running out of everything fast. We're running out of the thing we need most—blood. Ordinarily, the Department of Health and Human Services would be making a special nationwide and worldwide appeal for blood. That department no longer exists in any organized way."

Mayor Lincoln asked, "What should I do?"

"Get the word out somehow to Boston, Los Angeles, Chicago, and Dallas where the largest blood banks are to start flying plasma in. We can't screen blood here. We need red cells and plasma that've already been screened. And get Germany to start flying in red cells that have been screened—they usually fly in once a day because New Yorkers don't donate enough blood to supply the City. Ask them to multiply their shipments by . . . well, we can use the most they've got."

"What about doctors, nurses?"

"I got plenty of them. Four other doctors. Volunteers, but okay.

And Red Cross. And nurses who turned up out of nowhere. What the fu—I mean," she stopped herself from using her favorite four-letter word.

"Doctor Kelly, I'd like you to meet the man I've put in charge of the civilian volunteer effort, Sam Thorne."

Sam came toward her to shake her hand, but she turned her head just long enough for him to see her blue eyes and determined chin. She acknowledged him with a perfunctory glance, and then she trained her attention back on the mayor.

"I need you to get some people to go to the nearest hospitals and get us what we need. Now!"

"I understand, Doctor, but I'm going to turn you over to Sam. Sam. . . ." The mayor smiled, amused at putting these two unlikely individuals together, and relieved to turn Kelly over to someone else. "You help Dr. Kelly, will you? You can confer in the hallway. I have to use the phone."

"Okay," Dr. Kelly said, looking up at Sam. "Can you get me some supplies?"

"Have you got a list of what you need?"

"Shit. I never thought of that. Where's a piece of paper." She raced down the hall and he followed. She darted into an office where some policemen were looking at a city map, and grabbed a notepad off the desk. She glanced up at Sam again, but without really looking at him he realized. He could have been a stick of wood as long as he did her bidding. He was curious about her, this small, determined, tough young woman, but she did not care who or what he was, it was clear.

She jotted down a long list and handed it to him. "Can you read my writing? The nuns weren't too good at teaching penmanship where I went to school. I bet you write a beautiful hand."

He read the list out loud to her, thinking she was not as unobservant as he had thought and wondering why she seemed so hostile to him. "I managed to decipher it," he said to her drily. "Can't read most doctors' writing."

"Okay. Now let's get some of your civilians on the stick over to Lenox Hill or down to Roosevelt and get me what I need. I got people who are dying out there."

"Listen, Dr. Kelly. I just got my orders twenty minutes ago from

Mayor Lincoln. I haven't got any civilian volunteer force yet. I . . ."

She looked at him with contempt written all over her face. "Don't make excuses. Just get the stuff I need." She started back down the hallway.

Sam was angry. He followed her. "Listen, Doctor, I think you should save the ones you can save. Not waste time on the dying. In a few hours, no one underground is going to be searched for, we can only save those who—" He was matching strides with her as she, hands in jacket pockets, practically ran down the corridor. He grabbed her arm to stop her. "Jesus!" she yelled, clamping it to her side in pain.

"I didn't mean to hurt you. Just to stop you so I can explain . . ."

"It's okay. My arm got banged up when the quake hit. I heard what you were saying. I'm in a hurry. I don't like what you were saying, okay?" She started off again and he strode ahead of her and stood in her way.

"Dr. Kelly, wait a minute." He looked into her flushed face, noticing how pretty she was at the same time he wanted to throttle her. "We have to work together. And you have to face the fact that triage is in effect now. Not later. Now."

Her eyes darkened and she put her hands on her hips again. They faced one another. "Listen, buster, no big-time best-selling author dude is going to tell me who is going to live or die or who I'm going to try to save. I don't know why the mayor has you involved in this mess, just because your mug is on television, but I don't have time for you so get out of my way."

"I know about earthquakes." Sam heard his own voice and it sounded silly in his ears. "I'm a scientist."

Pat Kelly gave a mock laugh. "And I suppose you have a degree in medicine? Give me a break. And get me my supplies!" She brushed by him and he stood looking after her with amazement.

———

No one noticed or cared that Matt Devon and his team were bogus doctors. At first they had been worried that, once found out, they would be robbed of their newfound purpose in life, but they soon realized that in this crisis the sight of their medical jackets and their kind, reassuring manner gave them a passport no one was about to question.

Matt was on a high unlike any he had ever known, certainly since he had learned that he had AIDS. And he could tell that Scott, Guy, and Elliot shared his mood. Perhaps they had more love in their lives than he, though, and for him, self-absorbed as he had been all his thirty-eight years, with the desertion first of his father, then Bobby, and slowly over the past year all his glitzy famous friends from the fashion world making the pro forma call once a month to see "how he was doing," this role that he was playing gave him a sense of worth and purpose that he had forgotten existed.

When Matt had stored two bottles of Seconal in his Sub-Zero refrigerator in his opulent apartment in the Dakota, which his rag trade had afforded him, for the day when he would take them and his own life with them, he had felt, with that small preparation, a sense of power, of control. He had taken power away from the medical profession, power away from the disease. But that sense had left him soon thereafter, and only bitterness and despair and anger filled his days. He found no pleasure in his work, though he was certainly strong enough to plan the new spring season. He began making plans to get rid of the business, sell it to a big retailer. His acquaintances began to avoid him, not because he had AIDS, he knew that, but because he was such a downer for them.

And then this catastrophe beyond anyone's imagination had somehow given him back his sense of control over his destiny and others, and it had given him a sense of purpose and the camaraderie of these three young men.

The team worked its way up the drive, crossing over the divider, first the downtown side, then the uptown, helping people as they went along, using their young strength, intelligence, and humor to calm the wounded, reassure those trapped that more help was on its way. Though there was little sign of any official help. A few EMS workers, a policeman or two, but no organized aid was in sight. Matt figured that no one would have time to start checking the highways and bridges for at least a day. The skyline of the City told the tragic story. He saw small boats bobbing on the river, going from the East Sixties, probably the hospital, over to Tate Acres and back, and some helicopters doing the same thing. Smoke clouds rose over parts of the City signaling fires out of control. Dust from the fallen buildings had created a yellowish haze. There was an ominous silence, broken from time to time by a siren. One of the trapped, a young woman who told Matt that she had been on her way into New York to go to the Matisse retrospective at the Metropolitan Museum of Art, said, tears running down her bloodstained cheeks, "Is this the end of the world?"

By four thirty they had reached Diane. After futile attempts to break through the debris on the staircase, the firemen who, on foot and carrying a ladder, had been working their way up the block from Broadway, reached what was left of the theater. They managed to clear the sidewalk enough to be able to use the ladder, which extended to the window in Diane's dressing room. She watched the burly fireman climbing up the ladder.

"Are you hurt, ma'am?" he said when he got near enough.

"No, and am I glad to see you. How do I get down this thing?"

"I am going to put this harness on you, ma'am, and clip this rope so you're tied to me." He hoisted himself through the window and stood beside her. "If you slip, and you won't, I'll hold you safe. No problem. You got better shoes than those?" He looked at her slippers.

"Of course," and she put on her Reeboks she kept at the theater for when she walked home for exercise.

"Okay. Watch how I get out the window and then I'm going to talk you out and onto the ladder. Piece of cake."

"Sure, I'll bet." The knot in her stomach tightened. She had always been scared of heights. Maybe she was just hungry. Whatever, she had no choice. "I've got a boy in school up on Eighty-third between Park and Lex. I've got to get to him."

"Jesus, ma'am, I don't know." He towered over her. "It took us an hour to get from Broadway down this block. And two hours to get from our station house only five blocks away. The streets are filled up with crap, and it's real dangerous. Things still dropping off buildings. Glass ten inches thick. Where's your husband? Or maybe the teachers will get him home."

Diane stared at the young fireman while he talked. She knew

that she could not count on anyone. "My husband was midtown when it happened. He'll be trying to get to Danny too."

He shook his head. "Ready?"

"Yes."

He stepped out onto the ladder easily, having secured the halter around her torso. He went down a few rungs and said, "Come out backward, don't look down, and put your foot on the first rung, then bring the other foot down. Then just go slow, one rung at a time, and I am right here. You are safe. Start now."

She followed his instructions and in five minutes reached the ground. "You are quite a guy," she said and reached up and kissed his cheek. He blushed. "Now look, you've got to go back and get someone who didn't make it," and she saw the look of amazement cross the fireman's face. "Oh," she murmured. "I guess that's a crazy idea."

"Listen, ma'am. We have orders to rescue the living, and we can't even do that. I'm sorry."

"Where are you going now?" she asked. She felt very safe with him and hoped he was going uptown. Being above the street was one thing but down on the ground she looked around and was frightened. There were men with makeshift stretchers carrying the dead away. There were men and women picking through the rubble. Some people were sitting, bleeding, waiting for help. There were other firemen inserting what looked like a cable into the heaps and heaps of rubble.

"What are they doing?"

"I'm staying here to help. Those guys are from the Collapse Unit and that thing they've got there has a microphone built in so that they can hear if anyone is alive under that debris." Other firemen were hand digging and many people on the block were helping.

Diane hunched her shoulders under her fur coat. "I'd better start. Thank you again, and . . . good luck to us all."

The fireman shook his head as he watched the beautiful woman in the fur coat start trudging eastward, climbing over fallen bricks and stone, stepping carefully on the shards of glass littering the street. He sighed and tried not to think what might have happened to his wife and children in Brooklyn.

On one car the wheels had collapsed and it was flattened to eighteen inches. Guy and Scott managed to pull the man inside out by his hips, after an hour, and he was uninjured. In another car, Matt and Elliot looked inside and found parts of bodies. Many cars had burst into flames on impact and were too dangerous to go near. One car had been nearly crushed flat by the weight of the cross beam that had landed on it like a guillotine. In the front seat the mother and another female passenger were dead, and in the back two children, a girl and a boy, were badly hurt. The girl was unconscious with horrible head injuries, and when Matt managed to wedge himself halfway into the backseat through the open window he found the little boy, his legs crushed between two pieces of concrete that Matt could not budge. He wanted to give the boy a shot to ease the pain, but instead held his small hand in his own.

"What's your name?"

"José." The boy's huge dark eyes stared at Matt.

"We're going to get you out of here, José. You and your sister."

"Milagros."

"Yes, Milagros." The smell of gas was strong. Matt realized that any moment the car might explode. He stayed, holding José's hand and talking with him. "Where are you from?"

"Puerto Rico. We are visiting my aunt."

The boy could not see over the front car seats to where his mother and aunt lay.

"Do you feel better?" Matt saw the pain line across the boy's forehead ease.

José nodded. He gave Matt a faint smile, and his head toppled over on his shoulder. Matt thought at first that he had gone to sleep, but then he took the boy's pulse. None. Then he took the pulse of Milagros. None. He pulled himself back out of the car.

Matt had never witnessed such suffering before. The overpass had pancaked down on the drivers coming through the underpass in the East Seventies, and these people, the few who were alive, were in agony. Most of them could not be pulled out of their cars. When they could bring a person out, they tried to make him as comfortable as they could, but there were no blankets, no hot coffee, nothing to protect them against the cold nightfall to come. The team began to carry the wounded to the abandoned cars, wherever possible putting them inside, stretched out across back-seats or sitting up, if they were able to, in the front seats. They bandaged the wounds, and made tourniquets, and kept talking to the victims: "Here you go. A 1994 Mercedes we've got here for you. Big and comfy. You'll be warm until more help comes to get you to the hospital," Elliot told an elderly couple, who the four of them were carrying between them to a limousine.

Guy exclaimed when they had deposited the couple: "Look, a fully stocked bar!" They gave the old gentleman and his wife a swallow of brandy, and each of them took a swallow. "We can use these," Matt said, taking all the decanters with him.

Elliot sipped from the small delicate snifter he had lifted out of the holder in the bar: "By God, that's good. I'm a bit weary. Is anyone else?"

Scott groaned, but grinned, "I haven't had such sore muscles since rehearsing for *Chorus Line*."

"I think we've got everybody out of there that we can get," Matt said. "Let's go back and just check before we go on uptown."

They emerged from the limousine, pleased that the couple was out of pain, even sleepy, and their wounds were bandaged, at least the ones that were visible. "Hey, look fellows," Matt pointed. Back at the overpass they could see at least half a dozen Red Cross workers crawling up the remains of the overpass, carrying medical equipment. "That takes care of that." Matt started walking uptown, and the rest of them threaded their way between abandoned cars to follow him north toward the Triborough Bridge, which glinted in the late afternoon sun.

The sun was beginning to set and they had reached the Nineties. "I think we should find the biggest car we can, and rest," Matt announced to the obvious relief of the others. They found a relatively unharmed Chevrolet van within minutes, and inside not only two blankets but a half-eaten roll of Oreo cookies and a bag containing baby food, strained peas and lamb and carrots, along with a jar of water and some powdered milk. A jumble of toys in the back of the van and fishing gear, with a large high-power flashlight. They were gleeful. "What luck!" exclaimed Matt, who handed around the baby food. "First course. Pretend it's paté. With chocolate soufflé to follow."

They gobbled down the pap and munched on the cookies, too

exhausted to talk. Scott and Guy covered themselves with one Army blanket in the backseat and Matt and Elliot shared the other in the front seat. The moment he rested his head against the corner of the van's front seat, Matt Devon fell into a deep untroubled sleep for the first time since he learned he had AIDS.

The president of the United States entered the Cabinet Room of the White House. Geoffrey Collins, the secretary of state, thought he had never seen the man look so exhausted and careworn. Yet the characteristic spring in his step, his economy of motion, was still in evidence.

The president approached his seat at the head of the table and the men and women assembled in the room rose to greet him without words, for this was not a time for even the most subdued and innocent of conversations or comments. He stood at his place.

"A few seconds of silence, I think, would be in order before we get to the problems at hand. For all that will never be again."

One by one, the heads of even the most battle-hardened of the politicians, statesmen, and military officers in the room bowed in quiet prayer for the nation in its time of need and despair.

The president took his seat and looked around him at the others as they, too, sat down. He already knew which of his cabinet members were here, which were out of town, and he nodded to each of them in turn as he caught their eyes. State, Treasury, Defense (who had brought the chairman of the Joint Chiefs), Interior, Commerce, Labor—these he needed the advice of the most and they were all here. They and their principal aides. The other secretaries present were there more as a courtesy to their offices rather than out of necessity. They had all been asked to restrict themselves to bringing one senior official from their departments. The president had known seconds after he witnessed the destruction of New York City that he was going to have a battle on his hands with Congress; the fewer people who were involved with his thoughts and plans, at least initially, the better.

"Geoffrey, would you please give us a brief synopsis of the international reaction?" He turned from the secretary of state to the rest of the cabinet. "I'm going to ask you all to be as brief as possible. This crisis is going to produce a lot of verbiage; what the cabinet needs is speed and economy of words. Geoffrey . . ."

"In two words, Mr. President, incredible sympathy. Not, of course, from those like Khadafi, the Iranians, and Mr. Castro. But the expressions from around the world have been almost uniformly those of wanting to reach out to help, not take advantage of the situation. You have, I believe, heard from the prime minister?"

"Yes. He's offered unlimited assistance. Of course, with the British economy in its present state of repair, 'unlimited' becomes a moot point. In any event, he said their war secretary would be in touch with you, Tom. Has he?"

"Yes, sir," said the secretary of defense. "The Royal Navy has thirteen surface units in the central or western Atlantic, within forty-eight hours steaming time of the city. They've been ordered to stand off Cape May for an indefinite period in order to help whatever evacuation effort is gotten under way."

The president nodded, then turned to the secretary of the interior. "When we were flying back, I got some idea of the effects of the quake along the seaboard south of Manhattan. Bad, but not more than that. What can you add, and what about areas north of the city?"

The secretary stood and went to an easel on which had been set a large tablet of art paper. He drew back the first, blank page, to reveal a hastily drawn outline of the country east of the Mississippi with notations on it.

"From what we can tell now, the quake struck in this general direction." He indicated a southeastern-pointing arrow on the map. "It was probably centered almost directly under New York City, incredible as that may seem, then meandered on and out to sea. In the rest of the state, the Ithaca-Rochester-Buffalo triangle has taken a blow, one that's also extended into Canada. From Albany east in a line to Boston, there has been damage, but nothing that cannot be contained and quickly repaired. The harbors at Boston and Newport are already back in operation and can be used for any ship-borne evacuation immediately."

He flipped the page on the pad over. "South of the city the story is somewhat different, at least for the first hundred and fifty or so miles. New Jersey has been hit the hardest, after New York itself.

Both the Turnpike and the Garden State are impassable for miles at a stretch and there are massive fires at the refineries and storage facilities in the Newark area. The airport there is out of commission."

"What about the other airports?"

"I don't think we can count on them, sir. At least not for the next few days. To my knowledge, as of the time we sat down, contact had not been reestablished with either LaGuardia or JFK." He looked around the room, saw no headshakes of dissent, then went on.

"Philadelphia is out as a port facility and Baltimore and Wilmington probably won't be able to function up to capacity until Monday or Tuesday at the earliest. That leaves Norfolk as the nearest undamaged seaport. So I agree, sir, bad but not as bad as it might have been if the quake had struck in a different direction." He left the easel and returned to his seat.

The president nodded, then turned to the chairman of the Joint Chiefs of Staff. Although not a member of the cabinet, this career officer was almost invariably present when crises of this magnitude loomed. The president raised an eyebrow.

"Well, sir," the chairman began. "All branches of the military are on full Red Alert. We do not expect any overt threat from foreign powers, but we will not stand down until such time as that can be confirmed. We also can't count on how the terrorist nations around the world are going to react, how they might possibly take advantage of the situation. We're also ready to move in units to restore order in the City."

For the next forty-five minutes, the president listened as his top advisers gave their assessments of the situation. Those assessments ranged from bleak—Commerce—to hopeful—Treasury—but none ventured a positive step beyond the latter.

The president looked at the big clock on the wall. "It's getting on toward seven. I suggest we all take a break for supper. As a group, we won't meet again until tomorrow morning at seven thirty, but I'd like to meet with several of you individually later this evening. Tom, Geoffrey, Anthony. I trust the rest of you will be available on an around-the-clock basis for the next couple of days."

Heads nodded assent and the president continued. "I want to

know if any of you have immediate family who were in New York today." He looked around the room.

"Yes, sir, I have." Rose Compton-Reilly, the secretary of the treasury, spoke in reply. "My son, Julius, is at school at NYU."

So that's the reason she was so optimistic, the president thought. "I'll do everything I can, Rose, to find out what has happened to him."

"Thank you, Mr. President. I appreciate that."

"Come on in, Geoff," the president said to the secretary of state. The president was sitting behind a desk in his small, private study off the Oval Office. It was eight thirty that night, and his jacket was off, tie loosened, sleeves rolled up. He stood and walked to the green leather couch, indicating that Geoffrey Collins should sit at the other end.

"I know you well enough to know you haven't spent the last hour and a half eating dinner. What have you found out?"

"I've been on the phone with Moscow most of the time. In addition to offering whatever help they can provide in general, in specific they're going to clamp down diplomatically on all the potential hot spots—and hotshots—around the world. Khadafi has already begun to rattle his saber and Castro, not unexpectedly, has been on the phone to the Kremlin ranting and raving about how this is an opportunity that will never happen again, how Russia and Cuba must take advantage of our temporary weakness, and so on and so forth. The usual claptrap."

The president allowed himself a tiny smile. "And what did the minister have to reply?"

"As near as the translators could get it—remember, we're going from Russian through Spanish and into English—it was to the effect that if he wanted to keep his balls between his legs, he'd also have to keep his mouth shut."

The president grunted. "What did he have to say about the U.N.?"

"That it would probably be the worst possible forum to decide anything right now. He thinks the Security Council should move to Geneva temporarily, with new ambassadors if necessary. Nobody has yet gotten an accurate report of who's been killed and who's still alive."

"I agree. What were his thoughts about the General Assembly?"

"Keep them from convening for as long as possible, by veto if necessary. He thinks, and I concur, that endless speeches by ambassadors from countries with thirty-seven thousand people won't do anyone any good. The majority of the individual nations are solidly in sympathy with this disaster. Diplomats can only muck things up."

The president paused. "Tell me, Geoff, in straight terms. How do you think the world would react if New York City suddenly ceased to exist?"

The secretary reflected for perhaps sixty seconds. "To tell you the truth, after a year or so I don't think its absence would affect much of anything. In the short term, of course, a great deal would have to be adjusted, the economics of the world in particular. May I ask why?"

"You're being diplomatic, Geoff. You know perfectly well why. In the last hour or so I've taken several calls and refused literally dozens of others from senators and congressmen. The ones I've talked to were the most emotionally balanced members of each house—the ones I put off were the loons—and they're about evenly divided between rebuilding the City and abandoning it. When the loon factor is counted in, I think I'm going to have a great deal of trouble getting them to go along with appropriating the amounts of money it's going to take to get the City on its feet again."

Both men were silent for a while. Then the secretary said, "Is that what you're thinking, then? Get New York back on its feet?"

"I've talked with Bruce Lincoln," the president replied, avoiding a direct answer. "He's being stonewalled by Albany. Fleming told the lieutenant governor not to do anything until he gets back from Europe. When Bruce contacted me directly, I told him he could have the Eighty-second from Bragg tomorrow at dawn. I'll probably catch hell for that." He shrugged his shoulders. "I don't know, Geoff, it's a hard one to call. I've had preliminary estimates from OMB of up to seven trillion dollars over a ten-year period to bring New York back to where it was twenty-four hours ago. That's a hell of a sum to try to ram through Congress. However, since I won't be running again in 1996 . . ." He let the thought hang.

"Yes," the secretary agreed.

Throughout the night, the reports continued to pour in to the president in his small study, carefully screened to eliminate all but the most essential information. The cabinet secretaries whose advice the president most needed came and left with clockwork regularity, some more than once. The chairman of the Joint Chiefs spent fifteen minutes with his commander-in-chief and emerged red-faced and uncommunicative to the growing army of reporters waiting for news. Broadcast journalists reporting live could only surmise that he, who they all suspected of being a hawk in dove's feathers, had had his wings clipped in some fashion.

The president spoke to a handful of world leaders who he considered it essential that he not snub—Russia, England, Japan, France, Germany, the Vatican. The others who called were shunted off to the vice president's office. Only Peking remained strangely silent, but the president had been assured both by foreign leaders and his State and Intelligence departments that this was not necessarily ominous, so he put any thoughts of ill intent out of his mind.

At about 2 A.M. he picked up the receiver to be told that the one man in New York with whom he really wanted to talk was on the line, courtesy of several ham radio buffs.

"Howard," he said. "Good to hear your voice."

Rosemarie realized by Wednesday night that she could not possibly get from Oyster Bay into Manhattan. She would wait. Soon there would be a way. Long Island was not damaged half as badly as Manhattan. She would study maps and find a way. That night a runner came to the house and told her that Domenico was all right and would be in touch with her as soon as he could. She asked where he was, and the runner pretended he did not know. The same runner had checked on Angelica, who was alive and well, and very worried about her son, Alfredo, who had not turned up.

By Thursday morning, after a peaceful night's sleep, Rosemarie was serene with her plan. It was so simple. Why hadn't she thought of it before?

———

That afternoon Angelica's car drew into the driveway and the Irish wolfhounds raced out to greet her. She came into the house and threw herself into her mother's arms. "They found Alfredo, Mama. He's dead. My precious boy is dead," she sobbed.

Rosemarie comforted her, but felt nothing, not even a pang. Her grandson was better off in heaven, away from his drugs and the evil world. She offered Angelica some wine and candy, which her daughter refused. "Mama, are you all right? You know Daddy is all right, don't you?"

"Yes, the Lord spared him."

Angelica recognized the signs. Her mother was going off somewhere into her own head the way she had several times before. The pain of losing Alfredo made her furious with her mother for doing this again at such a terrible time. She stayed a few minutes longer, and then left to drive back to her house in Roslyn, where now there was no husband and no child. She wept bitter tears the whole way back.

———

Despite the tragedy that had struck New York City, there were many who found their way to street-level restaurants and bars that were not badly damaged, where lighted candles on the tables provided a romantic aura and liquor flowed.

It was reminiscent of the blackout of '77, Domenico Rizzo thought, as he waited at a table at the Bull and Bear at the Waldorf for David Hartnett. He had called for this meeting on his way uptown on foot to the Trump Tower, where he intended to make his small office in Nancy's duplex operational.

There was no water or ice, so Domenico nursed a glass of red wine. He surveyed the scene. There was a hysterical gaiety in the air. Young men and women stranded midtown drifting toward the warmth and lights, not knowing what they would find at their homes, willing to laugh and drink and kiss the stranger sitting next to them with abandon.

Rizzo was impatient. He had sent a runner up to Hartnett's apartment that afternoon to demand this meeting; at least the guy could get here on time. He had had to walk here himself, and he had managed to be on time.

Rizzo reflected. After he had spoken to Hartnett in the morning, he had had no illusions that the guy would be able to come up with the money to repay his gambling debts. But repayment wasn't what Domenico necessarily wanted. He wanted David Hartnett, whiz-kid Wall Street broker, in his pocket. For the future.

Now the future was here, borne on the back of an earthquake. And his pigeon was coming across the room to his table, dressed as if for an afternoon at the country club, as if the world hadn't fallen down around their shoulders. WASPs, Domenico thought, and nearly snorted aloud.

"Mr. Rizzo," Hartnett said when he reached the table. "Sorry I'm late. Lots of stuff to climb over."

"Yes, Dave, yes. And it's Dom, like I said on the phone this morning. I'm glad to see you survived in one piece. What was it like on Wall Street?"

They exchanged the banal pleasantries and stories of two survivors of a catastrophe for a few minutes. Hartnett's straight-up Chivas Regal came and he took a sip, then looked at Domenico expectantly.

"I want to go back to our conversation of this morning, Dave."

"Yessir. I need to tell you that with all that's happening I'm not going to be able to get my hands on the money to repay you quickly."

Rizzo smiled. "No matter. I'm sure we can work something out. In fact, I have an idea that might be beneficial to both of us."

"I'm open to any suggestion you might make, Dom."

"I know you are, Dave, I assure you of that."

Hartnett swallowed hard, then listened as Rizzo went on.

"I'm right in thinking that this is a time of unprecedented crisis throughout the financial world, am I not?" He waved his hand as Hartnett began to reply. "That being the case, I imagine that smart, well-educated, experienced men like yourself could take advantage of the situation."

Hartnett nodded, knowing better than to speak, and wondered what was to come.

"What would you guess the working capital of your firm to be? I mean money in banks that could easily be accessed—easily moved from one account to another?"

Hartnett made a few quick mental calculations. "Perhaps sixty million or so."

"So little? I would have thought more."

In fact, David Hartnett had lied to Domenico Rizzo, understating Kelly, Farnsworth's liquid capital by perhaps as much as forty million dollars.

"I don't believe so. Before I left the office I made duplicates of some of the most important financial records, and that figure is probably very close to accurate."

"Duplicates? Why would you have done that, Dave?" Domenico took a sip of his wine and waited for Hartnett to reply, sure that the younger man was lying.

"Only, ah, to have them in case generator power to the main bank of computers finally dies. That way, the most vital information won't be lost."

"Good thinking," Rizzo said. "And this 'vital information,' it would include account numbers and amounts in the firm's bank accounts?" Hartnett nodded. "Throughout the country?" Hartnett nodded again.

Rizzo smiled, a peculiarly sharklike grin in that otherwise cherubic face, and one that Hartnett found dangerously thrilling. He smiled back, only to see Rizzo's own turned off as if with a switch.

"And what can we do with this information during a time of chaos?"

"Most anything we want, Dom," Hartnett replied, and began to outline the plan that had been forming in his mind ever since the earthquake had struck and he had duplicated the banking information onto floppy disks.

At the end of Hartnett's explanation—and Domenico had had him go over individual points several times to ensure his own understanding—Rizzo was silent, turning the glass of red wine between his palms.

"What equipment do you need, where do you need to be to do this thing, and how long will it take you?"

Diane decided to go up to 52nd Street and crosstown to Park Avenue then walk up to 83rd Street. As she walked she tried not to look at anyone for she knew that she would have to stop if she saw someone hurt or asking for help. For most of the block no one paid any attention to her. She was in good shape, but soon it became clear that the fireman was right. She was walking an obstacle course. She saw groups of people digging with their hands and trying to hear cries from below. A man lay in front of her, wearing a navy-blue overcoat, his briefcase opened beside him with papers scattered. She bent down and touched him and realized he was dead. She walked on. Cars were tossed like toys, some up against buildings, some pancaked, some on top of one another as though picked up and placed there. A block farther, she saw three cars parked untouched, neat and orderly as if nothing had happened. Diane realized that what had happened was random, full of room for good luck and bad, one building pristine, the one next to it a death house.

It was getting colder. She reached Times Square. Her watch read five thirty-five. Twilight on the way, the area was swarming with people. She continued on, wondering if she would make it to the school before morning. It was clear that she would have to find a place to spend the night. She decided to go first to their townhouse on 63rd Street. She could change her clothes to something more practical, see if Sam or Mary were there, get some food, and go on. The darkness closed in. People had candles or flashlights, but she did not. She stumbled and fell. Picked herself up, feeling a trickle of blood run down her leg from a cut knee. Someone came alongside her and silently walked with her for a few yards, she glanced over. It was a young woman with a flashlight.

"Where you headed?" the young woman asked.

"Uptown. I'm trying to get to my son's school on Eighty-third Street. Thanks for the light. Where are you going?"

"My husband and I have an apartment on Ninety-sixth Street. We can walk together if you like."

"Would I ever." What incredible luck. She looked more closely at the young woman. About thirty, Diane guessed, well dressed, wearing a smart black cloth coat that looked none too warm. No gloves. "We could take turns holding the flashlight. That way at least three hands can go into pockets to keep warm."

The young woman stopped walking and handed the flashlight to Diane. "Thanks. My name is Karen Walker."

"Mine is Diane Taylor."

"You look awfully familiar."

"I know. I'm an actress. You may have seen me on television or in the show I'm in."

Karen Walker held out a hand and they shook hands. "That's it. I have seen you." They started walking again. "My husband and I were transferred here from Michigan for the computer firm we work for. We've only been here a year. He works down in the Wall Street area and I work on Seventh Avenue at Fifty-first Street. I walked down thirty-one flights. The building wasn't too badly damaged except for the glass that fell out into the street."

Diane shone the flashlight ahead of them as they scrambled over debris, trying to pick their way around the worst of it. The streets were filled with people, but there was an ominous silence in the late twilight. Murmuring. Groups of people moving bricks and stone away from fallen buildings. No sign of moving vehicles of any kind. How could there be, Diane realized, there is absolutely no way to reach any of these wounded, dazed, trapped people except on foot.

"I think my husband will be trying to get to Ninety-sixth Street, too," Karen said. "Don't you think so?"

"Of course. I know my husband will go first to the school."

"We haven't had any children yet. We keep putting it off. Until we make more money."

They had reached Park Avenue and 52nd Street. They paused and looked up the avenue. "My God." Diane felt her throat tighten. There were no words to express what she felt looking up Park Avenue and seeing the devastation. There was still enough light in the sky and now a full moon rising so that they could see. The Racquet Club with its Palladian arches and Greek Revival brick structure had collapsed in on itself and on the shops below it. The Lever House was standing but much of the glass was shattered, giving it the appearance of a skeleton. Across the avenue the Seagram Building stood intact, but particularly on the higher floors the glass windows had disintegrated. Up the avenue a fire blazed. Most of the large old apartment buildings were down.

Fallen onto the street. No bomb could have done more damage. "Oh, God, my beautiful city," she whispered to herself. Fear pushed her onward. She started off again and her young companion, silent now, came along with her.

An hour later they reached 63rd Street. "I'm coming with you to your house," Karen insisted. "You may need me."

"Thanks." They walked into the street and went to where the Thorne's brownstone had been. All that was left of it was a pile of debris and the front cement steps leading up to the front door and down to the kitchen door.

Diane stood on the sidewalk, tears streaming down her face. The makeup that she had applied before leaving the theater made dark smudges. Karen put her arms around her. "My Mary, oh God, Mary, is she in there somewhere? Was she going to get Danny at school? Did she go out shopping? Oh, no." Diane started to climb over the rubble, and Karen pulled her back.

"It's dangerous. You can't go in there."

She knew the young woman was right. Through her tears she saw people she knew from across the street, slowly picking the bricks and mortar up and tossing them into the street to try and reach whomever might be there. She called out, "Have you seen my housekeeper? Anyone?"

"No. Sorry. No one."

There was no option. She must go on to 83rd Street. There was nothing she could do here. "Come on," she said. "We've got to keep going. I'll be all right."

The two women went back to Park Avenue and started the walk up the middle of the avenue north, as the moon rose in the October sky.

More than half the people who had been at The Four Seasons for lunch had chosen to leave and find their way to various destinations they chose. Of the other half, seven were critically wounded, three were dead, and most of the others had superficial injuries. There were the staff of forty-one, including the partners, Margittai, von

Bidder, Julian—Paul Kovi had not been there that day. Dr. Gordon Keith and Kate Thorne, the twelve volunteers who had had some medical experience, and about twenty others who had decided to stay either to help or because they were terrified to go outside, made up the group. Meanwhile, from the offices of the Seagram Building, there was a steady stream of people walking down the stairs. Many of them were gathered in the plaza overlooking Park Avenue.

The people huddled together, some crying, some talking, all trying to come to terms with what had happened and the sights they saw from where they stood. It looked like a vast, smoldering wasteland, with occasional tall buildings rising from it. Smoke rose ominously from all over the city. The smell of gas stained the air. Many men and women were in the streets, trying to claw away rubble with their bare hands, knowing there must be people buried below, hearing faint cries for help.

The Red Cross sign hung from the awning of The Four Seasons, and a policeman came up the stairs holding a woman in his arms. "We just dug her out. Can you help?" Two waiters took her and got her to where Dr. Keith was working. They laid her down with utmost care. She was unconscious but breathing and covered with dust, so that her once dark hair was white.

Dr. Keith kneeled down beside her. He listened to her heart, took her pulse. "Her chest is crushed. Doubt she'll make it, but let's try anyway. Get her up on one of the tables, fellows." Keith had thrown his jacket aside. His white shirtsleeves were rolled up above his elbows. The chef's apron that Kate had brought him was smeared with blood.

The policeman stood for a minute while Keith worked on the woman. Keith asked him questions.

"Tell me what's going on out there? Any hope we'll get electricity or water anytime soon?"

"Jesus, no. I come from the Central Park Precinct, and we're cut off from each other, even our walkie-talkies don't work, and One Police Plaza is destroyed, I heard. Rumors are all over the place. Who knows? We got nothing. No communication, no nothing. And out there . . . it's hell, sir. I was in 'Nam and I've never seen anything like this. We're getting the dead and trying to carry them over to Central Park. The mayor's there and is trying to get the president to fly in supplies and men we need. Our precinct is the headquarters for the whole city. It's crazy. There's fires everywhere, and gas mains broke and water mains, big splits down the streets, people dead and alive under buildings and we can't . . ." He swallowed hard. "And there's already looters on Fifth. I've only been a few blocks each way on foot, and we're trying to organize workers out there from volunteers to help dig out and rescue any way we can."

Keith finished doing what he could for the woman and turned to the policeman. "What's happened to New York Hospital? Memorial Sloan-Kettering?"

"Don't know, sir. Haven't been up that far. The Fifties are terrible. All along Fifty-seventh Street and Madison those fancy shops and apartment buildings . . . they're in the street, just caved in on themselves like matchsticks."

"Good God." Keith rubbed his eyes. As though he'd asked, a waiter appeared with cups of coffee for him and the cop. On a tray. Keith started to laugh, but he stopped when he saw the shocked expressions. "Sorry. It is funny. The tray, I mean." Noncomprehension spread across the policeman's face, and the waiter grinned. "Got to keep up the standards, right?"

"Right." Keith took a gulp and felt better immediately. He surveyed the room. Margittai and the other partners were busy talking with the kitchen staff making lists of food. All the restaurant food was brought in fresh each day and there was not enough to last for more than twenty-four hours. Bottled water was rationed. The seriously injured were lying now off the floor on the capacious tabletops that had been covered with coats from the patrons and staff to make them softer, then made up with clean tablecloths for sheets. The not seriously injured were either lying or sitting in a group in the Pool Room or out in the marble lobby by the elevators or trying to make themselves useful. The dozen people who had volunteered some medical experience were all wearing aprons now, to identify them, and they were tending the patients. The women had kicked off their high heels long ago, except for one tall, statuesque beauty who had spent one terrible year at Harvard Med after she graduated from the then Radcliffe. She, head of her own publicity agency, was wearing her four-hundred-dollar five-inch heels from Charles Jourdan, as she rebandaged a man's dressing on his badly gashed leg. Ever gregarious, she was holding his rapt attention by telling him gruesomely funny stories about her early attempts to become a doctor.

Kate finished helping some people up the staircase and into the Grill Room where they sat down, exhausted. "We work on the twenty-fourth floor," one of them pointed up at the ceiling. "We had to walk down flights. You know, there are people trapped up on the twenty-fifth floor. The elevator got stuck somewhere and when I got out to the landing to go downstairs I looked back and the whole top of the brick stairwell had fallen in, like something had hit the wall there. I could hear them yelling through at us, and I couldn't hear what they were saying, but I yelled back that we were coming down and we'd tell someone that they're up there on the twenty-fifth floor."

"How many people do you think work up there?" Kate asked.

"Gosh, I'm Mr. Bates's secretary, I work on the twenty-fourth floor, and I don't know, but, Sally," she nodded at another woman, "what do you think?"

"I'd guess—well there are four offices up there, so I'd guess about fifty people."

"Fifty people trapped on the twenty-fifth floor of the Seagram Building. I suppose," Kate mused, "I suppose there are hundreds of people trapped in office buildings all over the city. And not a damn thing we can do."

Dusk had turned to darkness. Candles lighted the Grill Room, the hallway, staircase, the Pool Room, and bathrooms, which were, of course, of little use since there was no water for the toilets or the sinks. The staff had gathered trash cans from the kitchen, lined them with huge garbage bags, left piles of smaller garbage bags, for the people to use, tie with metal ties, and put in the cans to eventually move elsewhere. It was better than nothing.

People were leaving who had volunteered earlier to stay, and others were coming in to volunteer to take their places. Flashlights materialized from various sources, and as dusk came, many left to try to find their way home. There was a flow of people, in and out, quiet, not talking much, stunned, shocked into silence by what they saw around them. At the downstairs doorway and at the larger floor-to-ceiling glass doorway from Park Avenue in from the plaza, waiters stood with candles ready to show people in, say a few comforting words, get them a cup of tea or coffee, though Dr. Keith and Margittai had already started to ration both. One cup of water per person per day and they thought they could get through four days. Coffee and tea were forbidden by nightfall. Ironically what there was in great quantity were some of the finest wines in the world. They had settled on a leadership team, headed by Dr. Keith, Tom Margittai, and Alex von Bidder with Kate Thorne and two businessmen volunteers on it. All "survival policies" were to be decided on by this team, and so far no one had objected.

Food was to be rationed.

By eight o'clock that night, Gordon Keith had been on his feet for seven hours and he was exhausted. Kate watched him bend over a patient, straighten up, arch his back to ease the strain, and move on to the next table to check the person lying on it. She went to his side. When he finished, she took his arm. "You are coming over here with me." She led him over to a banquette. "Sit down and let me get you a drink." He smiled up at her.

"God, I thought you'd never ask. Whiskey, neat."

"I remember. Jack Daniel's." She disappeared and returned in moments with two glasses.

"To your health." He tapped her glass with his.

"My, what gallows humor you doctors have." She took a swallow. She shivered. "I'm cold, I suppose we all are. What the hell are we going to do? I mean, we can't just stay here. We have to go find our people, find out what's left of New York."

"Kate, there's nowhere to go. Haven't you realized that? Until there is electricity, phones, power to run the City, until the mayor or the governor or the president come up with some plan, we are all stuck here. Go out there? To do what? We're needed here with the people"—he waved an arm—"who are coming here for shelter and medical aid. It's not much, but it is better than them being on the streets in the cold, in the dark, with no law, no medical help, nothing but death and destruction around them."

"You know, I've listened to my son, Sam, talk about earthquakes for years, and I've never really believed him. Oh, sure, for the West Coast. But here? Never. I thought he was right to tell us it might happen, but I never really thought it would."

"Until today, when I was having lunch with that poor boring rich widow who was on the verge of giving New York Hospital a huge grant and now is sitting over there in her fur coat talking with some secretaries from upstairs, until that moment I had never given an earthquake a second thought. At least not here." He looked at Kate in the candlelight. "You are beautiful. As beautiful as you were the last time we met."

She looked at him without a word, remembering the one time they had met after that summer when, in New York, he had called her and they had spent the afternoon walking around the City, talking about everything except what they had on their minds, had dinner at Les Pleiades, gone to hear Barbara Carroll play jazz piano in the Bemelmans bar, and then they had gone up to her suite at the Carlyle. The next morning she had gone home to Colorado and they had not communicated since.

She took his hand and held it. "You're wrong, you know. Handsome, maybe. Good-looking, sure. Beautiful, nonsense."

"To me, Kate. I've never stopped loving you, not once, in all these years. And you?" He bent his dark head down so that it was very near her.

"You know the answer, Gordon. You don't have to ask."

He put his arm around her and drew her closer. They sat wordless for minutes. Then she said, "But I loved Daniel, too. The two feelings did not and do not seem contradictory."

He sighed. "I suppose not."

"I wonder about Sam, about my grandson, Danny, and, oh God, Gordon, everyone out there. It is too big to take in. This great city in ruins."

"Don't think. You know better, my darling mountain climber. I need you as my backup. Come on." He pulled her up beside him and kissed her. She tasted the whiskey on his lips, felt for an instant the years fall away, held him close. Then the moment was over. They made their way across the room.

Danny looked at his watch. It was early evening and through the crack in the door there was darkness and cold. He had given up getting through the door until daylight. There were no more sounds from Debbie. He shivered. His jacket covered his torso, but his legs were freezing. He put his hands deep into his pockets and curled up. Somehow, someway, he knew his dad would find him. With this certainty, Danny Thorne closed his eyes and went to sleep.

After meeting with David Hartnett, Rizzo made his way uptown to the duplex in the Trump Tower. He had walked up thirty flights and unlocked the door with apprehension, afraid Nancy might have been outside when the earthquake struck. He crossed himself and prayed as he opened the front door to the apartment that she was there and not hurt.

"Nancy?" He called out. No answer. He searched the downstairs with his flashlight. Many of the windows were smashed and the cold October night air was streaming in. She was not there. Heart pounding, he ran up the stairs. "Nan!" he called. He flung open the door to the master bedroom.

Candles burned in various parts of the large room. Her battery-operated tape deck was playing an Ella Fitzgerald tune. An open bottle of champagne sat beside it. Nancy was dressed in a blue silk caftan, and she was sitting in the armchair, one foot swinging in time with the music. "Hi, there, big boy." She pushed her auburn hair back and got to her feet. "Some earthquake we've got out there, haven't we?"

He took her in his arms in relief and felt her body go limp. He held her out from him. "Are you okay?"

"Sure. I took a nap and the next thing I knew windows were popping out into the air and I was sliding around my bed hanging onto the mattress." She giggled. "Come on, Rizzo, have a drink." She went to the champagne bottle and poured him a glass.

"You're drunk," Rizzo observed.

"Yes. I am very, very drunk." She gave him her most languid, slit-eyed smile. "Here's to us, Rizzo. We survived. People like us always survive." She raised her glass to him.

"I hate it when you're drunk," he said. "You leave me."

"Maybe. And I had a line of coke today, too. Got it from one of your bodyguards. All I had to do was whistle."

He threw the champagne glass against the wall. "No!" He went to her and grabbed her by the arm. "You can't do that to my boys. They don't understand. You're my woman, and you can't do that."

"Fuck off." She shrugged him away. "I do what I please, earthquake or no earthquake."

Rizzo stared at her. In the candlelight, her white face framed by her auburn hair, her green eyes glistening, her simple blue silk caftan flowing about her slender body, gave her the look of some unearthly creature. Even as he wanted to shake her, strike her, he felt the overwhelming desire to hold her so that she would not float away and leave him.

Calmly, gently, as though to a child, he said, "Let's go into the study where we won't be cold. Let's bring the tape deck and the candles and we'll open another bottle of champagne. Okay?"

She smiled. "Yes, big boy. Let's start a fire, and get warm and cozy and let the whole shitty world out there go to hell." She took two candles and, staggering slightly, made her way down the hall to the den.

He followed and they set candles about the inner room, he lighted the paper under the firewood and she went to the small refrigerator by the bar and selected a fresh bottle of Perrier-Jouët. With an expert touch, she uncorked it and poured the champagne into two flute glasses. She went over to him and set down his glass while she helped him off with his overcoat and took his jacket off. They sat down on the fur rug by the fire.

"Have you talked with your wife or daughter?"

As always, Nancy's swift changes of mood caught him by surprise. She sounded as sober and concerned as a priest, and yet, he knew in the next moment she could turn again into the drunken bitch-child. "No. I sent runners to the house in Oyster Bay and to Roslyn, and they'll get back here at some point. I've had to make my headquarters in this apartment for the time being. Down there, it's bad, Nan. It is real bad. I was scared that you might have gotten up early and gone out shopping or something . . ."

She put her hand on top of his. "You know I never get up if I've had a show the night before until late."

"Yeah. I was scared shitless." He looked at her. "I love you."

"You've never said that to me before."

"I know."

Nancy gazed into the flames of the fire. She turned her head and looked for a long moment into Rizzo's eyes. "I love you, too."

Rizzo opened his arms, and she moved into them and they held one another. "Damn it, babe, you scared me. I don't want to lose you," he muttered. "You drive me nuts. But I'm crazy about you."

"I know. You know," she pulled away and took her champagne glass and sipped. "You know, Rizzo, in the beginning it was just the kicks. You know, you were the most powerful Mafia boss in the City or maybe the country or maybe the world. I wanted to show you that I was able to humble you, mock you, do what I wanted with you." He tried to stop her words. "No. Don't interrupt me. I may never say any of this again to you. So listen, sir. At first it was just one great big ball. I mean you are sexy and the most secure guy I've known in the bed department. I mean you really think you are the best." She ducked her head and grinned at him and raised her glass. "And you are. But then," she took a swallow. "Then there was more. I never knew anyone, man or woman, who liked to take care of people more than you. It goes beyond a power kick for you. Yes, I know you're a killer." He reached for her to stop her from going on with a kiss, but she held up her hand. "Don't deny it, Rizzo. I know what goes on. Not from you, God knows. But Stefano told me a lot and I read the papers. I know you love the power and the crime and the big business you're in. You're not a thug, like John Gotti. You finished school, you haven't been to jail, you didn't steal cars or make book or fight in the streets on your way to the top. Of course, it helped to have had your father. But you're smarter than Gotti, smoother, and deadlier. And your family is clean, not like Gotti's brothers, who all helped bring him down." She put her fingers against his lips. "Shut up, I'm talking."

"I'll say." He grinned at her.

"You know you've changed. Two years ago you would have marched out in a snit if I'd said any of this to you."

"Where can I go? Have you noticed the earthquake below?"

"There is that." She emptied her glass and poured another. "Where was I? Oh yes. The history of Domenico Rizzo."

"Why don't you ever call me by my Christian name?"

She answered, "It's too familiar."

He shook his head.

"In the beginning, I never thought we'd last past the first month. But you kept hanging around, and I kept wondering what a nice, well-brought-up WASP like me was doing with a low-down killer like you. But then, you showed your other side to me, that take-care-of side, and I guess in my parent's house no one ever took care of little Nancy the way you do. If I have a cold you bring me a Kleenex and aspirin and chicken soup. If I feel lonely, you turn up with all that Italian charm and those strong arms to hold me. And if anybody does me wrong, you just send someone to kill him."

She grinned at him.

"Come on, babe, you know that's not true."

"No. Not yet. But you would, wouldn't you?" She moved closer to him. "Wouldn't you?"

He put his glass down and put his arms around her. "It all depends. I'll do anything to build up my image in your green eyes. If you want me to play the Godfather, I will do it for you, to keep you interested in me."

"Damn it, Rizzo, you're too smart." She nibbled his lower lip. "Let's go to bed and forget this city for tonight."

"I've got to do half an hour's work in the office, then I'll come to bed." He reached into his jacket pocket and took out the tickets for the Concorde. "There goes Paris." He tossed them into the fire.

They kissed and he went to the office to begin planning his campaign for the next few days. The opportunities he had realized were his until the City was back on its feet must be taken advantage of and quickly. One of the first jobs on his mental list was Stefano. At last, this was the perfect time to take care of getting rid of Stefano.

The sixteen floodlights that had been wired into the generator system in the park bathed the precinct house and the tents in bright artificial light. The scene was weird. With nightfall, their encampment became an oasis, reminiscent of a movie set, in the middle of dark, unimaginable chaos beyond the reassuring lights. People kept coming toward their precinct station out of the surrounding darkness, on foot, in shock, carrying the wounded, coming toward the light as for eons man had always been drawn by the promised safety and warmth of the campfire light.

Into the ring of light from the depths of darkness beyond strolled an African tiger. He stopped and looked around, somewhat blinded by the glare but drawn by the smell of blood. His proud head lifted, his nostrils flaring, he pawed the ground and moved silently into the light. Before one of the armed men could shoot him, he had leapt upon an elderly gentleman and mauled him. It took ten bullets to bring the tiger down, amid the screams of the terrified onlookers.

———

By midnight Sam Thorne returned to report to the mayor that he had set up teams in a twenty-block radius, and the civilian leaders would report to Sam each morning at an appointed time what the situations in their buildings were.

He had to walk by the medical tent. There, in the garish light, stood Dr. Kelly talking with another doctor.

"Did you get your supplies?" Sam asked.

She looked up, distracted. He saw that she did not remember the earlier scene. Then she gave him a grin. "I did indeed. Should I thank you?"

He felt the knot of anger start in his empty stomach. "Don't bother," he muttered and walked on. What a smartass woman. God, how he hated women like this doctor. About as feminine as a truck driver. He was at the precinct house door when he realized she was at his elbow. "I'm sorry. I really am thanking you now." She held out a hand.

He swallowed hard. "How're you making out?"

"Now that we've got the supplies, I'm in business. Got to go," she said, and went off to her tent.

He shook his head and went to see the mayor.

———

Danny was dreaming again. This time he was with his dad, who looked just like Harrison Ford, only with his dad's face. He had on the same clothes as the actor, including the fedora. His dad had him by the hand, and they were hiking over rough terrain, big sandstone rocks shaped like camels' backs, and tall ones like spikes planted in the desert. Everything was bathed in a greenish light. He was having trouble keeping up with his dad, who was very quiet and determined. "Where are we going?" Danny asked. "To find the Lost Ark of the Covenant." "Oh," said Danny, and held on to his father's hand as hard as he could.

Suddenly, from behind one of the great rocks came a huge bear, as tall as a tree, standing on his hind feet and waving his huge forelegs in the air. His dad took a pistol from the holster on his hip and dropped Danny's hand. Danny was frozen in fear and stood stock still. His father shot at the bear, who showed no signs of being hit and came at them. Three more shots rang out in quick succession and the bear was almost upon them. His dad shielded Danny with his own body, and then, just as the bear seemed to be ready to kill them with his huge bared teeth and long powerful claws, he dropped at their feet, making a terrible noise. "Come on," said his dad and took his hand once again. They walked around the bear's body, and Danny started to sniffle. His dad paid no attention to him but pulled him along, until Danny stumbled and fell. Then his dad kneeled down beside him. "Are you all right?" he said and gave him a hug. "It's not much farther. You are a terrific sport, Danny, and a first-rate hiker. I'm proud of you."

Danny felt a warm glow from his father's words, and he got up and put his hand back in his dad's big callused palm.

In the dream, suddenly it was night. And suddenly Danny's hand slipped out of his father's grasp and he was alone. He called, "Dad, Dad, where are you?" but there was no sound at all. The moon was out, and he could see the landscape, and way, way off he saw his father, out of earshot, walking on in that quiet determined way, to find the Lost Ark. Danny started to run after him, yelling, "Dad, Dad, wait for me!" The figure ahead of him got smaller and smaller, as Danny scrambled over the rocky ground, falling, bruising his knees, scraping his hands, and getting up panting, to try to catch up with the fast disappearing figure of his father.

Then, in front of him, as though by magic, there was another man, a tall, gaunt, evil-looking man who spoke with a German accent: "Young man, what are you doing here?"

"I'm Danny Thorne and I'm trying to find my father."

"Ah, yes, the young Thorne lad. And your father must be Sam

Thorne, the archaeologist. Well, I'm one too, and I believe we are both looking for the same thing, so you come along with me and we'll find him." The man stepped forward to take Danny's hand.

Instinctively Danny shrank back. "No, I don't want to go with you."

"Don't be silly." The skinny tall man scooped Danny up under his arm and started off after Danny's father.

"Help! Put me down. I don't want to go with you. Help!"

Danny woke up with a start. He lay curled between the toilet and the steel door, and he was cold and terrified. Hunger clawed at his stomach. He rubbed his eyes. It was a dream. He realized that, and he remembered where he was and what had happened to him. He sat up. It was nighttime and very still. He was very thirsty and scooped up a handful of water out of the toilet. He poked his head outside the door. "Debbie? Can you hear me?"

Silence. He pushed the door but could not get out. He sat back down on the floor and put his head on his knees. His dad would come and get them both soon. He knew that, and soon he fell asleep again, this time a dreamless slumber that lasted the rest of the night.

———

After Allen Young returned to the track bed, the small group of survivors he and Evie Lincoln were leading proceeded to walk north on the local tracks. The water continued to rise although the smell of gas that had assaulted Allen on the emergency exit ladder grew progressively fainter.

Their progress was painfully slow—several times one or another of the party fell—and it was after nine o'clock on the night of the first day by the time they reached the 23rd Street platform. Twice they passed parties of survivors headed in the opposite direction and both times paused to exchange information. The general consensus was that the unthinkable had happened—an earthquake had struck the City with such force that the entire subway system, and God knew what else, had been put out of commission.

The platform at the 23rd Street station was empty, whether because a train had just picked waiting passengers up or because those there had deserted it after the quake, they couldn't decide, nor, in reality, did it matter. What did matter was that huge amounts of debris had poured down the entrance stairways on both the uptown and downtown sides, leaving them completely blocked.

They sat for a while on the platform to rest. Fortunately the tunnel was, if not particularly warm, at least not cold. Even so, wet as they were, they all were shivering. Neither side of the station had a kiosk. They were without food and were very hungry.

Allen and Evie sat a bit apart from the rest of the group and close to each other. Allen had taken Evie's hand and was playing gently with her fingers. Evie's thoughts drifted from wondering about the fate of her family to an intense awareness of the man, the stranger sitting next to her. What if he hadn't been on the train, in the same car with her? Would she be here now, part of a group of survivors, or would she have fallen victim to the boy who tried to snatch her purse? And what would come of holding hands with this man? She couldn't deny, even to herself, that she felt an attraction to him. Was it simply because of the circumstances, or would she have been drawn to him even if they had met in court? Maybe this was the one she had been waiting for, the one who could soften her sense that she could only rely on herself.

"What should we do?" she asked, finally.

He sat quietly for a few seconds before replying. "I think we should move on. The people we've met so far hadn't been on a train any farther than the few blocks north of here and they had come directly downtown. So we don't know whether or not the stations in the direction we're going are just as bad as this one or might provide a way to escape. What do you think?"

"I agree with you." She placed her other hand over the two clasped ones and rested her head on his shoulder. "Staying here would be useless and we should push on as far as we can while everyone still has the energy. Of course, it would be nice to tell the rest of them to keep walking and we'll catch up with them."

"Ummm. Very nice. However . . ."

"Yes, I know. Duty calls. Once a Marine, always a Marine."

Evie kissed him quickly on the cheek, then stood up and walked to the small group huddled together. She was surprised when Allen didn't follow to take charge and decided she would talk with them herself.

"Allen and I think we should keep going. We can't accomplish

222

anything here, and who knows when rescue parties will start to look for people in the tunnels. Mary?" she said to the woman closest to her.

"Anything that will get us out of here, I'm for."

"Bill?"

"Let's go."

One by one the others agreed to leave the platform, though the thought of wading through calf-deep water held no appeal for any of them. Allen rejoined them and they made their way to the north end of the platform.

"It's five blocks to the Twenty-eighth Street station. At the rate we've been walking, it will take us about two hours to get there, provided, that is, that there's nothing blocking the tunnel. On that, we just have to take our chances."

"Won't we reach the train those other people left?" asked Jake.

"Yes. We can decide when we get there whether or not we want to board it, perhaps spend the night in one of the cars if they're not flooded. I know this sounds ghoulish, but one thing we should look for is dry clothing, not so much to change into as to cover ourselves with when we finally do rest for the night."

"What you're saying," said Gerta, "is that we should take what we can find from any dead bodies, yes?"

"Yes, in a nutshell. Let's not think about it and just get started. If we're lucky, we won't need to do anything of the kind."

The train the other groups of people had left was on the downtown express tracks, almost directly opposite the 28th Street station. Allen led them all to the platform on the uptown side. He looked at his watch, thankful that it had an LED display.

"Twelve thirty. I don't think we should try to get any farther tonight."

"What about the entrances?"

"Believe me, Peg," Evie said, "if there was an unblocked one, we'd know it." She turned to Allen. "You're planning to do something, aren't you?"

"Yes," he replied. "Bill, Jake, are you up to coming with me to explore that train? And the opposite platform, though I doubt there'll be anything different from what we have here."

Both Bill and Jake assented, and the three men descended once again to the trackbed.

Miraculously when they reached the train they found it upright and still attached car-to-car throughout its length. They climbed aboard through the first open door they found and Allen shone his flashlight around.

The car was empty. Several pools of drying blood were on the benches and floor. They walked to one end and passed through to the next car, which had been the lead one of the train. Like the one they had left, it, too, was empty. The motorman's door hung open and they decided that he had probably led one of the parties they had encountered on the tracks.

They turned back and, car by car, explored the entire train. While there was more blood, there was neither a living nor a dead soul on it.

Ten minutes later they were on the platform with the five women. Like the 23rd Street station, the platform of this one was a relatively narrow strip of concrete without a vendor's stall for newspapers and snacks. The women had established and already used a latrine area and the men had gotten rid of as much debris as possible from one part of the platform so that they would all have a reasonably smooth place to lie down.

Bill Cohen asked to borrow the flashlight and walked up the platform. "Hey," he called back. "One of you guys come up here."

Jake moved to join him and the rest of the group could hear them moving chunks of fallen concrete around. A few minutes later, stumbling as they came, they returned with a wooden bench that had been partially buried under the fallen ceiling.

"If we've lugged this damn thing down here and nobody has a lighter . . ." said Jake.

"I have one," said Marisa. "Juan was always losing his so I carried an extra." She gave it to Bill Cohen, who put it in his shirt pocket.

"First we have to break the bench up, make a pile."

"Just like Boy Scouts," added Jake. "What about kindling?"

Bill had begun to tear the arms off the bench, an easy job since it was rickety.

Gerta and Mary stacked a portion of the wood in the center of the cleared space and Bill put the rest of it to the side to be added later. Then he leaned over and flicked the lighter, adjusting the flame to a two-inch length. He had been right; the wood from the bench, which might have once been painted, caught quickly and they soon had a comforting and warming modest bonfire going.

"Well don't we all look a sight," said Jake. "But enough said. I need to get some sleep." He turned to Allen. "Are we rotating the fire watch, General?"

"Yes. I'll take the first four hours. I'd suggest we double up on the watch. Evie," he said, before anyone else could volunteer. "Would you take this one with me?" She agreed, and Bill and Peg said that they could be awakened at five that morning to take the watch over. Wood would be added sparingly to the fire in the hope that it would stay alight for the entire eight hours before they continued uptown.

They said their goodnights, each making him or herself as comfortable as possible, then settled down to sleep or at least rest.

Evie and Allen sat near the fire, feeding it from time to time with a piece from the bench. For the first hour or so they were silent, content with the nearness of each other and unwilling to talk and possibly keep the others from sleep. Finally, when the breathing from the rest of their group was steady and peaceful, Evie broke the silence.

"Do you think we'll make it?"

"Yes, somehow. Sooner or later we'll find an exit that isn't blocked, even if we have to walk up to—where is it, about One hundred twentieth Street—where the line goes aboveground."

"What about gas?"

Allen pondered before he spoke. "Gas, electricity, steam—we can't count any of those things out. But even with all the blockage, there's bound to be air getting in from small openings to the surface here and there. Those should draw the gas out, since it tends to rise."

They were silent again for a while, each wrapped up in thoughts of his or her own. Allen added several small pieces of bench to the fire. As he stared into it, he thought about fires he had sat around as a child growing up in the rural South, as a Marine on training exercises. How different. Not only because he had this beautiful woman beside him, but because all the ghost stories he had heard from his fellow campers and all the strategies he and his brother officers had planned had not really prepared him for the reality of what he was in. He did know one thing, though. Somehow he would get them out or, more accurately, get *her* out, and when he did, he would never let her be far from him again.

"Tell me about yourself," he said to Evie. "You managed to get my short history out of me before the wreck, but other than who you are and what you do, I don't know anything about you. And I feel I'd like to know more. When we get out of this, I'd . . ."

"Shh," Evie whispered. "Let's worry about what we're going to do when we get out when we really do get out." She paused, then started. "If you promise to tell me your story, I'll tell you mine." He nodded.

"By the time I was born, my father was already something of a force in New York politics, so my life has always been more public than I'd have liked. People always thought of me as Bruce Lincoln's daughter rather than Evie Lincoln, and as Bruce Lincoln's daughter, I had to live up to certain standards—certain *black* standards. I think they're harder than standards for white people because white people are always expecting black people to slip, to live up—or down—to what their expectations of black people are.

"It's made me a bit of a racist, I guess, or maybe *racist* isn't the right word. But I'm very aware of being a 'prominent black' "— here she let her fingers form the quotation marks—"in white society."

"Why law? And why criminal law?"

"Partly family tradition, I guess, the idea of going into public service. Also the realities of practicing law as a black woman in this city. You're relatively new here, but did you realize that in the twenty-five or so largest law firms in New York, there are scarcely a dozen black partners among over two thousand? Even at the level of associate, if all five thousand-plus were gathered in a room together, there wouldn't be a hundred and fifty black faces.

"When I was in law school, I spent my vacations working as a para for Conrad Harper, you know, he's the first black president of the City Bar Association, when he was with Simpson, Thatcher and

Bartlett. Conrad and my father go back a long way, and he spent lots of hours trying to convince me to go into private practice. Said that I could be one of the ones who could make it in that world, both as an African-American and as a woman. But I kept looking around me whenever I was there. Boy, you *know* that place was a hotbed of white Protestantism."

"Don't call me 'boy,' " Allen said, and they both laughed softly.

"They couldn't have been nicer—after all, I was Conrad's protégée, black, white, or green—but I still never felt entirely comfortable there. Nothing overt, just different."

Allen nodded as he stared into the firelight. "Like the Marines," he said.

"Anyway, I said a polite no to Conrad when the time came for making a decision and marched myself down to the D.A.'s office without any introduction from my father and got myself a job. I love it, I hate it, but it's made me think about things that I was always sheltered from."

"And you'll keep doing it?"

"For a while, yes."

"Politics?"

"In the blood, I'm afraid, but not right away."

"What's right away?"

She, too, had been staring into the fire. Now she looked at him, the light dancing across both their faces. "That remains to be seen."

San Francisco Chronicle,
October 5, 1994

MASSIVE 7.4 EARTHQUAKE DEVASTATES NEW YORK CITY.
THOUSANDS KILLED OR INJURED.
PRESIDENT SENDS IN TROOPS.
EVACUATION UNDER WAY.

At 1:21 P.M. this afternoon East Coast time a major earthquake registering 7.4 on the Richter Scale hit New York City. The earthquake's epicenter is thought to be on Manhattan and probably along a major east/west fault line along 125th Street, striking with devastating force both the heart of the city and Brooklyn and Queens to the south, as well as the Indian Point nuclear facility to the north.

From the early reports the major shock lasted about 90 seconds and was followed almost immediately by a lesser but still strong aftershock. All communication with New York has been cut off. At this time the loss of life is incalculable. The city is without electricity or water. Fires caused by broken gas mains are rampant. From aircraft reconnaissance ordered by the President many of the tall buildings, built on bedrock and constructed of steel, are standing, among them the World Trade Center, Empire State, Chrysler, and Pan Am buildings. Many more landmark structures such as the Seagram Building, Lever House, and Trump Tower are still standing. However, these buildings constructed since the late 1950s with glass façades have caused massive death and injury from the glass, which shattered during the quake and rained down on the people in the streets. Further fatalities and injuries have been caused by falling ornaments from pre–World War II buildings decorated with gargoyles, cherubs, and other attachments. Water towers have crashed into the streets. There are many crevasses running parallel to the fault line.

It is reported that Mayor Bruce Lincoln and other leaders of the City were able to fly by helicopter from a ceremony being held at Tate Acres to Central Park where they have set up an emergency headquarters. It has not been confirmed, but is believed that One Police Plaza, the Police Department's headquarters, which housed the City's formal Command Center for such an emergency, was destroyed, and that Police Commissioner John Mahoney is dead. Early reports are that the Central Park Precinct has been taken over as the emergency headquarters for the City. The devastation of much of Harlem, the East Side, Greenwich Village, the West Side along the Park and Riverside Drive, and much of Wall Street and the Financial District is complete.

All night long the lion made its stealthy way through the darkness of the park, stopping in a random way to kill two dogs and a cat that crossed his path. The lion had been in captivity so long that he was confused by his freedom, but the grass under his feet was a welcome change from cement, and he drank from the lake with pleasure. After one of his meals he lay down behind some rock outcroppings and napped. Some hours later he awakened, stretched, and padded off in a northward direction, toward Harlem, where by daylight he would reach the edge of the park and halt his slow progress, as frightened by the streets and milling people as they would have been of him had they seen him. Only hunger the next day would force the lion from the leafy glade in the park where he settled down to rest.

THE SECOND DAY

loyd's of London, the insurance underwriting group, placed damage at $200 billion in Manhattan alone.

Governor George Fleming, rushing home from a trade mission in Paris, said on Thursday engineers should have taken severe earthquake into their plans years ago. "I had assumed that most buildings in Manhattan were constructed with adequate standards so they could withstand a quake of this severity."

As emergency crews clawed through the rubble, workers thought they heard a woman's voice from a crushed car on the entrance to the George Washington Bridge. They found the noise came from a CB radio.

In another car crushed on the entryway to the Brooklyn Bridge, a child's dead mother was cut in half by power saws in order to reach and save ten-year-old Juan Rosario's life. His right leg was amputated in order to extract him from the wreckage of his family's car. "It was hell to be there," said Dr. Jim Backus, an emergency physician with EMS.

"Psychological aftershocks," that ranged from relief and disbelief to anxiety, anger, nightmares, and shock afflict the survivors. "It's like the rug is pulled out from under you—your world gets shaken," said Estelle Rubin, a psychologist with a practice in Manhattan, who has been treating victims of the earthquake. "It forces you to confront your own mortality, that bad things happen to good people, that you are not in control of many aspects of life." She added, "People who survive unscathed often display disbelief of surrounding destruction, followed by relief, then guilt that they lived while others died. There is no one to get angry at."

It was after midnight by the time Diane and Karen reached 80th and Park Avenue. They were slowed down by not only the obstacles in their path but by the cold and their exhaustion and hunger. Several times one of them would fall. Their legs were cut and bruised. They held on to each other now as they walked. Suddenly out of the dark came a voice. "Hold it, ladies." A flashlight shone in their faces. "You just hand over your money and jewels and there won't be any problem."

Diane had always had a problem with what her mother called "inappropriate laughter." It had tripped her up in church, in school, and often on stage. She burst out laughing now, doubled over until it hurt.

"Lady, are you crazy or what. Just hand over what you got."

She gasped and took a deep breath. Karen was already handing them a gold necklace and her money. Diane had left her pocketbook at the theater, putting her wallet in her fur coat pocket. "Here, cocksucker," she threw the money from her wallet on the glass-littered ground. "Take it." She felt the blow across her face and she fell.

"Don't you backtalk to me, you cunt. What have you got round your neck and on your fingers, bitch."

She unclasped the necklace Sam had given her for her birthday—diamonds and rubies—and took off the antique ring that she had lied to Sam about, telling him that her producer had given it to her for the play's first night, when in fact, Tony had given it to her. "Here." She got to her feet. "That's all we have. Sorry I offended you." She rubbed her jaw. She felt Karen's hand under her arm tugging her away. She was about to vent some more anger on the thug, but thought better of it, and he disappeared down the avenue.

"Come on, Diane. He could have killed us."

She could tell Karen thought she was a little mad, too. Well, why not. The world had gone mad.

Father Diaz had debated for a few minutes Wednesday afternoon about how to handle his situation. He had enough insulin to get him through a few hours. He was a brittle diabetic, one whose system was extremely sensitive to both insulin and the changes in his blood sugar. He had already had some fruit and cheese from the splendid kitchen. To monitor his condition was difficult but he knew he must eat, and eventually he must have insulin. Therefore, should he bring it up now to try to get a solution, or wait, in the hope of avoiding bringing his own physical problem, not yet dire, to the attention of people who could do nothing about it until help came? By nature he loathed bringing this kind of attention to himself. His brain told him that he had better begin trying to find a solution now rather than waiting if he wanted to survive.

The devastation in the city below them was horrendous. He yearned to get down out of the building to where he could be of some use. When the Saudi prince and his official group collected their wits and courage, they had gone into a small office room where for some reason the window glass was still intact. They looked through two sets of binoculars Prince Makthoum usually used at the great race tracks of Ireland and France, and they saw the City in ruins. Smoke rose over the City from east to west, north to south. The great towers of the Empire State, the Chrysler Building, AT&T, the Trump Tower stood in stark contrast to the flattened Plaza Hotel. The blocks where nothing stood at all. The Lever Building was like a metal scarecrow, nothing but steel beams, the glass walls gone, fallen into the streets. They could see through the binoculars people in that building huddled toward the walls, and below, a steady stream of those who could walk down the stairs and out onto Park Avenue.

By six o'clock, Father Diaz had drawn the prince to one side, told him of his problem, and they had enlisted the aide to the prince to try to help find a solution.

There was no way to communicate with the outside world, and no ability to judge when the situation would change. The aide came up with the idea to drop a note through the mailbox shaft by the elevators in the hope that someone in the lobby of the building would find it.

The message had been dropped and by midnight there was no response—though what precisely that response would or could have been there was no way to figure. As it was, a team of office workers had formed on the twenty-fifth floor and they were systematically removing the bricks that were blocking the viable staircase, though huge chunks of mortar were unmovable. There was a terrible sense of frustration, and moving the bricks helped.

Father Diaz was not surprised at the toughness and courage of these New Yorkers, but it was moving to him to see young secretaries, after a few moments of weeping, pull themselves together and set about trying to help others; to see the incredible humor of these people start to surface in the face of a disaster beyond any they could have known. He knew all about natural disasters from avalanche to earthquake to starvation. But these Americans were amazing. Every one of these people had loved ones below in the streets, in houses, wherever, and no way to know if they were dead or alive. Adversity seemed to bring out the best in these New York people. He was impressed.

He was also beginning to be afraid. He was not afraid to die. But he had so much left to accomplish for his beloved countries before he left this earth.

Below in the plaza facing Park Avenue people moved about, trying to clean up the glass, which in some places was still ankle deep. Some people bedded down for the night against the outer wall of the Seagram Building, huddling together for warmth. Father Diaz went to the prince. Soon the aide was tying a handwritten message to six paperweights: HELP! FATHER DIAZ TRAPPED ON 25TH FLOOR. DESPERATELY NEEDS INSULIN. TRY TO GET THIS MESSAGE TO EMERGENCY MEDICAL SERVICE. Then the aide threw the six messages out into the October air. One of the paperweights fell within inches of someone below. The person opened the message, read it, and looked upward—the moon was in his eyes. He started off toward 52nd Street and disappeared.

The prince said to Father Diaz, "I pray to Allah you are going to get your insulin."

"I wouldn't put anything past these Americans," Father Diaz smiled back. "They are very special people, are they not?"

"I think New Yorkers are the smartest, hardiest people I have ever met, except in the desert. The Bedouin are as good. But apart from the Bedouin, I'd rather have a New Yorker by my side in a fight than any other sort of person," the prince intoned in his clipped British accent picked up during his education at Eton and Cambridge. "Now, I think we should have a cup of tea, don't you?" He waved his guest ahead of him toward the kitchen.

———

Kate Thorne was making bandages out of cloth napkins. There was no point trying to sleep. The Four Seasons, lighted by candles, was filled with people. The Pool Room and the Grill Room were packed with wounded and people coming in from the cold. A man in a down jacket approached her.

"Someone from above in the building threw this down." He handed her the message, which she read.

"Thank you, young man. You look chilled. Go over there," she pointed to the open French rosewood paneled door to the kitchen, "and they will give you something to drink and eat."

She made her way to Dr. Keith. He was trying to talk a young woman into taking a pill for pain—her shoulder was dislocated and she was in agony but resisting. "I'll be all right. Give that to someone who needs it more."

"For Christ's sake, it's only an Advil, take it!" growled the doctor. "Then I'm going to try to pop your shoulder back in. You'll need the pill, believe me." He turned and looked down at Kate. "Tell her."

Kate smiled at the young girl. "Do what he tells you to do. I always do." She smiled up at Keith. "Read this, please."

"Oh, my God. Insulin. That's like asking for uranium. And how the hell would we get it to him?"

"We can ask if anyone here has diabetes and has a supply of insulin to share. Then we worry how to get it up there. Father Diaz is important, Gordon, he is more important to the world than almost anyone I can think of. We have to try."

Wearily, Gordon Keith went to Alex von Bidder. He, in turn, went to the balcony overlooking the restaurant and the waiters, alerted, went through the crowd asking for quiet. Von Bidder's accented voice called out. "Has anyone here got some insulin they don't need until we can get more tomorrow?"

No response.

"We have a man trapped on the twenty-fifth floor who will die by daybreak if we can't get some insulin to him."

A voice came from a waiter who was leaning over a banquette table. Someone who was lying on the table, his head bandaged, was speaking into the waiter's ear. The waiter listened, then stood up straight. "This man has insulin, and he has offered it for the man upstairs."

Kate Thorne was in the basement below The Four Seasons. The superintendent, Joe, was showing her the equipment the men who were working on the bank of stairs on the north side of the building had left. Joe thought this slender woman with short gray hair dressed in baggy green trousers and a chef's white jacket was crazy. She must be old enough to be his mother, and she was scurrying around the equipment like a teenager at a hop, picking up, studying, discarding bolts, screws, rope. She was talking to herself under her breath. Eventually she amassed a pile of equipment in a corner away from the great machinery that was normally used to heat and cool and light the building. "Now, for the kitchen," she announced to Joe. "Don't let anyone touch those things," she pointed toward the pile of coiled rope and other bits and pieces she had chosen.

"I won't, lady. Do you mind telling me what you're going to do with this stuff?"

"Not at all." She smiled her dazzling smile up at him, the tanned skin by her deep blue eyes crinkling at the corners. "I'm going to climb up the north stairwell to the twenty-fifth floor to take some medicine to a great man."

Joe shook his head. "Not on my watch, you're not. I know we're all a little nuts tonight, but I'm not letting any pretty lady like you get killed on some crazy mission. You just calm down and we'll get someone else to—"

Kate's eyes blazed. "Like a man? There is no man, or woman for that matter, here who can climb up that stair shaft except me." She raised her open palm for him to see the calluses ingrained. "The police are in the streets but no sign of a fireman and if they do arrive it is going to be too late, and even they are not prepared to free climb up twenty-five flights. I am. I climb mountains." She gave Joe a forgiving grin. "I know I don't look strong, but by God I am and if you want to check me out ask Mr. Margittai. Now I have to get some things from the kitchen."

Joe watched her slight form march up the short flight of stairs to the ground floor. He shook his head again. What a woman!

Kate cornered the Swiss chef, Christian "Hitsch" Albin, in the kitchen. He and the thirty-five others who worked each day in The Four Seasons kitchen had had their hands full since the earthquake struck. The two executive chief cooks, the two announcers, and the assistants to them had been following Tom Margittai's orders: all food was to be sorted through and rationed. There was fresh baked bread and rolls, large amounts of salad and soup, some already cooked meat and fish that had been about to be served when the earthquake struck; the service bar in the kitchen was being used as a command station for all liquor, wine, soft drinks, and food being dispensed under the careful eye of Julian. They had large stores of nonalcoholic beverages and every known kind of liquor and the best wine cellar in the City, or one of them. Alex von Bidder had ordered the latter put under careful guard, since the inclination to get roaring drunk in the circumstances was understandable.

Kate looked at her watch. It was 1:41 A.M. There was no time to lose. She spoke in flawless French to the chef. "I need your help. I think you may have things here which I can use. My name is Kate Thorne. I am an excellent climber and I must attempt to get through the north stairwell to the twenty-fifth floor. I choose that stairwell because it is under reconstruction of some kind and I believe I will have a better chance of finding places to hammer in my handmade pitons."

Forty-nine-year-old Chef Albin had his big red hands on his hips and he was leaning back on the balls of his tired feet. Now he had heard everything. He answered in perfect English.

"My dear lady, how can I help since I can see you're determined? By the way, please call me Hitsch. Everyone else does."

She smiled. "I intend to rappel up the shaft. I need heavier clothing. Better-fitting boots. I need loops for the rope and since I have no pitons I must make some. I would think some stainless-steel carving knives or forks would do if Joe downstairs had a good hammer and pliers. I can use a couple of your young men here to help me, if you can spare them. Try to give me smart young men, okay, my friend."

Chef Albin clapped his hands loudly and several waiters and busboys gathered around Kate and him. In minutes they had rounded up heavier trousers and a thick wool shirt for Kate and one of the women waiters had some excellent light boots she used to walk to work in that fit Kate perfectly. They had high, well-padded ankles and composition rubber cleated soles. The waiters chosen by the chef, Barry and Ted, had taken the most suitable stainless-steel dining-table knives and forks to Joe, who was bending them into loops. Kate was inspecting all the kitchen equipment for possible pitons. She knew that she would be using the cracks between the bricks both for friction for her feet and to pound the homemade pitons into the grouting. She chose the sharpest implements she could find and took two small hammers from Joe.

By this time a crew had been created by Kate, and excitement mounted. Joe, Chef Albin, Barry, and Ted were completely immersed in their tasks for Kate—they might just as well be my beloved Sherpas, she thought, as she took deep breaths in an attempt to relax. She had two vials of insulin and a hypodermic needle packed with great care by Barry in Ziploc bags lined with much paper toweling so that no blow or fall would break them. She knew she had to make a harness for herself and that it would not be very good, but she had to have one to distribute the force from the rope to her body in case she fell. Since she would be climbing alone without a belayer to help, to take in the rope and play it out for her so that it was neither too tight nor too slack, she needed to use one of her greatest skills—knot tying. She went over to the ropes she had selected and started practice tying.

Gordon's voice startled her concentration. "What in God's name are you doing?" He was still wearing the bloodstained chef's apron and his face was drawn with exhaustion. "What is this?" He gestured toward the piles of accumulated equipment.

"Darling, don't be upset. I'm just taking a little climb up to the twenty-fifth floor to give the insulin to Father Diaz."

He ran a hand over his brow in disbelief. "You must be mad. I missed you and asked Alex where you were and he said to look in the basement, for God's sake. You can't be serious, Kate. With this equipment?"

She took his arm and walked him away from the others. "Listen, I can do it. You know I'm not trying to break my neck. But without this medicine . . . well, Diaz is our best hope of stopping the endless corruption of drugs and terrorism that is ruining our world more than any earthquake could. I must try to save him, Gordon. You would do the same if you could." She held his arm and looked up at him. "You know you would."

He put his arm around her. "No. I don't think so. But you are Kate Thorne and nothing is going to stop you from doing what you think is right. Nothing." He held her close. "How well I know that nineteenth-century rectitude of yours and how much it has cost us."

Kate's voice was muffled against his chest. "I can't help it. It's the way I was raised."

He laughed and she stepped back. And then laughed too. "Wish me luck, darling."

"I love you."

"And I you." They kissed and then she left him quickly to return to her team.

On the twenty-fifth floor Father Diaz was lying down on one of the sofas in the office of Prince Makthoum. He was becoming drowsy and his breathing was heavy. A sweet smell lingered about his person. He had asked one of the aides to read to him to keep him awake. From time to time he forced himself to sit up and take some soup. He was fighting as hard as he could the lassitude that threatened to envelop him.

Kate had told them to leave her alone before she started the ascent. Many years of experience had taught her the importance of a few moments of meditation. She sat with her legs stretched out in front of her, her back straight, her eyes closed for ten minutes, her mantra repeated in her mind and then her mind at rest.

She got up and gave her equipment one last check. She unlaced her borrowed boots and made sure the two pairs of clean white socks were smooth around her feet. She laced the boots up again carefully, not too tight or too loose. She had fashioned a rope harness by passing it around her waist, making a loop on the "live" lower end, passing that end up through the loop, and tying a bowline. She backed up the bowline knot with a stopper grapevine knot. She passed the rope over both shoulders and down to her waist, securing it again with these knots, and fastening a steel loop made from a knife to the apex of the harness. It was fortunate the rope used by the construction workers was perfect for Kate's purposes, made of nylon, a smooth sheath of tightly braided fibers, fitted over a more loosely plaited core of straight nylon filaments. It was elastic enough to make her knots easy to make, and she knew that was the key to her safety.

She had worked out her method of ascent. The simplest kind of climbing without aid of a belayer above her, or nuts to fasten, or carabiners, a snap-link to clip the rope. Back to the essentials when Kate had gone on her first climbs with her grandfather up Pikes Peak in the early 1940s. She felt a strange sense of exhilaration. She felt this always before a climb, but the simplicity of this one, even though it was in a dark stairwell in a city and not in the stark sunlight and snow of the Alps, made her anticipation intense.

She checked her flashlight, fastened the row of pitons around her waist and the small hammer Joe had provided. She would place one piton as high as it would go above her and then another a foot below. Then if the one she was hanging from failed, there would be a good chance the top piton would hold. Each piton had been fashioned so that the sharp, knifelike end tapered back to a steel loop through which another loop hung—Kate would use an Italian hitch knot to fasten the rope through the loop as she ascended the face of the stairwell.

Now she carried the rope to the foot of the stairwell. She decided to use an Alpine coil and carry the rope on her back fastened by another rope over her shoulder and tied at her waist—she would need as much mobility as she could get for her arms and hands. She shone her flashlight on the brick façade of the stairwell. The earthquake had loosened much of it and some bricks had fallen into the stairwell, but she climbed over them and reached as high over her head as she could manage, tapping the first piton firmly into the cement grouting. Then the piton underneath. The rope tied through the loop of the highest piton and again through the loop of the lowest piton. With a sharp intake of breath, Kate Thorne used her controlling hand to hoist herself against the side of the wall, her feet braced against the wall. She maintained three points of contact with the wall—either two hands and a foot, or two feet and a hand—at all times. She put as much weight on her legs as possible and used them rather than her arms to lift her body—she knew that on this steepest of climbs it was imperative to conserve her arm strength. The bricks gave her feet traction. She brought her body close to the wall and took small steps up the face of the wall until she was level with the first piton. She took another piton, reached well beyond the top one, and tapped it in.

By the time an hour had gone by, Kate Thorne was halfway up the stairwell. It was strange, climbing in the dark. The stairwell was cold and dank. She could not wear gloves as they would impede her knot tying. Testing the grouting with experienced fingers, at times shoving her hands into cracks she found to pull herself up, her fingers were raw and bleeding.

As she shone her flashlight and saw the numerals nineteen painted in the red on the wall, she felt the lower piton give way and her body fell ten feet before she felt the higher piton hold and managed to swing her feet back to the wall. Her breath came in gasps. The harness had held but it had tightened around her rib cage and she was in pain now. It was one thing to fall as she had done many times with a belayer above her to hold the rope, climbers below her to yell encouragement, the crucial team spirit which invested each climb with special meaning for all climbers, and the beauty of the mountains surrounding her. A dark, dank stairwell, alone, hanging on for a terrifying instant over a twenty-story abyss, was quite a different experience. She forced herself to whisper the word *relax* over and over again. She knew that it was the climber's mind that made the difference. Her body was trustworthy. It was the mind that played tricks.

In a short time her breath calmed and she resumed tapping in the pitons and making sure but agonizingly slow progress. At last she reached the twenty-fifth floor and hoisted herself onto the landing. She stood up, flexing her knees for moments, then brought the rope up and coiled it on the landing for her descent. She unhitched herself from it and opened the door onto the wide gray linoleum of the twenty-fifth floor.

She went to the center office marked in gilt letters Aramdis Oil Corporation on its floor-to-ceiling glass doors, one of which had a large crack down its length. She pushed the intact door open with a bleeding hand and marched inside.

A young man in a dark suit looked at her with amazement.

"Hurry. I am here with the medicine for Father Diaz," she ordered.

"Come this way." He led her into a small office where candles lighted the room and the father lay on the sofa. She knelt by his side and took the hypodermic needle, filled it swiftly with a small amount of insulin—she had often provided medical care on climbs, as every mountaineer had to have this knowledge—and injected him with it. Too much would kill him. He could take another shot in a few minutes.

The prince stood watching this scene with disbelief. Where had this woman come from? It was a miracle. Tears began to run from his dark eyes down his plump cheeks.

The descent was much faster and easier a rappel than the ascent, and Kate Thorne arrived at the first floor by 4:25 A.M. As she came from the second floor down, she could hear the cheers from below. A chant that made her laugh with pure joy. "Kate, Kate, Kate." She dared a glance down and saw candles lighting their faces. She jumped the last two feet. Surrounded by her team, Barry and Ted, the chef and Joe, they put their arms around her and each other, kissing and hugging one another.

"My God, you are fabulous!" said the chef, now in French.

They stepped back as Dr. Keith made his way to Kate. He put his arms around her and hugged her. She felt suddenly faint, very tired, every muscle giving way. He picked her up and carried her into the restaurant, where people stood and cheered her. Tom Margittai rushed over and cleared a place for her to be seated and Julian appeared as though by magic with a mug of steaming tea laced with brandy. She sipped it and basked in the fame to which she was accustomed. After all, she had been on the famous ascent in 1970 of Annapurna's south face and in 1975 reached the summit of Mount Everest; when she descended in the first instance the Prince of Wales was there to greet her and in the second instance Sir Edmund Hillary and Sherpa Tenzing Norgay.

By candlelight, Alex von Bidder had shown Kate and Gordon up to the White Horse Tavern on the fourth floor. It was a sumptuous suite of rooms where the Bronfmans held special meetings and social events. All agreed that Kate needed to rest after her climb. She allowed them to think she did, even though after the drink Julian had given her, she felt extremely well. What she really wanted was a hot bath to iron out the muscle aches she knew she would have in a few hours.

"Here you are. There is a small refrigerator here with a few things in it that won't have spoiled. Make yourself at home, and rest," Alex said and left them. They set candles around the room.

"You are the one who needs the rest," said Kate and led Gordon by his hand to a long, ample couch. "You've been on your feet nonstop. Come on, now, lie down and put your feet up and I'll give you a back rub. I'm very good at it. My Sherpa showed me the best method I've ever found."

Gordon did not resist. He sat down and unlaced his shoes. "I should go back down soon. When morning comes a lot more people will find their way here. And I damn well hope the EMS gets here with some supplies and more medical personnel."

"Lie down." Kate went into the bathroom and came back with a bottle of witch hazel. She pulled off his socks and slapped some of it on her hands and began to massage his feet.

"That feels fantastic. Cold, but fantastic."

"Complaints, complaints. Just be quiet and close your eyes and pretend you're in Japan."

"Some geisha."

"Take off your shirt, please, and turn over."

"Hey, lady, wait a minute. Aren't you being fresh for the first date."

"Shut up and do as I say," she leaned down and kissed his ear. "Oh, all right, I'll help you." She unbuttoned his shirt buttons slowly, looking into his wide-open eyes. She leaned down again and kissed his nipples, running her tongue gently around each one, very slowly and delicately.

"Christ," he groaned. "I think I'm being seduced."

"You bet you are." Kate straightened up. He reached up and unbuttoned the man's shirt she had borrowed from the waiter. She undid her bra and tossed it aside. "Darling, I may have forgotten how, it's been so long."

"It's like riding a bicycle, so I hear." He pulled her down next to him and kissed her. "What about my back rub," he murmured as she unbuckled his belt. He pulled her pants off and his own and kissed her again. She moaned and moved beneath his touch.

"Darling," she breathed, "it's all coming back to me. Oh, my darling, I have missed you, oh yes, do just that."

Kissing her breasts and her lips, he whispered to her, "Kate, my Kate. You'll never get away from me again. Never. Tell me you like that, tell me."

"Oh God, yes. Don't stop."

They lay in each other's arms in the candlelight. Beyond the window lay the dark city. "I feel as though we are the only people in the world," she said. "As though if I play my cards right this moment will never end."

"Lady," he kissed her, "I can't think of anyone I'd rather share an earthquake with, if it takes that to get you into my arms."

"God, we sound selfish. Let's be, for now. Who knows what is ahead. I've found you again and that's all I can think about or feel." She raised herself on one elbow and looked down at him. "You haven't changed, you know that? Most people change. How do you account for that?"

"Doctors never change, they just go on and on until one day they drop in their tracks."

She grinned at him. "Nonsense. All those twenty years since that night at the Carlyle you've been having passionate love affairs and God knows what all else, but you haven't changed. Odd."

"I thought about getting married once. She reminded me a little of you. Strong. Bossy. Talented . . ."

"And beautiful?"

"Oh, hell, yes. Gorgeous."

Kate bit his earlobe gently.

"Tell me more, about her I mean."

"You know after my early lousy marriage until I met you I thought I'd never want to marry anyone again. And when you told me we were not going to see one another again after the Carlyle I hated you for a while, for making me hurt and being so damn righteous and for caring so much about Daniel."

Kate lay back in his arms and listened.

"I worked harder than ever and it didn't help. Seeing old and good friends didn't help. Sex didn't help. Nothing did. I was like an old dog pining away for the only person he ever loved totally, completely. I wanted to write you, call you. Every time I flew out west I had to keep myself from stopping off and getting a room at the Broadmoor Hotel and . . . well, I got over hating you, of course, and then you settled into my mind in a way. I talked to you, asked your advice, laughed at things I knew you'd find as ridiculous and funny as I, and when world events occurred I'd think of how you would respond, and shared the world's griefs and joys with you. I read Daniel's poetry and saw you through his eyes. I read about Sam's career and the other boys. And, of course, I read about you. The climbs. The speeches. Daniel's illness. And I had this kind of second life with you in my imagination." He was silent. She waited. "I met a woman who reminded me physically of you and in other ways and I couldn't love her, I didn't even like her much, but I saw her. And one day I thought, Gordon Keith, you old Scottish bugger, you are getting old and have no one to push the wheelchair so maybe you should marry."

"What a lousy reason for getting married."

"Yes. Well. Anyway, I decided the same thing. And besides, there was you, you see. Always you."

Kate turned and put her head on his chest. "I want to say something. It frightens me. To say it, I mean."

"You. Frightened. Never." He held her close.

"This time I'm not going to leave you. I can't." She sat up and he did too.

"Do you mean it, Kate? Don't break my heart again. It's too old to mend now."

"I mean it. With all my old broken heart to yours. When I saw you today—a million years ago now—it was as though we had never been apart. All the clichés in novels and romantic songs are true, you know. The years dropped away and we were back at the ranch that first summer, when we rode up the canyon and left the others behind."

"I remember."

"Remember the picnic. Under the aspen trees. High, high up the mountain, away from the world. You were a serious young doctor, and I very much married with three sons. How you had the nerve to pursue me, I'll never know."

"You gave me hints."

Kate was truly shocked. "*I* did?"

"Sure," he grinned at her. "I wonder if that refrigerator has any warm champagne in it. I think we should celebrate."

"I did not!"

She watched him cross the room, naked, and open the refrigerator. "Voila! And caviar. And here are some crackers."

"I'd rather have vodka, please."

"One warm vodka coming up." He returned with a tray.

"Here's to us," he said, clinking his champagne glass against her vodka glass. "I love you, Kate."

"And I you, Gordon. I want to hear you tell me about those hints of yours. I do not believe it. Of course, I did like you a lot. I suppose it was obvious I did."

Gordon laughed. She laughed too. "Yes, I think it was."

Even at twelve thirty in the morning the streets were still full of people. Dave Hartnett knew that the mayor couldn't very well impose a curfew; there were damn few places for people to go. There were more police visible than there had been when he walked uptown from his office. At least someone was trying to establish control.

He made his way to the retaining wall on the East River at the end of 85th Street. That's where Domenico said the boat would pick him up at one o'clock. He knew what to look for—a thirty-four-foot Hawk with a red lightning-shaped racing stripe, one of those boats that all real sailors disdained, a floating condominium— and what to do when it came alongside the wall. But what if it wasn't there? Well, he'd find a way.

At the retaining wall he was surprised at the number of people who gathered, most scanning the water for signs of boats willing to take them off Manhattan Island. Hartnett pushed his way up to the front of the crowd, looking anxiously about. Nothing.

Ten minutes went by, then twenty, Hartnett's anxiety growing as the time passed. Then, over the sounds made by other boats cruising the river, seeking to find passengers with money to pay to get off the island, Hartnett heard the growl of twin 800-horse diesels. Straining, he could make out the hydrodynamically perfect hull of the Hawk as it eased its way between the other boats and toward the wall. Hartnett moved to where it would land. Domenico had told him the code name of the boat's driver and he called it out, hoping his voice would penetrate over the sound of the engines. It did, and the driver called back the proper response. A second man aboard threw several fenders over the side to protect the Hawk's hull. When it had come to a rest against the wall, Hartnett threw down his backpack.

Several people had gathered on the wall where the Hawk lay at rest and two—a husband and wife—were trying to buy their way onto the boat. The captain repeatedly told them that he wasn't taking any passengers, paying or not, except the one he had come for. Still they persisted. As Hartnett made his way from the deck to the cockpit and the captain began to inch the Hawk away from the wall, the woman jumped. She landed on the deck and for a moment seemed to have her balance. Then the captain reversed direction and she began to lean sideways. As he increased his reverse speed, causing smaller boats to scatter, the woman screamed and pitched from the deck into the icy blackness of the East River. Her husband, yelling her name, jumped from the wall after her and the two disappeared from sight in the fast current.

Moving forward now, the captain swung the Hawk's bow upriver and toward Hell's Gate. Once through that stretch of rough water he pointed her toward the Sound, opening her throttles wide. The boat fled up the Sound at nearly fifty miles an hour, covering the distance to the private dock outside Northport before two in the morning.

At the dock of Domenico Rizzo's friend, which, protected, had suffered little damage from the tsunamis, Hartnett transferred to a waiting car. Less than an hour later he was at a small airfield outside Greenport. This far out on Long Island, the effects of the earthquake were barely evident, power had not been cut off, and things were seemingly normal. The aircraft waiting for him, a Lear 35, had the range to get at least as far as Chicago in one hop, even flying low enough to avoid radar. Chicago was where Rizzo wanted him to go, and that was fine with Hartnett. He knew the city well—his mother had family there—and knew that he could disappear quite easily once he had satisfied Rizzo that the money had been transferred.

Diane and Karen reached the Grove School by 2 A.M., and the scene there was desolate. The headmaster had not left and was still hand digging toward the crafts room in the basement, joined by many volunteers from the neighborhood. There were no police or firemen there and no rescue equipment. The moon shone down on the knots of people still gathered, talking in low voices, from time to time looking up at the top floors of the building where they prayed their children still, by some miracle, were alive. Mr. Thatcher told Diane that Sam had been there and said he would be back. And he told her that Danny was probably trapped up on the eighth floor where the roof had caved in.

"I'm not leaving you," Karen said.

"Thank you. But you must go on to your apartment and find your husband. I'll be all right." Diane gave her friend a reassuring hug. Somehow, now that she was near Danny she felt better and determined that he was alive and that they would rescue him.

"We'll come back. When I find my husband, we'll come back."

"I know you will. We must not part company ever. After this, we're joined at the hip." The two women embraced and Karen set off uptown.

Diane went over to Mr. Thatcher. He was resting and drinking a mug of coffee that one of the parents had given him from a Thermos. "We have to get up there. How can we do that? Can't we get a fireman or someone to climb up?"

"No one has come. Your husband said he would send some rescue people, but no one has come. There is no way for one of us to go up there. The building is very fragile and the least wrong move could collapse another floor or the walls or both."

Diane's optimism fell apart. She looked up at the ruined building. Danny was up there. Dead? Dying? Terrified. Hungry. Alone in the dark. But people did get rescued. How about the boy in Mexico City after ten days. And kids who fall down wells. It was possible. Her mind seesawed from hope to desperation and back. She looked into the eyes of the headmaster and saw exhaustion and sadness beyond words. "Oh, my God. What are we going to do?" she said.

Domenico's order to Bobby "The Shark" Corelli had been both cryptic and thoroughly understandable. "Federal Plaza. St. Andrew's Plaza. Get the names of the singers."

Now it was past midnight and Bobby and a few hand-picked men stood in front of the building at 26 Federal Plaza that housed the

New York offices of the FBI. Scarcely twelve hours had elapsed since the earthquake had struck and the City was still reeling from the blow. Confusion reigned and the normally tight security that encompassed the building was in disarray.

Domenico's "family" had long had a mole within the FBI office, as it had in the U.S. Attorney's several blocks away at St. Andrew's Plaza. Bobby led his men around the side of the building to a door used for deliveries. It was slightly ajar and he and three of the others slipped inside, leaving the fifth man to stand guard outside.

The mole met them, led them to a little-used set of stairs that ascended through the building. They climbed several flights before the mole said, "This is the floor."

His passkey let them onto the floor where the records were stored. A solitary guard looked up, startled, as they appeared out of the darkness before him. One of the men with Bobby shot him dead.

With the electricity off, the alarms that would normally have been triggered failed to function, and Bobby and his men were able to rifle through file cabinets without fear of detection. Finally one of the men said softly, "This is it." He held out a thick file for Bobby to see. *New Identities and Locations* was the simple label. Bobby glanced through it quickly. It was exactly what Domenico had told him to get.

Now to St. Andrew's. The singers would finally begin to pay for their songs.

———

The helicopters had begun to leave their pads at Ft. Bragg at two thirty on the morning following the earthquake. The four thousand men that the mayor had requested of the president plus medical and other emergency supplies were contained in a fleet of more than 300 helicopters—huge Chinooks for cargo, Blackhawks to transport the troops around Manhattan, and Cobra gunships for fire support in combatting the looters. In order to cause as little disturbance to the population as possible, the fleet headed first to the Carolina coast and twenty miles out to sea before turning north toward New York.

Flying in formations of six to twelve copters each, they followed the coastline until they were off Sandy Hook, New Jersey. Then, at six-minute intervals, each squadron peeled off the main body and headed for the City.

Normally the men and women of the 82nd Airborne would have parachuted to their objective. But because of limited space in Central Park for a landing zone, uncertain winds, and persistent smoke that made visibility a constant problem, the decision was made to helicopter into the Sheep Meadow, offload men and supplies, and take off again for one of several staging areas within a fifty-mile radius of the City.

The precision with which the fleet's pilots executed this order was awesome to watch. Brendan Ahearn had driven down from the command post to the meadow on a small police scooter to meet and welcome these much-needed reinforcements and their officers.

Even before the machines had touched down, doors and hatches had been opened. In four minutes, everything that each copter contained for the relief of the City had been disgorged and the copters had begun to rise once again into the dawn sky, only to be replaced by a new squadron.

Brendan had been told that the major-general in charge of the operation—a combat veteran of the late years of the Vietnam conflict—would be in the second squadron to land. In the hazy dawn light, Ahearn could just pick out the general's command copter with its two stars stenciled on its side.

As he watched, marveling at the precision with which the dozen machines were carrying out this new landing, his eyes widened in horror as one helicopter lurched out of control some five hundred feet above the meadow. It staggered to the left, then turned on its side and began to fall. As it plummeted earthward, its blades first sliced through the tail of the command copter, then the two airships slammed into each other. As they hurtled toward the ground below, men scattered in every direction. In a final, heroic effort, the pilot of the command copter, still able to exercise some control over his craft, aimed the two vehicles, now locked together in a final dance of death, at the shallow edge of the lake.

As they hit, they burst into flames with an explosion that rivaled many that had been heard in the City for the past eighteen hours. Bodies were tossed high in the air. Equipment that had been meant for the salvation of New York was hurled hundreds of yards in every direction.

My God, thought Brendan, no one can possibly survive that. No one had.

An hour later, Brendan listened wearily as the colonel stated his case once again.

"And I am saying to you, Captain," he sneered the title out in an Arkansas drawl, "that it is an Army operation and the Army will remain in charge of it. The general is dead, and I am next in line and have assumed command."

"I don't think . . ."

"You're not being paid to think, Captain. Just to follow orders. My orders. Now let's get that mayor of yours on the horn and get some order to this operation."

The emergency radio equipment had been set up in the colonel's tent and within seconds Bruce Lincoln was on the line.

"What seems to be the trouble, Colonel?" the mayor asked when the colonel opened the conversation by saying that he and Brendan were having a difference of opinion. Bruce Lincoln listened quietly as the colonel stated his case, then cut him short.

"Colonel, I appreciate your position. I'm an old Army man myself. However, in this city a deputy chief of police ranks at the level of brigadier general. Since I have appointed Ahearn temporary deputy chief of Police and Fire, he is your superior officer. While we are happy to have you in command at the line level, Chief Ahearn"—Brendan recognized the field promotion—"will be in overall command and will set policy for you and your men."

As the colonel began to bluster and protest, the mayor once again interrupted him. "Hang on a moment, Colonel. I have someone on the line who would like to talk to you."

The moment passed, then both the colonel and Brendan recognized the voice that came through the radio's speaker.

"Colonel, I've heard about the death of your commander. You and your men have my deepest sympathy. With his loss, the senior ranking officer will be whomever the mayor appoints. I expect you to follow this directive as you would any other from me."

The commander-in-chief had spoken. There was nothing more to say.

———

By nine o'clock the helicopters had landed all the men, supplies, and equipment that would enter the City that day. Once the colonel had heard the president's order, he cooperated without hesitation with Brendan Ahearn, and fifteen hundred men had begun to fan out through the City from the military encampment in the Sheep Meadow.

They would take a twelve-hour patrol, to be replaced at nine that night by fifteen hundred fresh troops. Most of them went on foot, but Blackhawk helicopters transported several companies of men to the northern and southern tips of the island.

The remaining thousand men and women were to remain in the park, to set up emergency medical facilities and temporary soup kitchens to serve the population.

Somewhat overawed by the efficiency of the 82nd, at noon Brendan turned over command to the colonel.

"I'll be at the mayor's command post. I'd appreciate it if you could report to me there at about six this evening and we can go over what has happened and what the next steps should be."

"I'll be there, Chief," said the colonel. Then, with a twinkle in his eye, he added, "and I hope to see that one star on your sleeve."

———

Sam Thorne had left the precinct headquarters after reporting to the mayor, to go back to a rental apartment building on the West Side where he had not been able to find anyone to coordinate rescue efforts.

Everything in him wanted to head in the other direction to try to find and rescue Danny. Everything in him wanted to use whatever influence he had with the mayor to try to get equipment of some kind to Danny's school to help reach the boy. He wondered if Diane were all right, and if she had been able to reach the school.

As he made his way over debris and blocked streets to Central Park West, he was cold, hungry, and exhausted. He had borrowed a jacket from one of Ahearn's men that he put on over the business suit he had worn to his television appearance that morning and lunch at The Four Seasons. He had managed to find a pair of sneakers at the precinct house in one of the officer's lockers. The moon was high and he cast a long shadow against the rubble in front of him. He checked his watch. It was after 3 A.M.

He reached Central Park West, and in front of him were the ruins of the Dakota. The once-magnificent turn-of-the-century building had crumbled in on itself, leaving only the first-story walls standing. It was cordoned off and smoke rose ominously from the back of the building where the circular driveway had once been. There were knots of people gathered outside the cordon, and inside several policemen were attempting to look for survivors. Sam walked on.

He passed another fallen building that had shops at street level and he heard a cry coming from below the stairs leading to its basement. He stopped and listened. Another whimper. He went to the stairs and shone his flashlight down into the darkness. It appeared a Chinese laundry had been there from the sign barely discernible through broken glass. He began clearing the mortar and brick from the stairs. Again. A cry like a child's coming from somewhere beneath the stairs. He called out, "I'm coming. Hold on, now. I'm coming to get you." There was silence.

For fifteen or more minutes, Sam struggled with the heavy chunks of mortar, hearing that thin child's voice from time to time, crying out in pain. It might be Danny, he thought, and at one moment, his back aching, the mortar dust filling his throat and nose and causing him to choke, he felt tears of anguish sting his eyes. Danny. He could not bear it.

He brushed his tears away and redoubled his efforts to free whomever was down there in the dark. Finally he was able to move to one side a big piece of the building's façade that had crashed down, and he shone his flashlight behind it. There, curled up in a fetal position, was a small Chinese boy, his face covered with dust, his legs bloody. Sam crawled into the cave without stopping to think how precarious the roof over them was and how easily the floor above could be disturbed by his movements and come down, crushing them both. He whispered to the little boy, "Don't be afraid. I'm going to take you to a doctor and you'll be fine." The boy's huge black eyes opened. "Mama. Mama." He must be about four years old, Sam thought, and he picked him up as gently as he could. The boy's head fell against Sam's chest. He had lost consciousness.

Sam carried the boy through the moonlit streets back into the park. He arrived at the entrance to the medical tent and looked for Dr. Kelly. She was in the middle of the tent, and he made his way through the cots and nurses and ambulatory patients to her. She was stitching a gaping cut on a young woman's thigh, a nurse holding a flashlight over it for her. More medical supplies would arrive at dawn, but now they made do with whatever they had found. A Red Cross volunteer saw Sam standing with the boy in his arms. "Sir, please, may I help you?"

"Yes. This boy is badly hurt. Can the doctor . . . ?"

Without turning her head, Dr. Kelly said, "Find a cot, I'll be there."

The Red Cross nurse led Sam to an empty cot. He noticed a row of dead bodies lined up near it, and a steady stream of policemen with stretchers carrying the bodies away to another part of the park where soon the crematoriums would be operational.

He laid the boy down on the cot and the nurse covered him with a blanket and took his pulse. "He's alive. Barely." She got up and went for something at the far side of the tent, where there was a jerry-built medicine supply depot.

Dr. Kelly stood by Sam, who was kneeling by the boy. She knelt too and began to carefully and gently go over his small broken body. "Give him five milligrams of Adrenalin," she ordered the nurse, who injected his arm. She took her stethoscope and listened to his heart. "He's going," she muttered, and ordered Sam, "Press his chest this way." She quickly demonstrated, then positioned herself so that she could breathe into the boy's mouth. In and out, in and out, Sam followed her lead and watched Dr. Kelly breathing life into the boy's lungs. Five minutes went by. Sam gave up hope. Not Kelly. She went on as though there were no question that their efforts were going to work, no matter how long it took. The thin little body seemed lifeless. Dr. Kelly motioned the nurse to give him another shot, but she did not interrupt her mouth-to-mouth resuscitation. Finally, unbelievably, the boy stirred and coughed. Kelly sat him up and hit him between the shoulder blades, and he spit up dust and water. His large eyes opened and he began to cry. Dr. Kelly put her arms around him and held him to her. "It's all right. It's all right now." She gave instructions to the nurse over the boy's shoulder and put him down on the cot. "You rest now, and we'll stop the pain. I'll be back soon. We'll find your mama, don't you worry. What's your name?"

Through his weak sobs came, "Thomas Lee."

"Okay, Tommy. I'll be back."

Pat Kelly stood up and stretched her aching muscles. She looked for Sam Thorne. The nurse said, "He's out there."

Dr. Kelly went outside and saw Sam standing with his back to the tent. She went to him ready to throw another sharp word or two his way at any opening he might give her. She went around and looked up at him. Tears streaked his lean tanned face, now as dusty as the boy's face, and his shoulders shook with sobs. He saw her and turned away, starting to walk toward the precinct house. She grabbed his arm.

"What's the matter? You're not allowed?"

He stood still, trying to get control of himself.

"Or is it me you don't want to show yourself to? A woman? I've seen strong men cry before, you know. My brothers. My dad." She led him to where crates were piled up near the soup tent. "Sit down. It won't do to have you collapsing on us."

He followed her orders like a child. He sat down and she put her hand on his shoulder. "You stay there. I'm getting you something to eat." He shook his head, but she disappeared into the tent and in moments returned with a bowl of soup. He took it from her wordlessly and she handed him a spoon.

"Eat it, Sam Thorne. Go on. I know you don't want it. Just do as I say."

She sat down beside him as he slowly started to sip the steaming soup. "The last time I saw my dad cry was when he was watching an old newsreel of the day Jack got killed."

"Jack who?" Sam asked.

"Kennedy, of course." She was surprised, then admitted, "I never met him, of course. I was too young. But to us micks, he was always just Jack."

"Why have you been so mad at me, doctor?"

Pat Kelly looked at Sam and grinned. "I don't know. Your type always gets to me. Rich and famous. WASP. You're the kind that starved us to death in County Mayo. I'm just a poor Irish kid from Queens. What do you expect?"

Sam smiled for the first time in hours. "Forgiveness."

"Never!" She smiled back at him.

"Are you married? Has any mere male been able to knock the chip off your shoulder long enough to marry you?"

"Sure. Brian Kelly. And two kids, daughters."

Sam and Pat stared at one another, thinking the same thing.

"I heard the girls are okay, hurt, but okay. At Roosevelt Hospital. Brian is okay, too. I'm lucky. How old is your boy?"

"Six. He's trapped up on the eighth floor of his school. The whole damn building is about to collapse. Danny is smart. If there's a way to get out, he'll find it."

"Why're you here, for God's sake? Don't you want to go to him?"

"Of course." Sam stared at Pat Kelly, into her bright blue eyes under the floodlight. "Of course I do, but I'm needed here."

She stood up, her small compact body's language showing her impatience with him. "The earth has come apart at the seams." Her hands were back on her hips. "There's blessed little you can do here. Someone else can do it, what the mayor asked you to do. You belong with your wife and kid. See! That's the difference. You do things by your head and I do things by my heart."

"You? A doctor?" He stood, too, and was tall beside her. "Well, I do believe you, Pat. Brains don't run your motor. They didn't keep you trying with that little boy. I would have given up. I admit it. You are some woman."

She looked up at him. "Thanks. A lot of men wouldn't have gone in and gotten that kid and brought him back here. You're not so bad yourself." She grinned. "I have to get back there."

"Thanks for the soup." On impulse, born of the moment they shared in time on this most tragic day, Sam leaned down and kissed her on the lips, gently, lightly, and then stepped back. "I'll see you." He turned and walked toward the precinct house.

At five in the morning on Thursday, the pink first light streaked the sky in the east. Matt awoke. His shoulder and neck were cramped. He blinked and rubbed his eyes. Where was he and what was he doing? He glanced over at Elliot and then into the backseat at Guy and Scott, who were curled up together under the blanket.

He looked up at the FDR Drive at the Triborough Bridge. The **V** shape. He wondered how anyone could survive in that **V** shape high over the cold river water, and if anyone had reached that place to find out.

"Wake up, troops. We have work to do."

The other young men came to slowly and stretched, yawned, got out of the car to relieve themselves and stretch some more.

"I'd like scrambled eggs, sausage, whole wheat with marmalade, and coffee, please," Guy said.

"Waffles and maple syrup," Scott answered. It was clear that these two had bonded.

Elliot did a little jogging step to get his circulation going. "What do we do now, Chief?"

"We could go inland and see what we can do there, but I think by now there are an awful lot of official people in the streets, a lot more than up there on that bridge. I say we should head up to the Triborough."

"Agreed," said Elliot.

"I'd like to get back to my apartment to see if my friend is safe. He works in a restaurant midtown," Scott said.

"Hey." Guy was disappointed in his new friend. "We're a team. If we break up now . . ."

"Correct," Matt said. "We all have people and things we're worried about." He paused, trying to think of anyone other than his mother he cared about. His cat, Leo? But where had his mother gone after she left the hospital? Probably took the subway back to Brooklyn. He forced his thoughts to stop there.

"Are we all agreed to keep going to the bridge?"

The other three nodded and they set off.

By eight o'clock that morning they had reached the curve to the Drive that led up the ramp onto the section of bridge that had collapsed from both of its ends, forming the huge **V**.

The approach of the **V** was semi-blocked by the highway, broken and tipped up slightly, forming a kind of pitched stretch of concrete, ending abruptly with a six-foot gap that yawned over the dark water of the Harlem River many feet below. Several of the aging concrete columns that held up the bridge had crumbled.

"How the hell are we going to get over that?" Scott asked of no one in particular.

It was clear that cars had fallen through the gap as it had opened under their tires some twenty hours earlier.

"I am not, I repeat, not athletic," said Elliot in such a way that they all laughed nervously.

"What am I doing here? I want to go home." Guy put on a false whine. Then, "It's a piece of cake, fellows." He walked up the ramp in front of them, stood poised on the brink of the gap for a moment, walked back a few feet, then turned and ran toward it while they watched, astonished, as he jumped with the ease of a cat and landed upright on the other side.

Matt was scared for the first time since the earthquake had hit. He hated heights and was terrified of them.

"Come on," Guy called to them. "I'll be here to grab you."

Scott made a run for it and sailed over, falling to his knees on landing. Then Elliot followed suit and just made it, Guy grabbing him as he crumpled.

There was no rescue effort being made for this bridge, Matt thought, and wondered why. He threw his Vuitton bag over the gap. He could feel the cold air and then the piercing cold of the river in his imagination. The terrible drop to a terrible death. He saw the other young men watching him, waiting for their self-appointed leader to show them he was not afraid. He decided not to go to the brink first. He would just make a run at it.

He clenched his fists and yelled to the others. "This is the ultimate chutzpah!" He ran toward them and sprang off the edge, his Reeboks giving him a good grip, and landed a split second later on the other side. They embraced him and each other.

"Well done, lads," chirped Elliot in a mock British accent. "Jolly good."

They started toward the break in the concrete that formed two slanting slabs and at their apex a jumble of cars. The toll gate beyond looked perfectly normal. All the cars they had passed before the gap were empty. Their occupants had walked off the bridge the day before, or the cars were burned out and, in some cases, filled with dead people. Rows and rows of cars, smashed up against one another or in perfect shape, not damaged in the least, but empty. Between them and the toll gate the cars that had not fallen into the break in the highway were filled with occupants who had been there since 1:21 P.M. the day before with no ability to go backward or forward because of the gap. The people in them were unhurt for the most part, though when they saw the young male medics they opened their doors and got out to greet them, some of them needing pills or bandages, all of them thirsty. The strip of bridge they happened to be on had been held upright by its concrete columns as capriciously as the other columns had disintegrated.

A man in blue jeans, sweatshirt, and a baseball cap approached Matt. "You jumped over? You guys must be nuts! Listen, I tried to do something about those people trapped in the pocket there, but it's too dangerous. Sooner or later the Marines or Coast Guard or someone will come and get us off here and help those poor bastards."

Matt nodded and proceeded on with the others behind him. The sight they saw froze them in their tracks. The giant girders of the bridge when the columns cracked and fell apart held the two pieces of concrete, but they had sagged to form a deep crevasse and numerous cars both coming into Manhattan or leaving it for New England or Long Island had smashed down into the artificial canyon, one on top of the other, some now completely upside-down, others front-ended or back-ended, all in all about a dozen of them across the width of the roadway. There were arms hanging crooked out of some car windows. A body lay on top of a car where it had been flung from the impact with the one in front of it and one behind smashing into it.

In the clear morning air, Matt heard cries, groans, weeping. A low hum of despair. He did not know much about engineering, just what he had learned about structure at Parsons, but he knew that the concrete sides of the crevasse were precarious, that any undue pressure could open it up at its weakest point and send all these cars filled with people, many still alive, plunging into the East River. These people had been trapped for almost twenty-four hours. Some of them must be dying, some dehydrated, others unhurt but unable to move out of their cars. A living hell.

Matt searched the faces of his team. He had grown very fond of these young men in the few hours they had been working together.

"I don't want any of you to come with me down there without realizing the risk. This is no jump." He put an arm around Guy and hugged him. "This is dangerous as all hell, and I don't think any one of us would blame the other for choosing to stay up here."

Guy said, "I'm with you, Matt."

"Count me in." Elliot smiled. "In for a penny, in for a pound."

Scott wavered. Then, "What the hell. I'll come, too."

"Good. I suggest that each of us take as much medical stuff as we can carry in pockets or strap to our backs, and then we go in twos so that our weights are equally distributed and all four of us aren't in one place at the same time. Two to one corner, two to the other, and work our way down to the apex and back up the other side, doing what we can for these people. Let's get started."

They divided what was left of the supplies. Scott and Guy went down one end of the **V**, Matt and Elliot the other. They began as they had on the Drive by putting their heads inside the car windows, ascertaining the condition of those within, and then trying to get into the cars to give first aid or pry the people out.

Matt approached a car that was under one that had landed upside down on top of it. He could feel the concrete sway gently under his feet.

"Can you swim?" Elliot murmured into his ear.

"Funny, funny." Matt turned and gave him a grin. "How about you?"

"Never learned."

The bottom car had been partially crushed but there was a three-foot pocket in it and two people lay inside. When they saw Matt and Elliot, the man called out in a weak voice. "My God, Alice. Doctors. Thank God. Can you help my wife? She's hurt real bad."

Matt saw the woman who had been thrown into the backseat and whose right arm was crushed between the top of the car and the window ledge. The man was pinned by the steering wheel.

Elliot, thinner than Matt, had managed to get into the pocket far enough to put a tourniquet on the woman's arm. She whimpered and sobbed with the pain and then, in moments, became quiet.

"I'm okay," the man groaned. His head slumped forward on the wheel. Matt pulled it back gently and the man's eyes opened. "I'm all right," he moaned. "I'm thirsty."

"You're a brave man. There's more help coming, and if you just hang on we're going to get you and your wife out of here. Sorry. We haven't any water."

"Okay," the man whispered.

They moved on from car to car, glancing from time to time over at Scott and Guy. Once a chunk of concrete came loose by Matt's foot and rolled over the edge, falling into the river. Matt watched its journey downward into the black swirl of the East River, and for an instant saw himself falling, his mouth opened in a silent scream, and then the icy water covering his face, suffocating him.

His heart pounded. His fear made him tremble, but he took a deep breath and went on to the next car. Soon, despite anything the doctor had said back at New York Hospital the day before, he was going to start giving these poor devils shots of morphine. Their pain was too terrible to witness. He had relief for the dying right in his Vuitton bag. He was determined to use it.

Danny awakened at 5:30 A.M. At first, in the total darkness, he didn't remember what had happened. He lay curled in the fetal position. As he came awake, he felt very cold and reached for his blanket. It wasn't there. And then his bedside light. It wasn't there, either. He sat up. Hunger gnawed at his small belly. He felt light-headed. He checked his watch again. It was October 6, 1994, at 5:31 A.M. Cautiously he tried to stand up, using the toilet-bowl rim to pull himself erect. He could just make it, his head almost touching the beam above him.

He opened his trousers to pee in the toilet and hesitated, remembering he had drunk from it earlier. There was clean water in the toilet bowl. He didn't want to but he directed his pee away from the toilet into the farthest part of his tiny space. Then he remembered that he had put two graham crackers in his jacket pocket to eat after gym. He wondered how long it would be before his father found him. Many TV shows and movies had taught him that he had better ration his food. He broke off one-half of a biscuit and ate it. He was not thirsty yet, but it was good to know there was a little water there.

He sat down again, munching slowly. He decided to yell at

fifteen-minute intervals, for as long as it took for his dad to find him and Debbie Murdoch. "Help," he yelled at 5:45 A.M. "Help, it's Danny Thorne. Help!"

He repeated his cries for an hour, every fifteen minutes.

There was no response. He sat in total darkness and silence. Tears began to trickle down his face and he put his head down on his arms and sobbed.

Now no one would find them. He tried to think what he could do. He thought about his mom and dad, and where they might be. They must be looking for him by now. He croaked out, "Debbie. Debbie Murdoch. Do you hear me?"

Silence. Then a moan. "Danny. Help me. I want my mommy."

Danny got up and pushed the stall door very gently, then turned sideways to try to wriggle through the opening. After a couple of tries he managed it, and he stood outside the stall door. Above him there were remnants of the roof, and open sky, the early morning sun casting a bright light on the scene before him. The roof had caved in on the gym floor and everywhere he looked there were heaps of cement, plasterboard, and beams. Off to one side where the stairwell once had been he could see a large, gaping hole in the floor. He moved slowly and cautiously and approached it. He could see that the drop was straight down, it looked like to the ground floor. Terrified, Danny drew back and moved toward his stall. He stood there, afraid to go in any direction, and then called out again in his croaking voice, "Debbie, I'm out now. Where are you?"

"Here," she replied, from not far away.

He looked in the direction of her voice and saw a heap of debris and a leg sticking out of it with a sneaker on the foot and a red sock above it. He crawled over to the debris. "Debbie," he said in as loud a voice as he could muster. "Are you there?"

"Yes. I can't see anything. But I can hear you and you sound close."

He touched her leg. It was cold. "Can you feel me touching your leg?" He had seen a movie once like this and someone asked the person who was trapped that question.

"No. I can't feel my leg at all."

He began to try to move the debris. At first he thought it was going to be easy. Then he got to the heavy beam and chunks of masonry. He pulled and pushed and grunted with his efforts, but he could not move them. He could hear Debbie crying underneath and he could not reach her. Finally he sank down on the gym floor and sobbed himself. He tried to stop, tried to think of his dad, but his head hurt and his fingers were raw and he was afraid.

At eight fifteen the morning following the earthquake, Brendan Ahearn climbed aboard the Bell Jet Ranger helicopter waiting for him in a small clearing south of the tent village.

"Head north," he ordered the pilot. "I want to start with the Bronx and the north end of Manhattan, then work our way downtown. Most of that incoming traffic should be done with by the time we're this far south again."

"Right," the pilot acknowledged, and he turned the copter uptown.

—————

They had already learned that, of the four boroughs other than Manhattan, Brooklyn and Queens had been the hardest hit by the earthquake. Staten Island had taken a blow, but being less built up than the others, had suffered less damage. The Bronx had been both destroyed and spared. While much of the South Bronx had been leveled, the Major Deegan Expressway could still be partially used, and though there was a monumental traffic jam, cars could move on it.

They followed the route of the number 6 train up to Pelham Bay Park, where thousands had gathered to find food and medical attention. City Island had been washed almost clean by the series of tsunamis that had thundered down the Sound after the quake— boats piled one on top of another like a handful of poker chips.

They turned west, and here the destruction was less. Van Cortlandt Park, like Pelham Bay, had become a makeshift refugee camp, but Brendan knew that it would hold many more people than were currently there. As they flew over Riverdale, signs of the devastation became more evident. Many of the stately old mansions in the area had survived, but several apartment buildings that had stood on the edge of the land overlooking the Hudson and across to the Jersey Palisades had toppled into the river. They passed over the broken Spuyten Duyvil Bridge and flew once again in the sky over Manhattan.

Crisscrossing the island, they made their way slowly downtown. The dominant feature was fire. Buildings everywhere Brendan looked were in flames, some burning brightly, others guttering out as flammable material was exhausted. The smoke was dense, but a mild breeze out of the east was pushing it toward New Jersey. Fort Tryon Park was below them and he could see that the Cloisters was intact and being utilized to care for the hungry and wounded.

As they approached Harlem, the full impact of the earthquake began to be evident. Brendan had already learned that the quake had centered on 125th Street, but he now saw what that meant in real terms. That street, Harlem's main thoroughfare, looked as if it had been smashed by a giant fist. Nothing—from the tallest buildings that housed State of New York offices, to the humblest of apartment buildings over storefront churches—stood, and the destruction was repeated for several blocks north. Up Lenox Avenue, the fifteen-year-old Schomburg Center for Research in Black Culture stood intact while buildings all around it were reduced to piles of bricks and mortar. Below 125th Street, all the way down to the northern boundary of Central Park at 110th Street, the Harlem that had existed twenty-four hours earlier was no more. Morningside Park was crammed with people who had no other place to go. Many of the buildings at Columbia University had collapsed, but some still stood, and Brendan could see people flowing in and out of them. Riverside Church had been badly damaged, its tall spire tossed down, but the cathedral of St. John the Divine, squat and imposing, seemed to be intact.

Brendan had decided that they would fly down the West Side of Manhattan to the Battery, then up the East Side to 110th Street again before doubling back to the precinct. There was some sort of police presence in Riverside Park at the end of what had been 108th Street, and Ahearn ordered the pilot to land.

A uniformed officer hurried over to the chopper. Brendan shouted down to him, "I want five sentences on the situation here."

"Bad, but not as bad as it might be. We've got a team of doctors here from St. Luke's and one of the Army choppers landed half an hour ago with medical supplies. Food is short and water is about to run out. We need cots and blankets badly, clothing also. And a way to start getting people out of here."

Ahearn acknowledged the officer's salute, and the copter lifted off. Food, water, blankets, clothing. And a way to escape the unthinkable.

The police helicopter continued south on its zigzag course over the West Side of Manhattan. Riverside Park continued to fill with people and Ahearn could see repetitions of the emergency facilities throughout its length. Good, he thought, the people are closing ranks.

Everywhere he looked, there were pockets of salvation in the midst of destruction. A high-rise here, a movie theater there. The earthquake had spared buildings, great and small, in a random, haphazard way. Opposite the park, the Museum of Natural History still stood; at Lincoln Center, the Metropolitan Opera was up but the Juilliard School had fallen.

The pilot was flying the copter at some two hundred feet when a blast from a ruptured gas main hurled them upwards. The pilot fought for control as the copter bucked and plunged in the updraft of heat and smoke. For long moments the small craft was flying on its side, and Brendan thought that the end was near. But the pilot's skill told in the end and they were able to right themselves and continue their tour.

Using Broadway as the dividing line, they continued their course back and forth over the West Side, and Brendan was gradually numbed by what he saw, by the sameness, the bleakness, the utter destruction of it all. The middle of the City was perhaps, with the exception of Harlem, the worst hit. Very few of the buildings between 34th and Canal Streets were of modern construction and whole sections of the City whose names evoked New York—Greenwich Village, SoHo, Little Italy, Chinatown—had been wiped out. The streets and avenues had been rendered impassable. If they had not been destroyed, they were so full of rubble that nothing could move on them.

As numb as he had become, nothing had prepared him for the devastation at Battery Park City. This new "neighborhood" of

Manhattan, with its architecturally inspired buildings and lovely open spaces along the edge of the Hudson River, had been built on a landfill. With another sort of underpinning for their foundations, the buildings might have survived. But the landfill, unlike solid rock, amplified the shock waves that the earthquake produced and the entire community had collapsed. Brendan found it impossible to imagine how many bodies lay under the huge piles of rubble below him.

They lingered over the site for several minutes. Then Brendan said, "Let's go."

On the second day, Copper had spent the night in the stairwell of an abandoned house. He was hungry and cold. He had found a piece of bread that day and gobbled it down. Before dawn he awoke to hear a scrabbling noise and he pricked his ears and strained to hear more. His nose told him. A rat. He stood up and then saw the creature, which looked almost as big as he was. Bred to hunt rodents, Copper went into immediate action. He raced toward the rat, his strong hind legs propelling him forward with sharp speed, and his large strong-toothed jaws clamped down on the rat's neck. He shook the rat from side to side, but because of the rat's size it managed to get free and sank its stinking teeth into Copper's shoulder. He yelped and pounced on the rat again. In a moment he had broken the rat's neck. He tossed the rat in the air and then, moaning, sank to the ground. The puncture wounds in his shoulder were very painful. Soon the pain got better and the sun rose. Copper trotted up the stairs and back out onto the street. He headed north toward Grove School and Danny.

Mattie Lincoln could hear the ticking of her watch—an antique handed down to her from her grandmother and one that she kept in good working order—but there was not enough light to make out what time it was. She had slept, and was as stiff and sore as anyone she knew who was unfortunate enough to suffer with arthritis. Still, she had always been a woman of infinite patience, and that quality served her now.

She began once again to recite the prayers of her childhood, the first ones she had learned at revival meetings in the rural Georgia of the first quarter of the century. But her body was old, even if her spirit and dedication to her Lord were young, and she soon drifted once more into sleep.

David Hartnett thought about the scheme as the plane crossed over the eastern third of the country. It was simple enough, which was its beauty. What he had copied from the firm's files contained information about the day-to-day activities of Kelly, Farnsworth— what had been traded, who wanted to buy, who wanted to sell—but that was fairly useless to him with the Exchange being shut down. He had had to copy it, however, in order to get to the information he wanted—the assets of the firm and particularly the amount of capital it had available in its various bank accounts.

Kelly, Farnsworth was small, but it could still lay its corporate hands on nearly a hundred million dollars in seconds if it had to.

Hartnett had low-balled his estimate of available capital to Rizzo, pegging the figure around sixty million. What the guinea didn't know wouldn't hurt him. Besides, he had extracted from Hartnett a sixty percent share in whatever Hartnett could steal in return for getting him out of Manhattan as well as the number of the account in Liechtenstein where the money would ultimately wind up. But Rizzo didn't know all the details.

Six months earlier, more as an exercise in possibilities than as a conscious plan to steal from his employers, Dave Hartnett had begun to construct a system for moving money. He had been on a winning streak then, and the few thousand dollars it cost to open up bank accounts in certain tax haven countries and create dummy corporations as the owners of those accounts seemed worth the investment, even if it remained only an intellectual one.

He had created a pearl exporting business in Nauru and one to import wool on the Isle of Man, both of which had very strict banking secrecy laws that the United States had been trying to force changes in, unsuccessfully, for years. Then, wanting the backup of a third corporate entity, he had created a tobacco importing firm in Liechtenstein. Continuing the intellectual exercise, he had moved funds from one to the other, sometimes lending himself money from one to the other, sometimes lending himself money from thoroughly unimpeachable international banks where the funds of his dummy corporations were lodged. It was all very small-time—he had never had more than fifty thousand dollars involved at once—but it had taught him that if he ever had the opportunity to lay his hands on a large sum, he would have the knowledge of how to manipulate it to his best advantage.

The opportunity had arrived.

The small group of survivors in the tunnel—with the exception of the Richardson children, asleep in the bed at the back of Joe Mazurski's cab—had stayed awake monitoring the truck driver's radio all night. At first they picked up only static across the entire band. Then Joe rigged up an extension for the antenna and real sounds began to drift into the tunnel from the outside world.

"An earthquake," Toby said as they listened. "No way we'll get out." His voice wasn't resigned, merely factual.

"Can't we call somebody, tell them we're here?" asked Vivian. She and Charlotte had spent the night reassuring each other about the future. Now it was morning, they knew what had happened, and such reassurances seemed empty.

"I'm going to try, ma'am," Joe replied. "Just as soon as I can find a band where somebody's looking for people trapped like us." For the rest of the morning, Joe played with the dial on the radio, speaking occasionally into the microphone, then listening for a reply.

Sister Constance brought him a glass of water and an apple from the Vanagon's refrigerator. She smiled at him. The order had given up habits for the nuns long ago, but Joe thought that even though she was dressed in street clothes he would be able to pick her and her vocation out in any crowd.

"Have you reached anyone?" she asked, her voice calm.

He took the glass of water. "No. Everyone's filling up the airwaves from here to hell and back. Excuse me, Sister." She nodded at him and he went on. "I need a better antenna to get through whatever it is we're buried under."

By midafternoon Thursday, Joe had further lengthened the antenna, using the ladder he carried with him to attach it to various electrical wires he found dangling from the tunnel's shattered lighting system. One wire, he figured, might just remain intact through the muck above them and be close enough to the surface to let his signal carry into the air.

Vivian had said to him, "I don't mean to sound grand, dear, but tell whoever you talk to that you're trapped with Mrs. Derek Gordon. My husband's been an adviser to every Republican president since Eisenhower's last term. If that name doesn't bring help, then nothing will."

After several frustrating failures, the radio with its improvised antenna suddenly worked much better than Joe had dared hope. Within minutes he was talking to another trucker, one who, luckily, hadn't gotten as far as the tunnel's mouth when the earthquake had struck.

"Yeah, I'm about twenty yards west of the toll booths. Can't move forward or backward. I've been using the radio once every hour to try to pick up people in trouble. I was just about to sign off when I heard you. Tell me again where you are."

"In the tunnel, maybe halfway through, in a section that got broken off and plugged up with dirt, river mud, whatever. We may have sunk some, too. I can't tell."

"Tell me your name again so I can write it down. And the names of the people with you."

Joe did so, ending with Vivian. "And there's a woman here who says her husband's name is Derek Gordon, some sort of adviser to the president."

"Well, I'll use that first. Might be worth something. How long do you think you can hold out?"

"We've got some food and water, not much, but enough for a couple of days. That's not the problem, though."

"Yeah, I'll bet. It's the air, huh?"

"You got it," Joe agreed. "I'll call you again in"—he looked at his watch—"two hours and seven minutes. That's seven by my watch."

"That's a roger, good buddy," said the other trucker.

Seven o'clock came and went and Joe was unable to raise the other trucker on his radio. He had told the rest of the group about his success and they had all crowded around the cab of his truck when he tried to call as scheduled. Their disappointment at his inability to contact the outside world again was apparent on the faces of all of them and, in their several groups, they returned to their own vehicles.

Every hour on the hour for the rest of the night, Joe switched the radio on and attempted to regain contact. And every hour on the hour, he was unable to.

The sun climbed in the sky above the Triborough Bridge. Matt and his team were still trying to help the several hundred people trapped when the bridge buckled, forming two giant concrete slabs of roadway which now slanted downward steeply to a very insecure valley held together over the East River only by the pressure of the two slabs jammed together at the bottom of the **V**. The dozens of cars that had toppled into this crevasse were filled with badly injured people, some dying, some dead, the living terrorized, thirsty, wounded, in pain.

The way the team was reaching most of the cars was by walking along the rim of the slabs, balancing precariously, on top of cars or concrete, whichever provided the most secure foothold. Then, inching along, holding on to whatever they could find, they climbed down, very slowly, the slanting slabs to try to reach as many occupants in the cars as they could. It had taken several hours to reach all those cars which had fallen into the near side of the crevasse. Now they were starting the upward climb of the far side.

Matt heard a high-pitched voice as he stepped from the roof of one car to another, a high child's voice speaking in Hebrew, words he could not understand. He knelt down and peered in the window of the tilted car. The man and woman in the front seat were dead. In the backseat was a young boy with curly dark hair and large solemn eyes. Matt was reminded of himself in a photo taken at age twelve. The young boy was all dressed up in a navy-blue suit, and his white shirt was soaked with blood. He was softly saying the same phrases in Hebrew, over and over, his eyes fixed ahead, and suddenly Matt knew that the boy had been on his way to a practice session for his bar mitzvah. He called out to him softly, "Hi, young fellow." The boy's eyes turned in his direction and he realized he must look odd, his own face upside down looking in a window. "I'm here to help you. Can you tell me where you are hurt?"

The boy shook his head. He started his chant again. Matt lifted himself into the backseat of the car through the open window, and just as he made it, the boy toppled over on his side. Matt put his arms around him and held him. He listened for a heartbeat but there was none. He held him for a minute, and tears sprang from his eyes and one terrible sob shook his thin body. Then he put the boy gently back on the seat and closed his unseeing eyes. He hoisted himself out of the car, careful to wipe away traces of his tears first.

There was a loud whirring sound overhead and two blue-and-white police helicopters flew toward them. Matt shielded his eyes from the sun with the palm of his hand and looked up. "High time," he muttered. He had not, in fact, used the vials of morphine in his Vuitton bag yet, but with every passing hour he was tempted more, and maybe the helicopters were carrying real doctors aboard. He looked over at his team and saw Elliot nearby bandaging a woman's arm.

Scott and Guy had reached the top of the slab, and were standing on a tipped-up car that, in turn, was balancing on the upturned car beneath it. Scott was holding on to Guy and Guy had hold of what looked like to Matt a piece of suspension wire. He saw all at once that the pilot did not see them. He yelled in vain. He started to jump from one car roof to the other, yelling at the top of his lungs. One helicopter, the noise and vibration from its main rotor deafening, hovered just above the bridge and a uniformed officer jumped onto the flat section near where Scott and Guy were perched.

Matt watched with horror as Scott and Guy tilted like acrobats on a tightwire. Slowly, very slowly they slid, their arms and hands flailing the air, trying to grasp anything to stop their sure descent through the bright October air into the swirling deep below.

Elliot heard Matt's terrible cry and saw his anguished face. "Oh, my God!"

"They're gone!" Matt yelled. He shook his fist at the helicopters. "Get them! Get down there and get them!" One of the choppers was already descending to the river. It landed with its pontoons on the rough water, and its crew searched in vain for Scott and Guy.

There was no time to grieve. Others' lives had to be saved. The two helicopters hovered over the bridge and lowered rescue cables. Matt and Elliot helped the single EMS officer carry the wounded to the dangling cables and eased them into the simple horse-collar harnesses attached to each cable, to be hoisted up into the helicopters. They worked through most of the day, battling the noise and downwash from the rotor blades and the ever-present fear that the entire precarious structure on which they stood could collapse at any second.

Finally, after they had lost count of the number of shuttle missions the helicopters had run and the number of lives they had saved, Matt and Elliot obeyed the EMS officer's request that they board a flight to the 61st Street heliport.

Matt said a weary good-bye to Elliot and picked his way up to what was left of York Avenue until he reached New York Hospital. He climbed up to the tenth floor and walked past rows of patients who lay on the hallway floors until he reached the nurses' station where Dr. Charles Lincoln was studying a chart.

Matt Devon, his face dusty and grease-stained, his clothes reeking of gas fumes, his white jacket smeared with blood, approached the doctor.

"Hiya, Charlie."

"Where in God's name did you come from? Where have you been? Where did you guys go?"

Matt pulled back his exhausted arm and threw the hardest punch he could into Charlie Lincoln's surprised face. Charlie staggered across the hall and into the wall, hard. Matt grinned at him. "I've been wanting to do that ever since I met you, Charlie Lincoln." And then the room turned around and upside down and Matt Devon passed out.

All over the City domesticated animals were running loose, hungry and terrified. Dogs of all sizes, cats, pet hamsters and monkeys and parakeets. One cheetah. Several pet snakes, one a boa constrictor owned by an eccentric artist who lived at the Chelsea Hotel. Many pets perished in the earthquake. Those that survived faced an uncertain and in most cases terrible future. They could not find their owners and in the chaos of the first few days they had to seek shelter where they could find it and food was scarce. By the second day, dogs had started to form packs, very dangerous packs because of the unusually high concentration of attack breeds favored by crime-wary New Yorkers. Akitas, German Shepherds, and pit bulls prowled the ruins, hunting small animals and in some cases, children, who, orphaned or separated from their parents, were wandering the city too. The lucky ones were taken in to church and school shelters until their families could be found.

Even rumor, and later, knowledge that the Army had been brought in to assert control hadn't stopped the looting. By noon on the day after the earthquake, it had reached its height—a frenzied lust. The rectangle bounded by 57th Street at the top and 34th Street at the bottom, and with Fifth and Lexington Avenues as the sides was the prime target for looters with upscale tastes. The boutiques, jewelry stores, and antiques and art emporiums were being hardest hit when the 82nd Airborne began to deploy.

The column of three hundred troops marched out of the park at the corner of 59th and Fifth, then split into ten squads of thirty men and women each. At as brisk a trot as they could manage amidst the rubble left by the earthquake, they moved together down to 57th Street, then started for their designated patrol areas.

The lieutenant in command of Alpha Squad had been with the 82nd for only two months. A June graduate of West Point, where he had finished twelfth in his class, he had no more expected that routing looters would be his first combat assignment than he expected to fly to the moon. But he had a mission to accomplish, and it was what he had been trained to do.

The twenty-nine men with him had proceeded down Fifth Avenue to 49th Street. Their assigned territory was from Fifth to Lexington, 49th to 45th. He devised a plan to sweep his area and enforce order, although not without some apprehension. Thirty was a damn small number to be trying this in an area of sixteen square blocks.

At first things went smoothly, and he and his troops were able to begin to restore some semblance of lawfulness. As they proceeded west on 49th Street, then back up 48th and down 47th, he left a man at every intersection in order to reinforce the sense of a police presence in the area. By the time he ordered his men to start eastward on 46th, however, his patrol had shrunk to thirteen men. Two more were left on Park, one on each side of that large, divided avenue, and another at the corner of 46th and Vanderbilt.

As they approached Madison Avenue a shot rang out. His remaining ten men dived for cover behind parked and stalled automobiles.

"Where do you think it came from, Corporal?" the lieutenant asked a grizzled, combat-seasoned trooper.

"Corner window, building to your right, second floor."

The lieutenant looked in the direction the corporal had indicated, saw the glint of sunlight on a steel barrel.

"Can you take him out?"

"Hard angle. Distance ain't bad, though."

"One shot's all you'll get."

"All I ever needed."

The corporal, in a crouch, began to move around the back of the car they were behind. Another shot ripped into a car further up the street. The lieutenant cupped his hands around his mouth and shouted, "This is the United States Army, 82nd Airborne. Cease fire immediately and surrender or you will be shot!"

The voice that shouted back had a hard edge to it. "I ain't gonna surrender, soldier boy. I'm in one of the best safari outfitters in the world and I'm gonna sit here firing away until I damn well get tired of it." The man leaned part of the way out the window. "What do you think about that?"

In one fluid motion that lasted perhaps a second and a half, the corporal stood, lifted his M-16 assault rifle, and fired. "This is what *I* think about it," he muttered, as the body hurled backward into the second-floor room.

The lieutenant stood. "Good shooting," he called out.

Charlie Lincoln bent over Matt Devon, who was coming to and trying to get up. Charlie put a restraining hand on him and called out to an orderly to help.

"Whatever you've been up to, you look like hell. I'm putting you in a bed if I can find one."

"Oh, no." Matt struggled to his feet. "No more beds for me."

"Okay. Will you come down the hall to a room where we can talk? And get you cleaned up?" Lincoln looked into the eyes of an angry man. "You look as though you could use some food."

Matt relented. He was starving. He followed Lincoln down the hall, and into a small storage room which had a couple of chairs in it. The orderly had gone for food. The hospital had had a good supply of staples and the patients were getting used to a high-carbohydrate diet of potatoes, cereal, pasta, and diet drinks.

Matt slumped into a chair. Lincoln got a basin with some water and soap and though Matt protested, he washed his face gently. "Let me take off that jacket." He slipped the bloodied medical jacket off Matt. The food arrived and Matt sat up straight and took the tray. He wolfed down the macaroni and cheese. Charlie Lincoln watched. When Matt finished and was starting on a piece of chocolate cake, Charlie asked:

"Now you tell me where you and the other guys went? And where are the others?"

"Why should I tell you anything, you stuck-up, arrogant faggot hater?"

"And why should I even try to be kind to such a bitter, spoiled, petulant child?"

They glared at one another. Then, suddenly, the ludicrousness of their situation hit them at the same moment and they started to laugh, both of them, first a little, then out of control, all the weariness and tragedy and pain of the last few days bubbling up and out of them, in uncontrolled laughter that was as close to weeping as mirth.

Charlie stopped first and wiped his eyes. He stuck out his hand to Matt. Matt got control of himself and took the hand in his, and they shook hands.

"Now tell me, man, what the hell have you been up to?"

It took Matt Devon less than ten minutes to tell Charlie what he, Guy, Scott, and Elliot had been doing since Wednesday at 1:21 P.M. Charlie listened in astonishment. When Matt described how Guy and Scott had fallen to their deaths, he choked up along with Matt. But he knew he and Matt were thinking the same thing— Guy and Scott were dying of a terrible and, in the end, humiliating disease. To die this way, saving others, living up to their best potential as men, was not such a terrible end after all.

When Matt had finished his tale, Lincoln sat in silence for a moment or two.

"You know, I was just thinking that you've been right about me. I was as bigoted about you guys as any Klansman about blacks. I hate to admit it. But it's true. And I am truly sorry." Lincoln looked hard into Matt's eyes. "Do you believe me?"

Matt grinned. "Sure. I guess I had you wrong too."

Charlie grinned back. "No. The truth is, you didn't."

Matt started to get up from the chair. "I've got to find out what happened to my mother. Any news about the subways?"

"Not good. We don't know too much. Though for a city knocked down to its knees, with no electricity, no phones, news somehow gets around. My sister was on the subway going to a dentist appointment from the Wall Street area up to the Seventies on the IRT."

"When Mama left here, she must have gotten on the same line to get back to Brooklyn."

"My mom works up in Harlem during the day at a child-care center. She's trapped under the building. So far no one has been able to reach her."

The two young men stared at each other.

Charlie took a deep breath. "Listen, how do you feel, really?"

"I'm tired, but other than that I haven't felt so good in months. Maybe years," Matt said.

"We need all the help we can get here. Would you be willing to work here for the next day or two? I mean, take a nap, and then I've got a lot of things you could do. Now that you are a 'doctor.' " Lincoln smiled.

"No one wants an AIDS patient taking care of them. What if . . ."

"You're not ready to be a surgeon, man. I'm talking nurses' aide stuff, nothing romantic."

"Give me half an hour to lie down somewhere and sleep, and then tell me what you'd like me to do."

"Great. Thank you, Matt."

———————

Sam Thorne had been on his way to the mayor's office to tell him he wanted to leave for a few hours to go to Grove School when an explosion thundered around the area. Brendan Ahearn, who had just returned from his helicopter tour, was walking toward him. A thick column of black smoke began to rise in the air, very close to the border of the park. Ahearn yelled at his pilot and Sam, "Let's go, guys. And fast."

———————

The Alwyn Court had stood on the corner of 58th Street and Seventh Avenue for eighty-five years, one of the true *grandes dames* of luxury apartment buildings in the City. Producers and stars of the Broadway stage, opera divas, artists, and sculptors predominated in the building, but its apartments also housed accountants and lawyers as well. No longer a building filled with twenty- and thirty-room apartments, it was instead divided up into more modest flats. On the ground floor, utilizing the building's original entrance, the restaurant Petrossian was now ensconced.

When the earthquake had hit on Wednesday afternoon, the Court had stood firm. While much of the decorative terra cotta on the outside of the structure had come loose and fallen to the sidewalks and streets, and while a certain amount of material falling from other buildings had damaged its façade, it had fared better than most of the notable buildings—Carnegie Hall and the Russian Tea Room in particular—in the immediate vicinity. Its water tower remained intact, and had provided its residents with a carefully rationed supply since the quake. Two small fires had broken out but had quickly been extinguished by residents and building staff. No one in either the building or the restaurant had been killed, and the most severe injury had been a concussion suffered by the restaurant's maître d' when he tripped and hit his head against the side of a table. All in all, the building had confirmed its reputation as a lucky haven for anyone fortunate enough to reside or visit there.

Now, on Thursday morning, the building was coming to life. Within its walls normalcy reigned, and its tenants and the friends and relatives that they had taken in after the earthquake were rising to face another day in the broken city.

Deep in a forgotten storage room in the Court's basement, gas had been accumulating steadily during the nearly twenty-four hours since the quake. The gas main that had ruptured was a small one, but one that had continued to leak after almost all the others in the City had been shut down. The air in the storage room had gradually been replaced, and the balance between oxygen and natural gas had reached perfect proportions.

A lamp in the apartment of the eminent conductor, Wladislaw Grobowski, flickered on, then died. Ah, thought the maestro, finally they are getting the generator on. It was the last thought that would ever cross his mind.

A wire to one of the electrical outlets in the storage room had pulled loose during the earthquake, its two ends touching together. The single spark that had been produced when the building's ancient generator had momentarily misfired was all that was necessary. The storeroom exploded, the force of its blast directed upward and through the Petrossian kitchen to the floors above. In an instant, the kitchen and then the entire restaurant were ablaze.

The newly installed, highly decorative doors between Petrossian and the lobby of the Court burst open, and the flames rushed to consume the paneling and paintings, the concierge's desk, and the concierge. In full control of the building now, the fire began to creep upward.

Brendan and Sam could see from the helicopter the Alwyn Court on fire. They landed in a small helicopter landing pad created by the Army at the intersection of 57th and Seventh. They could see flames curling out of the windows on the second story.

Adjacent to the helicopter pad at the intersection, fire equipment had been set up in a vain effort to combat a blaze that had consumed Carnegie Hall and the Russian Tea Room. The firemen at that site had finally given up the night before, and the hoses that stretched all the way to the Hudson River with pumps every block to keep the water pressure as high as possible were still there.

"You ever fought a fire?" Ahearn asked Sam.

"No. So I'll follow your lead."

"You do just that. Do what I do, and you'll be okay. If I think different, I'll order you out. Understood?"

Sam nodded, and they leapt from the copter.

The pumps were connected electrically, a generator at the edge of the river running constantly. "We need volunteers," Ahearn yelled, and he and Sam in minutes had rounded up a dozen men and women to help carry the hose up Seventh Avenue the one block to the Alwyn Court. Ahearn showed a volunteer which switch on the pump to press and then he and Sam stationed themselves at the hose's nozzle. "Now!" Ahearn shouted to the man, and the pumps throbbed into life.

The power of the water as it charged through the hose took everyone but Ahearn by surprise. Several men and women were thrown by its bucking but got up immediately to take hold of it once more. Sam held on to his section with all his strength and kept his eyes trained on Ahearn. Then he had an idea. He motioned to a man standing nearby to take his place and ran up Seventh Avenue.

In the absence of a fire engine with its ladder, Ahearn could only direct the stream of water into the restaurant, the glass doors of which had been blown outward in the explosion. A second stream of water appeared beside his own. He glanced briefly over his shoulder. Sam Thorne and a group of volunteers had run up the block and gotten the hose from the intersection of Seventh Avenue and Central Park South. "I thought I told you to stick right behind me," he yelled at Sam with a grin.

Though not a single person holding either of the hoses was dressed to fight a conflagration of this magnitude, no one shrank back as Ahearn and Sam advanced toward Petrossian's gaping mouth.

Water cascading before them, they mounted the few steps to the door and entered the restaurant. The fire, with little to feed on and no gas actively coming into the kitchen, had almost entirely exhausted itself, and the water from the hoses doused what few flames still flickered.

"How much hose do you think you have left," Ahearn shouted at Sam.

"Maybe two hundred feet," Sam yelled back over the racket made by the stream of water's effect on the restaurant's furnishings and cooking equipment.

Ahearn nodded. He thought he might have a bit more, but not much. When they had set up the pumping system during the morning, there was not another hose snaking to the river until 51st Street, and the 57th Street line had been meant to cover territory down as far as 54th.

"Let's keep going, then."

Slowly they advanced toward the doors to the lobby. Inside that room, they saw that it had been gutted, saw the charred body of the concierge. The fires that still burned in patches on the paneling were quickly extinguished, and they turned toward the flight of stairs that ascended through the interior of the building.

The gate to the stairs was locked, and for a minute all they could do was play their jets of water on the fire immediately in front of them. Sam said into Ahearn's ear, "Keep me wet." Then he moved toward the gate.

Ahearn aimed the nozzle of his hose toward the ceiling and Sam. The man to whom Sam had given his nozzle did the same. The water hit the ceiling then sprayed down on all of them, including Sam, with much less force than if it had been aimed directly.

The gate was old and well maintained, but its lock was no match for the karate kick Sam gave it. It gave way, and Sam was able to swing it outward.

Ahearn and Sam and the volunteers behind them could hear shouts and screams as they began to ascend the stairs, water shooting forward, then running back down over their shoes as they climbed. The hallway of the second floor was still burning fiercely and it was several minutes before the flames could be brought under control. None of the doors to individual apartments had been burned through.

"Take some men from hose detail and start knocking on doors," Ahearn ordered one of the volunteers. "If no one opens, break the door down. We have to make sure there's nobody inside overcome by smoke. Get them down to the lobby and outside. Then catch up with us and do the same thing on the other floors as we knock the fire down."

Ahearn motioned with his head to Sam and together they began to climb the stairs to the third floor.

The fire there was burning more strongly than on the floor below, and they had more difficulty dousing the flames. Doors to two apartments were open. Ahearn and Sam split up and each man took a hose into one of the apartments. Ahearn found the bodies of an elderly couple just inside the doorway of one apartment. Sam, having successfully put out the flames in the other apartment, retreated with a handsome blond woman in tow, conscious enough to walk with his help, and Ahearn recognized her as a film star from twenty years before.

Sam left the woman with a volunteer and joined Ahearn on the flight of stairs leading to the fourth floor. They reached the hallway. A window at one end of the hall had been broken, and the air coming through it was fanning the blaze to a high intensity. Ahearn aimed the jet of water at the base of where the fire was strongest and Sam followed suit. They moved down the hallway, fighting the blaze as best they could, and knocking on doors, telling occupants it was safe to come out.

Twenty feet away from where they had the fire temporarily under control, a door opened, and the flames pounced into the apartment. Sam went for the door, and Ahearn shouted "Stay back! There's nothing you can do." Sam stopped, horrified by the screams of the occupants as the flames enveloped them.

The fire was gaining strength, whipped along by the air from the window, and now through the open doors of a number of apartments from which people had escaped down the hallway to the stairs and volunteers who were helping them.

Ahearn motioned to Sam to retreat as the heat grew stronger. Behind them people were coming down the stairs from the upper floors, moving quickly as they saw Ahearn and Sam's inability to contain the blaze.

Sam and Ahearn backed up to the base of the stairs. "Let's go, guys," Ahearn yelled. "We can't hold on here."

There was no response from the volunteers who had gone

upstairs. No one appeared on the stairway. He shouted a second time as the fire advanced. The hoses were not enough. The water seemed a trickle in the face of the flames.

From above came a shout. Two men appeared on the landing halfway between the fourth and fifth floors. The flames had already begun creeping up the walls of the stairway. Within seconds the two volunteers were driven back up the stairs.

Ahearn looked at Sam. The experienced fireman knew it was hopeless. All twenty years of firefighting told him there was nothing he could do now, but he said to Sam, "Cover me."

Ahearn started up the stairs and Sam trained the water from his hose on a spot just ahead of him.

The fire had doubled in intensity. The heat was overpowering. None of them was wearing protective gear, and Sam wondered if his street clothes might burst into flames spontaneously. Sam and the volunteers behind him holding the hose made it to the landing where Ahearn was pulling the two men down the stairs. Sam gave the nozzle of his hose to the man behind him and went up the few feet to help Ahearn bring the men down. A scream from down the hallway caused Ahearn's concentration to waver. He turned toward the sound, as did Sam, and they saw a figure in flames, arms raised above its head. Ahearn started toward the figure and tripped over part of the hose. He sprawled face-forward, inches away from the leading edge of the flames. The end of the hose that he had been holding whipped violently about, sending water randomly around the hallway.

Sam had gotten the two men into the waiting hands of volunteers who were dragging them out to safety. He went back to help Ahearn. The volunteers trained water on him and he saw Ahearn try unsuccessfully to get to his feet. The figure engulfed in flames fell to its knees, then toppled over onto its side, hands curling into talons as the flames consumed the body.

A solid stream of water struck the hallway floor in front of Sam's feet, and he forced himself into the smoke to grab Ahearn around his waist. He saw coming toward him another man, his clothes on fire. "This way. Move, man, move." He hauled Ahearn away from the fire, and they stumbled into the safety of the stairwell. The man he had seen emerging from the flames was beating at his clothes and screaming. Ahearn yelled, "Don't go back!" Sam ignored him and plunged back up the few stairs, smoke engulfing him, flames scorching his face. He grabbed the man's arm and started to pull him down the stairs when the stairs collapsed under his feet. Smoke and fire seared his lungs as he fell and he knew nothing more except darkness.

The only way that Allen, Evie, and the others knew it was the first morning after the earthquake was from their watches; the blackness of the tunnel was unrelieved by whatever light might be shining on the City above.

They had made themselves as comfortable as possible through the night, though no one had gotten anything but a restless sleep.

"I know we're all hungry," Allen said, helping Gerta to her feet, "but we're just going to have to keep going forward until we find a way out of here. And we *are* going to find a way out." His young voice was strong and reassuring.

Mary said, "I need to lose ten pounds anyway. We won't starve."

They all agreed that they could stand to lose weight, and Bill Cohen added, "I haven't walked so much since boot camp in 1950. Hell, let's get going."

"Okay," Allen counted. "We're going to take turns at the back of the line. How about you first, Jake?"

"Sure. I hear there's alligators down here is the only thing. I'd hate to end up as a meal for one of them guys."

Marisa was genuinely scared at this thought. "Are you kidding?"

Jake laughed. "Yeah. Nothing to worry about. I'll go back to the end of the line and you'll see me. It'll be all right."

The others had formed up the line and Evie reached Allen's side. He shone the flashlight across her face. "Come on, girl. We've got to lead this line today. My, you are one good-looking woman, do you know that?"

Evie grinned. "I've heard it once or twice. Are you coming on to me in the middle of this scene?"

He squared his shoulders. "Hell, no, girl, what gave you that idea? But," he leaned down and gave her a gentle kiss on her cheek, "when we get out of this subway, I'm going to ask you to dinner at a place I know where there's great jazz."

"It's a deal." She took her place in the line.

Allen began to walk slowly forward, keeping his flashlight on so that he would not step off the end of the platform. He reached it, climbed down the ladder, and waited for the others to join him.

As the second day wore on, Allen led his group up the track. He had decided that he should not waste his time and energy trying to find a workable emergency exit in the roof of the tunnel. His earlier experience had been enough—the tons of rubble that had cascaded down the ordinary entrances to the system had told the tale of blocked exits.

They were headed toward 34th Street, and Allen reminded his group of the many entrances and exits in that station. They needed encouragement. The water level had not risen but it was cold and very tiring to walk in, and the faint odor of gas lingered in the air.

Allen's group could only cover the few blocks from 28th Street to the south end of the 34th Street station in something over three hours. It would have been faster, but now there were more obstacles in their path.

Evie asked Allen about the change.

"Earthquakes are strange," he replied. "When they hit, some things get it bad and some hardly get touched. I was in San Francisco back in 'eighty-nine. When it was over, if you were in the center of town you'd hardly have known that it had happened except for there being no electricity. Nothing fell down except some decorations on the outside of buildings. A few windows got broken. But if you went down to the Marina, it was a whole different scene. Looked like the area had been bombed."

He moved off to the left and crossed both the uptown and downtown sets of express tracks. Much of the tunnel's ceiling had collapsed. He reached the downtown local tracks and shined his flashlight again across the sheer face of a pile of debris that was twenty or more feet high. He swung his flashlight around to the downtown platform and played it about. There, lying on its side against the wall, was a ladder.

———

Rick, the boy from the subway, who had seen the lights, set off in their direction. Now he lurked some thirty yards behind Allen and waited until all the others in the group had climbed the ladder and gotten over the barrier, their way lit by Allen's flashlight. Then as

Allen himself began to climb up the ladder, he called out softly "Hey, nigger. I've got something for you."

The gunshot was deafening in the confines of the tunnel. Rick's lack of experience with a gun kept him from aiming properly and the bullet flew high and wide, embedding itself in the debris barrier. Allen extinguished his flashlight, then finished his climb as a second shot, then a third rang out. At the top of the heap, he pulled the ladder up after him, then slid down to where his group was waiting. Behind him, he heard a string of curses.

"Allen, my God, what's happening?"

"Somebody took a couple of shots at me. I'd say it was the punk from the train. Somehow he got hold of a gun. I think he's only after me. Otherwise he would have fired sooner."

They could see a glow coming through the opening in the debris wall that they had used.

"He's got a flashlight, too," Marisa said.

"Yeah. I suggest that we get out of here before he gets over the barrier."

Allen shined his own flashlight forward. The destruction it revealed was almost incomprehensible.

"Lord," said Evie. "It looks like Macy's fell into the station."

"It may well have. Come on, let's go."

As they hurried forward, Rick was trying to scrabble his way up the side of the barrier, tears of frustration streaming down his cheeks as he sought to find finger and toe holds. So close, and he had missed the target. Well, he wouldn't miss next time. And there'd be a next time.

Allen, Evie, and their group reached the downtown local platform of the 34th Street station. Looming up in front of them was a train that had evidently been picking up and discharging passengers when the quake struck. All its doors were open but it was as empty as the one farther down the tracks had been.

"They must have thought they couldn't get past the barrier and headed north," said Allen.

"Or maybe there's a way out of here," Bill Cohen replied. "Want Jake and me to reconnoiter?"

"Yes," said Allen. "In the meantime, we'll see if there is anything on the platform or in the train that we can use to protect ourselves from that crazy kid."

Bill and Jake went off to explore the station while the rest of them entered the train. Ten minutes later they were together again.

"No way out," Bill reported. "The stairs leading to the street are blocked, and the tunnel to Penn Station has collapsed. Can't even use the underpass to get to the other platform. Anything in the train?"

"Nothing. The people aboard probably weren't hurt at all— there's not even any broken glass—and left with whatever they had been carrying."

"What's that?" said Evie, and they all stopped to listen.

It was a voice, hoarse, ragged, screaming one word over and over again. "Nigger . . ."

"It sounds like he made it over the barrier," said Gerta.

"Yes," Allen agreed. "We have to make some quick decisions, people. I'm willing to take my chances with him, but it doesn't have to involve you."

"Don't be ridiculous, Allen," Gerta said. "We got trapped into this together and we're going to see it through together. Right?" she said to the rest of them, and they all readily agreed.

"Then the best thing you can do right now is find someplace safe. I'm going back and catch him by surprise."

"Allen . . ." Evie said.

"Just please do as I say. He may have a gun, but I have a lot of advantages that he doesn't. Now go."

As they moved toward the token-seller's booth at the north end of the platform, they could hear the boy's repeated cry coming closer. Allen ducked back into the train and began to move down through the cars.

Somewhere between the barrier he had crossed and the end of the platform he was now ascending, Rick had found a crowbar. As he approached the stalled train, he began to do what the earthquake had not done and used the bar to smash in the windows as he passed.

Allen and Rick reached the second car at the same time, and Allen ducked down below a bench as the boy walked along the platform swinging the crowbar. Glass flew about the car and Allen felt his ear nicked by one shard. He listened to the boy as he went past. The voice was the same—oddly pitched, on the edge of sanity—but the chant had changed.

"Nigger, I'm coming to get you, nigger." The phrase was punctuated by the shattering of glass.

When Rick had moved forward and began to break the windows of the next car, Allen stood and walked to the nearest open door. He stepped through it.

"Right here, white boy. Come and get me," he said, then ducked back into the car.

Rick, caught unprepared, was slow in his reactions, and Allen had time to slip into the next car before Rick had moved. The boy started back in the direction he had come, gun and crowbar in his hands. He passed the door at the end of the car and walked a few feet more. Then Allen stepped out behind him.

All of Allen's Marine training asserted itself and he closed the gap between the boy and himself swiftly. What he wasn't prepared for was the glass underneath his feet. His shoes crunched on it, giving the boy the warning he needed, and Rick turned and fired the gun blindly in Allen's direction.

The bullet caught Allen in the shoulder, threw him backward, and spun him around. He managed to catch the edge of the subway door he had just come through and pulled himself back into the car.

As it had on the tunnel bed, the gun's recoil sent Rick off balance. The crowbar flew from his other hand and clattered off into the darkness of the platform. He recovered and fumbled his flashlight out of a coat pocket, then switched it on, expecting to see Allen's body in front of him, for he was sure that this time he had hit his target. His surprise at its absence was replaced by elation as he heard Allen groan from somewhere nearby.

Cautiously Rick approached the door of the car where he thought the sound had come from, flashlight in hand, gun pointed in front of him. He reached the door and shined the light in. A pair of shoes, toes up, came into his beam. The body lying on the floor of the car was mostly obscured by the small bench just inside the door. Rick stepped in and shined the flashlight on Allen's body, letting it linger on the profusely bleeding wound. Blood covered Allen's chest and Rick was sure he had scored a mortal hit. He knelt down beside the man and played the flashlight over Allen's face. He giggled, then began to laugh in triumph.

"Got you, nigger. God damn, got you good." Rick threw back his head and roared with manic laughter, laughter that was cut off abruptly as a fist crashed into his groin.

"Don't count me out yet, white boy," said Allen, beginning to rise as Rick fell over backward, retching. As he went down, his body twisted and he landed face first in a pile of the glass from one of the windows he had broken. His scream of pain was accompanied by the muffled report from the gun as, involuntarily, his finger tightened around the trigger.

In the dim light cast by the flashlight Rick had dropped, Allen watched in disbelief as the boy rose to his knees, blood spurting from a gaping hole in his chest. He tried to move out of the line of fire as the boy began once again to raise the gun, but his body was not responding as it might have had he himself not been wounded. Then, slowly, the arm began to drop. As the gun fell from his hand, Rick leaned sideways. With a sigh that bubbled through the blood running from his mouth, he fell to the floor of the train.

Evie stood in the doorway, both sickened and frightened by the scene she had witnessed. Then, swiftly, she moved toward Allen.

"How badly are you wounded?"

"The bullet went all the way through, I think. It's beginning to hurt like hell, but it's probably better than it looks." He gestured with his head toward Rick. "I think he's bought the farm, though."

Evie glanced at the boy's still body, then gave a small shrug. "I want to look at your shoulder. Sit down."

Allen did as he was told and Evie carefully removed his suit jacket. Blood was still welling from the shoulder wound but she saw that Allen had been right—the bullet had gone in the front and out the back cleanly.

"Now the shirt," she said. "This is going to hurt, but it can't be helped."

He winced as she got him out of his shirt but realized through the pain how tenderly she was treating him.

"This isn't wonderfully clean anymore, but it will have to do," Evie said as she began to take off her blouse. She tied it gently around the wound and was pleased to see that the worst of the bleeding had abated, that the blouse was not immediately soaked with blood.

Allen stared at her in her brassiere. "You are, I believe, Counselor, what I think is called an incitement."

"And you, Counselor, seem never to lose your sense of humor."

"Gets me through the day."

Evie straightened up, then said, "Do you feel strong enough to walk?"

"Yes, but not much farther than back to the others, at least for right now. I want to take a look at him first, though."

They approached Rick's body. Allen stooped to pick up the boy's flashlight, then handed it to Evie. The gun that the boy had carried lay a few inches away from his outstretched arm. Allen picked it up, checked the chambers for bullets. "Empty," he said, and put it on one of the car's benches.

"What are those things coming out of his pants pocket?"

Allen looked at where Evie was pointing, then stooped to pick up several red cylindrical objects.

"Firecrackers, for Pete's sake."

"Firecrackers? What would he be doing with firecrackers?"

"Who knows. The kid was a nut case. It's a wonder he didn't have an Uzi."

Rick had been wearing loose jeans with multiple pockets in the legs. Allen reached into one of them with his good hand and pulled out a handful of firecrackers of all sizes and shapes. He put them in his own pocket, went through the other pockets of Rick's trousers that he could reach, then turned the body over and examined the rest. They yielded numerous objects that Rick had stolen from the passengers on their train, but only one contained any more firecrackers. Allen put these, too, in his pocket, then turned to Evie.

"You never know what might come in handy in an emergency. Let's get out of here."

Slowly, Evie and Allen made their way back to the others. Bill Cohen came to meet them.

"Jesus, Allen. Thank God you're okay. Come on. We've cleared a space and Jake's started to take apart the news vendor's stand. It's almost evening. We can stay here for the night, give you time to rest."

They built two fires. By now the rest of the group had realized the attraction that Evie and Allen had found for each other. Although they did not have the fire watch, Evie and Allen found it impossible to sleep. Instead they talked quietly, sharing those thoughts that two people share when they realize that they are falling in love.

"What would you have done if he hadn't accidentally shot himself?" Evie asked as sleep began to overwhelm her.

"I really don't know. When he started to get up I couldn't move. He would have had that one last bullet and we probably wouldn't be sitting here like this right now. Not that his aim was that great."

"Thank God for small things."

Allen's back was against one of the station's pillars, and Evie leaned more closely into him, resting in the protection of his good arm. He hugged her gently. They drifted off to sleep.

―――

"Mr. Speaker."

"The chair recognizes the Honorable Member from Missouri."

"Mr. Speaker, members of this esteemed house, there is no one, I submit, no one more in sympathy with the plight of those poor unfortunates in New York City and elsewhere in the East in their great time of travail. What has happened to them is beyond comprehension to all but a few of us. I myself was unfortunate enough to have been in San Francisco in 1989, and so I believe I speak with such sure knowledge. San Francisco is a beautiful and pure city, and one that was for the most part spared by the forces of God and nature. Not so New York.

"I spoke a moment ago of those 'poor unfortunates' in New York and yes, there are many of those. But they, sadly, are among the minority in that Sodom on the Hudson, that focus for all the evils that plague our great nation, that center of sin and corruption that festers in this otherwise noble land. For that is what New York is, and all the good people of America are perfectly well aware of that fact. As I am aware of it, ladies and gentlemen. As you are aware of it."

H. King Billingsley, fourteen-term member of the House of Representatives from Missouri, paused to let his words and the direction of his thoughts seep into the minds of his congressional colleagues. He sipped from a glass of water on his desk, adjusted his glasses, and gazed over them and around the House. It was nine thirty on Thursday morning, less than twenty-four hours after the earthquake had destroyed much of New York, and the House and, elsewhere in the building, the Senate had been called into emergency session to determine what the official response would be to the tragedy. H. King Billingsley had long been known for his opposition to federal support of "bailing out" urban areas in crisis. He was The Farmers' Friend, champion of all those values that it had become fashionable to refer to as outmoded, archaic, provincial, hick. The first two speakers of the morning had mouthed platitudes about duty-to-fellow-man-in-times-of-crisis, calling upon the House to vote large sums of money in aid of the City and other parts of the area that had been stricken. Billingsley had sat through them, his temper and blood pressure rising. Now he was ready to seize the golden moment.

"There are those among us who will say, 'Spend what it takes, but give us back New York.' I ask, 'To what avail?' For what was New York? What was so important about this place that all the wonderful people of America should be asked to spend, I am reliably informed, up to seven trillion dollars over the next decade restoring."

The fist crashed down onto the arm of the chair. "Who the hell let that out? How in God's name did that fool get hold of that information?"

The president's wife put a calming hand on her husband's arm.

"I know, I know, there aren't any secrets. And I know King Billingsley has informants tucked in every nook and cranny in this city. But even so, that information came to me on a Priority Need-to-Know basis."

The president and first lady were watching the congressional debate in her comfortable private sitting room. He had come up scarcely five minutes before after meeting with the cabinet for over an hour, receiving updates on both the national and international ramifications of the quake. He had hoped to have a half-hour respite. Now he reached for the telephone. In less than ten seconds, his chief of staff was on the line.

"Paul, did you hear that idiot, Billingsley? I want to know where he got his information, and fast." He slammed down the phone, then stood and turned to his wife. "Small minds like that are not, repeat not, going to have their way. That I can promise."

On the floor of the House, H. King Billingsley had continued to build up a head of steam. The "Sodom on the Hudson" reference had been only the beginning in an ongoing salvo against New York as the repository of everything that was corrupt in society. He had alluded to the fact that New York was a center for culture and the arts.

"But so, ladies and gentlemen, is St. Louis. So are many other fine cities, smaller cities, in this fair land. We have our symphonies, our museums, our libraries and ballet companies. But we, honored colleagues, keep things in scale. We do not let everything become overblown and grandiose."

"Except our politicians," muttered one New England congressman to another.

"And, ladies and gentlemen, we do not have, in the great Midwest, the overwhelming, the staggering problems of sin and corruption that New York possesses, or possessed until God took His rightful retribution. Where is there a center of harlotry like Times Square outside New York? Where else but on Wall Street does the corruption of money hold such sway? What other city deals in drugs to the extent that New York does?"

"The Tenderloin, the Merc, and this fair capital, in that order," the New Englander muttered again.

For another twenty minutes, Billingsley ranted in the way that the House had become familiar with. Then he summed up.

"I say to you, ladies and gentlemen of this august House, that we should, we will, we *must* spend the money necessary to help those people to evacuate that city. But *only* that which is necessary and not one penny more of the hard-earned money that the rest of the people of this nation strive so valiantly for. After that, the city should, will, *must* be abandoned, *must* be razed, *must* be left to die as such cities of the Old Testament were left. New York has been a blight on this nation's fair name. It shall be no longer."

"Listen to that applause," the president said to the few men in his private study with him. Geoffrey Collins, secretary of state, was there, as were the secretaries of labor, commerce and defense, the White House chief of staff and, somewhat in the background, the vice president. The president had left his wife's sitting room almost immediately after telephoning the chief of staff about the OMB leak and had watched the end of Billingsley's speech with these men.

"Yes, sir," said the chief of staff. "But remember, the House is only about a third full and most of those are from the South and Midwest. Only a handful of northeastern representatives are there. The rest are trying to figure out what has happened in their districts."

"That's true. What have you been able to find out about the leak from OMB, Paul?"

"I have two of my staff working on it now. I should be able to tell you something within the hour."

"In reality, though, what does it matter?" asked Collins.

"Nothing, Geoff, of course you're right. It's just symptomatic of what goes on around here. You ask for preliminary information and then a horse's ass like Billingsley gets hold of it and booms it out like God's truth." He paused, then turned to the secretary of labor. "What do your people think the unions' position is going to be about either abandoning or rebuilding New York, Anthony?"

"We've done some preliminary canvassing, sir. Most of the leaders that we've talked to see rebuilding as a golden opportunity for employment of their members. There's hardly a union in the country that won't be involved in some way. Abandoning won't do anything for them; rebuilding means jobs, lots of jobs, and for many years to come."

"I agree with Anthony, sir," said the secretary of commerce. "I've been on the telephone for most of the night with the heads of some of the largest corporations in this country. They've also been talking with high-ups in the unions. The general consensus seems to be that rebuilding would benefit everyone. It would provide jobs and be an impetus to American industry to show the world what it still can do. Tad Jackson, of National Steel, said that industry and labor haven't had an opportunity like this since Pearl Harbor."

"Which reminds me, Geoff. What about the Japanese? They have a significant amount invested in American business."

"There's no denying that," Collins replied. "So have the Germans, the Saudis, and lots of other nations around the world, just as we have in their countries. This is going to have to be a multinational effort."

"But the spearhead should be from America. Americans rebuilding America, not the Japanese, Europeans, or Arabs."

"I agree, Anthony," said Collins to the secretary of labor.

"As do I," said the president. "For lots of reasons, and not just because it will be good for business and labor. It will be good for the whole country. It will give all Americans a sense of pride that I think has been slipping away in the face of all the foreign takeovers we've witnessed in the past decade—pride in being able to take charge once again, do things that we thought we couldn't. Americans are going to find out again what it means to be the most inventive and industrious people in the world."

After the applause—unseemly with whistles and war whoops—had died down, the congressman from New England who had spoken softly to his colleague while Billingsley was orating asked to be recognized. Tall, gaunt, looking as if he had been chiseled from the stone of his native Maine, he had been in the House for three decades—longer even than Billingsley. Nominally a Republican, he had for the past ten congressional elections run on the tickets of both parties. The respect with which he was held in the House was enormous.

He rose and cleared his throat softly. "Mr. Speaker, my fellow representatives, I am fortunate to come from a state that has not been damaged by this disaster, much as does my esteemed colleague from Missouri. Unlike him, I cannot claim to have any special knowledge of the amount of money it might take to bring New York back to where it was a day ago. Nor am I particularly fond of the City itself. But I do take exception to Congressman Billingsley comparing it with St. Louis." The New Englander allowed a titter to subside before going on. "That would be, and I mean no disrespect to the people of my fair state—or the fair state of Oregon, for that matter—like comparing New York to Portland.

"New York has, perhaps, certain qualities not unlike those of the biblical cities that God caused to be punished for their sins. But those qualities are infinitessimal when compared to what, historically, it has had to offer in the way of beauty, culture, and enlightenment to this sometimes-lost age of ours."

The president listened to the rest of the reply of the congressman from Maine to Billingsley's speech. It had been short, well reasoned, and equally well stated, if not as well received as the previous speech had been. He glanced over his shoulder at the chief of staff.

"Ask him if he would be so kind as to stop over here when he's finished in the House. At his convenience."

"You're thinking that he would make a good point man, sir?"

"Yes. I've known him ever since I was a congressman and I've always liked him. But his reputation has come down through the years as being almost as insular as Billingsley's though hardly as rabid. If he's convinced, for whatever reasons, that New York should be saved, he'll be a powerful ally. And powerful allies are what we need right now."

The private line rang in the study of the governor's mansion in Albany at ten thirteen that night. George Fleming pondered a moment before picking it up, wondering which of the two dozen or so people who had this particular number might be calling.

He had had a hectic day. The plane from Nice had landed in

Boston and he had helicoptered from Logan to Albany to find turmoil in his administration. Physically, Albany had suffered little damage from the earthquake, though like much of the rest of the Northeast, telephone communications were spotty. The day had been taken up with a series of executive directives to officials in all parts of the state on what they could and could not do at this early stage of the crisis. Fleming, more cautious as a politician than as a man, wished for the appearance of no misstep in his handling of the emergency.

"Fleming," he said as he brought the phone to his ear.

"George, good to finally get you. King Billingsley here. Terrible tragedy, terrible. I want you to know that we in Congress will do everything we can to help you in this time of need."

"Yes, King. Thank you. I didn't hear your speech today but an aide reported to me the gist of it."

"And . . . ?"

"I think it's time to move with care, King. I believe both of us have the same agenda, as well as the same timetable. Do you think your, uh, supporters, will be able to block any attempt to send New York massive aid, aid that would get the City back on its feet as a city?"

"I am confident, George, from the way my short speech was received this morning, that you have nothing to worry about. New York City is dead."

"I'm pleased to hear that, King. Keep me abreast of the situation, would you?"

"Of course, George, of course. You know I'm always glad to do a favor for our party's leading presidential contender."

"Thank you, King. I appreciate that. It won't be forgotten."

George Fleming hung up. I wonder what this will cost me? he thought. Doesn't matter. It's in the future. The now is what's important.

———

Brendan Ahearn's helicopter landed near the medical tent and two Red Cross workers helped Ahearn get Sam Thorne's semiconscious body down onto a stretcher. Ahearn followed them into the tent and made his way through the crowded cots to Dr. Kelly. She was bent over a cot occupied by an elderly man who had suffered a heart attack, giving him an injection and giving orders to the nurse who stood by her at the same time.

"Pat," Ahearn stood before her, his handlebar mustache singed, his clothes and face blackened. "You got to come over here. This guy is hurt . . . I need you."

Pat Kelly straightened up. "Jesus Mary! Brendan Ahearn, you're the one that needs help. Where's the other one?" As he led her to Sam Thorne, she admonished him. "You go lie down on the first available cot and let one of our nurses give you some help. You must have inhaled plenty of smoke." They arrived at Sam's stretcher.

Pat Kelly knelt by the stretcher and started methodically checking Sam out neurologically, then, "Get the oxygen over here, stat." The Red Cross worker rushed the oxygen tank over and she put a mask over Sam's face, which was burned and bloody from a gash on his head. In a few moments, Dr. Kelly stood up and said to Ahearn, "He's got a concussion and without better equipment I can't tell how bad. What happened?"

"He was trying to save a man and he went up the stairs once too often. The fire had weakened them and they collapsed under his feet. He didn't fall far, but he inhaled a lot of smoke and hit his head. The guy he was trying to rescue died a few minutes after Sam reached him."

"Heroics, heroics, they'll be the death of us all," she said. "Go lie down. Your friend here is going to live. I need to do some work on him, and it's no help having you hang over me." She gave Brendan an affectionate push. "You there, take this brave fireman over there and give him some oxygen and make him lie down for half an hour."

"I can't do that, Patty. I'm needed upstairs at the mayor's—"

"You're needed nowhere for thirty minutes or you'll be no good to anyone. Go!" Kelly's blue eyes flashed.

Meek as a lamb, Brendan Ahearn followed the nurse.

"Jesus and all the saints, spare me from heroes," she muttered as she knelt again by the stretcher. "So, my fine friend, you bought some trouble fighting a fire, and what made you think you knew how to be an overnight fireman, you arrogant WASP male, you."

As she muttered, she washed his head wound, applied a topical painkiller in preparation for the twenty tiny stitches required. She took his pulse again and started to go over his body carefully this time for any injuries she had not picked up on the first time. The nurse helped her take off his torn and burned shirt and pants, and brought Pat the medical supplies she needed for the third-degree burns on his face and hands. As Pat Kelly thumped and prodded and felt his arms and legs, turned his neck from side to side, and listened to his heart, Sam Thorne's eyes opened. "Aren't you being fresh with me, Doctor?"

Kelly did not acknowledge her relief that he was fully conscious and without missing a beat or looking at him, she continued her careful examination.

"Am I alive or in heaven?"

"You're alive, buster, no thanks to yourself." She finished her examination. "No broken bones. No spinal damage. Just a minor concussion and some burns and a gash on your head. Damn lucky, you are, Mr. Thorne."

She stood up and looked down at him. He grinned up at her, his teeth very white against his sooty face.

"Okay, this shouldn't hurt too much." Dr. Kelly grinned back at him as he winced. "You won't feel a thing."

She got two volunteers to move him to a makeshift operating table and she shone a strong generator-powered light on his forehead. "Be quiet, and don't move your head, or you may look very funny tomorrow."

He put a hand on her arm. "Listen, Doctor, I can't stay here long. I have to get across town. My son." His expression was grim again.

She lifted his sooty hand off her arm and placed it gently by his side. "Sam Thorne, you are going nowhere until tomorrow morning. Maybe then you can leave. Depending. That concussion is no joke."

"As soon as you stitch me up, I'm gone, Pat."

She cleaned his wound with infinite sensitivity as she spoke to him, not in her usual tone with him, but quiet, gentle, as though she were calming a wounded animal. "I know how you feel. My kids are all right. Someone came and told me that my husband and kids are all right, all of them at Roosevelt Hospital being taken care of there. If I were you, wild horses couldn't keep me here." After giving him more topical pain medication, she began to stitch the wound. "But if you get up too soon and pass out in the middle of this chaos, what good are you to anyone?" She knew what Sam did not know and that was that she had already given him an injection to make him relax, and as she spoke to him, his eyes were closed. She finished stitching and turned off the bright light above him. His lean, angular face was calm, and his breathing under the mask was regular. "Tomorrow, my handsome friend. Tonight, you're here." She motioned for a nurse to start treating his burns, and Dr. Kelly made her way through the cots to see what priority case she needed to take on next.

———

The mayor took a call from Governor Fleming.

"Bruce, George Fleming here."

"Hello, Governor. Welcome back from Europe."

"My timing for being away was not good. What a terrible tragedy. I understand the president ordered four thousand troops into the City early this morning. Of course, I have called out the National Guard, and on the entire state to provide all the aid we can give the City. I'll fill you in on the details in a minute, but for now I want to tell you where I stand on trying to rebuild Manhattan."

Bruce was silent.

The governor continued. "I believe we must evacuate the residents and anyone else who was in the City on Wednesday. We must consider . . . well, we must for now, relocate rather than rebuild. There are many and diverse reasons to back up my opinion, Bruce, but the overriding one is money. This state and certainly the coffers of Manhattan do not have the money to undertake such a huge project as rebuilding the City. I'm not sure the federal government has the money. Every penny the state depends on would go to the City for years to come."

The mayor interjected, "But what we need now is not money. We need time. Things are already beginning to turn around. Not much, but some. Howard Tate is trying to reach the president as we speak. He has considerable influence with the president and Tate disagrees with you one hundred percent. As do I, I might add."

"Come now, Bruce. How can you—"

"Let me bring you up to date. Sitting in Albany it may be difficult to imagine, but the people of this City are already rallying. The Army Engineers are today attempting to build a bridge across the narrow part of the East River where the Williamsburg Bridge collapsed. We are getting our injured off Manhattan over to Tate Acres, where the medical center is caring for them, staffed by volunteer doctors and nurses from our hospitals here. Supplies, water and food, were helicoptered into Central Park early this morning, and now they will be brought in every hour of the day until we no longer need them. The police and the Army have begun to control the looters and other criminal elements. The evacuation effort is under way by boat, both pleasure boats and larger ships that are coming from every port in the Northeast, along the southern coast, and even from the mid-Atlantic. Our worst problems are the fires and those trapped—"

The governor interrupted. "I know. I know. But the subway system and power and water and sewer systems—all the things that make the City work—destroyed. God knows they were decrepit enough before this tragic earthquake. The financial district is going to have to set up elsewhere, Boston. Los Angeles. Chicago. I don't know."

The mayor sighed and tapped his pencil against his lower lip as he listened to Governor Fleming. When the governor gave him a chance, he said, "Governor, I was born here."

Fleming, irritated, interrupted. "I know, Bruce, I know. What has that got—"

"You wait a minute, George. Just listen to me. I was born here, a poor black boy with a drunk for a father who disappeared before I was six. My mother worked downtown as a housemaid and brought up four kids on what she made. On Sundays we went to the Abyssinian Baptist Church when Adam Clayton Powell was still preaching. I knew every drug dealer who hung around the schoolyard. My uncle was the top runner for the numbers game in my neighborhood. My pals used to wait on Fridays up by the

Hospital for Joint Diseases, you know, up at 126th Street, for the old black women orderlies to come out of the hospital. They'd stand waiting for the bus—no taxi, even driven by a black man, would pick them up—and my pals would grab their pocketbooks and run off with their week's wages. Somehow my mother kept my brothers and sister and me on the straight and narrow. I got a scholarship to Harvard, my sister is married to a top Army officer, one of my brothers is a retired ambassador, and my other brother was a New York City policeman killed in the line of duty. I came home to New York from Cambridge and went on from there. Now I've moved from Harlem to Gracie Mansion, which, thank God, still stands. Not much of Harlem does, but we can rebuild a better city, Governor. And if you think for one minute that I'm going to let a bunch of fat-ass politicians, yourself included, sitting in your cozy houses with your feet to the fire and the cat in your laps, dig this City's final grave, you've got another think coming. It will take more than you guys to bring New Yorkers down. Most of us were either raised here or got here because we knew this City is where it's at, Governor, and all these years, and all this work, and all this talent is not going to be abandoned. You hear me!"

The mayor slammed the phone down.

Across town on this, the second day, Thursday, Diane and the other volunteers were taking a break from digging out the basement of the school. A Red Cross worker had arrived on the block and set up a makeshift kiosk, where she dispensed soft drinks, candy bars, crackers, and blankets, supplies that had been distributed after the Army helicopters had landed in the park. An EMS van had managed to maneuver up the street, and it was equipped with many things they needed, including a Coleman stove, on which sat a huge coffee maker. Missing was equipment to detect the living under the rubble or trained rescue teams to attempt to reach children trapped on higher floors, like Danny Thorne and Debbie Murdoch.

Diane heard a woman call her name, and she turned to see who it was. Karen.

"Hey. How are you?" she asked, knowing the answer by looking at Karen's tear-streaked puffy-eyed face.

"Our building is down. My husband . . . no one on our floor has been found. They think they were killed. No one knows for sure because they are buried. Did you hear that the mayor has ordered all official rescue teams—the police, the emergency medical people—to stop trying to find anyone who is not above ground, by noon today." She fell into Diane's arms. "No one is even going to try to find him."

"You poor baby. Come over here and I'll get you some coffee." She led Karen over to the EMS van. "Why don't you lie down for a little while." There was a bunk in the back of the van. "Come on, you look exhausted." Karen obeyed as though any will of her own was gone. Diane sat on the edge of the bunk as they sipped their coffee. They were silent. Words of comfort had taken on an empty quality in the last few terrible hours. Finally Karen remembered to ask. "Your husband? Your little boy?"

"Sam is fine. He's working with the mayor's office. Danny . . . Danny is up there on one of the top floors of the school. We don't know . . ." she paused.

"Oh, Diane, isn't there anything, anyone who can . . ."

"Not yet. Sam is going to try to get some equipment, but with the streets the way they are, it doesn't look good." Diane got up. "Now you lie down and I'll wake you up in a while."

Karen put her head down on the bunk, and Diane watched her until the younger woman fell asleep.

The plane landed at a private field southwest of Chicago. Once again, a car was waiting, and Hartnett was sped quickly to a high-rise overlooking Lake Michigan. Perfect. He knew exactly where he was. They hadn't thought to keep his destination a secret from him, believing him to be safely in Domenico Rizzo's power.

The apartment was on the fourteenth floor, and Hartnett's first act, when they got there at around 6 A.M., local time, was to turn on the television news. It was as he had hoped. Trading was still suspended—it was, after all, less than forty-eight hours after the earthquake had shattered the financial district—but would be resumed on Monday when the Exchange would be transferred to Philadelphia . . . temporarily, it was hoped. He listened with half an ear to the rest of the news as he began to set up for the day's work. The country, the entire world, was still reeling from the blow that had brought Manhattan to its knees. The mayor was doing this; the governor that; the president something else. It all blended into the background as Dave Hartnett prepared to live like a king for the rest of his life.

Hartnett had told Rizzo what he needed in the way of equipment. Hours before Hartnett arrived in the apartment, the equipment had been moved in. The personal computer was the latest model from Seiko, a powerful, sleekly designed machine that Hartnett had long had his heart set on but had not been able to afford. With its fourteen-inch, high-definition screen and built-in printer, it was on the absolute cutting edge of modern computer technology. He had asked that Rizzo refrain from having the machine unpacked and set up unless he had access to an expert. Apparently Domenico had not, because it was still in its packing.

Hartnett checked his watch. Six fifteen. Seven fifteen on the East Coast. Lots of time. Even though the banks he was planning to raid operated electronically on a twenty-four-hour basis, he didn't want to arouse suspicion by tapping into the accounts too early in the New York day. Besides, while he had cracked all of the access codes necessary to gain entrance into the financial transactions programs, he hadn't dared enough in-depth testing to tell if the programs authorized financial dealings outside of New York business hours. If they didn't and he tried to invade them, he might well find himself with programs that had been wiped clean.

He took his time with the Seiko, lifting it carefully and lovingly out of its packing and setting it on the table in the small breakfast area off the kitchen. He took a damp paper towel and wiped it down gently, caressingly, and jumped visibly when a nasal voice said, "You gonna come, or what?"

Hartnett turned. A small, gopher-featured man stood leaning against the frame of the kitchen doorway.

"Wh-what?" Hartnett stammered.

"I been watching you for the last couple minutes," the gopher said. "You been stroking that thing like it's some pussy you're just about to put it to." His eyes dropped to below Hartnett's waist.

Hartnett reddened as the man grinned at him.

"Don't mess your pants, genius." Then the gopher turned and sauntered out of sight.

Hartnett had hoped that he would be able to be alone—for concentration's sake, he told Rizzo, when he was breaking into the accounts, but Domenico Rizzo merely laughed the request aside. Hartnett knew, however, that if Rizzo hadn't been able to find anyone who could unpack and set up the Seiko, whoever he had watching and guarding him wouldn't have a clue about what Hartnett was doing.

He turned back to the Seiko and unfolded the printer and the screen from the main body of the machine. Sweet. He checked the connections between the component parts to ensure that they were not loose before he switched on the power. Then he plugged the machine in and, holding his breath slightly if he had known it, turned the Seiko on.

At first there was nothing, and Hartnett almost panicked. Then he remembered that the Seiko had a series of delays built into it to keep power from any possibility of damaging the delicate circuitry within. One indicator light flickered on, then another. The printer hummed into life—odd that they hadn't been able to make it totally • silent. The screen grew luminous, then faded to a soft, eye-resting glow. Hartnett smiled, a small child with a new toy.

―――

Howard Tate kneeled by the cot on which Ingrid lay. Her head was turban-bandaged, her eyes closed. She had never regained consciousness. Dr. Kelly stopped by.

"She seems worse, doctor," he said.

"I'm sorry, Mr. Tate. We've done everything we could for her. Even if she were in a regular hospital setting, this kind of brain injury is difficult to treat and I am afraid she is getting weaker."

"There's no hope?"

Pat Kelly hesitated. "I'm a Catholic. We always have hope."

"Medically," Howard said with anger. "Not metaphysically. Will she die?"

"I think she is dying," Dr. Kelly answered. "Don't ask me when. I never know. But soon, I think. I am sorry."

Howard Tate ignored the young woman doctor. What did she know of his pain. Ingrid had not loved him, he knew that, but he had loved her, in spite of her hard, uncompromising, and avaricious character. She was young enough to be his daughter, and she had had a very bad time before she met him. He had been happy to give her all the things she had never had before. It gave him pleasure to see her greedy response, and to feed her ever more treasures of a material kind. She looked very young now, her pale face tranquil at last. Howard Tate got to his feet, his tall, distinguished form looking somehow diminished by sorrow. He left the huge emergency tent and made his way to the precinct house, where he had an important planning meeting with Mayor Lincoln.

It was Thursday night and Danny had slept, on and off, through the afternoon. When he awakened he tried his voice, and found that it was coming back. He checked his watch: 8:38 P.M., October 6, 1994. "Debbie," he called out. No answer. He had eaten his last graham cracker and his stomach ached with hunger.

He wondered if Debbie had died. "Debbie," he persisted. "Can you hear me?"

He went as close to the pile of debris where her voice had come from as he could and put his ear down onto the mortar.

"Help," a faint voice came.

He jumped up, yelled as loud as he could. "Hey, someone! We're up here. Come get us!" He dared not go toward the outside wall, most of which had disintegrated, in order to look down below. Instinctively he knew that there was no place where he stood that was safe.

He crawled close to where her voice had come. "Debbie, I'm getting help. Soon," he said in a loud voice.

He tried to think about his dad and figure out what he would do about Debbie. He was strong and would be able to move the stuff off her, unlike Danny, who felt very small and helpless.

He decided that his dad would use the time to do something that had a point. He sat down and went through his addition tables, then counted all his school friends by name, every one in the first-grade class by their first names. Then he started on the names of the states and their capitals. It was only 9:12 P.M. He was very tired, suddenly, and he put his head down on the cold floor, pulled his jacket up over his shoulders, and went back to sleep.

An hour later he awakened. He stood up and yelled, "Help!" at the top of his lungs. "Help! It's Danny Thorne. Help!" And this time he heard from far, far away the sound of voices yelling back. He couldn't hear what they said, but he knew then that he was going to be all right. His dad would come up and get him. His dad could do anything.

He found an opening in the debris where Debbie was trapped. He pawed at the material blocking it, and pulled a great deal of sheet rock and insulating stuff from it. Finally, lying on his side, his head almost touching the floor, he saw in to where Debbie lay. Her head was back and she seemed unconscious. "Debbie," he said loudly. "Wake up. It's Danny Thorne." She did not move. He could see blood on her face, and her body was twisted in a strange way. He reached in and could just touch her face. "Debbie. Don't be scared. It's just me." To his surprise her eyes opened. She made a funny gurgling noise. "Can you talk?" He tried to pry more material away so he could get closer to her. "Water," she moaned.

He got up and carefully went back to the stall and tried to figure out how to carry water to her. He looked around. Then he took off one of his shoes and dipped it into the toilet bowl and got it half full of water. He went back to Debbie.

He reached in and carefully dripped some water on her face and as near her mouth as he could manage. She opened her mouth and he poured some water into it. She choked, sputtered, breathed deeply and was quiet. Then she said in a very weak voice, "Thank you, Danny."

"Do you hurt?"

"No. I don't feel anything down there anymore." She opened her eyes again. "I remember you. The little kid who brings lizards to school in his pocket."

"Henry. That's the name of my pet lizard. My dad brought him back to me from California."

"Henry. That's a funny name for a lizard." She tried to turn her head toward him. "Do you think they'll find us?"

"Sure," Danny said. "My dad is going to rescue us. I'm sure of it."

"Good." She put her head back and closed her eyes.

THE THIRD DAY

O n the third day, Copper sensed he was getting near the school. He had had many detours, and his short legs were tired from climbing over debris, from losing his way and then circling back, over and over. He saw a Doberman coming his way, in a pack with some other big dogs. They were running from house to house, barking and grabbing any morsel of food they could find. Parts of an unfortunate cat still hung out of the mouth of one of them. Copper knew he was in trouble. He turned and fled, the big ravening dogs snarling and barking on his heels. He raced down the side street, dodging people's legs, and he crouched under a car. The hunters ran around the car, their lips drawn back, teeth bared in hunger and blood lust, but Copper was very still and eventually they ran off, after other small prey.

Sam awakened and looked at his watch. It was 3:21 A.M. on Friday, October 7. His head was splitting wide open with pain. His mouth was dry. He pulled the oxygen mask off his face and looked around by the light of a battery-operated lantern. He was in a tiny room made of packing cases on three sides with a sheet of plywood for a door. He touched his head gingerly and felt the stitches, and it came back to him. The moment when the smoke and fire took over. He lay back and closed his eyes against the pain and tried to think.

He heard the plywood shift. He opened his eyes and saw Dr. Kelly holding a flashlight. She took his wrist in her cool hand and put a thermometer in his mouth. He waited until she had finished taking his pulse, and then she slid the stethoscope under the sheet covering his bare chest, and he realized he was naked, except for his Jockey shorts. She finished and shone a small light into one of his eyes. "How do you feel?"

"Like someone hit my head with a baseball bat."

She took the makeshift pillow and raised his head on it. "Here. Drink some of this." She handed him a paper cup.

"Not if it's going to put me back to sleep. I have to get out of here." He tried to sit up and dizziness forced him back.

"It's not a sedative, just some juice. You need liquids. Drink it."

He did. She pulled over a packing case and sat down by his cot. "I don't want you to leave here for several more hours—"

"No way, Doctor. No way. I have to get across town."

She looked at him and he stared back at her. "I mean it, Pat Kelly. You've got to help me feel better so I can leave."

"You mean give you some recreational drugs to mask your concussion? No way, Sam Thorne, no way," she mocked him, instantly regretted it, but could not stop herself. His self-assurance, his will, whatever, galled her.

Sam did not answer. She took a washcloth and started to clean his face. He lay still. Then he opened his eyes and looked up into her eyes. "I need your help."

"Here." She handed him the cloth. "Clean off your hands. You can tell better than I can what hurts. You're lucky only the backs of them got burned. Superficial at that."

He did as he was told and handed her the cloth.

"I want you to drink some more of this, and I'm getting you some soup. Then we'll talk." She disappeared and he lay back exhausted.

Minutes later she returned and propped him up. "You need nourishment," she said. She put the bowl of soup in his hands.

He took a spoonful and then another. It tasted delicious to him. She sat and watched him while he finished the bowl. "I put a little something extra in there for you." She grinned at him. "A touch of whiskey never hurt soup."

He laughed and his head throbbed. "Can you amputate my head? Then I'd be fine." He took the two pills she handed him with some water.

"They'll help your head. But you mustn't go until dawn. I won't have you staggering around the streets in the dark with looters and Christ knows what all out there. When dawn comes, I'll check you over again and off you go. Deal?"

"Deal." He looked at Pat Kelly and thought again how pretty she was, with her jet-black hair tousled and her eyes dark with fatigue. "Why do you fight me, Doctor?"

"Because," Dr. Kelly reached down into a paper bag and pulled out a small bottle of scotch and poured an inch neat into a paper cup. "Because," she raised the cup and then drained it, "you are like the man my father would have liked me to marry instead of another mick like Brian. My dad would have liked me to have met and married a WASP, overprivileged fellow like you." Her bright blue eyes sparkled.

"Do I get some of that?"

"No. It's bad for your concussion."

"A swallow? It can't kill me."

She poured a tablespoonful into another cup and gave it to him, giving herself another inch.

"Here's to you, Doctor."

"May the road rise to meet you and may all your days be happy ones."

The liquid burned right down to his stomach. He felt light-headed, but his headache was much better.

"What do you do when you're not out finding earthquakes to study?"

"I go out and find other natural phenomena to study."

"Maybe I've found one thing we have in common." She squinted at him over her cup. "We do nothing but work. Right?"

"Maybe. I wouldn't dare speak for you, Doctor, or you'd snap my head off. But I'd guess you're as much of an obsessive career person as I am, sure."

"I think this week will change our lives." Pat stared down into her cup. "Nothing will be the same." She looked across at him. "Do you feel as though we're characters in a World War Two movie? I do." She reached out and drew the sheet that covered him down so that she could put her hand on his bare arm. She left it there, a strong, square, untanned hand, nails cut short, a doctor's hand. After a moment, he picked it up and turned it over and raised it to his mouth, and kissed the inner palm. He watched her face. She stared at him. "I knew this was going to happen," she said, and knelt by his cot.

"What? What's going to happen," he breathed, turning on his side toward her. He took both her hands and drew her down to him. They kissed. He could taste the whiskey on their lips, in their mouths, as their tongues explored, and he traced her breasts with his fingertips, running his fingers over the stiff nipples under her khaki shirt. He unbuttoned the shirt and she moved so that he could kiss her breasts.

"What the hell are we doing?" she murmured.

"Do you want me to stop?" When he drew away for a moment, she looked at him.

"I've never been unfaithful to Brian. No man has ever made love to me except him."

Sam wanted her, his body ached with fatigue and pain and passion and he pulled her close to him. "Besides," she whispered, "this isn't the Ritz. Someone's going to find us." She grinned at Sam. "Are you going to risk it, you serious, honorable man?" She lay down beside him.

He pulled the sheet over them, then took her in his arms and held her close. "I want you." He kissed the top of her head, nestled against him. "I want us to make love and . . ."

She pulled away. "When I go to my next confession, how am I going to explain that you weren't Irish?" She got up, rummaged for

a pen, and wrote in a big scrawl on a piece of carton, PLEASE DO
NOT DISTURB and propped it outside the plywood door. She came
back to the cot and crawled under the sheet, pulling off her pants
and shirt.

"God, your feet are cold. I wonder what this does to a
concussion?" He started to kiss her.

"Your feet are cold, too." He kissed her neck and then her
mouth. She put her arms around his neck and forgot everything in
the world except the feelings he was arousing with his mouth and
tongue and fingers and hard body.

Too soon, it was over and she lay in Sam's arms. "The nuns taught
us never to undress in front of anyone," she whispered. "It's the
one thing they taught me that I can't seem to get over." She raised
herself on one elbow and looked down at him. He opened his eyes.
"I feel wonderful, do you?" he asked.

"Yes. I think we're crazy, but I feel wonderful."

She bent her head to kiss his mouth. "You . . ." she paused.
"You made me feel things I've never felt before." She could feel
the heat in her cheeks.

He smiled up at her. "My feisty doctor, you are quite a woman.
Do you know how generous you are?"

"I don't understand you at all, you know that," she sighed.
"Generous?"

Sam was serious. He stared up at her with an expression that
tugged at her heart, that of a sad young boy. "Yes, you are all there
for me, Pat. Just me. No one else. I felt that and . . ." He pulled
her down beside him and kissed her. "And that's rare."

She gazed at him. "All I know is that we've had a strange special
moment, Sam Thorne."

"When this is over, I want to—"

She stopped him. "No. We're not going to be together again.
You know that, it wouldn't work." She smiled to soften her words.
"But this moment was terrific. I've finally been to bed with my
golden Protestant, and he was swell."

Sam kissed her. "You're mad. The mad doctor."

She sat up and started to pull on her clothes. "Soon you'll be on your way across town to find your son." She buttoned her shirt. "Here. I want you to have this." She slipped the gold chain with the cross on it over her head and gave it to Sam. "You don't have to keep it if it's embarrassing, but I want you to have something of mine."

He sat up and took her in his arms. He held her very tight. His throat ached. Something about this woman touched him beyond words. Slowly he released her. "I won't forget you, Doctor."

"Nor I you, golden boy. Have a good life. I know you'll find your son and he'll be fine." She kissed him on the cheek. She looked at her watch: 5:32 A.M.

"It's light out there. You can go. Promise me you'll go slow and get a doctor to give you a scan for the concussion as soon as possible?"

He nodded. She gave him a long look and quickly left him.

The Observer, *London*
Friday, October 7, 1994

HER MAJESTY THE QUEEN AND THE PRIME MINISTER CONVENE EXTRAORDINARY SESSION IN THE HOUSE OF LORDS AND THE HOUSE OF COMMONS TO UNITE THE EFFORT TO HELP OUR ALLY, THE UNITED STATES, IN ITS RESCUE EFFORTS OF NEW YORK CITY.

Her Majesty, Queen Elizabeth, and the Prime Minister convened both Houses of Parliament late yesterday, the day after a massive earthquake devastated New York City. The Prime Minister has put our armed forces on alert and our naval forces operating in the Atlantic have been ordered to New York harbour with all possible speed to help evacuate the wounded. H.M.S. *Ark Royal* is expected to arrive there by Sunday. Worldwide, the Royal Navy has rallied to speed its ships to aid the Americans. The Queen has mobilized all of our Red Cross and Emergency Services to aid in the relief effort. Emergency measures were taken by the City immediately to quell possible panic in the financial market.

Early reports estimate the number of those killed in the earthquake to be over two million people, and those injured over four million. The President ordered the United States Navy Base on Staten Island to begin evacuating the wounded, and the Army and Air Force have been dropping supplies into Manhattan's Central Park. Communication of any kind with the City is minimal, but the National Broadcasting Company has managed to activate one satellite uplink truck from heavily damaged Manhattan. Wall Street, much of which has been destroyed, is at a standstill. Many hospitals have been destroyed. The scene is one of chaos. Looting and more serious crimes of murder and rape have been reported.

———

The president, unlike many of his predecessors, was not much given to prayer breakfasts. His Protestantism was a comfortable, not an evangelical one, and he had never felt the need—for reasons of faith or politics—to reach out to the religious right any more than to his other constituents. But this situation, this extraordinary act of God, called for something more in response, and he had invited fifty-four key senators and representatives—including H. King Billingsley—to the White House, along with the Episcopal bishop of Washington, the chaplain of Georgetown University, and the rabbi of Washington National Hebrew Congregation to have breakfast at 8:30 A.M. on the Friday morning following the earthquake.

Meeting with the cabinet and a few other key administration officials the evening before, the president had made it clear to them that he wanted New York City to be saved and had asked, not for discussion but for any voice of strong reservation or dissent. Only Health and Human Services disagreed with the president's position, but not strongly, and the man had no problem with being suddenly called out of town and being unable to attend the prayer breakfast when it was suggested to him.

The president had made his position clear. "Until forty-eight hours ago, New York City was the most powerful city on earth, a symbol of America as the most powerful nation on earth. I am talking, ladies and gentlemen, about perception, not strictly about reality. If the most powerful nation can let its most important—powerful—city be defeated by a force of nature, what does that say about the nation? What signal does that send to other, lesser nations about our resolve, about our ability, about our strength and commitment at the end of this, America's century? More than half of the people from the Senate and House who have been invited for breakfast tomorrow are probably going to have a built-in prejudice against New York and the idea of restoring it to what it was. King Billingsley isn't the only one who feels that way—just the most offensively articulate. It's up to us to begin to change their minds so that, a few days from now when I go before a joint meeting of Congress, the vote to rebuild New York will be substantially in the majority."

After the meeting, he had taken Rose Compton-Reilly aside to talk about her college son, Julius, had had to tell her that there was still no word about his whereabouts or safety. As he would have expected of this brilliant economist and first woman to have held the Treasury post, she understood that he was doing everything possible and, despite his assuring her that she did not have to be at the breakfast tomorrow, said that she would be. "After all, Mr. President, there's nothing I can do for Julius from here. But we're New Yorkers, and if there is something I can do for our City, that's what I want to do."

The leaders of the three faiths had spoken and the assembled members of the administration, Congress, and the Supreme Court had prayed along with them for those who had survived and those who had not, for the city of New York and for the country. They had divided into separate groups of eight at individual tables. Not wishing to single out any individual senator or representative, the president and his wife sat at a table with the three members of the clergy, their two wives, and Rose Compton-Reilly ("my date," as the Georgetown chaplain said as he held out her seat). All three of the clerics were New Yorkers, and the president hardly needed to lobby them for their opinions, but each individually spoke of the need to rebuild the City and offered whatever help they could to the president's cause.

For strategic reasons, H. King Billingsley had not been seated at the same table as Edgar Smithson. The president had reasoned that the Missouri congressman was firmly fixed in his ideas; better to have Smithson lobbying for the president's position with members of Congress who might be teetering on the edge.

Billingsley's table was shared with, among others, Geoffrey Collins. Collins, a seasoned diplomat but also a renowned lawyer who had, in an earlier administration, been attorney general, had sparred with Billingsley in the House and on various handball courts for well over a decade. The two knew each other well and were aware of the other's strengths and weaknesses. The conversation, which included the rest of the people at the table, but only peripherally, never slipped below the level of politeness, but it was obvious that neither man was going to budge from his view.

At other tables, the quiet lobbying was going on with mixed success. Edgar Smithson, with his quiet Down East drawl, was talking quietly with the breakfast partner to his right, Aida Vasquez, a dour and purposeful congresswoman from San Antonio, who had long been an ardent supporter of federal aid to cities.

"It's too much, Edgar. Seven trillion. I don't know where King got his figure, but my own staff estimates indicate that he's not far off, and that may be low-ball. Think of what that kind of money could do—if it could be appropriated—divided up among a hundred other of the neediest cities in the country."

"There's no denying that, Aida. But the point is, it could never be appropriated. If you and your supporters spoke on the floor until you were blue in the face, the rest of the House still wouldn't appropriate money at that level for the needs of cities. But that's because the needs of cities are ongoing ones, recurring ones, and Congress has historically felt that such needs should be seen after by the cities themselves or their respective states. This is different, as I know I don't have to tell you. This is a catastrophe that has fallen on one particular city, something that no one could have predicted or foreseen in the way that you can predict subway renovations or the need for more homeless shelters. Yes, it's massive; yes, it will be horrendously expensive. But if we don't respond in a positive way—if we retreat from our real responsibility to the City, which is to give it new life—then we tell both the rest of the country and the world that, as a government, we are not going to be there in the time of our people's greatest need."

Aida Vasquez looked at Smithson. With her hair in a bun on top of her head, her large, liquid brown eyes, and her ample figure, she looked every bit the mother that the people of San Antonio who had elected her for the past twelve years wanted her to be. "Let me think about it, Edgar," was all she would say.

Throughout the room it was the same. Cabinet members and other high officials of the administration, along with Edgar Smithson and several representatives who were from the Northeast, lobbied quietly and intensely with those members of Congress who they thought they had the best hope of persuading. The president had chosen wisely when he had issued his invitations for this breakfast. With the exception of Billingsley, everyone invited from both houses was at least willing to listen to arguments in favor of rebuilding New York. If some went away unpersuaded, that was at least as much a fault of the advocate as it was an inherent stubbornness on the part of the congressman. To the credit of the advocates, most did not go away unpersuaded, or at least had opened their minds a little further to the need of saving the City. The money necessary—the president had neither confirmed nor denied the seven-trillion-dollar estimate (nor had he found out the source of the leak, but he hadn't really expected to)—loomed large in the thinking of these men and women as they left the White House. They had constituents after all, and it was the tax dollars of those plain people that would be used to bring New York back to life again.

Billingsley was not the only one who considered New York to be "Sodom on the Hudson." Indeed, as he had pointed out to Geoffrey Collins in their conversation at breakfast, lots of New Yorkers felt the same way. To ask people who had never been there, but who had heard endless stories of how dangerous and crime-ridden, filthy, and depraved the City was, to throw it a lifeline was to ask them, in his opinion, to throw their money down a sewer.

"That's over twenty-five thousand dollars a head for every man, woman, and child in this country," he said to Collins at the end of the conversation. "At least the way I see it. You can say what you want about insurance coverage and participation of the private sector; my experience is that the insurers will find some way to weasel out and the private sector will suddenly find itself strapped for cash when the time comes. Then who winds up footing the bill? The people, that's who. No, Geoffrey, this one I'll fight you tooth and nail, and you can tell the president that."

Edgar Smithson had, at the president's request, lingered after the other guests had departed. Now he and Geoffrey Collins were with the president in his study reviewing the morning. Collins had reported his utter lack of success with Billingsley, Smithson his partial one with Aida Vasquez.

"I've asked the others to give me brief memos on their conversations. I wanted you two to stay behind because I'd like you both to accompany me late this afternoon to Camp David. I've arranged a nonpublic"—the president hated the word *secret*—"meeting with Bruce Lincoln and Howard Tate for nine o'clock tonight. They'll be flown in via military helicopter, spend a couple of hours, then fly out again. To the best of our ability, the press won't know who has come and gone. I believe you both know Howard?" The secretary and the congressman nodded their assent. "He has long been one of the greatest champions of New York City. Almost ninety-five percent of the structures on Tate Acres survived the earthquake intact and it has rapidly become one of the focal points of the medical relief effort for the city. I spoke with him the night before last, told him that if he could present me a viable way of rebuilding New York that I could take to Congress the day after tomorrow, I'd go for it a hundred percent. He's promised that to me for tonight and I would like the two of you and Paul"—he mentioned the absent chief of staff—"and the first lady to hear it with me."

When he returned to his office on Capitol Hill, King Billingsley returned a few obligatory phone calls, then asked his secretary to get George Fleming. Told that Fleming would have to call him back, Billingsley had his secretary call again with the information that he would be in his office for only another five minutes. Within seconds Fleming was on the line.

"King? Sorry I couldn't take the first call. Not enough privacy."

"Better for you if we speak tonight?"

"No, no. I'm anxious to hear anything you can tell me right now."

Billingsley related the events of the prayer breakfast to him, how he and Geoffrey Collins had matched wits about the future of New York over the breakfast table.

"Sorry you weren't invited, George, though I'm sure you wouldn't have been able to come. Edgar Smithson was there . . ." Billingsley let the information dangle in the air.

"What's his game, King? He's never been a big supporter of urban problems."

"I'm not sure, George. Smithson plays his cards close to his chest, and he's been an individual thinker on just about every subject I can remember for the past thirty years. There was a rumor several months ago that he was angling for an ambassador- ship, but Edgar Smithson's not one to sell himself."

"Not cheap, you mean."

"Not sell himself at any price. Whatever the flea is up his ass, he's got his own reasons for it. And his opinion counts for a great deal, George, in the Senate as well as the House."

"Any chance of swinging him to our side?"

"Not after the short speech he made yesterday. Edgar's not one to change horses in midstream."

"Where do we stand, then?"

"I believe I still have the votes to block any extraordinary aid."

"Good, King. I'm counting on you."

No one in the broken-off section of the tunnel under the East River had slept well. The silence from Joe each time the radio was turned off had worn everyone's nerves raw. The four nuns had spent much of the night praying. Vivian and Charlotte, though Episcopalians, had joined them for a few hours, then retired to Vivian's Mercedes. Toby and Christine Riley had attempted to make love in the backseat of the Camaro. When that had proved impossible for a variety of reasons, Christine had collapsed, sobbing, into her husband's arms.

"We're going to die, aren't we, Tobe?" she said when the first flood of tears had abated.

"Yes, sweetheart, I think so," Toby replied.

"There's something I was saving to tell you for when we were at the Waldorf."

"What's that," he answered absently.

"I'm pregnant. About six weeks."

He looked at her, speechless. Then it was his turn to cry.

The Richardsons had spent the night attempting to calm the fears of their two children, but without much success. Kathy and George were good kids, but they were truly terrified, and no amount of comfort that their mother and father could offer was sufficient to keep the terror at bay.

Jim Richardson looked at the clock on his dashboard: 7 A.M., Friday, October 7. His window was open, and he heard Joe Mazurski's shout.

Joe was leaning out his own window. "I've got him again," he called. The doors of the other vehicles opened simultaneously, their occupants getting out to rush to the truck.

"What happened?" Jim asked.

"He says some troops came through and they finally got everyone on the expressway to move again, but it was a slow process and as he moved away from the tunnel, he couldn't pick us up. He's on one of the streets near where the tunnel goes into the river now. It took him all night 'cause everything's torn up from the earthquake."

"Is he still on?" Sister Mary asked.

"No. He'll call back in ten minutes. As soon as he's reached someone who might be able to help."

"What's his name?"

Joe looked puzzled. "You know, I never thought to ask."

At ten past seven on Friday morning, Joe Mazurski closed the door to his cab once more. The others could see him talking into the radio's microphone, gesturing occasionally. Then he hung it up. He rolled his window down and looked out at them.

"He says he can't get anybody to pay any attention. The airwaves are full of stories about people trapped all over the place. We're just a small part of a big crowd."

"Did you give him my name, young man?" Vivian asked.

"Yes, ma'am," Joe replied. "I'm afraid it didn't cut any mustard, but he'll keep trying. He's going to call back at eight and wants to know if there's anyone specific he might be able to get to in the government."

"Let me think about that," said Vivian, an icy calm descending over her. Ignore them? Impossible. After all, she *was* Mrs. Derek Gordon.

The eight o'clock call from the trucker—who had inexplicably refused to give his name—came through to the survivors in the tunnel. Vivian Gordon was ready, insisting on climbing up into the cab to talk to the man outside.

"I understand you do not wish to give your name, sir, and I shall respect that. Can you call a normal telephone from your truck?"

"Yes, ma'am, no problem. But I'm gonna have a heck of a time trying to get an operator. The airwaves are jammed and everything's a mess."

Vivian pushed the button on the microphone. "I am going to give you the personal unlisted number of Geoffrey Collins. I trust you know who he is?"

"Yes, ma'am. That is, if you mean the secretary of, um, state."

"Precisely. My husband and he go back a long way and we've both had this number for many years without having to use it. Now I think it's time."

"I'll sure try, Mrs. Gordon. Can I speak to Joe again?"

Vivian handed the microphone over and Joe and the other man confirmed that they would talk again in four hours, at noon.

"Well, that's done," said Vivian, and prepared to climb out of the cab.

At noon and again at three, Joe reported to the rest of the group that the other man had failed to get through to the secretary of state. The one time he had been able to get the attention of an operator—he had resorted to using a marine band—there had been no answer at the other end.

"Impossible," Vivian scoffed. "That line is always supposed to be monitored. Geoffrey has it set up that way."

"Yes, Mrs. Gordon," Sister Mary replied soothingly. "But we don't know the extent of the damage. Perhaps Washington itself had been hurt by the earthquake. Or perhaps the secretary has been injured."

Vivian contemplated these thoughts in silence. She took a deep breath, then coughed violently as the increasingly foul air entered her lungs.

Sister Mary patted the older woman's back until the coughing fit had passed. She was worried about their continuing ability to breathe. The children were already sleeping much too much; narcolepsy, she thought, brought about by the oxygen-poor air.

The children weren't the only ones Sister Mary was concerned about. Sister Constance, who all the other nuns thought of as so hardy, was in reality a mass of allergies, and she had spent much of the afternoon vomiting. Mrs. Gordon's friend, Mrs. Haskins, was suffering terribly. Mrs. Gordon had confided that Charlotte had a history of heart problems. Mary wasn't equipped to handle anything of that nature. She could only hope and pray that Mrs. Haskins would hold out. The young couple—what was their name? yes, Riley, the Protestant spelling—had remained in their car for almost the entire day, wrapped in each other's arms. The only time they had left was to use the area behind the truck that had been designated a toilet.

Vivian Gordon recovered from her coughing fit and smiled at Sister Mary. "You've been a great comfort, my dear. Now I think I shall go keep Charlotte company." She squeezed the nun's arm affectionately, then walked to the Mercedes.

Sister Mary turned the Coleman lantern down lower.

She didn't know how much longer they would be there—in any sense of the phrase—and wanted to conserve as much of its fuel as possible. The door to the truck's cab opened and Joe Mazurski climbed out.

"More water, Joe?" she asked.

"Yes, please, Sister. This stinking air makes me real thirsty."

"I know what you mean." She refilled his glass. "When will he call again?"

"In another twenty minutes. If he's going to call at all. Otherwise an hour after that, and so on."

Sister Constance emerged from the van and walked quickly behind the truck. They could hear her retching, the dry heaves racking her body.

"I don't think we'll all be here come morning, Sister."

"Perhaps not, Joe. But those who are not will be with God."

"Yes, Sister."

He turned away and climbed back up into the cab.

"Is Mrs. Gordon there?"

The voice, so long awaited, shocked Joe Mazurski when he heard it. He had been trying for hours to raise the other trucker with no success. The air in the tunnel had become so foul that he could barely breathe, and he suspected the Rileys in their Camaro had slipped peacefully away. Now, without warning, a voice was coming over the radio that he had been monitoring while dozing.

"Yes, yes, she is," he replied.

"Can you get her to the radio. I have the secretary and he wants to speak to her."

Joe opened the window of the cab. In the soft light below he could see one of the nuns kneeling by the side of the van.

"Excuse me, Sister, but would you ask Mrs. Gordon to come over?"

The nun—Sister Anne, Joe thought—rose and walked back toward the Mercedes. Within seconds, Joe could see Vivian Gordon approaching the cab. He opened the door.

"Here, Mrs. Gordon," he said, handing her the microphone. "Don't try to climb up. I'll turn the volume up."

"Hello," she said. "Geoffrey?"

"Just a second ma'am. I'll patch him through."

She waited, then heard the sound of the secretary of state's voice.

"Vivian? Can you hear me?"

"Yes, Geoffrey dear. I can hear you. Tell me the worst."

"You've always been a brave one." He paused, then cleared his throat. "The worst, old thing, is that we cannot do anything for you, at least not for several days."

"If it is going to take that long, Geoffrey, there's no point in doing anything at all."

The secretary was silent for several seconds. "I see," he replied finally.

Sisters Mary and Anne had come to stand by Vivian, one on each side. They knew what her next question would be.

"And what of Derek?"

"I'm afraid he didn't make it, old thing. But I'm assured that it was a quick end. Charlotte's with you, I believe. Would you tell her that Elliott is in the hospital but expected to make a full recovery?"

"Charlotte died about an hour ago, Geoffrey," she replied. Then she added, "Well, I expect there isn't too much more to say. You have the whole country to think about. Now don't start to sputter, Geoffrey. We all know perfectly well that there's nothing you can do. The young man who has, I believe he used the term 'patched us through,' has the names of all of us down here. I trust you'll see that proper notification is made."

"Yes, Vivian, of course. Well, old thing . . ." The secretary's voice trailed off. There really was nothing more to say. After her lifelong fashion, however, Vivian said it.

"You know, Geoffrey, I've always hated being called 'old thing.' " Then she handed the microphone back to Joe.

———

By dawn of the third day there were fewer people still at the Grove School. Many of the parents had left, either in despair, having found a child dead, or given up hope. Some lucky ones had left with their children mercifully unharmed. The headmaster, Mr. Thatcher, had stayed on, and there were volunteers still digging out the basement. Diane was one of them. There was no sign of rescue equipment.

Without makeup, hair uncombed, Diane's beauty was natural and now somehow refined by grief. The headmaster approached her where she knelt, her bloodied hands pawing through the brick and mortar, lifting chunks and tossing them behind her into one of the growing piles of debris from the building.

"Mrs. Thorne," he kneeled down beside her. "You look all in.

There's an EMS van over there now where you could rest for a while. I think he's got some coffee."

Diane looked up at the headmaster. "I have to stay busy. But thanks. Where is some equipment that could get up into the building? Is there any word?"

"Your husband left over twenty-four hours ago and I had hoped he could find some help for us, but . . ."

She frowned and stood up. The headmaster stood up, too. She said, "No sign of my husband." Her voice was low with anger. "He's never around when we need him. The great expert on earthquakes." She gave the headmaster a mirthless smile. "A lot of good all his expertise is doing Danny. Damn my husband and all his books and his know-it-all shit." Her voice rose, and the headmaster put a hand on her arm. He knew she was about to break. "Where is he when we need him? When it counts? The smug shit, I hate him!" Her voice shook with fury. "Our boy is up there." She shook her fist up at the building. "And no one cares and no one is doing anything."

The headmaster held her arm. In a reasonable tone, as though he were talking to one of the students, he said: "There are thousands of other parents in the same situation, Mrs. Thorne, and . . ."

Diane turned on him. Her face was contorted like a furious child's, and he held her out from him. "You're just like Sam. You smug bastard. Don't tell me about the other parents. That's Danny up there. My boy. You have to do something." Tears rolled down her cheeks and she spat out the words, "I hate your goddamn calm. If your boy was up there you wouldn't be so calm. Let go of me," and she wrenched free of his firm grasp. "I'm going up there, and no one can stop me!"

She started toward the front of the building. The headmaster followed her and grabbed her from behind and held her tight. He said in a loud, clear voice, "If you try to go up there you will surely kill him. The building will come down around him and you. I cannot allow you in there."

She fought against his restraining arm and then with a terrible sobbing cry turned and threw her arms around his waist and put her head on his chest. The headmaster held her and stroked her hair. "There, there. Help will come, Mrs. Thorne. You are a brave woman. We have to wait and pray. There, there." He led her gently toward the van where a few people had congregated to get coffee and some soup that the driver had provided. "Here," he fished in his pocket and produced a grimy handkerchief that he gave Diane. She stopped and blew her nose, her sobs subsiding.

She took a deep breath and said, "I'm sorry."

"Here's some coffee," he handed her a paper mug. "Drink it." He watched her sip the hot liquid and saw her thin shoulders shudder with the last of her sobs. "When you have finished that, try to get some rest. You can sit down inside the van."

A few minutes later, Diane went back to the building and stood looking up at the eighth floor. Through the early morning air like an arrow into her heart came a faint yell. "Help! It's Danny Thorne!"

"Oh, my God!" Diane cried. "Danny," she yelled back. "Can you hear me? It's Mom. We're going to come get you soon. Hang on, we'll be there." She stood staring upward. She ran over to the headmaster. "Danny's alive!" She threw her arms around him. "My baby's alive!" She stepped back and looked up at the gaunt, exhausted face of the headmaster. "We have to get to him, somehow, someway."

"We will get to him, Mrs. Thorne. You keep talking to him, and sooner or later, help will come."

"Oh God, do you think I'm being punished for being so selfish? I keep thinking . . ."

The headmaster smiled for the first time that day. "No, Mrs. Thorne. And I don't think you are a selfish woman. Believe me, I'm an expert."

"I said some things, I'm . . ."

"Better you said them to me than your husband."

They both looked at one another, as she nodded in agreement. "But where *is* he?"

"He'll be back as soon as he can. You know that."

"Yes. Yes, I guess I do." Diane thought a moment. "Where is your family?"

"My wife was probably at home. We live in a brownstone in the Seventies. My daughter goes to Barnard and my son is somewhere in the building. He is in the tenth grade."

Diane stared up at the headmaster. "Oh, my God. I . . . I didn't

know. I am . . . I am so very sorry. And for the way I've behaved."
She put her hand on his arm. "Then we must both pray. I know our
sons will be rescued. Now I know."

He gave her a faint smile and nodded. Then they both looked up
at the ruined building.

All the second day, Kate had worked side by side with Gordon
while the steady stream of homeless and wounded found shelter at
The Four Seasons. Medical supplies had arrived and two Red
Cross aides. The place was getting organized. A stairway had been
cleared in the Seagram Building and Father Diaz walked down the
twenty-five flights and came to thank Kate again for her remarkable
delivery of the insulin, which had saved his life.

"How are you, my brave friend?" he had said to her.

"Fine, Father. And you are too, thank God."

"Yes. He is on my side, it seems." Father Diaz smiled. "And
now, give me some tasks here to help." He had rolled up the
sleeves of his robe. "I was once a doctor," he said to Keith. "I am
here and ready."

Gordon Keith shook his hand. "We can use you, Father," he had
said. "Many thanks."

"What a man," Kate had said that night as they made their way
again to the White Horse Tavern. "Maybe he will pull off his
miracle after all. Maybe he'll save his people and ours, too."

Kate and Gordon's closeness was now unspoken. All that second
day Kate would catch Gordon's eye, or he hers, and they would
acknowledge by a glance their feelings. By nightfall, without a
word, they went to their hideaway again and collapsed into a deep
mutual sleep on the sofa. They awakened with the dawn of the
third day, and made slow rapturous love, achingly restrained, until
they could hold back no more.

The sun rose on the devastated city. Another beautiful October
day. "I've got to go to the hospital today," Keith said.

"And I must go find my family."

"Will you go to the school?"

"I'll go first to Sam and Diane's house, and if no one is there, I'll
go on to Grove School, yes."

"You'll be careful."

"Of course. And you."

"Yes. And we will meet as soon as we can. I have no idea whether my apartment survived. Or the Century Club. Or anyplace where you might find me other than at the hospital, so you'd better look for me there."

She kissed him. "I shall. As soon as I can."

Kate found what was left of the 63rd Street house early that Friday morning and went on to the school. By the time she reached it, a grisly scene had just ended. The first of the rescue teams had arrived and found a young girl on the third floor. They had heard her cries from their ladder and one of the EMS men had attempted to rescue her. The floor had partially collapsed, badly injuring the little girl. Diane was standing with the parents of the child when it happened.

Diane told Kate where Danny was. Kate looked up for a long time at the eighth floor. She walked around the entire building. Twice. Then she came to Diane.

"I'm going up there."

"No way." The headmaster intervened. "That's a sure death trap up there."

Diane looked at Kate. "How?"

"I'm not quite sure yet. But I know several things. I weigh just over one hundred pounds, and all these men weigh almost twice that. I can get up there without heavy equipment. And that's my grandson, Danny, trapped up there. I have to try."

"You're right. If I could, I would," Diane said. "Kate, what can I do to help?"

Copper ran down the sidewalk, his paws raw and bleeding, his coat matted, but his tail wagging. He jumped up on his mistress.

"My God, Kate! Look who's here. Oh, Copper, Copper." Diane scooped up the small red dog and kissed and hugged him. "Do you believe he's alive and came all this way to find us? Oh, you good, good dog."

Kate took Copper and kissed him, too, and found some sandwich leavings for him and some water. Then Copper sat down beside

Kate's and Diane's feet. He stared up at the building, up at the floor where Danny was, his bright dark eyes anxious and knowing.

———————

By the morning of the third day Domenico Rizzo had his office set up in Nancy's apartment. A runner had come there to tell him that his wife and daughter were unharmed and in their respective homes.

Bobby "The Shark" Corelli was waiting for him outside the door to the apartment, where two bodyguards sat on chairs every hour of the day, taking turns to walk down the thirty flights of stairs to get coffee and sandwiches. When Domenico stuck his head out the door to see if all was all right with the bodyguards, Bobby, who had been leaning up against the wall, sprang to attention. "Can I come in, boss?"

"Sure. Any unusual traffic out here, boys?"

"No, Dom. Nothing."

Bobby followed Domenico into the small office. He shut the door behind himself and stood in front of the desk. Domenico sat down and put his slippered feet on the desktop.

Bobby grinned. "Stefano. The job is done."

Domenico put up a hand to stop any further description. He did not like details. Never had. "Good, good." He opened the drawer, did not find what he wanted, and went to the wall safe, which he opened. He counted out five thousand dollars and gave it to Bobby. "Now, I want you to get Frankie Scarpino and his bodyguard, Tom Rufala, over here. Also, Sammy Gennero. Ask them to be here by this afternoon. Sorry about the climb up here, but they are all in good shape. Then tonight, I want everyone here who comes to our regular Wednesday meetings at the Da Vinci Club. All of them you can find, and who have good enough tickers to make it up here. By eight o'clock. I want reports from them on everything I asked them to do on Wednesday before the police got back in action."

"Okay, Dom. Any other special jobs?"

They both knew what the word *special* meant.

"No, no," Rizzo waved him out of the room, much as if he were the head of General Motors dealing with an overeager secretary.

Bobby walked to the door with a spring in his step. He could use the five grand. A shame the boss did not want to hear how he had offed Stefano. The drunken bum was in his apartment and Bobby had knocked on the door, saying he was the police checking to see if he was all right. Stefano had opened the door and Bobby had shot him in the face with his newest gun, a Beretta 9mm parabellum with a fifteen-round clip.

When they heard Danny call out again, Kate and Diane yelled back, threw their arms around one another, and held tight. Several minutes later reality struck them. Even before knowing Danny was alive, Kate had decided to attempt to reach him, but now the chances of her succeeding seemed minimal. They all stared up at the eighth floor, which was now pancaked down to the sixth floor and at what lay between—a building that threatened to collapse completely at any time.

Kate checked the time. Friday, October 7, 8:31 A.M. She looked up at the sky. Not a cloud in sight, and very little wind, thank God. She went to the van and found a young man trying to use his walkie-talkie. He looked up and said, "We need more help here. Ladders, crew, medical personnel. Damn it." He was burly, in his twenties, red-cheeked.

"My name's Kate Thorne. What's yours?"

"Hi, I'm Bob. Bob Kroweicki."

"Hello, Bob." She climbed into the van on the passenger side. "I need some equipment that I hope you have in back there. Rope, mainly. Some good nylon rope." She smiled in her warmest way at him.

"Sure. Not that it does one goddamn bit of good. My buddy just got himself hurt real bad an hour ago tryin' to get up there. My buddy and I go back to training school. I . . . ." He struggled with his voice.

"I know. It's terrible." She put a hand on the young man's uniformed arm. She waited a moment until he swallowed hard. "May I go back there and look around?"

"Sure."

Kate had not decided on her approach, but she was relieved to find plenty of nylon rope and some tools that she might need. If she managed to reach the floor Danny was on, her main concern was how she would get the boy down. She made some mathematical calculations. She weighed approximately 112 pounds. At six, Danny must weigh about fifty pounds, maybe a bit more, certainly not less.

She sat for minutes in the back of the van, thinking through her various options. She had approximately nine hours of daylight. One of the worst problems was that there seemed to be nothing stable for her ropes, either ascending or descending with Danny. And what if she discovered other children up there?

She thought back through her years of mountain-climbing experience, trying to remember everything that related to this problem. In her mind a picture of sheer walls of ice came back and, unbidden and unwanted, the memory of a Sherpa guide who had fallen to his death climbing up such a sheer wall in an attempt to rescue her from a high ledge where a blizzard had left her stranded. She forced her mind away from that ghastly moment when he lost his footing and fell three hundred feet, his body broken by the very rope which finally, too late and with too much force, held him hanging, his body limp, below her. Nothing anyone could do for him. Eventually one of the climbers higher up had come back for her when the weather had cleared.

No good, she told herself. It was no good to remember that moment, especially now when she needed every bit of concentration and wit she possessed to figure out how to reach Danny. Still, after all those years since it happened, the memory of the taste of salt tears on her frozen lips came back.

She would use the prusik knot, she decided. Not the best solution but the only one that she could work with lacking vital equipment. She knew she had to climb up the rope, not the wall of the building. She would make two slings from the rope in the van, tied so that the short one—about two feet—and the other about four feet long, would wrap around the climbing rope using the friction knot known as prusik. The prusik knot would grip when under the load of her weight, but release when she balanced her weight in the loops, so that she could advance the knot up the climbing rope. She would make a makeshift carabiner, a metal snap-link through which the rope would be clipped to the sit sling that she would fashion out of the rope. The short sling would fasten to her sit sling and the long sling would act as a foot loop, tied to the climbing rope below the short sling. She would make progress by advancing each sling alternately, standing in the foot loop so that the other sling could be moved up the rope, then the front loop would take her weight while the foot loop was advanced. It would work if she could find an adequate place to secure the climbing rope above her.

She emerged from the back doors of the van and went to Bob, who was still attempting to reach other emergency personnel. She was carrying a thick coil of rope.

"Ma'am, I just got word from the Central Park Precinct. The mayor has given orders. From now on it's triage—no official rescue teams will undertake missions involving anyone trapped or underground. As of noon today."

Kate nodded. "It makes sense. Well," she flashed him a grin, "I'm for it, I guess."

"What are you doing with that stuff? You aren't going to try to go up there, are you? That's crazy." Bob climbed down out of the van. "I'll go."

"Not on your life. How much do you weigh?"

"Two-oh-five, dripping wet."

Diane was at Kate's elbow. "What do you think?"

"I think that I have to make some more figures in my head, think a bit more, and then go it alone. Your weight is the factor, Bob. I know you want to help, but . . ." She gestured toward the school. "The walls left above when the floors pancaked down on each other are about to go at the slightest provocation. And Danny is on the top floor now. Any pressure, well, you know the rest."

While she talked, Kate was working with the rope, using a knife Bob provided to cut it, laying it out on the ground in neat circles.

"How are you going up?" Diane asked.

"I'm not sure. I think trying the outside wall is no good. My plan is to go up through the inside, hope to find a way to Danny, and prusik down with him."

"What the hell is that?" Diane asked. She had never felt so useless.

"I'll show you." Kate took two feet of rope and another piece four feet long. She wrapped them around the long climbing rope using prusik knots, tied by wrapping a short sling around the rope three times and joining the ends with the makeshift carabiner, and the friction knots, Kate showed Diane, gripped under a load. She pulled down on the knot. Then she released the pressure and pushed the prusik knot up the rope.

"See? I'm going to clip this short sling to a sit sling, which I'll make, and the long sling I'll use as a foot loop. I'll tie it to the climbing rope below the short sling. I'll make progress by advancing each sling alternately." Kate patiently showed Diane each move. "I'll stand in the foot loop, which allows the sling attached to the sit sling to move up the taut rope. The front loop will then take my weight while I advance the foot loop."

"I'll be damned. Kate, you are something else." Diane went over to her mother-in-law and put her arms around her. She held her for a moment, then held her away, looking into those clear, bright blue eyes. "I'd like to be your friend, you know."

Kate was embarrassed. Actresses were always actresses. But she was touched, too. "Of course. Of course we are friends. Now help me get this gear ready, both of you."

Kate told Bob and Diane what she needed, and miraculously Bob came up with all the tools she had to have or managed to make facsimiles of them.

People who were still waiting in the slight hope that their child would be rescued alive began to gather around the Thornes. They were silent. They watched the activity without question or comment. This tanned, good-looking woman seemed to be in command, and they knew without asking that if she could she would try to find any children who were still alive. It was as though they were superstitious. Leave her alone. Let her get on with it. Maybe, just maybe, it will work.

When she was ready, Kate put her arm through Diane's and walked her off from the gathered people.

"There are a few things I want to say, and please don't interrupt."

Diane smiled at Kate. No one ever interrupted her.

"You and I know that this has a less than fifty-fifty chance of working. Mountaineers don't attempt a climb at those odds."

Diane started to speak and Kate put a gentle hand up to her lips.

"No, I'm not saying this to scare you. There are a couple of things that I want you to do if things don't work out the way we hope. Okay?"

Diane nodded. "Let me come, too."

"No! And kill us both? Don't annoy me." Kate's eyes flashed. Her high cheekbones flushed with impatience. "I want you at the bottom when I bring Danny down, then you can help. Now listen. Time is running out. I want you to promise me a couple of things. If anything happens to Danny and me, you promise me that you and Sam will forgive one another and try not to give in to foolish, self-destructive guilt. Know that we Thornes gave it our very best. And"—Kate paused—"take a message to Dr. Gordon Keith. Tell him I love him." She touched Diane's cheek, then turned and went toward the prepared gear.

Bob moved all the gathered people back from the building and told them not to go too near the school until Kate Thorne was back with Danny. Diane watched Kate, carrying her ropes, disappear into what was left of the building.

Kate looked up. She was in the middle of the ground floor. It looked solid enough but she knew better. Three floors had already pancaked down on one another. The rest could do the same.

She had her plan. She must find something stable to throw her climbing rope up and over. There was no other approach since the stairs were completely blocked and the elevator doors were jammed shut. When she got to his floor, she would give Danny a quick lesson in climbing and get him to climb down the way she would climb up. She would follow and they would be home free. She hoped.

She peered up through the gaping hole, the sunlight slanting in, and she pulled her dark glasses out of a pocket and put them on, knowing they would probably fall off in the climb. She found a small piece of concrete and tied one end of her climbing rope around it firmly. She threw it as high as she could get it and it sailed over her target—a metal joist fastened to the precarious outer wall. The weighted end of the rope came back down to her as she gave it leeway. She pulled on the rope and it held. Would it hold over one hundred and fifty pounds?

She put the sit sling around her buttocks, her foot in the foot loop, and edged her body over to the inner wall and, using both feet cautiously placed against the wall, swung out. The metal joist above her held. She advanced the sling up the taut rope, the front loop took her weight, and she advanced the foot loop.

After finding progressively higher protrusions to throw the climbing rope around—she knew it was incredible luck—she was forty or fifty feet above the ground and opposite the floor on which Danny was trapped.

She hoisted herself up and onto the floor and looked around. Because the roof had caved in on it, most of the scene was nothing but beams and material upended onto the floor. There was little space to move. She saw the twisted frames of the toilet stalls and guessed that Danny must have been saved by being in one when the earthquake struck. Carefully, quickly, she searched.

She found him sound asleep where he had been trying to get Debbie to talk with him. She approached him and called his name softly. His eyes opened and Kate took him in her arms and held him tight.

"Are you all right?" She quickly examined him. He looked at her drowsily and held her hand tight. She realized that hunger and dehydration had probably made him very lethargic. Climbers had been known to go to sleep in similar circumstances and never wake up because of the cold. "I'm okay, Granny. I'm glad you're here."

"Did you get hurt at all?"

"My head hurts. It got bumped. But I'm okay." He held her by the hand and pulled her toward the heap of debris under which Debbie lay.

Kate knelt down and peered inside the hole Danny had created. She reached in an arm and put her hand on Debbie's neck feeling for a pulse. She felt nothing. She tried again. No use.

She stood up and put her arm around her grandson who looked up at her, his expression trusting. He knew she could do anything.

"I'm sorry, Danny. Debbie's dead. She must have been badly hurt at the beginning and over two days . . ."

"Are you sure, Granny?" His mouth quivered and he tried not to cry. "I talked to her during the night."

"I'm sure, darling. But you did everything you could for her." She knelt down and looked him straight in his eyes. "Remember that, Danny. You did your very best. Think how glad she must have been to have you talk with her and comfort her. We've had a terrible earthquake and thousands of people have been killed, but we are all trying to do our very best. That's all we can do." She gave him a hug and kissed his forehead and pushed his black hair back. "Now you and I have to get down to your mother and father and Copper."

"Copper!" Danny exclaimed.

"He found his way all the way here from the house. Isn't that extraordinary? He must love you very much."

"Where's Mary?" He was excited now.

Kate had not thought about Mary. She hesitated.

"We don't know exactly where she is, but we're sure she's okay." Better to lie right now than to tell more cruel truth.

His frown disappeared.

For the next few minutes Kate sat on the floor with Danny, going through again with him how the prusik knots worked up and down the rope. He was a smart child and learned fast. "For someone without food and water for three days you look pretty good," she said, her arm around him.

Then they were ready. It was only ten feet down to the next floor, through the open hole. Kate did not allow herself to think. With iron control she followed her plan. That was another rule of the mountains. Once decided, once in action, do not waver.

Danny started down first, carefully moving the knots, lowering his small body bit by bit. In ten minutes he stepped off onto the first floor ten feet above the ground and looked up.

"I'm coming," she said.

She put the sit sling around her again, and began the descent.

Something went wrong. One of the knots gave way. She would never know. Suddenly, inexplicably, Kate Thorne plunged through the gaping hole. The rope held, but the force of the fall was tremendous and she swung, unconscious, twenty feet above the ground floor.

Danny saw what had happened to his grandmother and he yelled for help. The headmaster, Mr. Thatcher, came into the building and looked up at Danny, then up farther at Kate's dangling, inert body.

"My God, stay where you are," he called up to Danny, and as he did several pieces of mortar and other debris fell down on him from high above. He knew the building was in imminent danger of crumbling, and every loud noise was enough to disturb its precarious balance. "I'll get help. Just stay quiet, young man."

Mr. Thatcher told Diane and Bob what had happened. Bob started toward the building.

"No!" Thatcher ordered. The young man paused.

"I know what we all want to do. But we must not. That boy's life and that of Mrs. Thorne depend on our staying out of there. One stupid move on our part and the building will collapse on them. We need an expert. We must get word to your husband, Diane. He's the only person who knows enough to get in there and save them. Danny could jump down, but the impact might be enough to . . ."

Diane said, "I'll go to the precinct house and try to find him."

Thatcher again ordered. "No, I don't think that's wise. You're needed here. Bob, you go."

"I'm on my way." And Bob started jogging westward.

Gerta woke Evie and Allen at eight on the third morning.

"The others are pulling themselves together, so we should get going now."

"Yes," agreed Allen.

They moved northward on the track bed, Evie leading, Allen bringing up the rear so he didn't have to hold somebody's hand with his wounded arm. Their shared hunger had made them light-headed. They were all mildly excited because the next station would be Times Square, with its multiplicity of entrances and its spur across town to Grand Central Station and the subway complex there. Surely, they told each other, we'll find a way out. There's nobody else down here with us. They must be getting out somewhere.

They trudged on. "The water's not so high anymore," said Marisa, who was directly ahead of Allen.

"Yes," he agreed. "It must finally be draining out somewhere. It's down at least six inches from yesterday."

Evie was walking mostly in the dark, unwilling to use the fading flashlight for more than spot checks to determine where they were. She switched it on and saw the end of a platform. "Times Square," she called back over her shoulder, and a ragged cheer went up from the group.

With a suddenness that caused them all to gasp and Peg to lose her balance and fall, bringing Jake with her into the water, a brilliant flashlight beam cut through the darkness of the tunnel, shining directly on them.

"Okay," a voice said. "Stop right there."

They stopped, blinded by the glare. Evie held an arm up to her brow, shading her eyes. "Who are you?"

"Doesn't matter who we are, sweetheart. All you need to know is that we're in charge."

Allen had come forward. Even obviously wounded, he was still a formidable figure.

"In charge of what?" he said.

"This station, man. And what we say goes."

The man was just outside the beam of the flashlight, but in its glow they could see he held something that looked like a rifle.

"Listen, mister," said Allen. "All we want to do is get out of here."

The man didn't reply but turned away. They could hear him talking to someone else, but couldn't make out the words. Then he turned back to them.

"Any of you armed?"

"No," said Allen, regretting that the bullet Rick had accidentally killed himself with during their fight back at 34th Street had been his last, rendering what would have been a very useful weapon, especially now, useless.

"Then use the ladder to come up here."

Ten minutes later, the group was assembled on the downtown platform of the Times Square station. The flashlight had been turned toward the ceiling, and they stood in its reflected glow surrounded by six men all of whom had a gun of some type or another.

"How do we get out of here?" asked Evie.

"How do you get out of here?" the man who had stopped them repeated. "That's funny, lady, very funny. Ain't it, Butch," he said to one of his companions, who agreed with a gap-toothed smile and vigorous nodding of his head. "Butch is dumb. He can't speak neither," the man said, to the amusement of the rest of his little mob. "Simple. You give us what you got, we let you keep goin'."

"You mean we've come all this way just to get robbed by a bunch of thugs," said Jake, outrage causing his voice to shake.

"That's about the size of it, pal. Pocketbooks, purses, wallets. Let's have 'em. An' any jewelry you're wearin', rings, watches, anythin'."

"Then what?" said Allen.

"Then you walk to the north end of the platform, get down on the tracks again, an' move out. Simple, huh? Now start throwin' your stuff into a pile right here," he said, and indicated a spot on the platform. "Now, I said," he added, menace rising in his voice.

"I don't see why—" Gerta started to say. Her words were cut off by a sharp slap across the mouth.

Peg took her watch off, then a gold cross that hung around her neck on a chain. She dropped them.

One by one the others followed suit and soon there was a small pile of valuables at their feet. Although the firecrackers in his pockets created small bulges, the men with the guns seemed satisfied when Allen dropped his watch, Academy ring, and wallet onto the pile.

"How about some food?" Bill Cohen said. "We haven't eaten in three days."

"You gotta pay for food, man. An' you ain't got no money to pay with. Or are you holdin' somethin' back?" He raised his gun, pointed it at Bill.

"Not me," Bill said.

"Then you don't get no food. Now start walkin' uptown."

They began to walk up the platform. "How about letting us go down the tracks toward Grand Central?" said Allen.

"No can do, man. That turf is controlled by another gang. They see you comin' along, they'll want to rob you too. They find out you don't have nothin', they'll prob'ly just shoot you dead. Look at it this way, man. I'm doin' you a favor."

A few minutes later, they were at the end of the platform. Another flashlight pointed upward, illuminating more armed figures.

"Have a nice trip," the man said as he pointed his rifle at the ladder to the tracks.

"Are you sure . . . ?" Evie began, but he cut her off.

"I'm sure, sister. 'Course, maybe you'd like to stay. You'd be real popular with the boys."

"She'll come with us," said Allen, and propelled her to the head of the ladder.

One by one they descended. The flashlight was now pointed up the tracks, illuminating them for perhaps a hundred yards until they curved out of sight. In its light they began to walk once again.

They stopped to rest at 51st Street for two hours, exhausted, hungry, and dispirited. Then they pushed on, planning to reach Columbus Circle before tiredness overwhelmed them.

Although smaller than Times Square, it still had more exits than the average station, and they hoped that one would be open. Before they finally came in sight of the platform they were aware of a glow from the direction in which they were traveling. Finally they came to it. There were people here, normal, everyday citizens, not the criminal types they had earlier encountered, willing hands to help Evie, Allen, and their group up onto the platform, but people who, nonetheless, were as trapped as they were.

Several fires had been built on the wide platform and they were led toward one of them. The fires had been fueled with whatever— theater posters, benches, trash—and offered little warmth, but they felt good after the time spent in the water walking from 42nd Street.

There were only about twenty people in the station. Allen learned that a group of them had gone north the day before, only to return with the report of a huge pile of rubble blocking the way.

"South's out of the question," said one man.

"Yes, so we found out," Allen replied.

"You, too?" the man said.

"Everything."

"Is there anything here to eat?" asked Peg. "We don't have any money. It was all taken at Times Square."

"Not much," the man replied after a moment. "We're rationing what's left, but the hotdog stand must just have had a shipment before the earthquake, because it was stocked full. There are eight of you? I'll get you something."

He returned with hotdogs which they cooked, or tried to, over the fire. Then, exhausted, they settled down to rest.

And wait.

Bob Kroweicki arrived at the precinct house just as Sam reached the Grove School. It had taken longer than he expected to get across town, since every time he started to jog he felt dizzy and had had to stop.

He found a cluster of people gathered outside Grove School, and he searched the crowd for Diane.

Then he saw her, standing alone, and he made his way to her. She saw him and came toward him. They threw their arms around one another and hugged. "Danny?"

"Oh, Sam, thank God you got here. Danny's all right. He's up on the first floor. It's Kate. And the building has collapsed more so that no one can get up to the fifth floor anymore. They won't let us into the building. And you mustn't go in there either, Sam. Please." Her red-rimmed, bloodshot eyes implored him. "I can't lose you."

He held her away from him and looked at her. "I'll be all right. I promise." He did not wait for her answer, and made his way through the waiting people into the building. He looked up.

He saw Kate's inert body swaying above him twenty feet off the ground held by the climbing rope. And Danny, flat on his stomach up on the first floor looking over the edge of the gaping hole down at his father.

Sam went over so he was directly beneath Danny.

"Come on, son, it's only ten feet. Jump and I'll catch you. Then I'll go get your grandmother."

Danny stood up and took the pose Sam had seen him take many times when jumping off a diving board, held his nose and took off. He landed on top of Sam, who broke the fall, and when Sam straightened up he saw his six-year-old son standing in front of him. He threw his arms around him and held him close. "What about Granny?" Danny was thrilled to see his dad, but scared at the sight of Kate.

"You go on out. Your mother and Copper are waiting. I'll get your granny down, I promise."

Danny looked up at Kate. Then he dashed outside into the sunshine and into Diane's arms. Copper leapt up three feet in the air, again and again, his rough red coat flashing in the bright light, barking for attention until Danny turned from his mother to greet him. Diane wept with relief.

Sam studied the situation. From his mountaineering experience, he guessed that two things had happened to Kate when she slipped or the knot slipped and she free fell, then was caught by the climbing rope, saved from crashing onto the floor of the building. He suspected that she had sustained serious damage to her spine and a whiplash to her neck which would have caused a severe concussion and resulted in her unconsciousness. To move her without a stretcher, to not be able to keep her absolutely straight on a stretcher, was going to risk injuring her further, but he had no choice. He went back outside and got Bob Kroweicki, who brought a stretcher from his van inside. "Stand here," Sam ordered him. "When I get down with her, as gently as you possibly can, brace the stretcher vertically on the wall and then we'll slide her onto it and turn it horizontal." Bob nodded.

Sam stood below where Kate hung for a few moments more and then made his decision. There was no way to reach her other than by using the climbing rope without the prusik knots. There was no time and no material from which to make a halter and sling for himself. Rapelling up the rope was the only way, hoping it would hold his weight and hers when he reached her. And hoping dizziness did not hit him at the wrong moment.

He wore gloves that Bob Kroweicki had given him and he rubbed dust from the floor on them and put more dust on his pockets. He pulled on the rope as hard as he dared. It held. He put all his weight on it. It held. He took a deep breath and swung his feet against the wall and started up, slowly, carefully, trying not to jerk the rope. Bits of debris fell on him from above. He felt the wall sway. Beads of sweat braided his forehead and ran into his eyes. Slowly, slowly, he inched up the wall. Then he was opposite Kate. Her face was white under the tan, her head lolled, her body clenched in the waist loop she had made for herself.

He realized that with their combined weight, they would be putting two hundred and fifty pounds on the climbing rope, held only by something forty feet above which Kate had fastened it around, or fastened it to, or God knows what.

He reached out with his left hand while clinging to her climbing rope with his right hand and he grasped the rope above Kate's head. He pulled her toward him with infinite care until he could slip his left hand between the halter and her body. More debris tumbled down on them, and his eyes were filled with dust and sweat.

Now he had a grip on the halter. The wall cracked above him and several bricks hit him with glancing blows. "God damn it," he swore. He held Kate by the halter with as little pressure as he could manage and very gently. He started the descent.

Twice his foot slipped on the wall and both of them hung for moments while Sam regained his balance. Kate came to and in a weak voice asked Sam, "Is Danny all right?"

"Yes, Ma, he's fine."

Satisfied, she closed her eyes. Sam put one foot below the other, and in a few minutes reached the ground where Bob was waiting with the stretcher.

"Try to keep her body as straight as we can," Sam said, his foot touching the ground. Bob and he lowered her very, very slowly the last few inches, placing her body straight against the vertical stretcher, and then carefully turned it horizontal. They carried her outside to where Diane, Danny, and Copper waited.

A cheer went up from the group of parents and others who had been there for three days waiting for their beloved children to be found. The cheer grew and filled the brisk October air. As the Thornes followed Sam and Kroweicki, who had gotten back, to the EMS van with the stretcher, the voices cheered again.

Suddenly Grove School collapsed completely. The floor Danny had been on crashed down onto the next and on and on pancaking down until the entire building was one great pile of debris.

Diane turned and watched the building fall as though in slow motion, and she saw the cheering faces change to frozen horror as the last of their hopes were extinguished. She left her family and ran over to Mr. Thatcher, who had come close to being trapped himself as the building disintegrated. He had been working still to get through to the basement. He was crying.

"I'll be back to do anything I can. I want you to know that," Diane said softly.

"It's too late." He rubbed his eyes. "Don't you see, it's too late. Oh my God. My child. All my children."

The EMS van was able to thread its way to New York Hospital through the streets that had been cleared for ambulances and other medical vehicles. Bob drove with speed just this side of recklessness. Kate lay unconscious on the cot in the back of the van. Sam rode in front with Bob, while Diane, Danny, and Copper rode in the back with her. "Step on it," Bob yelled out his window at a van in front of them. "For God's sake, *move!*"

By three o'clock that Friday afternoon, Dave Hartnett had succeeded in looting Kelly, Farnsworth of nearly seventy-five million dollars. Five hours earlier—at 10 A.M. Chicago time, eleven o'clock in New York—he had made his first computer linkup with the New Orleans branch of a large New York–based commercial bank. He worked the keyboard on the Seiko deftly but slowly, glad that he had never really learned to type. He was nervous, and using two fingers was safer than using all ten.

He accessed the Kelly, Farnsworth account and checked the

balance against the information he had copied after the earthquake had struck. Perfect, right down to the penny. He tapped in the proper codes to make an electronic transfer of funds to the import/export business on the Isle of Man, then watched the screen to see that it had taken place.

Nothing happened. He checked the codes again, then reentered them. Still nothing. Agitated now, sweating, he tried a third time, again unsuccessfully. He stared at the screen in disbelief. Somehow he was being barred from access to the largest single account Kelly, Farnsworth held. Why? Was his so-well-constructed plan going to fail him the one time he would be able to try it?

He brought the computer out of the program, tried to think. Then the reality hit him. Washington must have frozen the accounts of all New York City banks until the crisis had been dealt with. By extension, branches of those banks would not be able to carry out any transactions against those accounts.

Hartnett found the list of Kelly, Farnsworth bank accounts that he had printed out earlier. Damn. Most of them were based in New York. He scanned the list, looking for a Chicago-based bank with no ties to the City. The list swam before his eyes. Security National. No, an affiliate of Chase. First Farmers. A subsidiary of Morgan. Hartnett was beginning to feel sick. He had only the one day and already nearly an hour had been wasted.

Galveston. A bank he had never heard of, Gulf and Panama. He called the account up on the Seiko. It had deposits of slightly less than four million dollars. He accessed the account and the bank's computer responded positively with his request to transfer two-and-a-half million to the Isle. Double-checking, he let several minutes elapse, then called up the balance in the account. It had been reduced by that amount.

Excited now, he punched in the codes for his account on the Isle, asking for the balance. Where there had been slightly under ten thousand dollars, he was now richer by two-and-a-half million. He came out of the account, a smile on his face. He could let that money sit for now, transfer it elsewhere over the weekend. It was more important to find other Kelly, Farnsworth accounts that had no New York connections.

For the next four hours, Hartnett worked feverishly, invading banks around the country in which Kelly, Farnsworth had accounts. Whenever he was frozen out, he moved on to the next possibility, not wanting to take the time to double-check and perhaps expose himself. He knew that most banks had sophisticated security systems that traced the source of a request for moving money instantly. He did not want to risk exposing himself if anyone at the receiving end of a request was wondering why a New York brokerage firm, stopped from trading by the SEC and presumably unable to do business, was transferring money out of its account from a Chicago location.

But there were enough accounts for Hartnett to amass the fortune he had dreamed of. Nine hundred thousand out of an S & L in Dallas (An S & L, for Pete's sake! Putting money in one of those was almost criminal in itself). Three million from each of several banks in Los Angeles. A million and a half out of a Seattle account. He watched as the account on the Isle grew, his original smile changing to an ever-widening grin as it approached the seventy-five-million-dollar mark.

Finally, at a few minutes to three, he shut down. He was exhausted, shaking with the intensity of what he had done. He needed to shave and shower, go out for a good meal, celebrate with a really classy bottle of wine, maybe pick up someone to spend a few hours with. Everything could wait until tomorrow. Right now, David Woodbridge Hartnett, millionaire, was going out on the town.

Gordon Keith had left Kate on Friday and walked from 52nd and Park to 68th and York Avenue. The overcoat he had worn to his lunch date with the wealthy woman on Wednesday was long since misplaced, as was his gray pinstripe jacket from Savile Row. He had borrowed an orange down jacket from one of the waiters and was glad of it, since the early October air was brisk. He had not been outside since the earthquake struck. His eyes smarted. The sunlight was bright and the air was laden with dust and smoke.

He had decided to walk up Park rather than go immediately east to Lexington because he wanted to see what had happened to one of his favorite avenues in the City.

Fifty-second Street was busy when he emerged from The Four Seasons. Sanitation workers were picking up by hand and hauling away the debris that had blocked the street. Instead of their large garbage trucks they were using smaller pickup trucks, which had managed to come across 57th Street, one of the few streets that had been cleared, and down one lane on Park Avenue that had been opened that morning. Across the street was a cavernous hole filled with smashed and pancaked cars that had been in the parking garage. The Red Cross had set up a canteen, where the workers could get a hot cup of cocoa or soft drink. There was a sign hand-painted there that read, "WATER STRICTLY RATIONED. AVAILABLE ONLY AT FIRST AID STATIONS OR HOSPITALS." There were people still picking through the rubble of the fallen buildings on 52nd Street, hoping against hope for a sound of a voice underneath.

When he reached Park Avenue he gazed for a long moment up the avenue, and then turned and looked south. It reminded him of photographs of Hiroshima, though here, at least, a few tall buildings sprouted up out of the ruins. Heartsick, he walked uptown. The scene was much the same as it had been on 52nd Street. Every other block the Red Cross had set up a canteen, handing out food and soft drinks, blankets and other necessities. And on each block desperate souls were searching for loved ones beneath the implacable stones.

Fifty-seventh Street was clear, and Army vehicles, EMS vans, police cars, and other official cars moved slowly east and west. Gordon could see the East River from Park Avenue and 57th Street since there were no buildings left to obstruct the view. A few post–World War II apartment buildings stood, and a few office buildings. All the wonderful shops and Sutton Place area buildings were flattened. He walked on, realizing how many friends of his must have been killed or injured, the full reality of what had happened hitting him for the first time. The world inside The Four Seasons with people desperately needing medical attention, with Kate, with the ambiance of luxury surrounding them even when the world outside was shattered, nothing had prepared him for the sights he now saw. He remembered Tom Wolfe's novel *Bonfire of the Vanities,* and realized that Wednesday, October 5, 1994, had changed forever all that scene. The homeless, the rich and powerful, the mob, the drug dealers, the financial world, the yuppies or whatever they were called these days, he had lost track, all of us have been leveled. We are all homeless.

In spite of everything he was seeing, then he felt a lightness inside himself. Was it Kate? No, he thought, not just finding Kate, knowing that this time they would be together. It was being set free of possessions, of identity, in some strange way. He noticed that people walking toward him were in twos and threes, talking and animated, some even laughing at some joke someone said, and those people, not searching for loved ones but going somewhere to do some valuable job for the stricken city, seemed as lighthearted as he, like New Yorkers the morning after a blizzard.

When he reached Sutton Place, which turned quickly into York Avenue as he turned uptown, he saw the helicopter pad at 60th Street and the helicopters shuttling back and forth to Tate Acres. There was a long, long line of people who stood to one side and the line went for blocks north and south. Gordon stopped and asked a man what the line was for, and he said, "We're waiting for helicopters to evacuate us, and they say they're sending ships, too. We're leaving the City." He held a little girl by the hand.

———

For two days it had been known that Paula Lincoln was trapped in the building that had housed her beloved daycare center. Another worker in the center, who had been in the playground with her own group of children, told the first policeman on the scene that Paula had gone down to the basement just before the earthquake struck to check on food and other supplies before making up the weekly shopping list.

For two days, first with official help, then after the mayor's edict, without it, people had gathered to remove what was left of the building in order to get to her. They refused to abandon hope. Early on the day after the quake, one of the city's electronic victim locators had been brought to the site and had sensed heat from her live body radiating outward.

Now it was late Friday afternoon. Several dozen bodies had been recovered from the rubble, most of them small children whose mothers had dropped them off at the facility on Wednesday morning. Only Paula Lincoln was unaccounted for.

By hand, slowly, carefully, duplicating a scene that was taking place all over Manhattan, the volunteers dug ever deeper into the ruin. By now they had begun to call out her name, believing that they were only a few feet away from where she was trapped. Perhaps she was unconscious. She didn't answer.

Finally they were standing on the floor of the room over the one that Paula had gone to. Fearful of causing further collapse, they attacked the concrete under the linoleum with small hammers and light pickaxes.

At six ten a hole big enough to shine a flashlight through had been made.

At six eleven, they saw her body, its neck twisted in a way that precluded the presence of any life.

At six twelve, an aide to Mayor Bruce Lincoln gave him the news.

———

By five o'clock the men had gathered in Rizzo's office. Nancy, with nowhere to go and nothing to do, had been pacing around the apartment all afternoon, looking out the window at the activity below on 57th Street. Tiffany's had disintegrated and looters had stripped the remains clean by Thursday at noon. Now looters were going in gangs up and down Fifth Avenue, taking what they could from all the stores, most of which had suffered great damage. Today the first signs of law enforcement had appeared, and from time to time gunfire broke out. She poured herself a vodka and club soda with lime about four o'clock, no ice, and sat playing the piano desultorily. She was not a good piano player, but she accompanied herself adequately, and as Rizzo prepared for his meeting he listened to her low voice singing his favorite Cole Porter songs. He got up from his desk and went to the door.

She turned and smiled at him. Her straight auburn hair gleamed in the late afternoon sun from the window. He went over to her and stroked it. She leaned her head up against his jacket. "Do you tend to think of me as your favorite red setter?"

He sat down on the piano bench. "Could do worse."

"You've been so busy. Plotting and planning, no doubt." She struck a chord, then another. "I don't get to know about it."

"No. I don't want you to know about my business life. Any more than Stefano told you."

"God, I wonder if poor Stefano survived the earthquake. He's so helpless."

"I'm sure he's fine. That apartment building he lives in, it's solid. New. Like this one."

She sipped her drink. "Will we have dinner together? Whatever I can find to make with no electricity and no gas?"

"Late. I got people coming from five on until about ten. Then I'm all yours." He kissed her. "Get me a glass of red wine, will you? And I'll need the bottle for the guys."

"Sure. And I'll prepare a feast for us to have by candlelight at ten. Wine, cheese, crackers, and us." She took his head in her hands and kissed him back, long and lingeringly.

He got up. "Don't drink too much of that stuff. I have plans for us for later."

She raised her glass to him and went back to fiddling with the piano keys.

Sammy "The Bear" Gennero, Bobby "The Shark" Corelli, Frankie Scarpino, and Tom Rufala sat in Rizzo's office.

Gennero was talking. "Tonight up in Harlem we have platoons of at least twenty-five men to take out the Jamaican Posse. When we're through up there, the cocaine business is ours again. We haven't had it back since 1989."

Rizzo nodded, pleased at the news.

Bobby reported that five canaries had been dealt with, not including Stefano. Two informers to the FBI, three to the U.S. Attorney's office.

It was Frankie Scarpino's turn. "We got ten of our best raiding the basement, or what's left of it, at police headquarters. We know they got billions of dollars worth of cocaine stored there in the evidence room. No one is watching the place yet, and we stand to make a fortune."

"Good work," Rizzo said, laughing at the irony of that heist.

"Now later tonight the rest of the men are coming here to report on how we're doing on those files from the U.S. Attorney's office. We want more information on the informers. The men should tell us about the restaurants, too, the ones that have survived the earthquake, and I've asked them to stake out those that are okay with armed men. The looters are combing the city like locusts. What a fucking dirty thing to do," he said quite seriously. "I've ordered our guys to kill looters on sight." He got up and poured more wine into their glasses. "Now, tell me. How are your families?"

As he listened, he dealt with each situation, from sending a special team to try to find Frankie's mother who lived on Mulberry Street, to giving protection money to Tom Rufala so that he could pay off someone whom he knew would be gunning for him now. Soon the other capos started to arrive, and they moved the meeting into the living room. It went on until Domenico could see the full moon outside the window. He looked at his watch. It was ten thirty. He stood up and walked them to the door. "You all got places to stay?" They had. "I want you to come back tomorrow at the same time. Thank you. I'm sorry there's no elevator." Each one of them embraced Rizzo and then left.

He went to the bottom of the stairs. "Hey, woman!"

Nancy appeared wearing a slinky green satin gown. "Come on up, big boy. I'm famished."

Rizzo ran his hand through his black hair and bounded up the stairs, two at a time. She had disappeared into the bedroom. When he entered it, she dropped the gown from her shoulders and let it fall around her ankles. She was naked. "Let's take care of first things first."

The president and his small party reached Camp David only minutes before the helicopter from New York bearing Bruce Lincoln, Howard Tate, and several members of the staffs of each arrived. The terse official announcement had said only that the president was going to his retreat in the Blue Ridge Mountains for the night and would be back early the next morning. The press could not be accommodated and was discouraged from following along. Still, several of the more intrepid press corps members and their camera crews were on hand when, one after the other, the two helicopters landed. With long practice and experience, however, both pilots managed to position their craft so that the visitors from New York were shielded from press scrutiny.

Once inside, brief greetings were exchanged and the president led them all to the conference room in the compound's main building.

Howard Tate and his staff had come prepared with maps, charts, and a hastily produced but highly professional model of a Manhattan as it might be after reconstruction.

"My, Howard," the first lady said. "How did you manage that so fast?"

"I was lucky. I moved my architectural and engineering departments out to Tate Acres several months ago, well before the site itself was complete. Most of the people on those two staffs were on site when the earthquake struck, and many of them agreed to stay on once they knew what we needed and how critical the time factor was. I have one of the best model-making staffs in the world, though to tell you the truth many of these buildings are either stock items in our shop or have been cannibalized from other models."

The group stood around the scale model of Manhattan as Howard Tate and Bruce Lincoln proceeded to explain their vision of the City risen from the ashes. Both men were normally even of temper, but neither could suppress a rising excitement as they described what New York could be. Finally they were through.

The president was silent for a moment, toying with a model of the New York Public Library he had picked up. "So in essence what you would have Manhattan become is a city totally devoted to human interaction? The arts, commerce, religion, all within a twenty-two-square-mile parklike setting. No private vehicles. A very limited number of residential units. Hotels, theaters, restaurants, yes. Slums, crack dens, brothels, no. My God, Howard, Bruce—do you really think it could be done?"

"Yes, without question."

"What about the people who live there now?" asked Geoffrey Collins. "What would become of them? Where would they all go?"

"We estimate that there were about twelve to fourteen million people in Manhattan when the quake struck. We also estimate that four to six million of those were killed outright, will die later, or will never be found. The residential population of Manhattan is somewhere around one-and-a-half million. We can assume that half of them survived. My guess is that fifty thousand will be necessary to see to the actual running of the new city and surviving housing can be adapted to their needs, both wealthy and poor. This leaves us with some five hundred thousand to be relocated. A massive task, no question. But abandoning the island completely, plowing it under, would leave only more to be relocated," said the mayor.

"What about those who don't wish to leave, who own property and wish to rebuild on it privately?" asked Edgar Smithson.

"If they were talking about private housing, they wouldn't be able to. Draconian, perhaps, but there are laws of eminent domain. Much of the land for the Interstate Highway System was appropriated through such laws. And that's a lot more extensive than twenty-two square miles," Howard Tate replied.

"But you're talking about the twenty-two most valuable square miles in the world," said the chief of staff.

Howard Tate paused, then said, "Until last Wednesday at one twenty-one in the afternoon."

The discussion had gone on far into the night and the helicopter bearing Bruce Lincoln and Howard Tate back to New York didn't lift off until nearly two the following morning. By that time, however, they had convinced the president and the four advisers with him of the feasibility of their plan. The first lady, in particular, was enthusiastic about the prospects for the City's future.

"If this can happen the way you two men envision it," she said to Lincoln and Tate as she walked with them to the front door of the lodge, "you will have created the most perfect jewel of a city to be found on the face of this planet. What a wonderful beginning for this nation as it goes into the twenty-first century."

As the EMS van approached 68th Street and York Avenue, Kate drifted in and out of consciousness, and groaned with pain when she came to. Bob had taken her blood pressure, which was dangerously low, and put her on a temporary IV of saline solution and dextrose. He had put a collar on her neck as well. When they got to the emergency entrance to the hospital through 68th Street and into the back of the building, Sam rushed in to the office and asked for Dr. Gordon Keith to be paged, while Kate was put on a gurney and taken into a small room where a young intern attended her.

Diane and Danny and Copper sat in the visitors' section on folding metal chairs. Only in this chaos would a dog have been permitted in, but no one paid Copper any attention. He sat on Danny's lap, ears forward, looking at everything that was going on with intense terrier curiosity.

Sam stayed in the room with Kate and the intern, who was asking her questions. She was completely conscious by now, and, though weak, was aware of the fact that her legs were without feeling. In minutes Dr. Keith came through the door and bent over Kate. He took her hand and held it in his. "You're going to be all right, Kate. In a minute we're taking you upstairs for some tests. I hear you had quite a fall." He looked up at Sam and acknowledged him with a smile. "Are you in pain?" he asked her.

"No, my dear. Very tired. No sensation in my lower extremities. Reminds me of the time I fell on my way down the Matterhorn." She looked up at Gordon. "I'm glad you're here."

He kept holding her hand the whole way up to the x-ray and CAT scan floor, as two attendants wheeled the gurney up ramp after ramp put down on the stairs to assist with getting patients from one floor to another. Sam went along. When nurses took over to prepare Kate for the series of tests Dr. Keith ordered, Sam cornered the doctor.

"Tell me the truth, Dr. Keith. What do you think?"

"At this point I can't give you any kind of clear picture. She probably has internal injuries, how severe . . . I don't know yet. The legs? I think from the kind of accident she had two things happened simultaneously. The impact of the rope snapped her body so she may have a fractured backbone, subluxed, and the broken bone is pressing on the nerve roots. That would account for her legs being without feeling and very weak. Then the fall and the snap of the rope caused whiplash, and at her age she probably has a degree of osteoporosis . . ."

"None of this is life threatening then?"

Gordon Keith hesitated. "Listen, Sam, I'll know more soon. Your mother is in excellent physical shape and I needn't tell you she is tough . . . mentally I mean." He smiled at Sam, who nodded. "I suspect that I am going to want to operate within hours to remove the bone that is pressing on the nerves. We'll see as soon as these tests are back. My advice is for all of you to try to find somewhere to lie down and rest for a few hours. I'll get one of the nurses to try to find an empty corner of a room for you and some blankets and a little food. You look beat. I want the resident to look at that cut, and check you and your son. Though he looks amazingly well."

"Thanks, Doctor. Let me know the minute you know anything about Ma."

Gordon put out his hand to Sam. "I will. I want you to go upstairs for a scan of that concussion. And by the way, please call me Gordon."

Danny was given some medication for dehydration and Sam was given a thorough neurological check. All of them were given some food, including Copper, and they stretched out on the floor of a room filled with other ambulatory patients. People moved through the corridors at will looking for their loved ones. Sam tried to rest, but his mind was too filled with the sights and sounds of the last few hours and days. He had his arm around Diane, whose head rested on his shoulder, and in turn, Danny was in the curve of her arm with his hand resting on Copper's head. They did not speak. It was enough that they were alive and well and together.

In less than two hours Dr. Keith came to them and sat down on the floor beside them. He patted Copper and introduced himself to Diane and Danny. "I'm an old friend of Kate's," he said, and caught Sam looking at him. He wondered what Kate had told her son.

His expression was grave. Diane and Sam stood up. He talked slowly as though he wanted to make sure they understood what he was telling them.

"Kate is slipping in and out of consciousness. We're not sure yet what the reasons are, and there is evidence of some internal bleeding. I want to operate as quickly as possible to remove the fractured bone that is pressing on the nerve roots in her spine. The sooner the better for her chances of recovering the use of her legs."

"Oh, no!" Diane murmured. "Kate . . . she couldn't stand it." She buried her head against Sam's chest.

"There is risk. I need your permission, Sam."

"How much risk?"

Gordon frowned. "Let me put it bluntly. If I don't operate, she will very probably lose the use of her legs for the rest of her life."

Sam did not hesitate. "Go ahead, Gordon. You and I know what Kate would want."

Gordon was relieved. He looked hard at Sam, trying to say in his look that he was glad Sam understood his mother, and more. "Right. I'll get on with it then. We should know a lot more by tomorrow."

"And it's possible that the operation on top of her other injuries . . . that she might die?" Diane looked up at him.

"Yes." Gordon turned his gaze to this extraordinarily beautiful woman, whom he had seen on TV and the stage and in films many times. It added to his sense of unreality. "Yes. It is possible. I shall do my best."

"We were just getting to know one another."

Gordon patted her arm and left them.

"Oh, Christ, Sam," Diane sniffled. "I *never* cry. I've cried more in five days than in my entire forty years."

"Forty-two." Sam gave her a hug and she laughed through her tears.

———

The fire in front of which Evie and Allen were sleeping had burned low. Allen stirred, brought to consciousness by a sound he couldn't quite identify. He listened for a long moment, wondering if he should awaken Evie.

The scream that shattered the silence was one of pure terror. It had come from one of the women lying alone at the edge of the group, one whom neither Evie nor anyone else had managed to befriend.

Flashlights, growing ever dimmer, switched on and tried to pick out the person from whom the screams were coming. When they finally illuminated her, a convulsive gasp went up from everyone who could see.

The woman was standing, flailing at herself, dancing up and down in an effort to dislodge some half dozen rats that clung to various parts of her body. And there were more at her feet. Many more, and they turned their bright red eyes toward the rest of the group.

One flashlight shone over them and came to a break in the station wall through which they were streaming in what seemed to be hundreds.

The group, almost to a person, was on its feet now. The woman who was being attacked stumbled and fell, and instantly an uncountable number of additional rats mounted her body. She raised herself up once again and rushed blindly forward, tearing at her tormentors, heedless of the direction she was taking.

She went over the edge of the platform before anyone could help her—not that anyone was making much of an effort—and they could hear her, choking and crying, trying to stand upright on the track bed. One rat came sailing back up to the platform, landing with a smack amidst its brethren, which immediately turned on it. Then one of the flashlights penetrated the gloom of the track bed and they could see the woman, upright now and still covered with the terrible beasts, begin to run between the tracks southward, trying frantically to dislodge the creatures. Her screams continued to echo for many long minutes after she was out of range of their most powerful light.

"Watch out!" someone called, and those who had been following the woman's desperate flight down the tracks turned back.

"These suckers ain't afraid," another voice said, and they watched in horror as the rat pack began to move toward them. Slowly, purposefully, as if guided by one brain, they advanced. And the people shrank back.

"Who's got something that will burn, burn fast and hot?" asked a tall man with a cigarette lighter in his hand. "A piece of clothing, a shirt, a jacket, anything. They might not be afraid of us, but I'm damn well sure they're afraid of fire."

People volunteered almost instantly, ripping off articles of clothing and holding them out to be lit. Many of the items had been made fire-retardant, but enough were of flammable material that soon balls and sheets of fire were being launched at the rats.

The rodents retreated, several of them with their fur ablaze, but unless the people were prepared to strip themselves naked, they wouldn't be able to hold out for any length of time, and when the last piece of clothing had expired, the rats would move forward again.

"Evie. In my pockets," said Allen. He had been holding a flashlight with his good hand and had not been able to get at the firecrackers he had taken from Rick's body.

She reached into first one pocket, then the other. "Here," she said to the man with the lighter, as she held out a cherry bomb. "This will help."

As he took it from her and began to light its fuse, Allen said, "Throw it under them, not on top. Let it rip out as many bellies as it can."

The man with the lighter nodded, then concentrated. "Haven't set off one of these since I was a kid. Hope I don't blow my hand off."

The rats crept nearer, and the people in the group had backed as far down the platform as they could go without descending from it.

The fuse sputtered, caught, hissed like a small dragon. The man waited for what seemed to be an interminable time, then bowled it into the advancing pack.

The explosion, confined in the silent tunnel, shocked both humans and rats, but most of the people had prepared for it by putting their hands over their ears. The rats, taken unaware, flew screaming in every direction, including toward the people. But those that came within reach were kicked and stomped to death.

The man with the lighter held out his hand several times in rapid succession and each time, with the precision of a nurse, Evie slapped a cherry bomb into his palm. Slap, hiss, bowl, bang.

The rats began to retreat, shrieking in alarm. But there were so many of them that they soon jammed up against the station's wall, making the pack now scrambling frantically one on top of another an easy target.

"How many more of the big ones we have left?" the man asked Evie.

"About a half dozen," she replied. "Lots of smaller ones."

"We'll keep the bombs for if we need them again. Give me some small ones."

Evie handed him a rope of small firecrackers and he lit its fuse and tossed it into the roiling mob. It went off with a dozen small but effective shots and the pack disintegrated.

Biting and chewing at each other, the rats attempted to get through the hole in the wall from which they had come. But now the survivors on the platform, emboldened with their success, came forward after the rats.

"Kick any ones that you can off the platform!" The speaker was lost in darkness.

"Yeah," Allen agreed. "Then we throw a few more crackers through that hole and find some way to seal it up."

The man with the lighter complied. Then several people whose proferred articles of clothing had not been flammable stuffed them into the crack in the wall. They knew it wouldn't last long if the rats decided to return, but every one of them felt that they were at least safe for the night.

As a precaution, several people volunteered to rotate as guards over the rat hole. Then most of the others, weary beyond weary, finally lay down to sleep.

Sleep eluded both Evie and Allen. They sat in front of their fire for a while longer, and then rose silently and walked away from the others, into the darkness of the concourse that led from the IRT platform to the other lines in the station. By now they were used to the darkness of the tunnel and even the broad bank of stairs leading down didn't cause them any problem.

"We will get out of here," Evie said. "Barrier or no barrier, I want to keep going uptown tomorrow."

"We got over one. We can get over another." Allen took her in his good arm, pressed her against his body. "And when we do, when we get out of here . . ." He let the words linger in the dark silence.

Evie went up on her toes and pressed her mouth against his. Their kiss was long and deep, fulfilling rather than passionate. That would come later.

"I feel like a junior in high school," Allen said when they finally took time out to breathe.

"And like a high school junior's date, I'm telling you that it's time to go home."

"One of these days we'll be seniors."

"Yes. Very, very soon."

THE FOURTH DAY

t was day four, Saturday.

The report had come in at two twenty-six that morning from one of the Army units on patrol in Harlem to combat looting. There was a hostage situation at the Schomburg Center on 135th Street and Lenox Avenue. The Army unit had been fired on and was requesting backup.

Brendan Ahearn sighed when the news was relayed to him. So far there had been little armed resistance to the antilooting patrols that had fanned out all over Manhattan after the 82nd Airborne had landed nearly forty-eight hours earlier. Looting had been rampant. Initially valuables such as jewelry and consumer electronics had been targeted, but as the crisis continued looters began to focus on staples— food, clothing, bedding, and the like—to keep themselves alive and intact.

In some cases, store owners and shopkeepers whose businesses had remained standing had willingly opened their doors, handing out supplies to those in need rather than wait for the inevitable pilferage.

There had been sporadic instances of violence, but the troops had quelled them efficiently—ruthlessly, some might say, but ruthlessness was what was called for if control of the City was to be maintained. The report of the problem at the Schomburg was different. Whatever was going on was more calculated than the random occurrences that the City had seen up to now.

"Sorry, Major, lots of static. Tell me again the situation."

"Briefly, Captain, there's a gang of what I understand to be drug dealers—someone says they're known as the Jamaican Posse—that have taken over the center. They're holding a lot of civilians who went there for shelter after the earthquake."

"How many men do you have with you?"

"Sixteen, but two of those are wounded. I don't know how many of the Posse are inside, but that place is like a fortress."

"Yes, and one that we can't attack." Ahearn knew that the Schomburg held the largest collection of African-Americana in the world. Books, photographs, art, sculpture—the collection was priceless. That the Schomburg had survived the general devastation to Harlem was itself a miracle. Nothing could be allowed to put that collection in danger.

"I'll have reinforcements for you ASAP." He broke the connection.

Brendan apprised the mayor of the situation and received permission to go to the site and personally take charge of the operation.

"I realize, Mayor, that you wouldn't ask me to, but I hope to find out something about your mother while I'm there."

The mayor nodded. "That would be a kindness, Brendan."

The additional troops—some four hundred men—had been landed at one of the temporary helicopter pads created in Mt. Morris Park. Now they began to make their way up Fifth Avenue in the predawn darkness. A wooden bridge had been built over the crevasse that ran the length of 125th Street, and they walked north in the eerie silence that enveloped the ruination around them. The column of soldiers made a left turn onto 135th Street and moved toward where the Schomburg Center stood on the far side of the next corner.

"Major, I'm Brendan Ahearn." The two officers—Army and police—saluted. "How are your wounded?"

"One's fine. The other's pretty bad. I'd like to get them out of here."

The troops had brought a dozen stretchers with them, and the two men were quickly evacuated to Mt. Morris Park and given first aid.

"What's the next step, Captain?"

"We wait until dawn. Then we see if they'll talk to us."

One of the first things Domenico Rizzo had done when the earthquake had subsided was to order men to Harlem to kill as many of the Jamaican Posse as could be found. Throughout the next two days, his trained killers stalked the ruined streets and avenues above and below the crevasse at 125th Street, picking the West Indian drug dealers off in ones and twos. By late Friday night, it had become evident to Philip T'Frere, the Barbadian boss of the Posse, that his men were being killed off systematically, eliminated by a rival who had long had his eye on the increasing amount of trade the Posse controlled. Domenico Rizzo came to mind.

His men were scattered throughout Harlem. "Call them to me." The order went out, flying as if by Caribbean magic from one gang member to another. "Tell them they should assemble at the Schomburg. At midnight."

The Schomburg Center for Research in Black Culture had been completed in 1980, a low-rise, fortresslike structure that had become the symbol of Harlem's renaissance. With reading and exhibition rooms as well as several rooms devoted to research with microfilm readers and computer equipment, the Schomburg drew like a magnet any resident or visitor with a thirst for knowledge about African-American culture.

Although the earthquake had centered its force barely ten blocks away, the Schomburg's solid construction and lack of height had helped to preserve it intact. While buildings around it collapsed into dust, it had stood firm and become a beacon for survivors. Its small kitchen facilities had worked overtime to provide food to the needy, tables in the reading rooms had been given over to the injured, and several doctors and nurses from the damaged but functioning Harlem Hospital a block away had come over to administer first aid. The center would turn no one away, black or white, if that person needed food or temporary shelter.

From ten o'clock that night, members of the Posse began to drift in. Few of them had affected the dreadlocks of their leader, and it was easy enough for them to enter the Center as simply more of the refugee population of the area. No one in the first floor lobby of the building registering these destitute persons in—even in the midst of destruction, bureaucracy held sway—thought to check for concealed weapons.

At seven minutes past midnight on Saturday morning, a young boy led a man whose face was hidden by dreadlocks into the Schomburg's lobby. "The earthquake made him blind," the boy said, while the man remained mute.

"Take him downstairs to—" the security guard began when the man grabbed the boy and put a small handgun to his head.

"Lock the door," he said in a deep voice to the unarmed security guard, who quickly complied. Then, summoning the witchcraft of the Caribbean islands that he had practiced since the age of eight, he cried out in the commanding tones that had bonded the members of his gang to him, "To me! I desire that you come to my side."

Altogether, Philip T'Frere had seventy-six men. Hundreds of the Posse had been killed during the quake, and the more recent depredations by Rizzo's gang had reduced it to this core. T'Frere had herded the ambulatory survivors—hostages now—to the upper three floors of the five-story building, where they were guarded by seven of his men. In a short, impassioned speech, he told them that he had no desire to see them come to harm but that he and his people would soon be under attack and it was their bad fortune that the Schomburg Center was the best place for the Posse to defend itself.

Thirty of the men bearing the longest-range weapons were sent to the rooftop. The balance of the Posse was told to eat and rest for the battle that T'Frere knew must come. Then he went to one of the executive offices on the corridor off the main lobby. He took the pipe and the ganja that were always with him and smoked until the trance descended.

Sammy Gennero knew he didn't have enough men for the job. Domenico's order had been clear enough. "Wipe them out. Now. There's a vacuum and we can fill it before they recover."

Sammy had set about the task with his usual plodding thoroughness, and at first things went well. His hit men reported murder after murder with no reprisals from the Posse. Then suddenly the Posse members had disappeared, were not at their usual hangouts when the hit men arrived. Sammy had been stumped at first, but had hesitated reporting back to Domenico until he had a more complete picture.

He got it just before one o'clock Saturday morning when one of the runners arrived, breathless, at Sammy's temporary headquarters in a partially destroyed building on 95th Street.

"Well?" Sammy said.

"You know that building up on Lenox and 135th where the jigs keep all their historical stuff?" Sammy nodded. "That's where they've gone. I was about to hit one of the Posse when he began acting all funny, like he'd been smoking that shit they smoke when they want to communicate with each other." Sammy made a derisive noise and the runner shrugged his shoulders in agreement. "Anyway, he went to that building, went inside. I hung around to see if he'd come out again, but I recognized some others from the Posse going in. Then T'Frere showed up, his hand on some kid's shoulder. The next thing you know the door was being locked."

The runner went on to tell Sammy about the guards on the roof. Shit, Sammy thought, I don't know how the fuck many people he's got in there. Sammy had some thirty men he could use, knew that Domenico couldn't or wouldn't spare more, knew what the reward for failure would be.

"Get the guys and let's go."

The sun had barely begun to rise when the first shot rang out. Brendan Ahearn swiveled around on the balls of his feet in time to see one of the rooftop guards plunge to the street below.

"Where the hell was that from?" said the major.

"Damned if I know. Damned if they know, either," he nodded toward the Schomburg, "or they'd be returning the fire."

A volley erupted, sounding to Brendan as if it had come from a machine pistol. It was south of them, but not far. Brendan had had the major position his men up 136th and 137th Streets. He did not want to expose them on Lenox Avenue to attack from the Posse if he could avoid it. On those two streets, they were out of the Schomburg's direct line of sight.

Now the gunfire was being returned from the Schomburg's roof, as well as from windows along its Lenox Avenue front. The sounds of shots filled the air along with screams of men on both sides who were hit. Several RPGs—rocket-propelled grenades—sailed up and onto the Schomburg's roof, tearing holes in it and starting fires as they exploded.

"Whoever's after those guys wants them real bad," the major said.

Whoever, thought Brendan. Then it struck him. Domenico Rizzo. There had been a few rumors before the earthquake that Rizzo was planning to make a move on the Posse. Unofficially that had been fine with both Ahearn and the mayor. If the gangs wanted to fight it out, let them do so. There would be fewer for the police to mop up when it was all over. But now the operation had changed. The Posse was holed up in a building where they had God-knows-how-many innocent civilians with them. On top of that, the building had incredible significance for the African-American community. Rizzo wouldn't care about either the culture or the individuals, and whichever one of his lieutenants was leading this assault would have instructions to act accordingly.

"Major, I want you to take the men who are on 137th Street back down Fifth Avenue to 135th. Whoever is firing on the center is concentrated in the block on 135th between Fifth and Lenox. While you create a diversion, I'm going to rush the building with the rest of the men." The major signaled his understanding of the order and Brendan went on. "The men that you're going to come up against are dangerous, among the most dangerous in the City. They're professional murderers and they do their job well. Good hunting, Major."

The firing between the street and the Schomburg Center was now a full-scale battle. Even though the Posse's men had the advantage of the center's height, they were not as heavily armed and had suffered more casualties than had the mobsters on the street below.

The fires that the grenades had started had been put out with extinguishers, but if they were subject to more volleys like that, the extinguishers would give out and the center would burn. Thirteen of the thirty men who manned the roof had been killed or wounded and their assailants had been positioned well enough that the Posse member in charge thought that little damage had been done in return.

They had known since before dawn that soldiers had arrived to reinforce the existing troops outside the building. The soldiers had made no attempt to conceal their coming, and T'Frere had told his men that he thought they would try to starve them out. The hostages would have been a useful defense against this tactic.

T'Frere's attention—the attention of all of the men on the roof—was diverted by the sound of increased gunfire on 135th Street. The Posse swarmed to that end of the roof. From their vantage point, they could see perhaps a dozen of Rizzo's men backing up into the intersection of 135th and Lenox, firing down the street in the direction of Fifth Avenue.

"Shoot the bastards," the leader said, and the men in the intersection were caught in the crossfire from the Posse and the major's troops. One by one they began to go down.

Brendan Ahearn, on the opposite side of the building, had been waiting for the Army's assault to begin. He heard the staccato burst of gunfire from the Army M-16 assault rifles and saw the rooftop members of the Posse rush to the southwest corner of the building and begin to fire down.

"Let's move out," he said, and the two hundred men behind him started across Lenox Avenue.

One of the soldiers with Brendan's group was a young black captain who had grown up in Harlem and been in and out of the Schomburg almost every day during his teenage years. When they had discussed the assault of the building, the captain had made a rough diagram, had shown them where there was a small courtyard off the octagonal research room in the basement. To reach it, they would have to go around the back of the building, but these men were trained to move over the worst terrain, and the ruined buildings between 135th and 136th behind the Schomburg presented few problems for them.

Ahearn knew that T'Frere, if he were inside, would know that the octagonal room was vulnerable, would position men with his heaviest weapons there. But it was the only way. A frontal assault would have been suicide; they would be exposed to gunfire from both the Posse and the mob and probably also to stray bullets from their own men advancing down 135th Street. He knew that he had to take out whoever might be in the octagonal room quickly and without either a great deal of gunfire or something that might set the center ablaze.

Brendan Ahearn was in fighting trim, though not trained in this kind of police work. Still, he managed to be almost at the head of the company of soldiers when they reached the wall overlooking the small courtyard.

"Ready?"

"Yessir."

"Then do it."

Two men picked up the largest piece of rubble that they could handle. Now they heaved it at windows that opened from the room onto the courtyard. The glass shattered and Brendan and the others could hear mingled shouts and curses from within the room.

"Now."

Two more men stepped forward and lobbed tear gas grenades through the gaping window.

"Okay, guys, masks on."

They waited two minutes, then Brendan and the black Army

captain dropped down into the courtyard. It had been agreed that the captain would lead the way and that the shoot-to-kill order applied to anyone in the building who showed the least sign of resistance. Several carefully measured shots rang out.

The smoke from the gas grenades had begun to dissipate and Brendan and the captain could see several inert bodies on the floor. More men had dropped into the courtyard and were beginning to fill up the research room.

"This way," the captain said, and began to lead them out of the room. They moved toward the narrow flight of stairs that led up to the lobby. The door to the women's room just beyond the stairwell was suddenly thrown open. A man stood in the doorway, gun in hand. Before anyone had time to react, the gun had been fired and Brendan Ahearn was on the floor. The captain fired a burst from his M-16 that riddled the figure in the doorway, then bent over to help Ahearn.

"I'm all right. My arm. Just a flesh wound. Guy wasn't much of a shot, considering the distance." He rose somewhat shakily to his feet. "Let's keep going," his voice muted by his gas mask.

The carnage at the intersection of 135th and Lenox was nearly complete. Caught as they were in the crossfire from the Army and the Posse, Sammy Gennero's men could only die. Three managed to dive down the stairs into the IRT station below the street, pursued by several soldiers. Eighteen bodies littered the intersection. It was enough. Domenico couldn't want this.

Sammy Gennero stepped out from behind a ruined storefront waving a white handkerchief, first in the direction of the troops, then toward the Schomburg.

"Cease fire," the major roared over the sounds of gunfire.

In the abrupt stillness, Sammy stepped forward into the street, walked toward the major.

"Drop your weapon." Sammy did so.

"How many more men do you have?"

"Seven."

"Call them out. Tell them to leave their weapons behind."

Sammy called out the order and, one by one, his remaining men came out from their places of concealment empty-handed.

"You're all under arrest," the major said. As he turned to the captain next in command of his troops to issue orders, a single shot from the roof exploded through Sammy Gennero's body.

The remaining mobsters bolted but most were not fast enough for the soldiers, whose bullets cut them down. Only one managed to sprint down Lenox Avenue, bobbing and weaving as he dodged gunfire from the soldiers and the Posse. Someone had to get word of the massacre back to Rizzo, and he was determined to be the someone.

Brendan Ahearn and the black captain had decided to let tear gas precede them as much as possible, and a soldier tossed a gas grenade up the stairwell to the top landing. They waited for it to take effect, then began cautiously to climb the steps.

When they reached the top, the lobby was completely empty. Brendan sent small details of soldiers to search the exhibition rooms and executive offices, but the reports all came back negative.

"Someone's been in the offices, and recently," one soldier said. "Place stinks of pot."

They heard sounds of running feet above them, then silence. Ahearn, his arm bleeding slightly, looked at the captain. "Man's gotta do . . ."

The troops on 135th Street had dived for cover as some members of the Posse on the Schomburg's roof began directing their fire at the soldiers. "Hold your fire," the major called out to the several of his troops still attempting to pick off the last, running member of the Rizzo hit team.

He looked up at the roof across the street. A half dozen black faces were staring out over the roof's wall. Then, in one fluid motion, he saw them disappear.

Inside the Schomburg Center, the soldier with the gas grenades heaved another up the stairwell between the first and second floors. Then they moved upstairs once again. The second floor, too, was deserted, the silence in the building oppressive.

"We can wait them out, let them get hungry enough to want to surrender. Or we can try to get troops onto the roof, catch them between us."

"Either way," responded the black captain, "there's going to be bloodshed. They won't surrender without a fight, and they'll take innocent lives with them. Not much of a choice."

"But one we have to make anyway," Ahearn said.

"Why, gentlemen? Why you have to make such a choice?" The stairwell door leading upward opened slowly. A man with dreadlocks stood in it, a young woman clasped tightly against him, gun to her head.

"I say you don't have to make this choice. You," he nodded toward Ahearn, "probably know who I am. My fight was not with you but with that evil mon, Rizzo. My people have not harmed you," he said, pointedly ignoring Brendan's bleeding arm. "They are upstairs with the others now, prepared to kill and to die. But it is not necessary. I say you should let me go. I am the only one you can identify. My people look like the rest of them upstairs. There is no need for more death." T'Frere paused.

Brendan Ahearn weighed the choices. Ordinarily he would have flatly refused T'Frere's offer. But a protracted standoff would tie up several hundred troops badly needed elsewhere in this crisis. He had thousands of civilian lives to think of. He looked at the black Army officer and they exchanged the wordless commentary that fighting men had always used when faced with hard choices. Then Brendan made his decision.

"Captain, escort this man downstairs and outside. No harm is to come to him." He turned to T'Frere. "You will let the woman go?"

"Word of honor, mon."

After Philip T'Frere had disappeared into the Harlem morning and the hostages had been set free—along with those members of the Posse who Brendan Ahearn declined to try to identify—the police captain ordered the Army troops back to Central Park. He kept two policemen with him and, remembering the pledge he had made to the mayor, walked the few blocks up and over to the Abyssinian Baptist Church.

The mayor had known that his mother, as she always did on Wednesdays, was part of the Ladies' Auxiliary that kept the altar area of the historic shrine in immaculate shape. He had not, however, been able to learn whether his mother had actually been there when the quake struck, only that the building had suffered a great deal of damage.

When Brendan reached the first of its bright red sets of doors on 138th Street, he saw just how bad the damage had been. The spires that had dominated the low skyline of the surrounding neighborhood had fallen. The roof had caved in, how far he could not tell. The façade of the church had remained standing, but the middle set of red doors had been blown open to reveal the destruction within.

Because of its historic significance, the church had been a focus of the rescue attempt in Harlem before twenty-four hours had elapsed after the earthquake. Now, two days later, firemen from the local station were still directing neighborhood residents as they carefully picked through the rubble, taking pains not to disturb anything that might cause a further collapse. As bricks, stone, timbers were removed, they were passed hand by hand down to the street and placed carefully in an abandoned lot. The citizens of Harlem had already decided that the church would be rebuilt, and when it was, it would be with as much original material as possible.

"Any bodies recovered so far?" Brendan asked the NYPD lieutenant in charge of the operation.

"No, sir," the man replied. "If there was anybody up around the altar it will take us another eight to twelve hours or so to reach them. This was my church, sir, I know it pretty well. That altar's a long way away."

"You know why I'm asking?"

"Yes, sir. Mrs. Lincoln. Everybody around here knew her, knew she'd have to be on her deathbed not to be here on Wednesday sprucing up the church." He cleared his throat. "If she was there, Captain, we'll find her and bring her out. She was one loved woman. Tell the mayor that."

"I will, Lieutenant."

"Miss Mattie, Miss Mattie."

Mattie Lincoln woke once again, sure that she had dreamed that someone was calling her. If she were lucky, it would be an angel, calling her to come greet her Lord.

Terrible to leave Bruce and the others this way, especially Charlie and Evie. But if it were to be the Lord's will, if it was an angel coming for her, she was ready to face her Maker and His judgment.

Her face slipped into peaceful lines and her mind into that peculiar clarity it always took on when she thought of her Lord.

"Miss Mattie. Are you in there somewhere?"

"Yes, Lord, I'm here," she murmured. Then she wondered why He wouldn't know where she was.

Suddenly awake, she could hear the sound of digging, and the voice calling her name over and over again. So it's not my time yet, eh, Lord? Well, then I guess I still have a few more things to do for You here.

With all the energy that she could muster, she called out. "Miss Mattie's right here. Now stop your hollerin' and get me free of this mess."

Ten minutes later, sunlight streamed in toward Mattie Lincoln in her little cave in the Abyssinian Baptist Church. The light of the Lord, she thought. *My* Lord. She turned her face to the light and smiled.

Dave Hartnett woke up on Saturday morning feeling like a new man. He had spent much of the previous evening indulging himself with a few purchases on his Kelly, Farnsworth American Express card, then had taken himself off to an extravagantly expensive meal at the Pump Room. A bit of pub crawling after that and a few hours spent with a college student he had met at a gay bar ended his night. He had called a car service from the young man's studio, promised to stay in touch, and returned to Domenico Rizzo's apartment at around three.

Now, with six hours of sleep under his belt, exercised and showered, and having eaten a small breakfast, Hartnett was ready to begin moving the money he had stolen around. He switched on the Seiko and waited a few seconds for it to warm up. Then he checked the account of his dummy import/export operation on the Isle of Man. Nearly sixty-million, eight hundred thousand dollars. He smiled to himself. What Domenico Rizzo didn't know was that his Nauru and Isle of Man corporations weren't the only ones he maintained. During the raid on Kelly, Farnsworth accounts yesterday, he had transferred over fifteen million dollars directly into the account of his tobacco importing firm in Liechtenstein. He didn't want to double-cross Domenico for more, afraid that the mob capo would become suspicious. With his forty percent of the Kelly, Farnsworth money that Domenico was allowing him to keep, he'd have well over thirty-four million, enough to keep him in boats and boat boys for many years to come.

He accessed the purchasing department of the import/export business on the Isle of Man and wrote up an order for $58,999,999 worth of gem-quality pearls from his business in Nauru, then sent it speeding along the electronic pathways to that small Pacific island.

Dave Hartnett then called his pearl-exporting operation in Nauru up on the screen. The order had been received and the paperwork was being automatically written up. He watched as the programs he had written performed flawlessly. The shipping department in Nauru informed the purchasing department on the Isle of Man that the pearls would be shipped upon receipt in its bank of the payment for them and gave the import/export business the correct account number in Nauru in which to lodge the funds.

Hartnett quickly switched back to the Isle of Man company in time to see the purchasing department acknowledge the requirements from Nauru. Fascinated, as he always was, by the combination of his own skill and the electronic capabilities available to him, he accessed his account in the Isle of Man bank. For perhaps ten seconds, the balance he had seen earlier was there. Then it was suddenly reduced by fifty-eight million dollars.

Wondering if he could move faster than the transfer—and knowing that he couldn't—he came out of the Isle of Man account and went into the one in Nauru, but the transfer had beaten him and that account now showed the figure that had been transferred.

Hartnett laughed out loud, gleefully. One final step. He called up the shipping department in Nauru one last time and watched as it acknowledged the receipt of funds and informed the Isle of Man company that the pearls would be shipped as soon as the proper export documents had been received but certainly no later than ten days from now. Home free!

Domenico Rizzo picked up the telephone and dialed the number of the apartment in Chicago from which David Hartnett had made his raid on the Kelly, Farnsworth accounts. Hartnett picked it up on the third ring.

"Dave? Domenico. How did everything go?"

He listened as Hartnett detailed for him the amounts of money he had stolen and transferred to the account on Nauru.

"Fifty-eight million. That's a nice sum. You did good work, Dave."

"Thanks, Domenico. I'm thinking of leaving in the next hour or so. See if I can get a flight to Mexico or one of the islands. I'll let you know as soon as I've landed somewhere."

"You do that, Dave."

Yeah, buddy boy, you just do that. Domenico picked up the phone once more and dialed a different number in Chicago. When it was answered, he said, "The guy in the apartment has served his purpose. Take care of him for me, would you. Then bring all his equipment back here. I want it within four hours. The boat will be waiting at the usual spot on Long Island."

Fifty-eight million wasn't bad, but Domenico wondered how much Hartnett had skimmed off for himself. In half an hour it wouldn't make any difference. The guy was history.

On Saturday morning in New York, while Dave Hartnett was moving around the money he had stolen from Kelly, Farnsworth, Brian Kelly was making his way downtown to his office in the World Trade Center. He hadn't been back since the earthquake because he had been seeing to the care of his daughters at Roosevelt Hospital. Pat had managed to take a few hours off to join them this morning. Brian had spent Thursday and Friday nights with them, but now it was time to see what was going on at the building that housed the offices of Kelly, Farnsworth and Klein.

He hadn't rushed to return to the offices right after the

earthquake because of two pieces of information he had received through one of the office's messengers at the restaurant where he had been having lunch. The first was that the SEC had stopped trading, which he had known would be the case. The second was that a skeleton staff would stay on duty through the night in case power was restored, then lock up the offices if trading were still suspended the day after the quake. What he hadn't realized was that the skeleton staff would include Dave Hartnett. The confrontation between them on the morning of the quake had been ugly, and he was sure that Dave would resign from the firm. Too bad. He was a brilliant kid. But they couldn't afford to risk having him stay.

As he trudged south, Brian was amazed at how much cleanup had already been done in the seventy-two hours since the earthquake had struck. As usual, New Yorkers could rise to the task at hand like no other people on earth. Very little had been done to make real repairs, but most of the fires had either been put out or were being allowed to burn themselves out, paths had been cleared on the sidewalks and it was possible to move without having to climb over piles of rubble.

The financial district, when he got there, was not in as good shape as the rest of the City that he had seen, and for a moment Brian wondered why. Then he realized that few people actually lived there, that there was no real feeling of neighborhood or community, and that very few people were available to do the work that was going on elsewhere.

The building in which Kelly, Farnsworth had its offices had suffered little harm from the earthquake. While larger structures around it had been reduced to nothing, their seventy-story structure still stood, relatively unscathed. Brian used his passkey to unlock the front entrance, then walked up the three flights to the first of the Kelly, Farnsworth floors.

He let himself into the mailroom and flipped the light switch. The generator system was designed to provide power to only twenty percent of the available lights in order that most of it could be conserved for the firm's computers, and Brian found himself in semidarkness. Good. At least the generators were still operating. If they failed or ran out of fuel, a further backup system of batteries would keep the memory in the computers intact for an additional forty-eight hours. It had been estimated, in that event, there would be enough time to copy all the stored information before memory was lost. However an alarm was supposed to go off at the homes of all three partners, carried by telephone wires, in the event of a switch to battery power, and Brian knew that this fail-safe aspect of the system had failed. It was a relief, therefore, to know that the generators were operating smoothly.

He went from the mailroom to the computer room, on the same floor. The skeleton crew that had stayed on after the quake had done its job perfectly, and the computers were as alive as they would have been if Con Ed were providing the power.

Brian decided to work from the terminal in his private office rather than one of the ones in the computer room, and he walked up the final three flights of the internal stairway to the top floor of the building and the executive offices of Kelly, Farnsworth and Klein. There was sufficient light coming in from the tall windows of his corner office that he decided not to turn on any of the lamps that sat on tables and his desk. He hung his trench coat on the antique rack that Pat had given him several years earlier, then sat in front of the carrel on which his computer terminal lay.

For the next two hours, Brian Kelly checked as many of the critical aspects of the firm's financial life as he could. Nothing had been traded since the SEC-ordered shutdown, and with the lack of ability to utilize the telephone system in the City, the information the computer called up was precisely as it had been up to the moment of the quake. The computer was holding buy and sell orders for the time when it could again transact them.

Brian went deeper, trying to check the firm's bank accounts around the country, but quickly realized that without telephone service, modem communication with bank computers was impossible. Nevertheless, it seemed to Brian that for a medium-size brokerage house, they were in a very solid financial position, and once this mess had been straightened out, they would bounce back better and stronger than ever. Satisfied at last, Brian Kelly turned off the power to the terminal and left.

Bruce Lincoln had refused to take any rest, even though Dr. Patricia Kelly had threatened him with all sorts of dire repercussions if he didn't. He had catnapped from time to time since the earthquake had struck over three days earlier, but that sleep probably didn't amount to more than a few hours in total.

He was racked with worry. His beloved city had been brought to its knees; the governor of the state was actively campaigning against reviving it; congressmen from the Midwest were flocking to the governor's support; the aftereffects of the earthquake—fire, lack of water, absence of electricity, spotty communications with the outside world, the potential for disease—were never-ending and gnawing at his gut like a nest of rats. Underlying all of it was that, of the four people he held dearest in the world, he knew for sure that only his son, Charlie, was safe. Paula, his dear wife, was dead in the rubble of her child-care center; Brendan Ahearn had told him about his mother, Mattie, when he had returned from Harlem; and only hours ago the police reported finding the wallet of his daughter, Evie, after a shootout at the Times Square IRT station—she, too, could be dead or alive. It was becoming too much, and Bruce Lincoln knew it.

He looked at the battery-powered clock that someone had put in Brendan Ahearn's office to replace the dead electric one. Nearly nine thirty at night. He stretched and a stab of pain went through his chest. Damn it, another stitch, he thought. Then he collapsed to the floor.

They left the 59th Street station at eight o'clock the next morning, this time with additional people from the platform, moving out in single file once again on the track bed. The water had almost disappeared and the track bed was littered with the corpses of rats, and more than one person vomited dryly as a rat body was stepped on. Evie was once again in the lead and Allen brought up the rear.

Lighting the way was increasingly difficult. Of the six or seven flashlights they had started out with from 59th Street, only three had any power left after an hour or so, and that was minimal, so they were walking along the track in utter blackness, saving the flashlights for when they might need them.

Evie came up against a wall of debris from a cave-in. Although she had been walking slowly, she still crashed into it painfully, uttering a cry and then another as the person immediately behind blundered into her. The line tottered as its members were brought to a sudden halt, then recovered its balance.

"What's happened?" Bill Cohen called out.

"A barrier of some kind," Evie replied, loud enough for the entire group to hear. "Whoever has the flashlights, come up to the front. We have to find out what this is."

"Jesus," Peg whispered, as the lights were shined on the obstruction. "How the hell do we get past this?"

Evie turned to them, though few could see her well in the glow reflected off the wall of debris. "We're going to get past this if we have to dismantle it piece by piece," she said. "We know what's behind us. Nothing. No escape. We don't know what's on the other side of this. It looks solid but a lot of it has to be loose, not too thick in some places. So we dig."

"How?" Gerta cried. "We don't have anything to dig with."

"Something wrong with your hands?" Bill Cohen replied gruffly.

Five hours later they had accomplished what Evie had hoped they would. Tapping and listening to the sound their tapping made, they had found a place that seemed less solid, less dense than any other part of the wall. Carefully they had begun to move the rubble, each person working at the wall for ten minutes at a time. Slowly and painfully, with hands cut by the bricks and masonry they encountered, they tunneled a small hole through the wall, big enough for the largest of them. Their biggest fear was that it would collapse.

When the lead man was halfway into the hole they had created and which they tried to shore up as best they could, they heard him yell something. Then, furiously scrabbling, he backed out of the hole.

"Did you get through?" Allen asked.

"Shit, yeah. But there's gas on the other side of the wall. Thick. Real bad."

Now they could all smell it, for it had begun to flow through the opening they had dug. They shrank away from the hole, and most tried to put some article of clothing over their mouths and noses.

"Christ," said the man who had lit the firecrackers the night before. "It's a good thing I wasn't trying to see anything with my lighter. That wall would have come down quick."

The smell of gas was stronger now and many of the group were beginning to gag on it.

"Move away from the hole, but don't go too far. And try not to touch the rails. None of us can remember if something might be on the bottom of our shoes that might cause a spark."

The speaker was a young man and his voice carried authority. "Unless we're really unlucky, that's going to be a pocket of gas rather than something live and still pumping. I've been waiting for this ever since we started out."

"Who are you?"

"Tom Fellowes," the man replied. "I work for Brooklyn Union. I've been surprised all along that we haven't encountered more gas down here. If I'm right, that pocket will slowly seep out through the hole we dug. There's enough air here for it to dissipate without doing us harm. Except that at a certain point, the mixture can explode. Everyone should stay as quiet as possible."

"What if you're wrong?" Evie asked.

"If I'm wrong, if there's a live main leaking gas on the other side of the wall, then we're either stuck here or we have to go back. Or we're dead."

Evie approached Tom Fellowes as the group settled down on the tracks to wait to see what the gas leaking from the other side of the wall would do.

"How long do you think this will take?"

"Hard to tell. I don't have a meter with me that would tell us the level of the gas in the atmosphere and whether it's rising or falling, but I've been smelling the stuff for long enough that I can pretty much tell if it's going up or down. In the few minutes since the wall was breached, it doesn't seem to have changed very much."

"Does that necessarily mean anything?"

"Could. Let's wait an hour. Then I'll tell you what I think."

They waited, mostly in silence, most of them continuing to cover their noses and mouths with cloth. Finally Tom Fellowes got up and went to the hole in the wall. He sniffed several times, then crawled into it and went completely through. "Evie," he called back.

She moved to the wall and tried not to notice the smell of the gas as it came through the opening. "I'm here." She could see a soft glow from the flashlight Tom was shining about.

"I'm in a cavern about twenty feet long. A second section of the tunnel fell along with the one we've already opened. It's created a little room but it's not as complete as the wall we had to dig through. I can see areas along the top where there's space between it and the roof of the tunnel. That'll be why the gas we got hit with when we went through the wall wasn't too strong. It rose, and when we opened a hole on the other side of the room, most of it has been flowing out away from us."

"Can we get through?" Allen had joined Evie.

"Yes, I think so, but it's going to take some work. I'll need some volunteers who have strong stomachs and who can work for a few minutes at a time in this atmosphere to help me widen one of the spaces. See who wants to help."

Evie turned to the others. Most of them had approached the hole in the wall and had heard Tom's comments, and a half dozen of the men and several women immediately volunteered. They and Evie clustered around the hole and Tom told them what he wanted them to do.

The closest space between the second wall and the roof of the tunnel was only about three feet higher than the tallest of the volunteers. When they had assembled in the small room, Tom told them that what he wanted was a ramp built up to the space with debris from other parts of the wall. Two or three people would work at a time while the others stayed near the first hole to breathe the fresher air that was coming through it. Tom had decided that there was some live leak, but had also decided that it wasn't enough to keep them from going forward, and wasn't going to do more than make some of them mildly nauseated.

Over the next four hours, the ramp took shape, three feet wide and starting fifteen or so feet from the wall so that the slope to the opening would be reasonably gentle. When it was finished, Tom sent his volunteers over it to the other side—the jump down wasn't very far and two of the taller men stood by to catch the ones who were apprehensive about leaping off the top. Then he told Evie and Allen to send the rest of them through.

One by one they entered the room, then started up the sloping ramp and crossed over the wall. Evie and Allen brought up the rear. She had sensed his frustration when, with his injured arm, he was unable to be of much help in building the ramp. Not used to inaction in a situation like this, she thought. But we'll be out of here soon. I hope.

By the time they had reached the top of the ramp, Tom Fellowes had sent the others in their party up to the track but had waited behind to assist them off the top of the wall. Allen made the jump first, stumbled, and was steadied by Tom's hand on his good shoulder. As they turned to help Evie down, she hissed softly at them to be quiet.

They waited for thirty or so seconds while she listened. Then, impatient to be on his way, Tom said, "What do you hear?"

"Voices," she replied. "Fairly close. And I can see a light flickering as well through the first hole we made in the wall."

"Well, we've made it a lot easier for whoever it is than it was for us. Come on down. If they've gotten this far they can get along without us."

Evie made the small leap to the track bed and the three of them started north after the others, several of whose voices they could hear in the distance.

"Not that it particularly matters," Allen said, "but are you sure that you didn't hear people from our own group? A tunnel like this can play tricks with sound."

"No. I'm positive. Besides, I could see light coming through the opening on the other side. I told you that."

The three of them were silent for a moment, trudging forward. Then Tom said, "Tell me what the light looked like again. Didn't you say flickering?"

"Yes," she said. "Why?"

"Not steady like a spotlight or even a flashlight might shine?"

"No. Why?" she repeated and was going to add more, but Allen cut her off.

"Jesus. Let's move."

Evie looked at him questioningly. Allen grabbed her by the upper part of her arm and began rushing her up the tracks. Tom Fellowes, understanding the reason for Allen's alarm, moved out quickly ahead of them.

"Allen, what are you . . ." Evie gasped.

"That flickering light is probably a torch," he yelled.

Evie, Allen, and Tom had managed to scramble far enough up the tracks that the blast caused by whoever had ignited the gas-filled chamber that they had recently passed through didn't cause them any injury. The roar in the subway tunnel had been deafening, though, and it was many minutes before the three of them stopped shaking. Characteristically, it was Allen's sense of humor that returned first.

"Lincoln Center's next."

"I know," Evie replied.

"Want to take in a concert?"

"I prefer the ballet."

"Amazing the things you learn about the woman you love."

Gerta was walking just ahead of Evie. "I knew he'd say it sooner or later," she said. "I'm coming to the wedding."

"You're all invited to the wedding," said Allen.

"Hey, hold on. Don't you think you ought to ask first."

"I will just as soon as I can get down on my knees."

Suddenly, Tom Fellowes's voice rang out from the front of the line. "I see light."

"So do I. Yes. He's right." The chorus of replies was unanimous.

As the Lincoln Center station came into view, they could hear the generator that was powering the emergency electricity in the station. They began to rush forward, yelling and laughing and crying all at once.

There were several people coming toward them and as they got closer they saw uniformed policemen from the Emergency Services Unit. The rescue squad had been able to open up the entrance in front of Avery Fisher Hall and had established a base of operations on the platform.

When they reached one another, the survivors and the cops embraced and wept and clapped one another on the back and everyone talked at once. An officer strode up to Evie and Allen and surveyed the latter's wound critically.

"Water and food are on the platform. Watch it. There's lots of twisted metal along this stretch."

Allen grinned. "You think we've been walking through a field of lilies since Wednesday? Any coffee up there?"

"Sure, but go easy. You don't want too many stimulants right away."

"Oh, I don't know," said Allen, and looked directly at Evie.

"I want to get word to my dad that I'm okay," Evie said. "How can I do that? I'm Evie Lincoln, the mayor's daughter."

"Miss Lincoln! Jesus and all the saints be praised. We knew you were in the system, but by now we thought . . ."

"I know."

"You come with me, ma'am, and I'll get you to the command post where the mayor has been since the quake. He's some guy, that Bruce Lincoln."

Holding Allen's hand, Evie turned to the others to say good-bye.

"Here's my address, sweetie. Remember that invitation," Gerta said.

Evie and Allen rode to the Central Park Precinct House on a policeman's scooter. She did not ask anyone about her mother and brother. She would rather hear whatever news there was of them and her grandmother from her father.

They were led to the first-aid tent. A young woman came forward. "I'm Doctor Kelly. Pat Kelly. How are you both feeling? That looks nasty," she said, indicating Allen's wound. "I'd like to check you both out. You're first," she indicated Allen. "And then you, Ms. Lincoln, once you've seen your father."

"Where is he? What's wrong with him?"

"He's fine. He suffered an angina attack this morning but he's doing well. We can't keep him off the phones or from the rest of his workload. Come on." Pat Kelly led the way through the rows of cots to Mayor Lincoln, then returned to Allen. The mayor was propped up by makeshift pillows, sitting cross-legged on the cot, with two phones by his side, one of which he was on.

Evie went up to him and waited until he looked up.

"Yes. I want those boats to start up the Hudson to help out across in Nyack. Okay?" He hung up.

"Hi, Dad." Evie flashed her wonderful smile and he uncrossed his legs and jumped off the cot in one motion to throw his arms around her. They hugged tightly for a long time.

"Are you really all right?" she asked him.

He stood back. "I'm one hell of a lot better for seeing you. You look pretty good for being down in a subway tunnel for half a week." He took her by the hand away from the cots where they could be private.

"Mother?" she asked.

He shook his head. "She was at the daycare center, and the building collapsed. She wasn't one of the survivors."

Evie stared at him and he struggled to keep his composure.

"Charlie and Grandma?"

"They're fine. Charlie's been working at the hospital and your grandmother was found at the church."

Evie felt her knees go, and her father caught her. "Get something to eat and drink for her, please," he called out to a passing volunteer. He made her sit down on a cot and he sat next to her.

"I can't believe it. Not Mother . . . I, oh, God." She turned to him and buried her head on his chest. He held her tight as sobs racked her body. His tears flowed with hers as they rocked back and forth, overcome by their loss.

The closed-door joint session of the Senate and the House of Representatives had been in session for much of the day. At the direction of the Senate majority leader and the speaker of the house, congressmen and women were limited to having one aide with them in order to keep as much confidentiality to the proceedings as possible. At that, there were still over one thousand people privy to what was taking place on the Saturday following the earthquake, and what was taking place had on more than one occasion degenerated into outright hostility.

To their credit, no one on either side of the fence—and the nature of and response to the crisis had transcended party lines—had stooped to filibuster tactics. Every member of both houses knew that whatever decision was made had to be arrived at as quickly as possible. Some amount of money had to be appropriated to the relief of New York City. It was a question of how much.

H. King Billingsley had spoken early in the proceedings, and vehemently, to the resounding applause from his supporters. But this applause was nowhere near as impressive in the midst of a full joint session as it had been two days earlier with only part of the House in attendance. Of the hundred senators and 435 representatives, all but one of the former and three of the latter were there, and those four were all missing in the aftermath of the quake.

Billingsley's opening salvo had come after several speeches from northeastern congressmen calling for as much aid to the afflicted areas as the nation could provide. Each speaker, however, had deftly avoided the issue of what to do about New York City, had instead spoken in general terms about the needs of the region. After four of these, Billingsley asked to be recognized. He made his salutations and then seized the bit between his teeth.

"I have listened for the past hour to my colleagues from the eastern half of the country talk about devastation and destruction and the need to repair and rebuild. None of that is at issue here, ladies and gentlemen. I would be the first among us to extend the hand of help to those who have been ruined by this act of God. Just as this mighty nation has always reached out in times of other natural disasters— floods, hurricanes, tornadoes, and earlier earthquakes—so will it now stretch forth its hand to succor its people in their time of need."

"Why does he always sound like a bad movie?" Edgar Smithson whispered to Aida Vasquez as she passed by, intent on some purpose of her own. The congresswoman merely smiled.

"But, ladies and gentlemen, there is an issue far larger to be addressed here, the issue of the survival not of people but of a city, of a man-made thing. This, my esteemed colleagues, is where we will be asked to open the pockets of every citizen of this country and take their hard-earned money to bring to life what is and should remain dead.

"New York City for the past forty years has been a blight on America, has been an open sore festering on the coastline of this mighty nation. It has been a magnet drawing to it all the worst elements that a society in transition can produce.

"That it has been out of control for many years is a fact against which I believe none of you can argue. The crime rate is the highest in the nation; its educational system is in shreds; municipal services operate at a level that would not be tolerated throughout the rest of the land; its government seethes with corruption at every level. In short, ladies and gentlemen, it is a city, like

Babylon and many others before it, that has run its course. It has been destroyed by God.

"Yet the administration will soon ask this august body to begin to pump trillions of dollars into the rebuilding of that Godforsaken place—and I use the word *Godforsaken* advisedly, for God has, truly in His Wisdom, forsaken that sin-ridden city. And why? Why, my friends? In order that those same sinners who brought New York to its terrible pass in the first instance can have it back to continue their vicious ways."

"He's warming up," Smithson said to his principal legislative aide, who replied in a laconic, Down East manner that he had always wanted to attend a revival meeting.

The fire and brimstone poured forth. For another quarter hour, Billingsley in ever more colorful terms excoriated New York. Finally, though, even he knew that he was beginning to repeat himself and that, in so doing, he would begin to lose momentum with those whom he needed to sway to his argument.

"And so, ladies and gentlemen, I say this to you. This country has been given a unique opportunity in its history to rid itself of a cancer that is eating into the very fabric of our society, to cut it out cleanly and make the body of the nation whole again. It is an opportunity not to be missed. Money for people in need, yes. Money for the resurrection of a city that God wants dead, no. No and never."

"He's effective, you have to give him that," said the president to those members of his staff who were with him in the Oval Office watching the proceedings in the House.

"So's a rattler," said his private secretary, a woman from the Southwest of middle years who had spent years terrorizing everyone around the president except the first lady.

"But like a rattler, his tail can be cut off. The question is not so much how, but when."

"When?" repeated Geoffrey Collins several hours later when the president put the question to him. "Quite frankly, I have been watching the meeting only sporadically. Most of my day so far has been taken up with trying to fend off well-meaning but basically useless offers of aid from Third World nations that cannot even feed their own people. Has Smithson spoken yet?"

"No. I've thought several times about sending him a note, but he's wily enough to know what he's doing."

"And irascible enough that you don't really want to send the note to him."

The president nodded. "Bruce Lincoln called a few minutes ago. He's confirmed that they've gotten a handle on the fires and the looting at last."

"How much of the City is intact?"

"The buildings? Probably only about twenty percent are still standing in Manhattan, and it will be weeks before it can be determined how many of those are structurally sound."

"So most of it is rubble."

"Yes. But as Howard pointed out last night, that rubble doesn't have to be carted off in their plan. It can form the basis, the foundation of the new New York."

"If there is a new New York."

On the floor of the House, where the joint meeting was taking place, Edgar Smithson had been asked repeatedly when and if he was planning to speak. All through the afternoon, he had deftly avoided giving an answer. Now, however, Aida Vasquez had taken him aside.

"I am telling you, Edgar, Billingsley's forces are on a surge like some vast tide. I don't agree with what you said at the breakfast yesterday completely, but I know that if King gets his way today, it will be the beginning of the end for aid to cities. You *must* speak. So far, no one except the New York members of both houses have been able to present a cogent argument for doing anything other than abandoning New York."

Smithson looked at his watch. "It's almost five thirty. We'll be having a break soon. When they come back with their bellies full and their passions somewhat less aflame, I'll ask to be recognized."

When the joint session reconvened at seven thirty that evening, Edgar Smithson was the first speaker recognized by the chair. Word of his position on the crisis had spread throughout both houses after the prayer breakfast of the day before, and an expectant hush settled over the chamber.

Smithson opened by saying that he had listened attentively to all the arguments presented for and against doing anything more than the minimum for New York City. Now he felt it was time to look at the matter in as dispassionate a manner as possible.

"Most of you know that, like many folks from Maine and other rural areas of this country, I have little use for big cities. To tell you the truth, they frighten me more than a bit. They're generally noisy, dirty, overcrowded, and the pace of life is too fast for us country boys. But whether or not I like them personally has nothing to do with the issue at stake. I recognize, and we all must recognize, that a giant urban metropolis performs certain functions on a global scale—it serves as a focus for the eyes of the rest of the world in terms of a nation's culture. Think of England without London, France without Paris, Russia without Moscow, Japan without Tokyo, and a dozen other countries that we automatically associate with their principal cities. If one of those cities were suddenly removed from the scene, that country would somehow, indefinably, be lessened in the eyes of the world.

"So it is with America. Like it or not, ladies and gentlemen, much of the world thinks of America as New York. Not Washington, or San Francisco, Chicago, Miami, or Boston. Or," he added after a pause, "St. Louis or Portland—either of them." He waited for the gentle laughter in the chamber to subside.

"Because New York had grown so vast, because it had attracted loonies as well as geniuses, criminals as well as good people, the lazy and the industrious, it had become for many the representation— the hub, if you will—of everything that is wrong with our society. 'Cut out that cancer and America will once more be pure,' I believe my esteemed colleague said, or words very close to that. I do not believe, I cannot believe, that if you think about it for more than a few moments that you will agree with him. Those few things that are wrong with this society are wrong with it *generally*, not specifically because of New York. To take just one example, closing up shop in

New York would not end the drug problem in our nation, for it is truly a *national* problem. And that is true for virtually any problem you can identify in New York. Except, of course, the subways."

Smithson paused to take a sip of water as quiet laughter again rippled through his audience. He had always had the ability to bring a certain tension-relieving lightness, but never levity, to even the most serious topic, and it did not fail him now.

"But there is an even larger issue at stake here, and that is the government of this nation's response to a national crisis, no matter where in the country that crisis occurs. If we allow New York to slip into history when it is devastated by an earthquake, will we next subject Atlanta to the same fate if a hurricane leaves it in tatters, or Honolulu if one of Hawaii's volcanoes explodes?

"We must send a signal to every citizen of this country, and every country of the world, that we as a government will be there for our people, for *all* people, at their time of greatest need."

Smithson waited until the applause—much greater than that accorded Billingsley, he was pleased to note—had quieted.

"Tomorrow the president will ask permission of the speaker and the majority leader to address this combined Congress. He will at that time present the preliminary draft of a plan to bring New York City back from the ashes. I urge all of you to listen openly to what he will have to say, not harden your hearts to the mercy that this government should, *must* show at this time of great need. Thank you."

The gopher-faced man had brought the Seiko and Hartnett's disks to Rizzo at the Trump Tower. He had taken care of Hartnett. Now, on Saturday morning, one of the electronic whiz kids in Rizzo's organization was opening the computer in his presence. He exuded all the confidence of a twenty-three-year-old who had always known computers.

Hartnett, compulsively, had labeled his disks clearly enough for anyone to understand what pieces of information were stored within, and the whiz kid selected one that was marked BANK ACCOUNTS: NAURU; ISLE OF MAN. He inserted it into the waiting machine.

The screen came alive. The whiz kid studied it carefully, for he knew that it could be booby-trapped to allow access to no one but Hartnett. He took out the code book that they found with the disks and punched in the appropriate codes for the Nauru account. Once he had the actual bank account number, they could transfer money into one of Rizzo's private accounts.

The screen darkened, then showed the balance in the Nauru account along with the account number. The whiz kid turned to Domenico.

"What now, Mr. Rizzo?"

"Move it to Switzerland." Domenico handed him a piece of paper with a bank's routing information and his account number on it.

The whiz kid checked the code book again. He had studied it carefully for several hours after the gopher-faced man had brought everything from Chicago, but it never hurt to double-check.

He began pressing keys, entering the correct codes from the book to effect the transfer. Then he pushed the SEND button.

The screen went blank and stayed that way for a few seconds. Then, as Domenico stared in disbelief, centered in the middle of it flashed the words, FUCK YOU, GODFATHER.

The lion had awakened in his glade and felt the sharp pangs of hunger that were usually assuaged by the arrival of a keeper with his dinner.

Beyond his hiding place the sounds and movements of 110th Street assaulted his sensitive ears. He decided to roam the park in search of food instead of venturing out into the streets. Hunting was almost forgotten, but hunger stirred his memories of his early life in a different place. He padded along the bicycle path in the moonlight. He heard voices and stopped, his magnificent head held still. Instinctively he followed the sound. There in the moonlight were two human bodies, half-naked, involved in some activity that made them moan and call out. The lion paused for an instant. Then he let out a roar and leapt upon the couple, killing them both very efficiently. He devoured their extremities with great speed.

Sated, he wandered away, heading toward the center of the park. In a few minutes, his belly full, he found another hidden spot to lie down, and shortly he dozed off.

THE FIFTH DAY

Sunday, October 9, 1994

P aul Diamond's column, in the *Washington Post* by invitation (since *The New York Times* is unoperational):

Late last night Congress in an emergency session failed to pass a bill to provide New York State with emergency funds in the amount of ten billion dollars to start putting New York City back on its feet. This is a major defeat for the President, who has been fighting since Wednesday, when the massive earthquake struck, to turn the tide of majority opinion in Congress that the cost is too high and New York City should be razed. Senate Minority Leader, Robert Hill, said last night "Billions of dollars are at stake, but if we allow New York City to go under, the cost to the nation is incalculable."

The question remains whether or not money will

have an appreciable short-term effect on the fate of
Manhattan. In a nation used to the Federal checkbook
being the first resource turned to when disaster hits—
Hurricane Hugo and the San Francisco earthquake in
1989 being the last most dramatic examples—ironically
this great city built on bedrock, a tiny vertical city on an
island, inhabited when the earthquake struck on a cruel
weekday afternoon by over twelve million residents and
commuters, this city, which in recent years has been
seen by many as the symbol of unbridled greed on the
one hand, glitz and glamor and riches not seen since the
pre–World War I era, and on the other the center of
corruption, the homeless, the crack citadel of the world,
some called it Sodom on the Hudson, may not now be
able to be saved by mere money.

Rescue efforts have been frustrated by many factors,
but none so great as the very structure of this island city.
Many thousands of survivors have walked through what
remains of the subway system up into relatively unaf-
fected areas of the Bronx. Many more survivors have
been put on ships from many nations to be taken to
hospitals in Maryland and other states along the seaboard, and the ships head back to pick up more survivors
who wait in makeshift hospitals dockside. Tsunamis kept
any ship from entering New York harbor for two days
after the earthquake. Fires raged unchecked in many
areas of the City. Three thoroughfares have been
cleared: Second Avenue, Fifth Avenue, and crosstown
57th Street. Most other streets and avenues remain
partially blocked. Mayor Lincoln, after consultation with
the President and all major officials of the City, made a
decision on Thursday that all rescue efforts would be
concentrated on those survivors above ground. All official efforts to rescue those trapped in the rubble ceased.

From the poorest section of Harlem to the Silk
Stocking District on the Upper East Side of Manhattan,
many thousands have perished, and we are humbled
before those forces beyond comprehension which have

killed and destroyed so many and so much in sixty seconds last Wednesday. When I file this column, I intend to go with my wife to our temple to pray.

I am going to pray for all those who have lost their lives, all those who have suffered grievous injury, all those who live and must bear the burden of this great tragedy. I am going to pray that our leaders reconsider their decision. While the financial problems this nation faces have never been more perilous, we are still a rich country. To allow a city to perish which is a symbol to the world of aspiration would be the worst kind of tragedy. We have learned once again that there is much we have no control over and our destinies surely are written in the sands and stars. But to relinquish the control we do have over our fate, to abnegate our dreams and hopes, to turn away from the human task at hand, that would be the greatest tragedy of all, one from which I do not believe this nation would recover. For this country more than most lives by its symbols. Presidents who have understood this not only intellectually but emotionally, Roosevelt and Reagan to name two, have been able to tap the American soul, born and raised in freedom, even the poorest and most ill-treated of us, a freedom that no other country in the history of the world has rivaled, and this American soul needs the symbol New York City has become from the days of the immigrant waves in the last century when its streets were said to be paved with gold for those who worked hard, made sacrifices, aspired to greatness.

The earthquake of 1994 has leveled more than a great city. We are all part of the family of man struck by this natural event and we must convince our government to help New York City rebuild. It will never be the same, but perhaps there is a way to rebuild that would help eradicate the ills of the City and enhance its greatness. You in government who would take a bulldozer to New York must try to look beyond the cost of saving the City, its ills of the past, to a future which this country needs as much as England needs the monarchy—not because so much of what it *does,* but because of what New York *means.*

Sunday morning. The fifth day of the disaster that had overtaken New York. Brendan Ahearn, the Police Department's newest deputy chief, sighed, then pushed his chair back from the desk at which he had been working.

The mayor told me on Friday to take a break, to get some rest, find out what's happened to my boys. So what am I doing here? Dedication, or what?

No, it's something different. It has nothing to do with duty. I'm scared, scared to go home, scared of what I'll find.

"Brendan," he heard a soft voice say, and he looked up from the paperwork he had been staring blankly at. It was the mayor. If he had admired the man before last Wednesday—and he had—it was nothing compared with what he felt for him now. Despite his own losses—the death of his wife, the ruination of his city—he had managed to find the strength not only to go on but to triumph.

"Yes, sir," Brendan Ahearn replied and started to rise.

The mayor motioned him down, then came to sit on a corner of the desk. "I thought you were going home to get some rest, find your sons. Do I have to make it an order?"

"No, Mr. Mayor. I was just about to leave."

"Good." The mayor smiled, a kind, wise, weary smile, that of a man who has finally faced all his personal demons and gotten the better of them.

"Now get your ass out of here, Chief, but be back in seventy-two hours, rested, showered, and shaved."

"Yessir."

Brendan Ahearn was helicoptered out to Port Washington along with some other firemen and policemen who lived in the area, had been injured, and were given a day off to try to find their families and get some rest.

He decided to go home first rather than to Holy Name. Nicky

and Willy would have gotten home somehow from school if they were all right.

He realized that in the past three days he had not allowed himself to think of them or the memory of JeanAnne. If he had, he would not have been able to stay on the job. Now, faced with the possibility of losing the boys or finding them seriously injured, he hated to open the front door of his house. Before he reached it, a yellow Labrador leaped up from the pathway and bounded over to him. "Timmy!" Ahearn greeted the dog and allowed him to kiss his face with wet, all-encompassing Labrador kisses. "You old devil. I'll bet you're hungry." The house was undamaged. The sun was out. It looked here as though the earthquake had never happened.

He pushed the door open. It was unlocked. There sitting at the kitchen table were his sons, Willy's blond head bent over a cereal bowl and Nicky, who looked up, one hand in his catcher's mitt, and jumped up from his chair. Suddenly both his sons were climbing all over him and he was clinging to them, and he heard himself bawling like a baby, the tears streaming down his face. The boys were yelling and asking questions, and he held them close and sent a prayer to JeanAnne in his mind. Thank God, babe, they are safe. I love you always. And as he thought the words, he knew that he was finally, after such a long time, saying good-bye to her.

On Sunday morning, Dr. Keith came to them and beckoned them to follow him.

Kate was conscious, intravenous needles in both her wrists, and four bottles of intravenous substances were held high above her, two on one side of the bed, two on another. She was pale, but her blue eyes were bright and she managed a weak smile as they entered her room.

"Thank God," Sam said and kissed her forehead.

"Oh, Kate. We love you," Diane said, and Danny reached up and kissed her on the cheek.

"I love you, Granny."

She nodded.

"Come on, that's enough for now," Gordon ordered. "You can come back later when she's a bit stronger. You go to sleep, Kate."

"Bossy," she murmured, and closed her eyes.

Out in the hallway Sam asked Gordon many questions, and all the answers were positive. "She's going to be fine. She'll have to be here for about two weeks. Then she can go into intensive therapy at Gaylord up in Connecticut. After a couple of months there, she'll be fit. No more mountain climbing, I fear, but able to play tennis, do what she wants."

The Thorne family hugged one another and thanked Dr. Keith. "Diane. Danny. We've got to make some plans. Let's go back to our room and sit down and discuss what we do next," Sam announced and they set off down the hall, Sam in the middle with his arm around his wife and a hand on the back of his son's neck.

Dr. Keith went back to Kate's room.

He sat down by her bed. A close call; only he knew how close. He put his large hand over hers. She opened her eyes and looked at him.

"Bossy."

"I know. Doctors are, you know. Don't you talk. I have to go back to surgery in a minute but I just wanted to sit here and look at you first."

She murmured something and he couldn't make it out. He got up and leaned down and put his ear near her mouth. "I love you," she whispered.

He kissed her cheek. "And I love you, my darling Kate. My intrepid Kate."

"Will I be all right? Tell me the truth."

He sat down again beside her. "You are going to be fine. In two months or less as good as new. Your legs are going to be fine. They won't carry you away from me again, will they?"

She smiled. With effort she said in her real voice, "I told you. Never. You're stuck with me."

"Kate Thorne, we have a great life ahead of us." He held her hand as he spoke. "A great life."

For the next two days Matt Devon joined the army of volunteers who had come from all the surrounding blocks to offer their help taking care of the injured. He found great satisfaction in seeing what he was doing make a difference. Once, a good-looking, middle-aged woman whose manicured scarlet nails and excellent facelift and perfectly colored ash hair put her immediately into the world from which he had come, looked up at him from her hospital bed and said, "Don't I know you from somewhere?"

"I don't think so."

"Oh, yes I do. You're Matt Devon, the dress designer."

"No. Afraid you've got the wrong guy. I'm Moishe Dersowitz."

On Sunday morning Charlie Lincoln found Matt in the emergency room.

"Things are more or less under control," the doctor said. "I'm taking a day off. So are my father and my sister and grandmother. We're going to have a reunion up at Gracie Mansion. Lunch. That old house wasn't hurt at all and the chef's got something good for us. I'd like it a lot if you would join us."

"You all should be alone together, shouldn't you?" Matt was touched.

"Not really. You see, it would be a lot easier if we weren't right now. With you there we can talk about a lot of things, and have a few laughs. With just us we're going to sit and cry a lot about Mom. You'd be doing us a favor."

Matt had had word that his own mother had been killed on the subway. He had no one now.

"I'd love to come."

"Great. We'll walk up there in about an hour. I'll come by and pick you up."

Matt watched his new friend hurry down the hall toward another doctor's task. He thought for a moment about how amazing life was, full of agony and joy. Even if the moment of joy was fleeting, a shaft of light then darkness again, it made the struggle worth it.

After Sam, Diane, and Danny had visited Kate, they sat in their room at the hospital and talked about what to do next. They did not have a change of clothes, let alone anything that had been in the house, from Sam's notes on floppy disks for his new book to Diane's jewelry and clothes, to Danny's toys.

"I suppose we ought to go back to the house and see if we can find anything in the rubble." Sam hated the idea of looking at what once had been a handsome nineteenth-century brownstone.

"Yes," sighed Diane. "I guess so. Then what?"

"I have to report back to the mayor this coming week, after we hear what the president and Congress decide to do about the City. There is a monumental job ahead. I think you and Danny should get to California as soon as it's possible. At least there you can rent a place for us, and Danny can go back to school. I'll come out as soon as I can."

Diane nodded. It seemed to make sense. She resisted the temptation to make a wisecrack about taking refuge in California from an earthquake.

"What about Mary?" Danny asked.

Diane glanced at Sam. "Well, we have to find her. Then we'll see if she wants to come back out to California."

Danny held Copper on his lap. His brow was furrowed. "Do you think she's all right?"

"We're not sure," Sam admitted.

Danny's mouth quivered and he fought back tears. He buried his face in Copper's wiry coat.

Later in the morning, Sam found Diane sorting medical supplies at the nurses' station. "Come on over here. I want to talk." He led her into an empty supply room and closed the door. "We haven't been alone at all."

"I know." She sat down on a folding chair. "Are you as tired as I am?"

"You bet. Listen, is it really okay with you to take Danny and go out to the coast until we know what's what? I mean, we left things sort of . . ."

Diane gazed at him. "You tell me."

Sam leaned up against the wall. He thought a moment. "I love you, Diane. I always have. I want us to stay married."

"Oh, Sam, so do I." She stood and they embraced. "I promise

not to be away as much," he said. And she said, "I promise not to put my career ahead of you and Danny ever again."

They stood back from one another and burst out laughing.

"Did you just hear us?" Diane said. "Do you believe us?"

"Seriously," Sam grinned, "I mean it. And so do you. But it isn't going to be easy."

"No. But we'll try," she said and kissed him.

He held her, and asked, "What about the guy?"

"What guy?" She hesitated. "It's over, Sam. Believe me."

Serious now, Sam searched her face and saw a beautiful, tired woman whose eyes were full of pain. "That bad," he murmured.

"Yes. He was killed."

Sam put his arm around her shoulder. "That's terrible. I'm sorry, Diane. I'm really sorry."

Her eyes were filled with tears, but she smiled up at him. "I know you are, and that's why I love you, Sam, my darling best friend, lover, husband. Let's go find Danny."

That afternoon the Thorne family walked uptown to their house. Their street was half cleared of rubble, and they passed people they knew on the block who were searching through the ruins of their houses.

Two houses still stood, badly damaged, but still erect. As they approached their address, Danny saw a figure huddled in what was left of the basement steps area. He and Copper broke into a run. "Mary!" he yelled, and Mary stood up and opened her arms to him.

Sam and Diane started to run, too, and soon the four of them had their arms around each other, laughing and sobbing as Mary told them that she had been at the fishmonger's when it happened and they had all gotten under the marble table he used to clean the fish. Copper jumped higher and higher, barking for attention, until Mary, her broad face beaming, reached down and picked him up. "You little rug rat, you!"

"We're going to California, Mare," Danny exclaimed.

She put her hands on her ample hips in mock dismay.

"Oh, my goodness, we're parking our brains on a shelf again, are we, and going out to lotus land."

Sam and Diane roared with laughter, as Danny looked bemused. "Yes, well," Diane gasped, "it's better than this." She indicated the ruin that had been their house.

Mary shook her head. "Now, are you *sure* about that?"

———————

"Ladies and gentlemen, the president of the United States."

Once again, except for the four congressmen missing as a result of the earthquake, the floor of the House was packed with senators and representatives for the second day of the extraordinary joint session. This time, however, the doors were not closed, cameras from all the principal networks were in operation, and the press was in full attendance.

To the left of the speaker's podium, a table had been set up and tilted toward his listeners. A crisp white sheet covered it, placed over a framework that did not allow people even to guess what might be underneath. A large screen loomed behind it. The president had never had much time for theatrics but, if he were going to convince his audience that his recommendations be adopted, he wanted to have as much ammunition as possible.

"Ladies and gentlemen, I wish to express my appreciation to you all for allowing me to address you. I know that many of you have been affected and afflicted by this terrible tragedy that has overtaken the nation, and I mourn with you for those whom you have lost and pray with you for those who have suffered injury.

"But mourning and prayer must now be temporarily put aside or, if not put aside, at least relegated to the background as we begin to reconstruct the life of this great nation. A mighty city has fallen, and with it some of the most wonderful and brilliant facets of our American culture, indeed of the culture of the entire world. Is it New York's fate, is it America's fate, is it the fate of the world, that the City not rise again? I say no, and I call upon all men and women of good heart and good will to say no with me.

"What we have lost can never be retrieved in entirety nor, I imagine, would any of us wish it to be. There were many things wrong with New York, as there are many things wrong with this great capital and every other city, large and small, in America. But there were also many things right about it, and those merits outweighed the City's faults.

"You in the Senate and House heard Congressman Smithson yesterday. You also heard Congressman Billingsley. One, ladies and gentlemen, is looking forward. The other is not, or has perhaps deluded himself into thinking he is."

There was a slight sense of shock in the audience. This was not a president known for personal attacks on senators and representatives. As if he knew what his listeners were thinking, the president went on.

"I mean no offense to the honorable representative from Missouri. But forward is the only way we can go. The status quo, where it concerns New York City, cannot be maintained. It is not enough simply to rescue the survivors and allow the City itself to perish.

"But, you will ask, what will the cost be? Will it not be a great financial burden to impose upon our people?

"I say to you, yes, it will be great. But our people are greater. Already there has been a massive groundswell of help from individuals from every area of this country. We have never historically been a people, nor are we now, who can turn away from need.

"Will the government of this nation turn its back when its people are so inclined to help?"

The president took a sip of water, then gestured to the two men who had been waiting quietly out of sight of the audience. They moved toward the speaker's podium, Howard Tate and Mayor Bruce Lincoln, in a wheelchair, and a smattering of applause broke out as they were sighted. The applause grew steadily in volume until it was a roar that nearly deafened those who were clapping. While the president was waiting for it to subside, he leaned toward the two men.

"I imagine you've never been clapped for quite so hard, Howard?"

"True. I might even give Bruce a run for his money in the next election."

The mayor smiled. "And there will be one, Howard. You can bet on that."

"I am betting on it."

The chamber grew quiet and the president went on.

"Obviously, you all know these two men, each of whom is, in

many ways, emblematic of New York. Both were born there, grew up there, have been lifelong residents of the City. Bruce Lincoln came from one background and culture, Howard Tate from another. They are on different sides of the fence politically, and they have publicly disagreed on more issues than I care to remember. But they have one thing in common: a love of New York City and a desire to see her whole again.

"In a very short time, in the space of less than ninety-six hours, they have developed a plan to bring the City back to life. Not the City as we knew it—that can never be. But all the best aspects of that mighty metropolis without the terrible problems and evils that came to sully it over the years.

"New York is a clean slate. This is what can now be written there."

The president turned to his left as Bruce Lincoln and Howard Tate drew the sheet back from the model they had shown the president at Camp David two nights before.

In the thirty or so hours since the president and his party had seen it, the model makers in Howard Tate's organization had refined this three-dimensional representation of the City. As large as it was close up, however, people at the rear of the chamber had trouble seeing it. The president asked that the House lights be dimmed and a slide of the model was cast onto the big screen behind it.

There were exclamations of appreciation and a smattering of applause. The president held up his hands.

"In a short time this model will be set up so that all of you, and I include the press, can view it. For now, I ask your patience for your inability to see it well. I am now going to turn this presentation over to the mayor of New York, the Honorable Bruce Lincoln, and to my good friend, Howard Tate. They will explain their—our—vision of New York City as it can be in the future. When they have finished, the three of us will welcome any questions that the members of Congress care to put to us. I hasten to add that there will be a separate press conference at four thirty this afternoon, so you ladies and gentlemen of the press corps won't feel excluded. Bruce and Howard . . ."

For the next forty-five minutes, Bruce Lincoln and Howard Tate took carefully orchestrated turns explaining the reconceptualized New York City. When Tate said, "Our belief is that the City should not only be saved, but rebuilt along completely different lines from its historical past," the Congress was rapt with attention.

"We propose a new New York City," he continued, "one in which all buildings will be built sturdily enough to withstand the seismic stress of an earthquake." Howard paused a moment before launching into the most radical element of his plan. "In the heart of the city, Manhattan, virtually all residential areas will be abandoned." A collective gasp echoed through the chamber. "Manhattan will become a self-contained island of culture, medicine, education, commerce, and finance. There will be magnificent hotels, theaters, restaurants, museums, and office towers. A revolutionary new transportation system will transport workers and visitors to and from the new Manhattan."

Howard paused a moment to let suspense build.

"Let me digress a moment. The natural evolution of the transportation system in Manhattan over the last century or so got things exactly backward. People were sent underground into dark, noisy tunnels to get around. The freight necessary to provision and supply the city was delivered on the streets, usually by large, loud, pollutant-belching trucks. There will be no trucks in the new Manhattan and no people underground. The subway system will be restored, but will be used strictly for the transportation of foodstuffs and merchandise and all the other goods needed to keep a great city running. The surface, the air and sunlight, will belong exclusively to the people.

"People will arrive in Manhattan from the suburbs and the city's other boroughs via high-speed monorail to one of three new terminals, Uptown, Midtown, and Downtown. From there, they will travel to their destinations in new, electric, computer sequenced surface trams, all free of charge. They will move smoothly, quietly and efficiently past gleaming new buildings, manicured green spaces, parks and pedestrian esplanades. Gone will be the noise and foul air that were the constant companions of anyone in Manhattan, since no trucks or cars or any vehicle with an internal-combustion engine will be permitted on the island.

"There will be no slums, no homeless, for now that we are all homeless we are finally forced to solve one of the overriding problems of our City." Howard Tate turned to Bruce Lincoln, who took over.

Lincoln said, "We intend to build new public housing for the homeless in the City's four other boroughs. These new complexes will be constructed with an aesthetic practicality never before used in public projects. We feel we should also assist those who lost their homes and wish to move farther out from the City, to do so."

He searched the faces of the senators and representatives. Their attention was held. He continued, "Imagine New York as we envision it. Yes, some of its character has been erased by the earthquake. The old beautiful brownstones and eighteenth- and nineteenth-century buildings, the wonderful ethnic areas—but imagine that the Italians, Chinese, Greeks, and all the others will build pockets of fine places to eat and shop once again. We have lost a great deal. Much of it cannot be replaced. We can only build for the future. If we will admit it, New York City was not meant in the first place to encompass millions of residents and commuters. Its streets were crumbling. Its subway system and water systems and electrical systems—all outdated. Our bridges and tunnels needed major repairs. And the growing distance between the very rich and the very poor was ruining the City. Crime made our parks unsafe and our streets equally so. The drug trade corrupted our youth and was ruining our society.

"Our new City will be free of the criminal element, its streets clean and new and green. People from all over the world will still come to the City to work and visit. It will still be the cultural center, the financial center."

At this point Tate's people began to show the Congress the graphics on the screen. There was hardly a person in the chamber who was not dazzled. Some graphics showed potential vistas up and down the island of Manhattan; others indicated existing buildings that they thought and hoped could be saved as well as new structures that would go up in the future; still others went into the economics—pro and con—of attempting to rebuild the City along these lines.

"And so, ladies and gentlemen," said the mayor in summing up, "we give you New York as it might, should, and must be by the beginning of the next century. Six years is perhaps a short period of time within which to carry this plan forward to reality. Or six years would be, for any other people on earth. But we are Americans. And Americans can do anything they set their minds and hearts to."

The applause was a rolling wave of thunder that echoed back and forth in the chamber. It was later reported in the press to have lasted for nearly eight minutes, spurred on by the calculated flashing on the screen of the most startling and evocative of the slides Howard Tate had provided. Finally, though, it began to dwindle and Bruce Lincoln cleared his throat to go on.

"I would ask the president to join Mr. Tate and me and, as promised, we will respond to questions from the floor."

The president, Bruce Lincoln, and Howard Tate had planned to field questions from the floor of the House for a two-hour period. Virtually every senator and representative had at least one question to ask, point to make, or criticism to get on the record. At the beginning of the session, it was decided that the speaker of the house would choose the questioners and, if a question seemed to him to be a repeat of something that had come before, he could choose to dismiss it.

As if waiting for a cat to pounce on a mouse, the first few questions put by congressmen and women avoided the topic of the cost to reconstruct New York along the lines Lincoln and Tate were proposing. Fifteen minutes after the session had begun, H. King Billingsley asked to be recognized. He wasted no time getting to the point.

"I address this question to you, Mr. President. What the mayor and Mr. Tate have proposed is most impressive, most impressive indeed. And, I would imagine, very costly. Can you tell us, sir, just how much the federal government is going to be asked to pay in order that New York might continue on as a city?"

"When the crisis was twenty-four hours old, the Office of Management and Budget put together some rough figures—and I emphasize the word 'rough'—indicating that approximately seven trillion dollars would be necessary to rebuild New York. I believe you have already used this figure when you spoke to the House two days ago."

"So then, sir," Billingsley bellowed. "You propose to spend four times the annual budget of this entire nation on one city alone?"

The president let Billingsley's question hang in the air. Neither the senator from Missouri nor any other member of Congress could see the slight smile the president could not suppress.

"Preliminary figures are, of course, almost always misleading," the president said evenly. "In many—perhaps most—cases they turn out to be too low. There has not been an administration in modern times that has not been plagued by cost overruns. However . . ." the president looked around the chamber, then continued. "The seven-trillion-dollar figure was a first rough estimate by OMB of the full replacement cost of everything that was damaged or destroyed in the metropolitan area. Every office building. Every apartment building. Every private home. Every bridge, tunnel, and roadway. An entirely new subway system. The entire water system, gas system, and electrical system.

"As you've just seen, we are not proposing to rebuild New York City just as it was. Not by a long shot. For one thing, Howard Tate chose monorails as the only links to Manhattan not just because they are much faster than trains or cars. They are much, much cheaper to build. Its simplicity of construction makes a monorail river crossing cost less than one-tenth what a conventional bridge costs to build, and one one-hundredth the cost of a tunnel. Not that we'd get anybody to use a river tunnel again, anyway," the president added. When the grim laughter died, he continued.

"Additionally, ninety-nine percent of the new construction will be financed not by the government, but by the private sector. Howard assures me business people from all over the world will practically kill to buy up property and build in the Manhattan he envisions. And let me say a word about insurance. Even though few New Yorkers carried specific earthquake insurance, I expect the insurance industry to honor its commitments to home and apartment owners, to all property owners who've suffered losses. For the record, the attorney general assures me that legally, much of the destruction was caused by fire and water damage, which are commonly insured against.

"So what the federal government, the American taxpayers, must do is pick up some of the slack where insurance leaves off and also help finance a new infrastructure. Transportation systems, water, power, and so on. And even here, the private sector is willing, even eager to participate. The cost to the taxpayers, then will not be seven trillion dollars, as the distinguished senator from Missouri has indicated."

Again the president paused. There was dead silence in the chamber. "It will be far, far less. Less even than one trillion dollars." Murmurs filled the chamber. "The federal share of the cost of rebuilding New York City will be no more than seven hundred fifty billion dollars. I might point out, ladies and gentlemen, that that is less than what the final cost of the Savings and Loan bailout proved to be. And unlike the S&L money that simply replaced deposits, the money for New York will be a shot of adrenaline for the economy, creating millions of jobs and millions of dollars in new tax revenues.

"I must also point out that the seven hundred fifty billion dollars will be disbursed over a six-year period, and can largely be financed by federally backed tax-free long-term municipal bonds. The actual annual cost to Washington, will therefore be around ten billion dollars the first year. Or if you prefer," the president added with a hint of sarcasm, "for that same amount we could instead purchase ten new Stealth bombers."

There was silence for a moment as the senators and representatives looked in astonishment at each other. Applause erupted, filling the chamber for more than five minutes. When it began to subside, a red-faced Senator Billingsley, inexplicably not yet ready to accept defeat, stepped up to a floor microphone and snapped, "With all due respect, Mr. President, that seems like a bit of creative accounting to me."

"Not at all, Mr. Billingsley," the president replied smoothly. "As I believe most of you know, Mr. Tate runs one of the 'tightest ships' of any business or industry in this country. He is known for bringing in projects on time and at cost. It is my plan to issue an Executive Order creating a temporary commission to oversee the reconstruction of New York City and appoint Mr. Tate as its head. The appointment would be for a ten-year period so that it would not be subject to the shifting political climate in Washington. Mr. Tate has agreed to take this job on, giving up his position at Tate Industries. He has also agreed to put his own personal assets in escrow for the duration."

Billingsley's eyes darted around the room for support. He saw none, but pressed one last attack.

"But then, Mr. President, you are pinning all of this scheme, I will not for the moment say 'wild scheme,' on the abilities of one man."

Howard Tate reached out and touched the president's sleeve. "May I?" he asked quietly, then stood.

"I understand your concerns, Mr. Billingsley, and I appreciate them. I hope that what I am about to say will relieve them if not erase them entirely.

"I am no longer young and, with Tate Acres, I had assumed I had achieved the capstone of my career. As you may know, my late wife and I were not fortunate enough to have children, and the business that I have built up over the past forty years has always been privately owned. It is my intention—and I have already had my attorneys begin research into how it can be done—that Tate Industries be reconstituted as a nonprofit organization and that the reconstituted organization, some twelve hundred men and women strong, be hired by the new commission to be the core staff overseeing the reconstruction of the City. In this way, not only will start-up time be kept to a minimum, but the task will go forward smoothly even if I am not here to guide it through the whole ten-year period. I believe that salaries for the existing staff of Tate Industries, with built-in performance and cost-of-living escalators, can be covered for the foreseeable future by the judicious selling of certain corporate assets and investment of the profit from those sales. Which is to say that no part of the monies needed for the actual reconstruction of the City—whether from the government, the banks, or the issuance of bonds—will be necessary for staff overhead which, as you all know, is treacherously high at the government level."

Billingsley took a moment to find his voice. "Do you mean to say, Mr. Tate, that you would do all this—dismantle your own, if I may use the term, financial empire—in order to bring New York back to life again?"

"I would, Mr. Billingsley. Yes, sir, I would."

Howard Tate smiled at Billingsley. The wily politician was stymied by Tate's response, and little did he know, or would he ever know, that generosity was easy when one had had the verdict Tate had received from Dr. Gordon Keith only four days earlier. Yes, Howard Tate smiled at his adversary, Billingsley, glad to see the disbelief on the politician's face. No one but Keith and he knew how easy it was to be generous when time was running out. Besides, the gesture he was making toward his beloved New York City, Howard Tate knew, would give him a certain kind of immortality. Trump put his name on dozens of buildings; it wasn't the same as actually building a city with your own money and power. Howard Tate said again, this time with more emphasis, "I would, Mr. Billingsley. Yes, sir, I would."

George Fleming had been disturbed the day before when King Billingsley had failed to return his calls after the closed-door session of the combined houses. Now, having watched this televised session and heard the president, Bruce Lincoln, and Howard Tate state their reasons for saving New York City—and the positive response from Congress to their reasoning—he was thoroughly alarmed. King Billingsley's exchange with Howard Tate had not gone in favor of the representative from Missouri, Fleming was sure of that. Tate's selflessness in combination with Lincoln's passion and the president's bombshell about the cost and his ability to convince or strong-arm wavering members in favor of their cause would be difficult to overcome.

He hit his intercom button. "See if you can get Billingsley for me. He's on the floor of the House, but tell whoever you get that it's urgent I speak with him."

Fleming drummed his fingers on the desk while he waited. Fortunately he had not publicly come out to say he was against the reviving of the City. Whenever he had been asked, he had waffled the question, adopting a let's-wait-and-see attitude. But the press had picked up on his indecisiveness, and several newspaper editorials outside New York City (whose newspapers were still at a standstill) had already taken him to task for not throwing himself into the survival of the City as had Bruce Lincoln. Billingsley and the votes he could muster were Fleming's only line of defense. If he lost this battle, he lost the war.

His intercom startled him. "I have Congressman Billingsley, Governor. Line four."

Fleming punched the button, picked up the phone. In the background he could hear the applause that was still going on for Howard Tate.

"George?"

"Yes, King, right here."

"Well, Governor Fleming, a great day in the history of this nation."

"What do you mean, King?"

"What you should be proudest of. The federal government moving with all dispatch to come to the rescue of the citizens of its greatest city."

"But, King . . ."

"Now, George. I'm sure you have been watching the televised proceedings this morning. The president, Mayor Lincoln, and Mr. Tate have convinced us, all of us, that saving New York City is in the best interests of this country. There will be a vote in a little while, but I can tell you that it will only be pro forma. I believe this joint session will vote unanimously, or nearly so, for the plan those gentlemen have presented. As I say, a great day, George, a great day. Have to be going now, but I'm sure we'll talk soon."

Fleming began to say something, then realized he was talking into a dead phone. Damn him, he thought, damn all politics and politicians to hell. Then the realist in him took over and he began to devise a way to retrench.

Rosemarie drove as far as she could toward Tate Acres, and walked the rest of the way. She wore her jogging clothes with a heavy sweater tied around her ample hips and sneakers on her feet. The helicopter pad at Tate Acres was busy, choppers taking off to Manhattan with doctors and nurses aboard and landing with evacuees going to the hospital on Tate Acres every few minutes. Rosemarie had planned her story. She was a nurse, no one bothered about uniforms at this time, and she was on her way to

New York Hospital. There was no difficulty getting on a helicopter, and within minutes she had walked across town from the 61st Street and helicopter pad on the East River. By noon she was within a block of Trump Tower. She felt under her sweater for the Beretta. It was snug against her rib cage, loaded, ready.

She climbed the thirty flights of stairs to the duplex she knew was Domenico's. His bodyguards exchanged worried looks but didn't try to stop her. She rang the bell by the front door. In moments a woman not much younger than she opened the door. Rosemarie stuck out her hand. "Hello. I'm Rosemarie Rizzo. You must be Nancy Thayer." She brushed by the astonished woman and walked into the living room. Domenico got to his feet.

"I've been so worried about you," she said and went over to him.

"How did you get here?" he asked.

"What does it matter, I'm here." Rosemarie's cheeks burned as though she had a fever. She looked at Nancy Thayer, who had come into the room and had folded her arms in front of her and was looking at Rosemarie with curiosity and something else. Rosemarie was not certain what she saw in those large, luminous green cat's eyes.

Rosemarie reached inside her sweatshirt and took out the Beretta and pointed it at Domenico's stomach.

He started to move toward her. She waved the gun as she had seen thugs in movies do. "Don't move an inch or I'll shoot you," she said. Then she moved the gun in Nancy's direction. "Move over here next to Domenico." Nancy went to Domenico's side.

"You make a beautiful couple," Rosemarie said.

Rizzo stood stock still and then put a hand on Nancy's arm, trying to move her behind him. "No," Nancy whispered. "No, big boy, we're in this together."

"Rosemarie, you can't do this," he began. "Let's talk. We can talk and fix anything. Think of Angelica."

"I've thought of Angelica. She's a grown woman. She doesn't need her whoring-around father anymore. I'm going to do to you what they did to Capri." Tears started down her plump cheeks.

"What happened to Capri?"

"She got killed. She fell on her neck and they shot her."

"No. No. I don't believe you," Rizzo muttered.

"She was too beautiful and she shouldn't have been asked to race that day. She didn't feel well. But you and Factor went ahead and put her in the race. You men don't care what you do as long as you can kill beautiful things. You've killed everything, Dom."

He started toward her, and when the bullet hit him he stopped, his black eyes widening in pain and horror. The next bullet hit Nancy, who fell to her knees, her arms outstretched.

"Now, I kill you." She emptied the rest of the bullets into their dying bodies, crumpled on the floor, blood pouring from each new wound. She threw the gun down. She went to the window. The breeze blew in through the broken glass.

Rosemarie Rizzo climbed onto the steel frame of the window, and as the bodyguards crashed through the front door, her body hurtled thirty floors down to the ruined street below.

THE SIXTH DAY

The City's houses of worship—those that had survived—had rallied more quickly than any other institutions in New York. Members of congregations throughout Manhattan had flocked to their churches and synagogues both to receive aid and to give it. By midafternoon on the day of the earthquake, several hundred of these temples and churches of all denominations were functioning as emergency shelters, dispensing medical care and food to anyone who was in need.

The four most prominent religious leaders of the City—Cardinal O'Connor, Rabbi Jacob Samuelson of Temple Emanu-El, Pastor George Stevenson of the Abyssinian Baptist Church, and the Episcopal Bishop Andrew Goode—had all been kept abreast of Mayor Lincoln's negotiations with Washington, and all had watched closely the televised proceedings of the joint session of Congress. When it was finally obvious that the federal government was going to back the plan to save the City, the cardinal realized that something more than the ordinary was called for.

He picked up the telephone in his private study and asked if communications were in good enough repair that he might make a conference call.

"A bit spotty, Your Eminence," replied one of the cathedral's operators in an Irish brogue. "But let's see what we can do. Who is it you'd be wanting now?"

He gave her the names, then sat back to wait while the calls were attempted.

Five minutes later Bishop Goode was on the line and, shortly after that, Rabbi Samuelson and Pastor Stevenson. Greetings were brief; none of them had the time for more than basic politeness.

"What this City needs now is something that only its churches and temples can provide," the cardinal concluded. "But not each of us clinging stubbornly to our own brand of faith. A true ecumenical service. What do you each think? Jack?"

"I'm in complete agreement, John. Your cathedral and my temple are both large and both in the center of the City, but St. John's can hold as many people as our two put together, and then some. Besides, Harlem has been hit the worst. It will be several weeks before George's church will be up and running again. I think the service you have in mind should be held as close to that part of the City as possible. Andy?"

"I don't have any problem with that. Just tell me what time you think would be best and I'll get moving on it."

Word of the service had been spread by mouth and by the time the great bronze doors of the Cathedral Church of St. John the Divine on 112th Street and Amsterdam Avenue were opened, there were over one hundred thousand people on the cathedral grounds and in Morningside Park waiting for it to begin. Already the surviving young men and women from Harlem who had been trained by master English stonemasons had begun to make repairs to the cathedral. The damage to this largest of Christian churches, however, had been held to a minimum because of the quality of workmanship that had gone into it for the past century since the cornerstone had been laid down in the 1890s. Other residents from the Morningside Heights area had helped to set up an extensive public address system in the park, so that everyone could take part in the service.

Many of the people not in the cathedral itself had brought blankets with them and had spread them on the lawns and under the trees of Morningside Park. Matt Devon looked around him. He had not really wanted to go into the cathedral but he wasn't sure whether Elliot, the philosopher king, would find him in the mob that was filling up the park. He heard his name shouted and turned toward the sound. Elliot was pushing his way through the crowd carrying a wicker basket. Trust Elliot, Matt thought. Only the finest. The P.A. system hummed to life.

In the cathedral, five men moved to take seats in front of the altar. The cardinal, the bishop, the rabbi, and the pastor flanked Mayor Bruce Lincoln. Like him, the four clerics were dressed simply, in black, and each wore a skullcap and had a band of purple silk around his right arm in mourning for those who had been killed in the earthquake.

Bruce Lincoln sat with the others and looked out over the nearly five thousand people thronging the nave and transept of the cathedral. His thoughts drifted for a moment to Paula. Then he brought them back into focus as he watched the choirs from all four houses of worship assemble in the cathedral's stalls. As the crowd grew silent, the thought went through his mind that these were his people and that everything that he had gone through in the past days, including Paula's death, had been given meaning by their presence.

The massed choirs of the temple, the church, and the two cathedrals lifted their voices in an anthem by the great Jewish-Italian Renaissance composer, Solomone Rossi. As its final tones drifted away in the cavernous cathedral, Jacob Samuelson rose from his chair to deliver a benediction.

Halfway down the nave, a lovely woman who people thought they recognized but had the courtesy not to approach stood between a man and a small child, holding their hands. Diane

Taylor, dressed simply and without makeup, squeezed those hands gently, thankful that the two who she loved most in the world had been spared. Danny felt the pressure and looked up at his mother, then wished that his granny was there with them. He knew Kate would be in the hospital for a while yet, but was glad that the nice doctor whose name he couldn't remember was with her.

Sam Thorne's thoughts had also turned to the hospital, then made the leap from his mother to Pat Kelly. Wonderful and liberating, he thought . . . and over. He squeezed Diane's hand in return, then bent to kiss the top of her head.

The benediction was over and the rabbi resumed his seat. In the Armed Forces Chapel at the front of the nave, Brendan Ahearn stood with one young son on each arm. He was poignantly aware of how subdued they were. The neighbor with whom they had stayed had described their torment at the thought that their father might not have survived. He hugged them more closely. No way, he thought. No way they're going to lose me.

As the choir began the Sanctus from the Mozart *Requiem*, Cardinal O'Connor stood and walked to the cathedral's pulpit.

Cardinal O'Connor cleared his throat quietly and leaned in toward the microphone. His talk to the assembled thousands in the cathedral and the park would be brief and to the point.

"As has been the fate of man since the beginning of time, tragedy has struck. And as has been the *will* of man since the first tragedy, we will overcome. Each one of us has suffered loss, but that loss has made us all truly brothers and sisters. Now it is time, as a family, to face the future, to grasp it in our hands and mold it in the best possible manner. In facing the future, we become the future.

"I would ask you now, all who are able, to kneel while Pastor Stevenson gives you his blessing. Then go forth in peace and love."

The blessing that the minister of Abyssinian Baptist gave was spare and simple. As the great organ hurled forth the opening bars of Handel's "Hallelujah Chorus," those who had been kneeling stood. As one huge voice, they joined the choir in the *Messiah's* great song of praise and thanksgiving.

The echo of the final "Hallelujah" died and, as the cathedral's bells began to toll, the people within began silently to depart. At the back of the nave, near the huge bronze doors that had been thrown open to admit the crowd earlier that morning, an elderly black woman stood with a young couple who were very obviously in love with one another. Absorbed as they were with each other, they failed to hear the few words she murmured.

"Thank you, Lord," Mattie Lincoln said. "For everything."

Six days earlier, the forces of the Metropolitan Opera had been in the midst of a dress rehearsal for the revival of Verdi's *Nabucco*, had been, in fact, in the middle of the very scene in which God sends Nebuchadnezzar of Babylon mad. The sudden darkness, the roaring and shaking of the earthquake had stunned everyone into silence. Chandeliers fell on the empty seats in the hall, interior damage had been massive. It would be many months—if ever—before a performance could be staged there.

The building itself had held firm, as had all of those surrounding the plaza with its dried-up fountain. The plaza had been cleared of debris and chairs for the Met's orchestra and risers for its chorus had been set up.

Pamphlets had been circulated throughout the City during the day, and a huge crowd had gathered in front of the plaza, spilling over into the broken streets all around the center.

The A-440 pitch was sounded and the crowd fell silent. Maestro Levine strode to the temporary podium in the midst of this unaccustomed silence. He raised his baton and the music and words from *Nabucco*'s great prayer came forth. *"Va! pensiero, sull'ali d'orato . . ."* Indeed, the maestro thought, indeed.

The Lady had fallen forward when the base that she stood on for so many years had split. Now she lay face down, the lower part of her body on the plaza in front of the base, the upper part extending out over the island's lawn.

The work to raise her again had proceeded feverishly throughout the weekend and well into Monday. In the midst of the larger tragedy that was New York, she could not be allowed to lie sprawled out for the world to see.

The huge cranes on the floating barges had been positioned.

Steel scaffolding surrounded her, to which cable from the cranes had been attached. A rough foundation had been created on the plaza. All was ready.

Slowly the cranes began to winch in their cables. As the cables tightened, the groan of metal was audible to those who watched, breath held, from a distance.

Slowly, painfully, the scaffolding began to rise, bringing with it the figure cocooned within it. There could be no hurry, no haste, for no more damage could be allowed to occur to the Lady.

The scaffolding inched upward, the crane operators acting in perfect tandem to keep the whole structure balanced. Two hours and twenty-seven minutes after the lift had begun it was complete.

The Lady was secured to her temporary base, then workmen swarmed over the scaffolding. What had taken a weekend to construct was dismantled in slightly less than four hours.

As the sun rose out of the east that morning, the Statue of Liberty raised her torch once again to greet it.

EPILOGUE

The Woolworth Building, built from 1910 to 1923 and designed by Cass Gilbert, long a landmark of the Lower Broadway area, had been dubbed a "Cathedral of Commerce," because, like a church, it had been built on the nickels and dimes of its parishioners. It cost thirteen million dollars, and Woolworth had paid for it in cash. The building collapsed in on itself when the earthquake struck, killing most of those people who worked within its walls.

Trinity Church on Rector Street, built in 1846 and designed by Richard Upjohn in Gothic style, long the tallest building in New York, survived, and many Wall Street workers found refuge there.

Rockefeller Center was designed by Raymond Hood and was built from 1931 to 1940 between West

48th and West 51st streets. Mr. Hood's dream of designing a complex of buildings of classical composition, a city within the City, was realized. The seventy-story RCA building suffered severe damage, and the statue of Atlas in front of the International Building, though bent where falling concrete had hit it, was still there.

Tudor City, built in the 1920s by Fred F. French Co., was destroyed.

Columbia University, designed by McKim, Mead & White and built from 1893 to 1913, was badly damaged. Low Library's Ionic pillars disintegrated, and its domed roof crumbled down onto the top floor. The Acropolis-like campus buildings were mainly destroyed.

The New York Public Library, built from 1897 to 1911, and designed by Carrere & Hastings in Modern French style, still stood, but its triangular roof over the main section collapsed, and the façade decorated by Corinthian pillars turned to dust. Its foundation was badly damaged and the west wing was destroyed by fire. The lions that graced the front entrance suffered cracks but were able to be mended.

Temple Emanu-El, built in 1868 and designed by Leopold Eldlitz and Henry Fernbach, stood, but its Saracen minarets fell into Fifth Avenue.

St. Patrick's Cathedral, built on rock, survived as well. Built between 1850 and 1888, it was designed by James Renwick, Jr.

The Cathedral of St. John the Divine was built on a high, rocky outcropping in Morningside Heights, and survived, though its many gargoyles and other ornaments hurtled to the ground, killing and maiming passersby. Heins & LaFarge designed the cathedral in Norman Romanesque character. The cathedral is still under construction.

The Metropolitan Club and the Century Club were completely destroyed by the earthquake and the subsequent fires.

Grand Central Station Building, designed by Warren and Wetmore, disintegrated onto Park Avenue, leaving the Pan Am building towering alone, its windows gone but otherwise intact. The great hall of Grand Central Station was devastated when the roof above caved in.

The Chrysler Building, designed by William van Alen in 1930, and the Empire State Building, built in 1931 and designed by Shreve, Lamb & Harmon, survived without severe damage.

Battery Park City, situated on a landfill area at the southern tip of Manhattan and built between 1986 and 1989, designed by, in part, Yu-hwa Hung and Vladimir Arsene, was modeled on the early twentieth-century apartments on the Upper East Side and West Side—masonry-clad buildings with punched windows, stone bases, and uniform façades. The entire project was leveled by the earthquake, and the tsunamis carried its debris out to sea.